AWAKENING

Center Point
Large Print

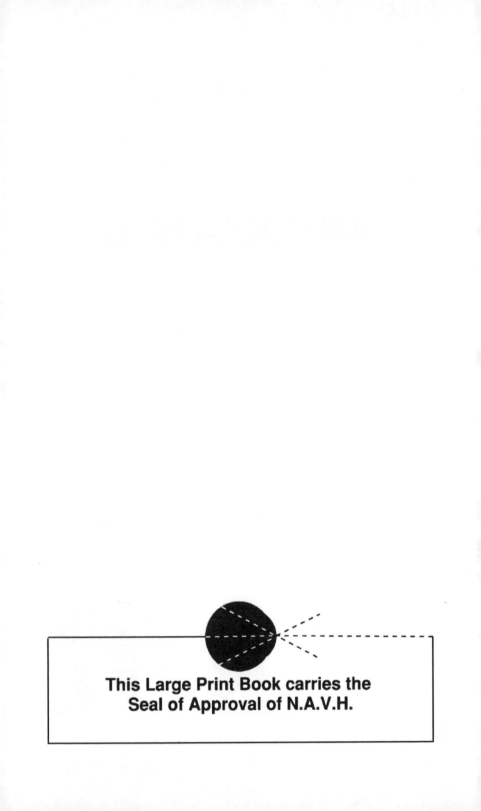

**This Large Print Book carries the
Seal of Approval of N.A.V.H.**

AWAKENING

Tracy Higley

CENTER POINT LARGE PRINT
THORNDIKE, MAINE

The text of this Large Print edition is unabridged.
In other aspects, this book may vary
from the original edition.
Printed in the United States of America
on permanent paper.
Set in 16-point Times New Roman type.

ISBN: 978-1-62899-692-0

Library of Congress Cataloging-in-Publication Data

Higley, T. L.
    Awakening / Tracy Higley. — Center Point Large Print edition.
        pages cm
    Summary: "Seven years ago, Kallie woke up in a New York City
museum with amnesia. Now leaving her job as an assistant curator at
that museum, she joins a mysterious billionaire and his team on a global
quest to find the key to the ancient Minoan language—and a personal
quest to find her true identity"—Provided by publisher.
    ISBN 978-1-62899-692-0 (library binding : alk. paper)
    1. Amnesia—Fiction. 2. Large type books. I. Title.
PS3608.I375A97 2015
813'.6—dc23
                                                                2015020460

To John Olson

For giving me courage to write
the book of my heart,
no matter where it took me . . .
For walking and plotting
and walking some more . . .
For your friendship,
worth more than any story.

→ 1 ←

The world outside Kallie's apartment was unreal —a hazy fairy tale sucking her into itself as she dashed from her building into the gray morning chill and descended rain-slicked concrete steps to the city street.

Not a happily-ever-after fairy tale.

Kallie hesitated on the sidewalk, turned, and eyed the massive door to her apartment building, then ran a hand through the dark waves of her hair, flattening quickly in the damp. Should she bolt back upstairs for an umbrella?

Overhung with scudding clouds and wrapped in an evil mist, the murky streets had all the feel of the Brothers Grimm about them—tales of step-sisters who cut off parts of their feet to fit the glass slipper and wicked queens forced to dance in fiery iron shoes until they dropped dead.

But she was late already for her Yearly Ritual. And the portal to the underground labyrinth of subway tunnels yawned only three blocks east. If she hustled, she could descend into their protection before the clouds fractured and soaked her through. Better to push forward and attempt repairs to her hair when she reached the museum.

She flipped the collar of her white trench coat upward and soldiered on. She clutched her soft-sided laptop case to her body, kept her head down, and wove through sluggish pedestrians, dodging wayward umbrellas and stepping over puddles. The wind was strangely warm for March, with a hint of salt impossible this far from the sea. The kind of peculiar wind that dampened the soul and whispered of longings unfulfilled, of desires just out of reach.

The three blocks stretched, and the metallic-rimmed eyes of a hundred windows seemed to watch her rush to the subway. The streets smelled of rotting leaves and garbage in corners and sausages cooked by street vendors braving the elements—a combination of ordinary odors trapped by weighted air and the city fermenting, composting around her.

Such black thoughts.

But it was always this way—on this day.

March twenty-first. Vernal equinox. Her *birthday,* as Judith called it. And if so, only her seventh birthday, with the rest lost in mist thicker than the New York air.

Her mouth tasted of three cups of bitter coffee and her nerves jittered to match. She'd needed over-caffeination to face the day, but it had been a mistake. Her stomach swirled in uneasy rhythm with the unpredictable sky. She reached the subway entrance at last, already swallowing people at this early hour, and sighed in relief.

She'd left her apartment late. The six-fifteen

train would have come and gone. It meant standing on the platform, pressed into the restless crowd, staring like a single, many-eyed beast down the dark tunnel, waiting for the tremor underfoot to signal rescue.

She followed the red-painted stripe down the stairs, into the tunnel, and ran her gaze along the chipped and peeling red line as it disappeared into darkness—Ariadne's thread leading into the labyrinth.

A middle-aged man in a floppy-brimmed wool hat slouched against the wall, some kind of stringed instrument in his hands. He played, but the discordant, jerky plucks on overtight strings sounded more like cat howls than music. Kallie stood apart from the crowd, closer to the wall, and fished a few dollars out of her bag. She stepped across to the open case beside him, dropped the money into a pool of coins and scattered bills, and gave him a quick smile. The musician ceased plucking and brought his gaze from the lyre-like instrument to Kallie's face.

A sudden shiver ran through her, like the vibration the train would soon cause, but there was no train. She checked.

He was dressed in grays and whites, with clean-shaven, plaster-colored skin. Beside him lay a wooden cane, intricately carved with twisting snakes. He wore sandals over large bare feet. Sandals with oddly placed decorative pieces on either side, like tiny wings. She shuddered again.

Kallie knew her Homer well. Not only the *Iliad* and *Odyssey*, but the lesser-known works and hymns. Winged sandals, stringed instrument, the snake-twined caduceus staff.

Hermes. Messenger of the gods.

He watched her still, not unkindly. She took a step backward. The look in his eyes had more of pity than gratitude. The hollow silence of the tunnel pressed against her, and she steadied herself with a shaky hand against the grimy wall.

He opened his lips, held them open as though summoning speech from another world. When he spoke, the words were quiet, earnest. Had she expected the booming voice of a prophet?

"Shattered mirrors can be mended."

Kallie swallowed, looked toward the empty tunnel, and stepped away. To anyone else, his words would have indicated mental imbalance.

Not to her.

The platform began its quivering and the commuters shifted, prepared for the battle of the daily commute. Kallie joined them, welcoming the train and the escape it provided from the sandaled stranger.

The inside of the car smelled of fumes and people and neglect. Kallie stood alone and apart, as though untouchable in her immaculate white coat. She forced herself not to think about the odd stranger, the Yearly Ritual even, and focused solely on tonight's big bash.

The grand reopening of the museum's Greek and Roman exhibits would be celebrated by a fund-raising gala—an invitation-only, black-tie soirée. As the department's curator, Judith would give an impassioned plea for funding, with special emphasis placed on Kallie's pet project, the *Minoan Collective*. She let her mind drift to the wonderful possibilities the funding could bring to life. She could truly focus her passions on the Collective, set aside the more mundane duties of assistant department curator, and spend her days digging through the fascinating past, uncovering secrets long buried.

The past. Like shattered mirrors. What did the man say? *"Shattered mirrors can be mended."*

She tried to visualize mending a mirror while absently studying the subway map posted above the darkened windows. The red thread twisted and trailed under the city, a faithful guide through the maze, a sure path to her true home: the museum.

Yes, home. For it was the museum where seven years ago she was truly born.

The subway shrieked to an abrupt stop and the doors swooshed open, sucking commuters onto the next platform. Kallie held the strap of her case against her shoulder and stepped across the narrow gap between train and concrete, her toes just across the universal yellow line of danger. And stopped.

Around her, passengers jostled and flowed like river water around a jutting stone. Kallie could not move.

Across the platform, against another red-striped filthy wall, sat a musician with a strange instrument and winged sandals.

He met her eyes. Of course he did.

Did no one else find it strange to see him there again? They hurried up the steps, up into the world, as though the gods had not broken through to mortals.

She heard the doors slide closed behind her, felt the rumble of the train as it surged away, pulling air into the vacuum it created. A dizziness swept her, threatened to drag her backward into the void. Her mouth was plaster dust. Would this messenger give a different message?

Ariadne's thread was unraveling.

Kallie teetered backward, a black fuzziness at the edge of her vision, hand gripping the strap at her shoulder as if it could anchor her to the floor. The tracks below were magnetic, pulling, pulling her downward.

It was the sort of damsel-in-distress moment that screamed for a hero to swoop in and save her.

Kallie yanked her unruly thoughts together and rescued herself.

She was headed home—and nothing would stop her, including hallucinations. Sidestepping Hermes without a glance, she bounded up the steps to the city block, hurried along the street, then stopped at the foot of the museum.

The clouds still hoarded their rain, thankfully. She stepped inside and sped past the wide stone stairs of the visitor's entrance to a half-hidden door marked *Employees Only*. A swipe of her card and she was across the threshold, safe from imagination and paranoia, hair still wavy, white coat still immaculate. She exhaled, then shook her head to center her thoughts. Yes, it was only the Yearly Ritual. It did strange things to her mind.

She hurried through the empty corridor to the elevator, her mind skittering over the past, the subway, the gala tonight, and finally settling on the present moment as the elevator deposited her at the entrance to the third-floor Greek and Roman exhibits.

Compared to the squalor of city and subway, the pristine white glow of statuary with its clarified air and holy hush of empty halls felt more like temple than museum. Kallie's shoulders relaxed, her breathing evened out, even the caffeine seemed to leach out of her system.

She drifted through Andreas Hall, absently pulling thin white gloves from her bag and slipping them over her chilled fingers. She ran a reverent hand over the foot of Zeus, the robe of Athena as she passed. The tracks of myth ran heavy through time, through all cultures of the past. If the divine could be known, surely it would make itself known here.

The statues and friezes called out their connection to something beyond mortality, but it was the marble relief at the end of the hall that drew her to itself. This time she did not resist its magnetic pull. Not today.

The relief was anchored to the wall, a solid piece of marble measuring thirty-one inches wide and nineteen inches high. Carved in the Hellenistic period, circa 320 BCE. Garlands of flowers, grapes, and pomegranates. Beneath the swags, Theseus slaying the Minotaur.

She stopped before it, lowered her laptop case to the floor, and traced its contours first with her eyes, then her gloved fingers. Searching, as she always did, for answers. The museum dropped away and she closed her eyes, sleepy and trancelike, and drank in the stone through her sense of touch alone, a blind woman desperate for truth.

Why here? Why then?

The gloves were not long enough to cover her wrists, and when she opened her eyes, her gaze strayed from the marble relief to the faint red markings that striated her skin. Markings of her past. Her unknown past.

Seven years ago, doctors suspected she had attempted suicide. Upon further study, it was decided they were rope burns. Angry, deep rope burns that suggested captivity and torture and unnamed horrors.

The burns had healed to pink scars. How could the unknown be healed? It was a shattered mirror.

Brisk footsteps advanced behind her. She needn't turn. She knew the gait, expected the arrival.

"Happy birthday, Kallista."

Judith never used her nickname. Always the full name, Kallista.

Kallie inhaled, dropped her hands from the relief, but did not turn.

The curator had a right to formality. It was Judith who had named her. *Kalliste*, the ancient Minoan name for the island of Santorini. *Andreas,* for the family whose charitable contributions over many generations had funded the holdings, the research, and the staffing of the museum's Greek collections. *Kallista Andreas* was a product of the museum, through and through.

"Anything this year?" Judith's New York accent carried eager curiosity.

At her question, Kallie's thoughts fluttered over the heraldic weather, the subway hallucination, her jittery emotions. None of it connected or made sense. She shook her head and turned. "Nothing."

Judith Bittner was a short woman, slight though exuding power, refusing to age past sixty. She wore her salt-and-pepper hair short and spiky around her face, dressed exclusively in black, and had eyes the color of steely blue sapphire. To the interns and newer staff, she was a force of nature to be feared and obeyed. The museum was her life.

For seven years Judith had been a strange mix of fairy godmother and wicked stepmother to Kallie, in turns gifting her with a name, an education, and a job—all the while goading her to work harder, work longer, for meager pay and even less affirmation. For Kallie, it was hard to say whether she hated Judith or loved her.

The older woman held out a package in her hand and stretched it across the space between them.

Kallie accepted the red-wrapped square with both hands, then removed her gloves before pulling off the wrapping. A leather journal, tooled with intricate swirls. She feathered the pages— blank, with thin blue lines.

Judith's voice was oddly uncertain. "I thought, perhaps, you might want to begin a journal. Start a story."

Kallie felt the outline of something else in the wrappings and removed a lovely wood-grained pen. Both items were clearly expensive. She raised moist eyes. The gift was unusually sentimental for Judith. "Thank you." Her voice wavered with uncertainty at the idea. The journal and pen felt heavy in her hands, substantial. As if they held power to create a story for her, one that could not begin any further back than seven years, but perhaps was worth the telling all the same.

Judith shrugged one shoulder, all business again, and jutted her chin toward the marble relief. "Take as much time as you need." Her clipped footsteps echoed away and she disappeared around the corner.

Kallie returned her attention to the relief, but the spell was broken. There was no use taking more time. Despite her faithfulness to the Yearly Ritual, this corner of the museum never yielded answers. She hoped—and feared—one day there would be a staggering revelation that would change her life forever. But it never happened. She was reading too much into weather, people, any variation in her life for clues.

She tossed the journal, pen, and wadded red paper into her bag, shoving everything mystical into the dark tangle of her soul, and strode purposefully toward her office. There was much to do before tonight's event.

She crossed the entrance hall and slipped through a small door marked *Private*. She bypassed several small offices, each one cramped and overflowing with shelves of books, reams of paper, and lesser-valued museum pieces in transit, including Judith's, and entered her own tiny space with a sense of reprieve. She closed the door and exhaled. The Yearly Ritual was over. She would not go near the marble piece again until the first day of spring next year.

Kallie pulled her laptop from its case, mulling over the final details of the brochure she'd been working on for the past week. She needed to get the file to the in-house printer in time for tonight. Maybe glossy paper for the tri-fold piece, to show off the high-resolution images of the collection's latest Minoan acquisitions. It was the text that needed work, needed crafting into the perfect combination of fascinating fact and passionate plea to open the pocketbooks of the wealthy for the funding she desperately needed for the *Minoan Collective.*

Then perhaps she could let go of the past. The Collective was her future—a reason to exist. A repayment to Judith for all she'd done. Kallie could be part of a team, find a place to belong. And in the process, she would become the world's foremost authority on Minoan culture, for the good of this research community and the museum, of course.

A photo of a terra-cotta tablet lay on her desk, and she squinted at the ancient, unknown script. Linear A, still a lost language, had been her passion since grad school. The mysterious language fed her obsessive desire to understand the past and flowed through her veins like a life-giving river. Tonight's event could be the key to unlocking the symbols. Eagerness shot through her. She would transfer her passions so powerfully in the brochure that others would be ignited as well. She sat down and poured herself into communicating through words and pictures the very essence of her heart's longing.

Two hours later, she e-mailed the brochure file to the printer, but heightened anxiety over its perfection drove her out of her office to speak personally with the print staff.

The museum had opened to the public while she'd been holed up in her windowless office, and now in Andreas Hall, the sun dissolved the morning mist and streamed through the huge, high windows flanking the room. It was a glorious sight, and she drank it in as she walked. She passed Judith, speaking to a group of school-age children. Judith could have delegated the duty to Kallie or another assistant, but the older woman seemed to thoroughly enjoy educating the school groups.

Her eyes immediately flicked to Kallie. She wrapped up her comments with a big smile, directed the group to the next hall, then hurried to catch up with her protége.

"Kallista, a word."

Could she run? "I was just going to the printer, to make sure—"

19

Judith waved away the explanation. "Yes, yes, your precious brochure. People aren't moved by brochures, Kallista."

Kallie locked eyes with her, raising her chin and frowning at the insult. "That's why we have *you,* Judith. To close the deal."

Judith's blue-bright eyes bore into her. "Passion, Kallista. It's *passion* that moves them, gets them opening their wallets and writing their checks." Her eyebrows drew together, a dark V that made Kallie nervous. "And no one is more passionate about Linear A than you."

Kallie shook her head, anticipating Judith's next words. "My passion's flowing through the entire brochure, Judith. As soon as they look at it, they will feel the excitement, understand the need. I'm the visionary. You're the speech maker."

Judith struck like a viper, her fingers biting into Kallie's arm. "Do I need to remind you how important tonight—?"

"Exactly!" Kallie winced. "That's why it needs to come from *you.* You have the credentials, the reputation, the respect." She yanked her arm from Judith's grasp and glared at her. "The funding is far too important to have an *assistant* make the plea."

Judith sniffed and lifted her chin, meeting Kallie's gaze. "Passion trumps position."

Kallie crossed her arms. "Money trumps

everything. They are thinking first about their money."

"Dimitri Andreas will be here."

If she thought her announcement would sway Kallie, she was mistaken. All the more reason for Judith to make the speech. The mysterious, newly appointed patriarch of the Andreas family—for whom the Greek collection's hall had been named—had just returned from years in Europe. It would be his first visit to the museum that had benefitted immensely from his family's generosity. Kallie narrowed her eyes. She was done with this conversation.

Judith glanced left and right, then spoke quietly. "Supposedly, he has information about the Key."

Kallie's breath sucked inward and she leaned forward. "What information?" The question came out as a whisper, conspiratorial and urgent.

Judith's eyes glowed in victory as she shrugged. "You'll have to ask him. Tonight. After you speak."

The curator spun around, sauntered off, and rejoined the schoolchildren who were filing into the corridor outside Andreas Hall. Her arms flung upward as she extolled the virtues of a statue of Apollo.

Kallie sighed. She would deal with Judith later. Make sure she knew Kallie would *not* speak. She was better suited for behind-the-scenes research, not a public platform. The professional periodical article she was putting together had a better chance of gaining her funding than any speech she might make.

Right now, she needed to get to the printer before he could make a mistake with her brochure.

On the wall above the room's exit, a strange shadow wavered, thrown there by the sunlit window panel behind her. She turned in time to see an enormous bird sail past, its wings nearly unmoving. A hawk?

Shaking off the obvious myth-born significance, she escaped Andreas Hall.

Hours later, eyes blurred from research, she lifted her head from her desk to find the clock reading four. Time to get home and get ready for the gala. But first to find Judith and remind her that Kallie's role would be secondary tonight.

She gathered up her laptop, bag, and papers and was about to leave the office when her desk phone rang. She hesitated, deciding whether to let it ring to voice mail, then swung her bag against her hip and grabbed the receiver.

"Kallista Andreas." Her professional voice automatically kicked in.

There was no sound but soft breathing on the other end. She half smiled. A prank call? To a museum?

But then a raspy hiss. "I know who you are."

Kallie froze. It was most likely a woman's

voice. But who? The laptop bag slipped from her shoulder, hit the floor with a *thunk*.

The voice sizzled. "Stay away from what is not yours."

⇥ 2 ⇤

A shiver ran up Kallie's spine, gripped her neck with icy fingers, prickled the hair on her arms. "Who is this?" The words choked in her throat. Nothing but a click that severed the connection. Kallie set the phone down slowly, replaying the cryptic words. It didn't have the feel of a prank. But what else could it be? She was an assistant curator of a single department. An academic, buried in a tiny office, with a pathetically nonexistent social life. But there was no mistaking the meaning or the tone. She had been warned.

But it was not the cartoonish warning that burrowed like a stone into her chest.

"I know who you are."

She tried to shake off the nonsense, retrieved her bag, and marched straight to Judith's office. It was already locked for the night, and Kallie growled at the unyielding doorknob. The woman probably left early to avoid Kallie's objections. There was nothing she could do now but go home and get ready for the evening.

Thankfully, Homeless Hermes was in none of the subway tunnels on the long trip across the city to her apartment, nor when she returned two hours later, refreshed and dressed up like a princess headed to the ball. She felt attractive yet still professional in a black satin sheath that fell to midcalf, complemented by agonizingly high-heeled strappy sandals. She'd tamed her hair into a chignon, but already a few wisps trailed her face and tickled her lip.

Judith would complain at Kallie's crossing the city alone at night, but she wasn't worried. It was only seven o'clock. She'd take a cab home when the gala ended.

When the train pulled up and the doors beeped apart, she hurried into the car, grabbed a pole, and took a deep breath of stale air.

And tried not to think of it as the most important night of her life.

Yeah. Right. She glanced around, trying to divert her thoughts. There was the dingy East Line map, the pretty young girl and her prince—headed into the city for Friday night fun, the old crone hunched into her faux-fur-lined hood, hoarding shopping bags at her feet. The couple and the woman lifted narrowed eyes to her as if she was annoying them. Oh. How long had she been tapping the inside of her rings against the metal pole?

Another deep breath. *Chill, Kallie.* She only

needed to show up, let Judith introduce her to the big money, smile, and shake a few hands. She could do that easily. Charm the money out of a few gray-haired philanthropists, keep from falling off her spiked heels. It would be over quickly enough. Long before it grew unbearable. None of them need ever know she was only seven years old.

Twenty minutes later she reached Andreas Hall and gasped. Even though she and Judith had planned every particle of this event, seeing it was like stepping into another world. Museum staff had placed braziers along the sides of the long gallery, and their shimmering flames danced along the walls between the sculpted forms of gods and mortals. The hall had become a mysterious, alluring, ancient palace. A portal to the past.

Breathtaking.

She let it wash over her, soothing and still.

The murmur of wealthy conversation drifted from the gallery to her left, a low current of sound rippling gently across white travertine floors. At the far end of the hall, a shadow, too solid to be flame-induced, shifted.

Judith?

Curiosity lured her farther, body slanted toward her toes to keep the stilettos from striking tile. Definitely a person. A man, judging from height. He stood with his back to her, facing the glass-

25

enclosed display of Late Minoan artifacts. A soft metallic sound echoed.

Ten feet from him, she paused and a furious flare of heat surged to her fingertips. He was picking the lock on the glass case! She'd happened upon an art thief, bold enough to do his work with a hundred witnesses in the next room.

"What do you think you're doing?" She rushed at him, the words spilling out with a righteous fury, in spite of a flicker of fear.

He spun to face her. Brazier light glinted from something in his hand.

But it was his eyes that caught her. They did not betray surprise, nor guilt. They spoke of pain. Deep, perhaps bottomless, pain.

But then his expression hardened and he straightened.

She glanced to the item in his hand. A paper clip. Not exactly the tool of a master thief.

And if he was a thief, he was cut from the Pierce-Brosnan-Thomas-Crown mold. Expensive tux, heavy gold ring on his finger. Her fear evaporated and indignation triumphed.

She pointed to the paper clip. "You'll have to do better than that. It's not some teenage girl's diary."

He slid the paper clip into his pocket and half smiled, the confident look of a man fully aware of his charm. "Yes, I've discovered as much. Perhaps you have a key?"

Of all the— Why did attractive men always think they could get whatever they wanted?

"And I'm not some teenage girl." She glared at him. This was *her* museum, *her* home.

He graced her with a full smile then, though somewhere behind it was the pain, still the pain. His eyebrows lifted as he appraised her from chignon to sandals. "Clearly not." His mouth quirked with humor.

She forced down the blush, grateful for the dim light. "What is it you're looking for?"

He turned to the case, giving her an instant to breathe again, regain her equilibrium.

"The truth."

Taken aback, she almost laughed. Weren't they all?

But she didn't laugh. The display case, or perhaps its thief, subconsciously drew her to his side to study the three glass shelves of artifacts, lit by a single small bulb.

She glanced sideways at her companion.

He leaned his forehead against the glass, where it would leave a smudge.

She said nothing.

His voice was soft, reverent. "Do you know what it is?"

She followed his eyes to a carnelian-colored, amygdaloid seal. The orange stone was smaller than her fist, etched with a palm tree and Linear A script. Her voice softened. "A seal. It was used to stamp one's personal imprint in wet clay."

His nod was nearly imperceptible, his head still braced against the glass.

She studied his profile. He was shockingly good looking. Like a sculpture, fleshed out. Square chin and strong jawline. Just the right amount of fashionable stubble. Expensive cologne, spicy and sharp. She spoke to break her mesmerized gazing. "Why do you want to steal it?"

"I wasn't stealing it. I only wanted to touch it. To hold it."

She bit back a reply about oils on the fingers, about cotton gloves and proper handling techniques. She said nothing because . . . she understood. She turned back to the seal, suddenly connected to this stranger by mutual admiration of the artifact. "It was most likely used by someone on the island of Crete, about 1500 BCE, the Late Minoan IA period."

He straightened, then used the cuff of his tux to wipe the glass. "Those are its facts." He looked at her, his eyes intense, smoky. "But what is its *story?*"

A flutter of something—part fascination, part excitement—coursed through her blood and she met his eyes. "You feel it, too? The way every piece has a story." Her voice grew zealous, urgent, heating up to match the flame in his eyes. "Something to be unlocked, discovered, celebrated." She reached her own fingers yearningly toward the carnelian seal. "If we could decipher the script, an entire civilization would open up to us. A new world, with all its passion and glory, its deceit and greed, its lives and loves and contributions to humanity." She licked dry lips, felt the breathlessness that always accompanied her obsession. "It's all right there, waiting to be pried open, like a long-buried vault of secret treasures."

He nodded, wide-eyed, and they stood in companionable silence. Kallie traced the contours of the seal with hungry eyes and felt he shared her intrigue.

Footsteps clicked behind them and they both turned, startled. Kallie smoothed down her dress and fumbled at her hair. Somehow the encounter had left her feeling disheveled, though every-thing seemed to be in place.

"Kallista?"

"Here, Judith." She stepped forward into the light, distancing herself from the enigma at her side. "I was just about to come in. Do we have a good crowd?" She spoke quickly, too quickly—like someone covering guilt.

Judith glided toward their end of the hall until she was a few feet from Kallie, then looked over Kallie's shoulder and stutter-stepped. Her eyelids flickered and her lips opened wordlessly at seeing the man.

It was only a sliver of a moment, and perhaps he didn't even see it.

Kallie reached for Judith, grasped her arms. "What is it?"

But she had already recovered. Chin lifted and mask of serenity back in place, she gave the stranger a cool smile, once more the priestess of her temple.

He stepped from the shadows and extended a hand. "You are Judith Bittner, I take it?"

She dipped her head in acknowledgment and gave him her small, heavily jeweled hand. "And you are?"

"Dimitri Andreas."

Kallie's lips parted in shock, but thankfully no unprofessional expression escaped.

Judith's face was stone as well, but Kallie knew her well enough to catch the flicker of surprise behind her eyes.

"Mr. Andreas, how lovely to meet you at last." Judith brought her left hand to enclose their handshake, her voice as warm as her encircling grasp. It was her most effective and charming greeting. "And may I say how sorry I was to hear of the loss of your father. He was a great man, and such a devoted benefactor of the museum."

"You are very kind. I assure you it is my intention to carry out his work *and* his philanthropy in the way he would have wished."

From Judith's flush one would think the man

had just declared his undying love. Perhaps for Judith, they were one and the same.

"And I see you have already met our most promising researcher, Kallista Andreas."

Dimitri glanced at her, his dark eyes sparking more with concern than any curiosity over their shared last name. Did he fear she would reveal the hidden paper clip?

"Yes, she was giving me a most informative and passionate lesson about the Late Minoan period."

Judith beamed. "As I told you on the phone, she is the best and brightest our institution has to offer."

So. Judith had already spoken of her to the man. From his lack of reaction, Judith must have also mentioned the strange coincidence of their shared last name.

Dimitri extended a hand toward the gallery, including them both in his gallant gesture. "Shall we join the party, ladies?"

Kallie followed Judith, intensely aware of the walking, talking Greek god at her back.

At the entrance of the gallery she paused, taking in the room full of old money, black tuxedos, and jewel-toned gowns. Again, the weight of her blank past, her lack of connection to anyone or anything, squeezed against her heart. She was a fraud in this room, and she had to make sure they would never discover that truth.

A gentle pressure against her low back

surprised her. Dimitri's hand, encouraging her to enter.

His head was just above hers and he spoke into her ear. "They are waiting to be inspired, just as you inspired me."

Her limbs grew both cold and hot at once, a mingling of terror and joy, dread and anticipation "I'm only a researcher." She said it more to herself than to him.

Then they were in the gallery, weaving among the wealthy, with Dimitri introducing both himself and Kallie to guests who nodded their greetings, their hands full of champagne flutes and napkins of hors d'oeuvres.

Dimitri disappeared as she spoke with a software company president and her husband, then returned with two glasses of champagne.

She accepted, grateful only for something to hold. No alcohol for her tonight.

At some point she found herself eating a cracker with a tiny shrimp curled over cream cheese, but the edges went down sharp and the shrimp was tasteless. So far, no questions about her family, her past. But how long could her luck hold?

Finally, the clink of metal on glass drew all eyes to the front of the gallery and settled a hush over the socializing.

Judith stepped onto a tiny platform, placed there especially to accommodate her tiny stature.

They hadn't wanted anyone to miss a word. She signaled Kallie with her eyes and a slight inclination of her head.

She wanted Kallie to stand beside her, a visual aid. No problem.

Kallie weaved through the crowd to the front of the room, only slightly dwarfed by Judith on her dais, and faced the crowd with a pasted smile and twisting stomach.

Dimitri had disappeared among the patrons.

Judith's introductions and gracious welcome flowed through the room like perfumed music. She could be venomous with employees during the day, but with children and with donors by night she became the snake charmer. She mentioned the elder Andreas's passing with the appropriate amount of respectful regret and hailed the younger Andreas with delightful warmth. She spoke of the importance of history, of knowledge, of research, with smooth persuasion that would make a politician envious.

"But we are here tonight not only to celebrate the renovations your generosity has made possible, but to look to the future, to what *new* funding and new research will bring us." Her eyes were bright as she held the crowd in her palm. "And for the future, you do not want to hear an old woman speak." She winked, and the crowd chuckled obligingly. "No, it is the passion of the next generation that will carry us forward.

So I give you the future! I give you Kallista Andreas."

With a grand flourish toward Kallie, she stepped off her platform, leading the room's polite applause, and joined the crowd looking expectantly at Kallie.

A light-headedness swept her, not unlike the feeling this morning when she'd nearly fallen into the channel of subway tracks.

Don't do this, Judith. Do not do this to me.

But it was done.

She lifted a leaden foot to the platform, then another, because it seemed strange to speak from her place on the floor when Judith had addressed them from above.

She faced them, all of them, looking to her. For inspiration, Dimitri had said.

Who was *she* to offer inspiration? She was a researcher, nothing more. She knew books and analysis and facts. She did not know people. Her breath was coming too quick. She was going to hyperventilate.

This panic, it was more than a lack of self-confidence. It was a phobic fear of standing before an important crowd who held expectations she could not fulfill.

Kallie swallowed, a tight, dry swallow. Where was that champagne? The gallery had grown so silent. That uncomfortable sort of silence when one hears the stray coins jingling in someone's pocket at the back, the subdued throat clearing of a woman to the left. The clink of ice in glasses. Of a cork popping at the open bar.

Small and distant with black shadows at its periphery, the crowd seemed to telescope away from her. She was alone. Friendless.

And she did as she always did in moments of heightened stress—she flashed into her imaginary world.

A disfavored queen, I stand before my people with one last plea for fealty, while the executioner waits in the wings. One chance to convince them all I should lead, convince them they should trust me with their kingdom, with their lives. Knowing they will reject me, will find my claim to the throne spurious, and I will die alone.

She dragged her thoughts back to reality and forced air and sound into her throat. "I—I am glad you are all here."

A terrible opening, but at least she had spoken.

"It's an important night. As Judith said. An important night."

She sounded like a first grader. Her mind screamed curses.

"The next project—the project that needs funding—is research into the Minoan period." Her lips had gone numb, but they were moving. "We know a lot about the later Greek period, of course, but not enough about the people who lived in Greece before them. Before the classical period, I mean." Were her lungs constricting? Could one suffocate while speaking? "So that's what we want to do. Study the Minoans. And try to figure out their language. Because we haven't yet."

The room was tomb-silent now. Even the ice seemed to have melted down in the heat of her failure, and the corks and coins and coughs retreated with shame.

Big finish. She needed a big finish. This was her moment, her chance to step into all she was supposed to be.

She opened her mouth as her mind went blank and the world started spinning. Quickly, she stepped down and forced herself to breathe, her back to the crowd.

The silence stretched, and then there was one slow clapping, the kind of slow clap that follows a shocking and yet profound speech. She had shocked them, to be sure. But she'd been as profound as a child's picture book.

Judith took the platform again without meeting her eyes. A bad sign.

Within seconds, Judith regained the crowd and had them laughing, the tension draining from the room.

Kallie didn't wait for her to conclude. She escaped through the tiny door at the head of the gallery, back into Andreas Hall, back to the marble relief of Theseus and the Minotaur where she'd spent her morning and braced her back against the wall beside it, panting like she'd run across the city, her neck clammy with sweat.

She heard the footsteps at the end of the hall but did not raise her head, even when they grew close. Her teeth and jaw were locked in tension.

"What was that?" Dimitri's voice was angry, demanding.

Kallie shook her head, still staring at her feet. "She shouldn't have done it." The words were bitten off, an attempt to stem the emotion. "She knew I had nothing to say."

"Nothing to say?" He thrust a thumb toward the case that held the carnelian seal. "What about all that? The passion and the glory. The vault of secret treasures. Why didn't you say any of that?"

She raised her eyes, straightened her spine. "Why do you care? What is it to you if those people open their wallets?" The fire was returning. Where had it been when she needed it?

He made a sound like a growl and spun away from her. "It's not about them. It's about you."

Kallie inhaled, a sharp intake of breath that seemed to ignite her blood. "And who am I?"

He turned to her again, arms crossed over his wide chest. "That's the question, isn't it? Who is Kallista Andreas?"

She'd told him. Judith had told him of the vacuum.

"Judith insists you're the future of Minoan

research. I came here tonight to find out if this is true. To learn if my money would be well spent—"

"It would be!" Kallie surged toward him, grabbed at his sleeve, heedless of the inappropriateness of the gesture. "I promise you—"

He pulled away and jerked his head toward the gallery where Judith was still speaking. "After that stunt?"

"So I'm not a public speaker. Who cares? I belong behind the scenes—"

"Well, that's not what I'm looking for, Kallista. I'm looking for a leader. Someone with passion and vision and strength."

She backed off but continued begging. "Will you take two out of three?" She needed this. She needed him. Her life, her future depended on it.

He exhaled, a tiny breath of amusement that seemed to deflate his anger. "I don't know if that's enough." His eyes found hers and studied her for a moment that felt like a month of knowing. When he spoke, his voice was sober and deep. "You *have* strength, Kallista. You only need to find it."

Her heart expanded to swallow up the praise, but she couldn't accept it. Not truly.

And then Judith was there, a firestorm of wrath, spitting rage in tiny, short bursts, the veins across her forehead like bas-relief. "Kallista! Shocking! Idiotic."

Kallie faced her, burning with humiliation under the heat.

Dimitri disappeared into the shadows, like the gentleman she'd already discovered he was.

"Judith—"

Judith raised a furiously waving hand and cut her short. "Do not even try to say you warned me. Your reticence is unacceptable."

"Can't I just—"

"Just what? Stay in that tiny office your whole life? You could be the curator of this museum one day, Kallista."

Kallie fought back the sting of tears at the unexpected tribute.

"But not like this. Hiding behind research, never connecting with people. You must learn how to work the public, especially the rich ones. Learn how to be a passionate leader. Instead of this—this—untouchable, ivory-tower snob!"

Dark spots flamed behind Kallie's eyes. How dare she? Never mind that Judith's words echoed Dimitri's.

Judith's voice spewed venom and fire. "You've put your own project in jeopardy tonight. You know that, yes? And perhaps even the department's funding!"

Kallista cringed, her whole body shaking, only the wall holding her upright.

At the entrance to the gallery, a quiet cough

severed Judith's diatribe. Henry, another of Judith's assistants.

"What is it?" Her bark was subdued so only Kallie and Henry heard it, no doubt mindful of the guests in the next room. Another figure appeared beside Henry.

"Mr. Wilton was searching for you."

Judith was all smiles and extended hands. She deserted Kallie at a brisk walk, her smooth stream of pleasantries carrying her to the gallery entrance. "Ah, Mr. Wilton, I am so glad you found me. I've been wanting to say hello to you and your charming wife all evening. It's just not a proper gala without the two of you here . . ." The rest of her magic was lost to Kallie as they disappeared into the other room.

Kallie wasted no time. She'd glad-handed enough donors and done enough damage for one night. She stumbled toward the cloakroom, retrieved her wrap, and fled the museum through the main visitor's entrance, seeking the city's elusive shadows.

After closing the museum's massive doors, she stopped to catch her breath. The sharp March air jabbed through her clothing like an icy knife, and she stopped before descending the grand stone steps that led down to the street. On either side of the wide platform, huge stone sphinxes guarded the entrance, like a warning to the unworthy. The vinyl banner above the doors, with three-foot letters proclaiming the grand reopening, snapped in the stiff wind.

Since no one had followed her out, Kallie's stomach began to unknot. She strayed to the gargantuan sphinx and leaned her head against its roughened paw, absently watching the passing vehicles. The park across the street was a tangle of shapeless limbs and shadowy paths, unlit by the cloud-banked moon. The city smelled of fumes and rain. She swallowed against the salt of tears at the back of her throat.

She'd made a fool of herself and, by extension, embarrassed Judith and the department. Dimitri's anger over the debacle was no doubt only the beginning. Though a significant one. His money was important, and he'd never give it to an idiot like her.

A strange sound, one she couldn't immediately place, drew her attention skyward. A huge shadow passed across the lights atop the museum.

Wings?

There it was again—the shadowy form and the flapping sound.

And then the dark thing was spiraling down, down, down to light upon the head of her sphinx-sentry. It peered at her with a glassy bead eye. A hawk. Like bookends to her day—the Hermes character in the subway tunnel and now this mythic symbol. Hawks were always messengers.

The bird shifted on its twiggy legs, raised and

lowered its wings twice, and rotated its head, still looking at Kallie. For an insane moment, she was certain it would speak.

The day, with all its omens and disasters, pressed upon her, and she *wished* it would speak, give her some understanding of past and present, and even future.

But hawks did not speak, even on nights such as this, and when it flew off into the park, Kallie watched it till it vanished in the blackness. Forcing herself out of the trance, she dug around and pulled her cell phone from her clutch bag.

There were good reasons for keeping one's shrink on speed dial.

⇒ 3 ⇐

The line-drawing maze lured her eyes, then her finger, to wander through its impossible channels in a futile search for its center. In the year of seeing Dr. Newsom, the solution had remained a mystery. If only she could take down the frame, remove the glass, sketch a path with a pencil . . .

"Kallie!" A door slammed.

She jumped, whirled, sucked in her breath.

"Still trying to solve the puzzle?"

Kallie stretched the tension from her neck,

fighting gritty-eyed sleeplessness. Dr. Newsom had agreed to the emergency Saturday morning session, but the promise of relating yesterday's disasters had not relieved her insomnia. In truth, she avoided sleep to avoid the dreams. "One of these days, I'll get it."

Her psychiatrist crossed the room to his desk, confident and casual. Newsom was in his mid-thirties, with no wedding band, no pictures of a wife and kids on his desk. But they never talked about him, so Kallie knew nothing about his personal life.

"Sorry to keep you waiting."

"I appreciate your seeing me at all today." She resisted the pull of the unsolved maze.

He dropped to his desk chair, waved her to an overstuffed seat, and grinned. "When my service gave me your message, I could hardly ignore it. Something about going off the deep end?" He leaned back, bracing his hands behind his head. "We like to avoid those terms in my profession, Kallie."

He was joking, trying to put her at ease as he always did. With his unflustered smile and slightly dimpled chin, he seemed anything but an academic. More like a big brother who liked to tease.

Kallie succumbed to the red and yellow cushioned depths of the "patient chair" with an attempt at a smile.

"Still having the daydreams?"

She snorted. "Daydreams, nightmares, hallucinations."

The doctor leaned forward, elbows on his desk, eyes contracting. "Hallucinations?"

Kallie shrugged one shoulder. "Maybe. I don't know. I guess that's the problem with hallucinations, isn't it?" She avoided his eyes and scanned the familiar office. Newsom had a knack for making patients feel comfortable, from the cheerful décor to the intriguing desk gadgets that seemed more like toys. Her favorite was a moving metal sculpture of two children on a seesaw, perfectly balanced in a perpetual up-and-down. The little girl's head lifted and fell, her laughter almost audible.

"You're afraid that what you are seeing may not be real?"

She relayed the incident with the homeless man in the subway tunnel, skipped briefly over last night's public speaking disaster, and ended with the hawk that hadn't spoken.

He steepled his index fingers and pressed them against his bottom lip. "Interesting . . ."

If he'd said it with an accent, it would have been a decent Freud impersonation.

She picked at loose threads on her seat cushion and let the silence lengthen. Outside the windows, behind Newsom's desk, a garden courtyard languished in the cold, its fountain silent. All she heard was the hiss of the forced heat through floor vents.

"And the subway man's reference to shattered mirrors—what did that mean to you?"

Unable to remain seated, she got up and paced the floor. "Nothing. I don't know."

"You know." His voice was gentle, coaxing.

"The past, I suppose. When I look in the mirror, I see nothing. Like my past has been smashed into a million pieces and I can't make sense of it."

"Can't you?"

He had that probing-question thing down to a real science.

"I've tried! You know I've tried."

Yes, years of trying. First with the aging Dr. Freinhauer, who had finally retired. Now Newsom, whose playful approach to therapy felt like a kid drawing fake mustaches on works of art.

"So we have Hermes and we have a hawk. Both messengers. Both emerging from Greek myth."

"Emerging from my messed-up mind, you mean."

"From your subconscious, Kallie. Which, of course, is steeped in Greek history and culture and images. Very natural."

She paused in her pacing to watch him drag a little rake through a sand-filled Zen garden. "Doesn't feel natural."

"Can you sit?" He raised his eyebrows slightly.

"No." That didn't feel natural, either.

"All right." He continued to contentedly rake his minigarden.

She huffed. "If you want me to sit, just say so. You don't have to agree with everything I say!"

"You're an adult, Kallie. You can make your own decisions."

It was a familiar tune. For all his childlike banter, he was always reminding her she was not actually seven years old. Urging her to believe in herself, in her own strength.

She grabbed a handful of bright pastel chocolate mints from a bowl on his desk and plopped into the chair with a huff.

"Any new men in your life?"

She crunched the candy coating of a hot pink mint too hard and jarred her teeth. It was an unexpected question, and coming from an attractive man it felt invasive, accusing. Did he find her perpetually single status indicative of something deeper? "Why are you asking me that?"

He half smiled, as though holding a secret. "Just trying to see what has changed, what might have triggered this new phase we're about to enter."

The candy went sour in her mouth and she swallowed too soon, jagged edges scraping at her throat. "What new phase?" The words came out panicked.

Dr. Newsom inhaled slowly, leaned away, tilted his head to examine her. "It's time, Kallie. Surely you see this?"

"I don't need anything to change—"

"But of course you do." He rolled a pen between two fingers, then tapped a rhythm against the edge of his desk. "It's time to come to terms with your past. If you don't make this choice intentionally, your subconscious will force you. I believe this is what happened yesterday. This is what the heralds are making known. It's time to remember what happened to you, to bring it into the light."

Kallie circled her left wrist with her fingers, rotated her arm to rub the phantom rope burns. "I—I have already—"

"You've resisted. But you can't resist any longer, not if you want to be whole."

The rest of the candy was melting in her hand, leaving traces of pink and blue and yellow. She dumped them on the edge of his desk.

"It's not uncommon for people with PTSD to be challenged by their subconscious—"

"Post-Traumatic Stress Disorder." She jumped up and resumed pacing. "I've told you, I've done the research. PTSD should only cause repression of the traumatic event, not wipe out my entire life."

"Amnesia is not an exact—"

"Amnesia!" She waved a hand dismissively.

"I'm not some TV movie-of-the-week, Doctor."

He laughed, but sobered at her steely look. "We don't need to argue over terminology. That's simply avoidance. We need to face the truth. The repressed memories are part of your Self along with your Shadow, which you fear so much. You have to face both to be whole. Let the old identity, the old Self die and the new Self be reborn."

Kallie inhaled and blew out her breath through tight lips. "Carl Jung and all that?"

"You *have* done your research. Yes, you're prime material for Jungian analysis. These ancient motifs are charged with meaning and common to all human beings. You're steeped in the archetypal myths already, and anything born of your subconscious will naturally have deep spiritual significance."

"You believe the divine can be known?"

He spread his palms. "There is something beyond the simply physical and mortal, of course. Every myth, every part of ourselves, our experience, tells us this. But whether the divine exists outside of ourselves, how can we know?" He leaned forward, his forearms skimming the desk. "The important thing is to discover your part of the collective divine."

She heard the excitement in his voice, the fascination of a child with a new plaything, and it burned a hole in her stomach.

"I suppose you'll write a journal article or something about me, then?" Her voice came out spiteful, sarcastic, and she closed her eyes at the unkindness.

His voice sparked. "There'll be nothing to write if you never find any courage."

"So I'm a coward?"

He said nothing, in that shrink-silence meant to draw the patient out, get her ranting all her secret, angry thoughts. But Kallie had mastered the game over the years. She sat in the chair, crossed her legs and arms, and waited him out.

"Kallie, of all my patients you should have an understanding of the motifs we find in dreams, in delusions and myth—those preexistent forms that are part of the inherited structure of our psyche. They can manifest spontaneously, anywhere—"

"The phone call." She straightened in the chair, twisted her hands together. How had she forgotten? "I got a phone call yesterday—or at least I think I did. It wasn't any kind of archetype or mythic symbol. Just a weird call, warning me to stay away."

Dr. Newsom's lips tightened for a moment. "Stay away from what?"

"I don't know. From something that is not mine. As if I was being watched."

Again, the flicker of heightened concern flashed in his eyes.

She tried to lighten the incident. "Maybe I'm

part of some kind of mind-control experiment or something—"

Newsom stood, and his chair rolled backward with the sudden movement. "Kallie, stop." He circled to stand in front of her, leaned against his desk, but his body was rigid, tense. "We aren't going to indulge those kinds of thoughts. No one is watching you. You are not being controlled."

Cold fingers of fear tightened around her heart. She had come for reassurance, but his demeanor gave none. "What aren't you saying, Doctor? You think I'm crazy?"

He folded his arms, seeming to weigh the wisdom of telling her some awful truth. "We need to consider the possibility your situation is becoming more serious, perhaps something other than repressed—"

"Just say it."

He sighed. "Schizophrenia often presents at around your age. The sleep disturbances, social isolation, paranoia, hallucinations—they can all be symptoms."

The words bounced inside her head like stones dropped into a deep cavern. Schizophrenia? Would she be wandering the subway tunnels soon herself, muttering and smacking her head to still the voices?

"But there is also research suggesting strong ties between psychotic symptoms and PTSD. Either way, it's time to face the past." He crouched in front of her chair now, bringing his face to her level, the way one would soothe a child. "We'll face it together, Kallie. I promise."

She chewed her lip, scanned the room for a place to hide. Swallowed against the acidity in her throat. She couldn't be crazy. Not on top of everything else.

Newsom was back behind his desk. "I'd like you to start recording your dreams." He rolled his chair forward and leaned his elbows on the polished mahogany. "All of them—the day-dreams, anything you suspect as a hallucination. And when you wake, try to get the nightmares down on paper immediately. Bring your notes with you when you come next week."

Judith's birthday gift flitted into her mind—the handsome pen and leather-bound journal, with its blank pages calling out to be filled. Perhaps it was meant to be a dream journal. Something to anchor her to reality, to keep the hounds of mental illness at bay.

But thoughts of dredging up the unknown past were more like saber-toothed tigers than hounds and threatened to shred her sanity into bloody pieces.

She shook her head, eyes focused on her tight fists. "I—I think it's best not to dwell on the past. To focus on the future, on my work—"

"Then this refusal will destroy you." Newsom's voice was full of foreboding, an omen in itself.

Their time was finished. Kallie half stumbled from his office, barely hearing his final warnings. She had begged for this emergency session so he could tell her she wasn't crazy. Instead, he'd implied it would get worse, or that her imaginings meant something more terrible than she suspected.

The reception area was empty and no one sat at the front desk. She was Newsom's only crazy this morning.

Kallie hurried through the glass door, barely noticing the insistent chirp of her phone. On the sidewalk she fished the phone from her purse, glanced at the unfamiliar number.

"Yes?" The syllable burst out sharp, angry.

"I—I'm trying to reach Kallista Andreas?"

"Yes. This is she." Kallie retreated to the office building's outer wall and turned one ear away from the street.

"Hi, Kallista. It's Dimitri." A pause. "Dimitri Andreas."

The angry heat generated in Newsom's office deflated into a clammy chill. Her heart dropped to her stomach, but professionalism kicked in.

"Yes. What can I do for you, Mr. Andreas?"

"Dimitri."

"Right. Kallie."

"I was hoping, wondering, if you were free this evening."

The heat resurged. And confusion. She couldn't handle being criticized again. Not right now.

"Uh, I think so. Did you need something?" She tensed.

"I have something I want to discuss with you. Regarding your Minoan research."

"Ah." She winced. Everything in her wanted to run down the street. His censure the night before had been quite enough. But perhaps she needed to tell him to stand down.

"Kallie—are you there?"

"Yes . . . well, where would you like to meet?"

"Would you mind if I sent my driver for you? I'd like to meet in my office."

"I don't need a driver—"

"I know. I just thought it would be easier than a taxi."

"Okay, yeah, sure." She closed her eyes. After last night, she could imagine *exactly* what he wanted to discuss. But she'd keep her head up, insist that she was a researcher—an excellent one, and she *would* find the Key if he would give her a chance. If he refused, she had no idea what she would do next. She couldn't think about that now.

"Your address?"

She numbly recited the address and agreed to six o'clock.

"Thank you, Kallie. I look forward to seeing you this evening."

"Right. Thanks." She tossed the phone back into her purse, leaned the back of her head against the office building wall, and felt herself slipping, falling into her dream world . . .

I walk through the stone arch, across the marble atrium, the dim recesses of its lofty ceiling lost far above. The coolness of shadowed stone greets me, caresses my skin.

It's not imposing, though. Not intimidating. I am confident here, sure of myself, my purpose, and my belonging. I stroll through the atrium, past the central fountain, the goddess pouring water from her horn in a never-ending supply of abundance. I run fingers through the crystal water as I pass, then flick droplets into sun-dappled air and dry my fingertips on my robe. Across the atrium, the entrance to the throne room beckons, but I linger a moment. I sense a presence in the throne room and approach with careful, silent tread.

The windowless throne room lies mostly in shadow, for the royal audience has ceased for the day and all but one brazier has been doused. The remaining bowl of fire flickers in the front corner of the room, behind the throne platform. Illuminated by its fitful light, I see two figures, shrouded and indistinct. Shards of conversation glide to me across the white marble. Two women, one dressed in dark robes and hooded. The other in white, her face strangely blurred in my vision.

"I fear for them," the white-robed woman is

saying, hand pressed against her heart.

I cannot hear all of the black-hooded one's words. " . . . test must strip them . . ."

"But they might come to harm—"

"—together or apart—against each other—"

I strain to hear the other's answer but do not enter the throne room. Instead, I press against the rough stone wall at the entrance, the smell of plaster dust in my nose, and hope to remain unnoticed. Somewhere behind me, I hear the shout of one palace slave to another, something about a delivery of grain. I lean into the throne room.

"They are so young." Again, the white-robed woman, her voice full of fear, of love.

"No younger than you, when you were called to rule." This phrase comes to me fully from under the black hood and fills my heart with dreadful anticipation.

Her head is dropped to her chest now, the woman in white, a sign of submission. I cannot hear her whispered words, but a black cloaked arm reaches for her, and a bony hand covers her head. More whispered words. A blessing or a curse, I cannot tell.

And then the throne room is rushing away from me, sucked into a vortex that leaves me swaying and alone, empty and abandoned . . .

Kallie blinked and swallowed, swiveled left and right, shot an arm out to steady herself and pawed empty air. A rippling blueness sparkled under her shoes, sunlight striking water in a thousand bright beads.

The air whooshed from her lungs in a sudden terror of realization, at the very moment a white sedan screeched to a stop on her right and the driver jumped out.

"Hold on there!" His voice roared over the din of bridge traffic. "Let's talk a bit. We can talk."

She turned her head slowly, taking in the white car, the metal struts of the suspension bridge, the three-foot drop to the asphalt behind her, and the dizzying plunge to the river below her concrete perch. The wind tore at her hair, and the numbing cold of shock wrapped around her limbs. Her teeth tapped each other—a jerky hammering that threatened to jar her from the wall.

The man slid beside her, his hand extended, his smile genuine and unintimidating. "Can you step down, please—just for a minute? We can talk, if you'd like . . ."

She gazed at his large hand and pleading eyes, still confused. But she reached down and gripped his hand with her own icy fingers, then tightened her grasp as though she already dangled above the river. Her body vibrated like her teeth, twitchy involuntary movements as though her limbs would fly apart.

He pulled her to the asphalt, hands clasping her forearms, and steadied her beside the waist-high wall. Cars continued their rush, heedless of the scene on the narrow shoulder.

"We should get off the bridge," he was saying calmly. "Let me take you somewhere—do you have family nearby? Friends?"

She shook her head, more shudder than answer. "I—I want to go home."

"Good. That's good. I'll take you home."

He led her to the passenger side of his car, her Good Samaritan, and placed her carefully inside.

Moments later they rejoined the flow of traffic and she was forcing out her address. He tapped it into his GPS and they rode in silence for a few minutes.

"Do you have someone to talk to? About what just happened?"

Kallie tried to steady her breathing, tried to loosen the grip of the choking, unnamed terror. "I wasn't going to jump. I don't think. I don't know what happened. I just sort of—woke up. And I was on the bridge."

The words tumbled from her lips even as her eyes focused on the green LED lights of the dashboard clock. Her appointment with Dr. Newsom had ended at eleven this morning.

"Is that—is that the right time?"

He followed her glance. "It's a few minutes fast, I think. It's probably only about two."

Two o'clock. Three hours since she'd left Newsom's office. Three hours, and how many miles?

PTSD. Amnesia. Schizophrenia. Whatever it was, Newsom was right.

It was going to destroy her.

⇢ 4 ⇠

The black Lincoln Town Car slid along the curb in front of Kallie's building at six o'clock, exactly. Kallie waited inside the entryway, avoiding the damp evening chill, and reached for the door with a suddenness that jammed her index finger. She shook off the pain, jerked the door open, and dashed down the steps to the curb, where the driver had already opened the back door of the stretch automobile.

He was an older man, pale-skinned and white-haired, with the deep lines of a lifetime worn into the face under a black cap. He lowered his chin in a slight nod but did not speak. Kallie slipped into the backseat and hugged her briefcase to her side. The door *whooshed* closed, vacuum sealed. Beyond the two rear-facing seats, a partition separated her from the driver.

She was like an artifact sealed into a glass case. She sank into the supple tan leather and tried to relax.

Had she dressed appropriately? What did one wear to meetings with wealthy philanthropists who were about to criticize you and probably fire you? After three wardrobe changes, she settled on a white turtleneck sweater and khaki-colored linen pants. Hopefully not too casual. She'd debated about bringing the briefcase, but it gave her sweaty hands something to hold on to. Plus, she was determined that he see her as a professional researcher, regardless of the public-speaking fiasco.

She tangled tense fingers in her lap, forced her thoughts to her research. Perhaps she still had a chance to redeem herself after last night. Convince Dimitri to fund her project. She rehearsed her plea from various angles.

Low-hanging clouds obscured the sunset, and the twilight passage through the city was awash in a murky drizzle. Was Dimitri's office in Manhattan? She hadn't even asked.

It soon became clear the office wasn't in the city at all. Crossing the East River, the car sped farther east across Long Island, its green dashboard lights lit up like a plane's cockpit. By six forty-five, they'd traded concrete for tree-lined vistas and finally slowed at a massive iron gate with an intricately worked *A* at the peak.

The Andreas Estate.

The driver punched in a gate code, and the Town Car passed onto the long private drive.

Tall maples blocked most of the house for a few hundred yards, but then a slight bend in the drive revealed the estate, glowing in the ebbing daylight with a dozen golden lamps mounted in arched recesses and above-window balconies. She studied the property through misted glass, watched a long, tall hedge of boxwood slide by, cut with a curious series of openings through which she glimpsed another tall hedge.

They circled a huge stone fountain and pulled onto a white concrete pad. Her driver had the door open promptly, then escorted her up wide stairs, past classic statuary of Zeus and Apollo flanking the double doors, and into the foyer.

He pressed a tiny button on a square panel inside the front door, and Dimitri's voice answered, a bit muffled but distinct.

"I have Ms. Andreas, Mr. Andreas."

Too weird.

"Thanks, Martin."

Martin dipped his head to her. "He will be with you momentarily, miss." And then he was gone, leaving her stranded in the center of the high-ceilinged foyer, complete with a scarlet-carpeted sweeping staircase wrapping around an enormous antique-brass chandelier.

The estate, the interior, it pressed down on her with all its grandeur—unreal, all of it. Less real, in some ways than her foray into an imaginary palace this morning. Perhaps she would awaken from this moment and find herself perched on the roof of her building or wandering unknown city streets. She straightened her spine, lifted her chin, and pulled her shoulders back, forcing herself to breathe deeply and calm down.

"Kallie."

He didn't descend. Simply stood at the top of the stairs, smiling down into the foyer. He wore a short-sleeved black polo and jeans—even more casual than her choice. "Thank you for seeing me. Will you come up?"

"Of course." She followed the stairs, sinking into the plush carpet, and ran a light hand over the smooth banister that topped iron scrollwork. It was the kind of staircase that made a girl want to trade her sweater and pants for a ball gown and glass slippers, but Dimitri's eyes were on her, and she met his gaze. She would not be intimidated, even if her worst fears came true.

On the second level, he ushered her past an open door, where she glimpsed polished tile, a wall of windows, and a glossy black grand piano in the center, and drew her through the next set of doors, into what he must have called his "office" on the phone.

Dark walnut-paneled walls deepened dying light. Heavy Persian rugs and hanging tapestries absorbed sound. Music played, somewhere and everywhere at once, softly sophisticated.

Kallie relaxed as the music saturated her with soothing waves. She spoke to Dimitri's back. "Miles Davis?" The lyrical trumpet over muted piano and snare drum was unmistakable.

He turned, eyebrows raised. "You know jazz?"

She shrugged and smiled, then took in the rest of the room before answering. River-stone fireplace, mantel empty of photos, a rounded bay window with a cushioned seat half-hidden by red-and-blue plaid drapes. A very masculine room. It fit him, even if he had only just arrived home from years abroad. "I enjoy jazz." She remembered the grand piano. "Do you play?"

It was Dimitri's turn to be evasive. "I fool around a bit. On nights like tonight, when dreary weather and an empty house have me feeling a bit—introspective, I suppose."

She gave him a quick smile. "Shall I expect a concert, then?"

He laughed and crossed to the fireplace, already laid with preparations for the next blaze. "Not why I invited you, no."

Her heart sank and the panic rushed back. This was about business—the business she botched. To stop herself from descending into whatever insanity she'd been experiencing, she forced herself to focus on her surroundings as though she were doing research.

The room smelled of wood smoke and spice. How many nights did he sit in that upholstered reading chair before the flames? She attempted a casual glance at the books tossed on a nearby side table. Homer's *Odyssey*. Hesiod's *Theogony*. They were no more for show than the fireplace. Worn paperbacks, not leather-bound collectibles, with a bookmark jutting from the midpoint of Homer.

Rich, great-looking, intelligent. Greek. Powerful. Was there anything this guy didn't have going for him?

"What can I get you to drink?" He glanced at a small marble bar at the side of the office.

"Oh, nothing. Thank you." She adjusted her briefcase strap on her shoulder and drifted to the window. How would the property look from this height?

Behind her, a match struck, with the sharp scent and crackle of kindling and paper catching fire.

He joined her at the glass and peered over her shoulder at the expanse of near-dark lawn.

"Is that—is it a maze?" Her voice tripped over the final word. The hedges along the drive took on new significance from the second floor.

"You should see it in daylight. Even after the long winter, it's beautiful. It's one of the reasons I chose to return to this estate rather than either of the other two family homes."

He hovered close at her back, trapping her between the cold glass and the heat of his chest.

Too many questions, and it felt wrong to ask any of them. Two other estates? Why did the hedge-maze draw him to New York? Where had he been all those years his family had lost track of him?

"Why did you stay away so long?" The words slipped out. She felt his intake of breath behind her.

"Been Googling me, have you?"

She half turned, smiled. "I like to go into battle prepared."

His eyes were still on the half-lit maze, his expression lost in the past, in some sadness that excluded her, some guilt that haunted him. It was clear he was not going to divulge his past.

She turned back to the window and nodded toward the hedges. "I would love to explore."

"Then you should return, as soon as spring makes itself felt."

Had it sounded like she was fishing for another invitation? Regardless, his words melted the glacier of fear that had avalanched over her since last night. He wouldn't invite her back if he was pushing to have her fired, would he? He seemed casual, relaxed—not at all angry like she had expected. A warmth crept across her throat. He still had her pinned at the window, preventing escape. Unless she leaned back into him. This was not at all like she had imagined the evening, and, like the tide pulled toward the moon, she felt herself being drawn to him.

Crazy thoughts.

The jazz piece crescendoed and ended, and in the slight pause before the next, he shifted away from her, toward the fire.

Kallie turned. She couldn't make sense of all of this. "Why did you ask me to come?"

Dimitri sank into the reading chair and waved her to occupy its partner, with the book-strewn table between. "I didn't intend to sound mysterious. I wanted to talk about your Minoan research, as I said on the phone."

"I think you heard enough at the museum gala." She mumbled, hot-faced, and fell into the chair.

He smiled, that knowing, appraising smile she'd noticed last night. "Enough? Yes and no." His voice was low, and firelight painted shadows across his face.

"Hmm . . . cryptic. It suits you."

His gaze was on her, approving. "It's the house. Too many dark corners and skulking statues. Everywhere the ghosts of the family Andreas."

She had to ask. "Did Judith explain the coincidence of our names?" A coldness gripped her insides.

He studied her in silence, then nodded, though a bit uncertain. "She said you—ran into some trouble—a few years back and needed to make a change. You were already interested in Greek and

Minoan cultures and loved the museum, so you chose my family name."

Close enough. She licked dry lips. "It feels a bit presumptuous, now that you're flesh and blood rather than simply a wall engraving."

"I'm happy to share." He rubbed the stubble along his jawline. "And glad my family's name brought you some comfort in a difficult time."

A leading statement, fishing for more of her story. He'd be waiting a long time. She nodded once. "Thank you."

A few beats of awkward silence. Kallie stared into the burgeoning fire, unwilling to ask again why he'd brought her to his mansion on a cold Saturday night but desperately wishing for the suspense to end.

Finally, Dimitri spoke. "So, tell me more about this collection you wish to fund, Kallie."

Ah, at last. She pitched him her well-rehearsed thirty-second spiel about bringing the best of the Linear A tablets to a central location for study and comparison and assembling a team of linguists, then added a few intriguing details about the more recent pieces. Dimitri nodded through her explanation, and she relaxed a little and warmed to her favorite subject.

When she stopped to breathe, he smiled—a smile of amusement at her verbosity, perhaps—then held up a hand.

"Those are all the practical considerations.

Tell me *why* you want this project so much."

"Because I—" she stumbled and paused, searching for the words she should have spoken from the platform last night.

"Just your heart, Kallie. That's all I want to hear."

She breathed out the anxiety and leaned forward, her gaze penetrating his dark eyes for understanding. This was her final chance. "I believe in scholarship, in what history gives to the world. I believe in honoring the past, in searching out where we came from to comprehend where we are going. I want to devote my life to something bigger than myself." Why did agony pour from the same fountain as passion in her soul?

"Why wouldn't you speak last night?" Dimitri's question was soft, the tone entreating.

She sank back into the chair. "Because that's not where my passion lies." At his silence she continued. "I don't want to lead a movement, to be an impressive public speaker. I just want to be left alone to study the mysteries and make a difference from behind the scenes."

Dimitri paused a few moments, gazing into the fire. "What if I told you there was a key to the script, and I knew where to look?"

Her heart seized on itself, then expanded and flipped in her chest. She tried to dismiss the bold statement. "There have always been rumors—"

"More than rumors, Kallie. Much more."

Her years spent scouring the Internet for whispers of the key to the lost Minoan language had yielded little. Like the Rosetta stone that had unlocked Egyptian hieroglyphs because of its parallel passages in Greek, and the Behistun Inscription that gave Old Persian cuneiform to the academic world, the key to Linear A, if it existed, would be inscribed with known languages alongside the unknown.

Kallie sat straighter, eyes wide. "What's it supposed to be? A stele like Rosetta? A cliff face like Behistun?" She fought the rise in pitch of her voice, forgetting everything except the thrilling hope that the elusive mystery might actually be solved.

"I don't know exactly. Not a wall inscription, though. Whatever it is, it's been on the move for many years."

Again, a list of questions too lengthy to speak all at once tripped over her tongue. "Where is it? Who has it? Have they donated—?"

Dimitri stemmed the tide with raised hands. "This is why I called you. You're the one I want to *find* the Linear A Key."

Her heart rate slowed. "Find it? But you said you knew where it was."

"I said I knew where to look. Or at least where to begin looking, which I suppose is not the same."

She shifted back in her chair. What kind of game was he playing? "Not the same at all. You want me to go on a treasure hunt? I suppose you have a map, with a big, red *X* on it?"

Dimitri pressed his fingertips together and pursed his lips. When he spoke, it was still low, with that same gravitational pull. "No map. No. But a few clues. Solid clues."

He was serious.

"Why don't you do it yourself?" She tried to decipher his face.

"Several reasons. For one, I need to personally see to my father's estate here, and it will take some time. But mostly because I want to know what I'm buying, and you're the expert in everything Minoan. You can spot a forgery, authenticate the real thing."

"Hold on." Irritation and a bit of outrage pushed her to her feet. "What you are *buying?* Black market?"

"Sit down, Kallie."

She raised her eyebrows and put her hands to her hips. "Don't tell me to sit down. You ought to know better! Black market antiquities harm all scholarship."

"Please, will you sit? Listen to my explanation?"

She sat on the arm of the seat. "Only to be certain you don't do something stupid."

He smiled and closed his eyes briefly. "If it

exists, the piece has been on the black market for years. I want to locate it, make a good offer, and then acquire it as a donation to your museum."

She glared at him. "So the end justifies the means."

It was an old debate, actually. There were thousands, perhaps hundreds of thousands, of valuable pieces changing hands every year, sold by one mysterious collector to another and hidden away in private estates like Dimitri's. Unprovenanced items whose origins were unknown. Did scholars overstep ethical bounds when they offered money to disreputable dealers to acquire pieces for museums? Opinions varied and were often heated.

Dimitri held eye contact with her. "Yes. The end justifies the means. Especially if we are talking about the Linear A Key. I will do whatever is necessary to put this piece in the hands of those who can best use it."

Kallie would not admit it, but so would she.

Still, the black market. It fired off every nerve ending in her body to think about complicity with such a system. Or with one of the rich collectors who perpetuated it.

"Think what you want of me, Kallie. I probably deserve it. But don't pass up this chance."

"So you expect me to leave my job, go traipsing about the back alleys of Europe or the Middle East perhaps, to search out smarmy antiquities

Cass County Public Library
Pleasant Hill Branch
****

User ID: 20022001237262

Item ID: 0002203949801
Title: Love finds you in Sunset Beach, Hawaii
Date due: 5/3/2018,23:59

Item ID: 0002204850370
Title: Come home
Date due: 5/3/2018,23:59

Item ID: 0002205025493
Title: Awakening [text (large print)]
Date due: 5/3/2018,23:59

Item ID: 0002205017615
Title: The readers of broken wheel recommend [text (larg
Date due: 5/3/2018,23:59

Thank You

dealers and pass them wads of cash?" She folded her arms across her chest.

"I've put together a team for you."

It was such an unexpectedly serious answer to her sarcasm that it pushed her backward. A swirl of excitement rippled through her, raised the hair on her arms. "A team?"

His dark eyes were trained on her as though to root out any hesitation, any fear. "You'd be the antiquities expert. But I have a language specialist for Greek and Linear B, assuming they'd be the parallel languages, and an assistant for travel arrangements since you might be moving around a bit. Also a bit of muscle. For protection." This last was said with a hesitant, even nervous, tenor to his voice.

"Protection?"

"I wouldn't ask if I thought there was any real danger—but—just to be safe."

Kallie blew out an overwhelmed breath. Her mouth had gone dry and her skin felt clammy. "I don't know, Dimitri. There is more than one concern here. Besides safety, I'm not comfortable with black-market dealings. And how can I leave my job?"

He crossed one leg over the other and draped an arm over the back of his chair. "As for your job, I have a bit of pull at the museum." A little smile emerged. "You'll be on sabbatical, and they'll welcome you back. And to your ethical concerns," he waved a hand, "you must see the provenance of this piece isn't nearly as important as its authentication. Where it's been, where it was originally dug up, if indeed it was ever buried, matter very little. It's the language decipherment possibilities that make it valuable. Besides," he leaned forward, his eyes bright, "wouldn't you rather see a dedicated Minoan historian deciphering it than some old man in Prague or Belgium adding it to his private collection?"

"You know the answer."

"Exactly. I know your passion, Kallie. I saw it at the gala." He spread his palms. "I had hoped to see a bit more natural leadership, since I'm asking you to take charge of this team and I'm funding your efforts . . . but Judith believes you have what it takes." He rested those smoky eyes on hers again. "And I think perhaps *you* are the only one who doesn't see it."

Kallie rubbed her wrist, studied the fire. "And what about my research project? The funds needed to bring the pieces . . ." She let the question evaporate. Getting Dimitri to sponsor an inferior project was hopeless. Not when he had the rumored "Key" in his sights.

He unfolded his long frame from the chair, stepped to the fire, and rearranged an errant log with an iron poker. With his back still to her, he braced his hand on the mantel, then leaned his forehead against it. "It must be done. We can't allow the Key to be lost again."

"Why are *you* so committed to it, Dimitri? Why Linear A? Why the Minoans?"

He didn't turn at once, didn't speak. But when he faced her, his eyes held some of that pain she'd sensed last night when she'd found him trying to get closer to the carnelian seal.

"I don't know, Kallista." The words were whispered with the intensity of a boy who feared monsters behind closed doors. "I don't know. I just—I have always been fascinated—" He turned away and said no more.

Heart racing, she joined him at the fire, touched a gentle hand to his shoulder, and murmured, "You don't have to explain. I understand." She did. All too well.

It was like the soul's search for God, too personal for words. The lure of the Greek islands of Crete and Santorini, of Knossos with its golden palaces, of the stories of Minos and his Minotaur, Ariadne and Theseus, Daedalus, and Icarus flying too close to the sun—all of it had enraptured her for as long as she could remember. Which was to say, all seven years of her life.

Dimitri clasped her hand in both of his own, part handshake, part entreaty. "You'll go then?"

She frowned. "I don't even know where—"

"Egypt."

She pulled her hand away and breathed the

word. "Egypt." Desert and camels, temples and tombs and pyramids. The very thought was at once exotic and thrilling.

"The rumor is the Linear A Key was part of the Abd el-Rassul family heist in 1871."

"The royal cache in Deir el-Bahri?"

He smiled, affirming her professional capacity, even if the personal still felt a bit off balance.

"Yes. And if it *was* part of the cache they uncovered, it would have ended up on the black market when they sold off everything they'd raided."

"But why would the Key be in Thebes? That burial site dates back to at least twenty-first dynasty, right?"

"Eighteenth. And I don't know how it would have gotten to Egypt."

Kallie's mind spun with possibilities, and she turned from Dimitri to pace the reds and grays of the Persian rug. "There *was* trade between Crete and Egypt. And there are some indications that those who escaped Santorini before the eruption may have gone to Thebes. They could have taken it with them, or at least taken their language and created it there later . . ." She stopped pacing. Was he following her garbled ruminations?

But he was nodding, as though he'd thought it through already. For a businessman, he knew his history.

She bit her lip. "But the el-Rassuls sold off their

finds nearly 150 years ago. It could be anywhere by now."

"But it's not." He swallowed and looked away. "At least, that's what my sources tell me."

No need to ask about his sources. His hesitance told her he preferred to keep them private.

"I have a name." He ran a hand through his dark hair, leaving it a bit ruffled. "A contact for you, who can put you in touch with another—someone with some shady dealings. He's off the grid, apparently. Can't be contacted through usual channels. It needs to be in person."

He was giving her details. As though she had agreed. Had she?

"I'll think about it, Dimitri."

He blinked twice and rubbed at his forehead. "Well, Judith told me you were a hard nut to crack. I suppose that's all I can ask."

Another awkward silence. Maybe he could play that piano for her. Or show her the rest of this magnificent house.

"I'll have Martin drive you home."

Right.

After a stilted good-bye in the foyer, Martin ushered her into the backseat, and they glided past the hedge maze, through the iron gate, and into the night, speeding toward the city.

It had been a night of surprises. Was it excitement or dread that left her hollowed out, her stomach knotted? The Andreas Estate and its enigmatic owner disappeared behind her, but the smell of wood smoke and cologne, the sounds of soft jazz, and the wonderment of the chance she'd been offered clung to her like the raindrops on the car's dark windows.

Dimitri Andreas was most likely a man without principles, who stood for everything she hated. And the quiet security of her museum life was all she knew.

Could she give it up to chase a rumor across the globe?

⤜ 5 ⤛

In the open courtyard of the palace danced a mesmerizing interplay of soft light and cool shadow, of fountain-water melodies and sighs of sea breezes, of exotic blooms both living and invented. In this joyous and open place, I chose to pursue my studies and my sister pursued her art.

Kallie shoved Judith's journal away, tossed the pen against its cover. She should be working on the article she was writing, pushing forward in her argument for the *Minoan Collective*. Instead, those blank pages called out to her imagination, and she had succumbed. That first paragraph released some long-held fear. Where had the words come from? Where would they go, if she allowed herself the freedom to follow? She slowly picked up the pen and touched it to the paper. Perhaps only a few more minutes . . .

She had great skill, my sister, with all manner of dyes and paints, and she tied luxurious brushes from the hair of the black goats that clambered at outrageous angles on the island's sun-splashed hills. I studied her this morning, my head raised from my texts, her fat brush dipping, dipping into a dish of cerulean blue, mixing with plaster, spread in confident strokes along the west wall, which transformed into a dolphin leaping across pale-blue spirals, spirals that called to mind the waves that caressed the white strand far beneath the palace. Melayna loved to paint dolphins.

My older sister's hair flowed down her back in its own dark waves, loosed and wild, not yet plaited. I had attended to hair and dress before leaving chambers, knowing that once my texts claimed my attention, I would think of little else.

Melayna seemed to sense my gaze and turned, brush upraised. "Something amiss?" Her tone was suspicious and sharp.

I smiled. "Beautiful. As always. I love the water."

Melayna raised her eyes to the cloud-strewn heavens and exhaled heavily, as if calling on the goddess herself to give patience with my stupidity. "The waves are barely begun, Chloe.

Much more ornamentation is needed. Here," she jabbed at the lower border of the fresco, "and here."

"I prefer simplicity."

She gave me her back. "Of course you do."

With this inscrutable agreement ringing in my ears, I returned to my clay tablets and the history of our people. The artistic was my sister's domain and clearly I had no eye for it. Ours was a living, breathing art—full of whorls and spins, beauty drawn from tendrils of plants, tentacles of octopus, coil of snake—a curvilinear art that spiraled along our walls and our pottery and more than anything, deep under the massive hills of our island, where the rainwater of millennia had worn intricate, lacy mazes through the limestone.

This history of stone I understood, but the art it birthed, I only appreciated. No, it was language where I excelled. The loops of logic and tangential stories like tide pools swirling along the edges of the greater sea of our people. This was all the art I needed.

I ran light fingers over Bardas's most recent tablets, still heavy and damp, still formable. A trill of excitement surged to my fingertips. I could change history with the merest pressure of my stylus, rewrite what had come before and thus change what was still to come. Bardas had honored me by asking for an early reading, when corrections could still be pressed into the wet clay. And he had risked Mother's censure, for royal daughters had no need of the past, only an eye on the future and on the kingdom.

But I am only the younger daughter.

This I repeated to myself twice more, as though thrice-stated it would erase the words of the Oracle who had spoken over me at birth, words still whispered by aging palace servants and time-worn priestesses who clung to the old ways.

The Oracle's words—conferred but never explained.

"The younger shall rule the elder."

We had never spoken of the Oracle's prophecy, Melayna and I. Nor would we, I expected. But it remained there between us, a rocky cliff jutting up, keeping us ever apart. She eyed everything I did with distrust. If she had seen my heart, seen how the thought of rulership terrified me, perhaps it would have changed her affections. But revealing my heart had never come easily.

Two sharp claps drew our attention from tablets and tableaus. The queen glided into the court-yard, followed by her ladies. She wore a heavy dress of pale pink today, flounced in four over-lapping layers descending from her waist, swishing as she moved.

"White sails at port. Twelve horses on the Marina Road, girls. Coming fast." The words were clipped, nervous, and her glance darted from my dress, my plaited hair, to Melayna's disarray and blue-stained fingers. My sister's gaze met my mother's, wide with concern.

"Make haste, Melayna!"

Melayna threw her brush into the paint bowl, deposited the bowl at the fresco's base, and fled the sunny courtyard. Mother flicked a hand toward the servants and they hustled behind Melayna, ready to attend.

Her attention shifted to me. "Put away the tablets, Chloe. Tend to the flowers or something. I won't have suitors believing you prefer the deeds of men already dead to the living, breathing—"

"But I *do* prefer—"

"Hush!" The word was not spoken harshly. Mother silenced me with an upraised hand. "The suitors will be here to woo both of my daughters, and I won't have you unmarried all of your days."

A fear I sometimes shared.

She disappeared, perhaps up the Grand Staircase to the royal quarters, to assure herself that Melayna would present herself well, and I gathered the tablets with a low mutter. Would the clay still be damp when this newest spate of suitors departed?

They came in waves, and on the waves, to vie for the hands of the island's royal daughters. Succession to the throne of Kalliste had always been through the female line. Marriage to the king's daughter made one a king, and the queen held the reins of power as tightly as her husband.

Which was why the Oracle's prophecy made little sense.

Melayna wanted a husband, and she wanted to be queen. I wanted only to study. And perhaps to love. But only if love did not mean the sacrifice of my studies.

With the mainland people of Mycenae ever increasing their military strength and threatening our way of life, a marriage alliance for the second daughter was also a priority. My father had even attempted to offer me to the prince of Mycenae himself, although I had taken secret measures to ensure that marriage would never occur. Would my parents yet force marriage upon me—to one of the fools who blundered across the sea in hopes of becoming King of Kalliste?

Not today.

I stashed Bardas's tablets in a storage room off the courtyard, alongside the great earthenware jars filled with oil and grain, then fled along a corridor, past massive columns like inverted tree trunks, their bases narrow and elegant and their capitals impossibly splayed, as if rather than earthbound they were stretching toward the heavens.

Built upon the rocky summit of Kalliste, the far-flung palace was a study in constant fluid movement, just as in our art. I ran down several levels, past openings into courtyards and corridors, along light-shafts and down dark flights of steps, through halls and colonnades and across terraces, and finally down a crumbling set of wide, shallow steps to the welcome feel of grass beneath my bare feet. The scent of vineyards and olive groves perfumed the air. The morning mists burned away to reveal the earth sloping sharply downward to the water. To my left was the sacred High Place, where we worshipped the goddess, but it was the sea below that called to me.

The men would come, and they would first present themselves to our parents. Melayna would see them, one by one, in a sun-bright receiving room ornamented with frescoes of our people resplendent in daily life, reminding the suitors that to rule Kalliste was to rule a peace-loving, joyous people who worked hard and loved well.

And I would be at the sea's edge, avoiding false flattery, or brutish manners, or the smell of too many days since port. Biding time until they were sent on their quest and did not return.

The grass thinned, gave way to coarse white sand that scraped at my feet, but this is how the sea welcomes, and I did not slow until the foamy lip of water tickled my skin and the roar of waves filled my hearing.

I gave myself to the cocoon of harmony that

was Kalliste and walked along the water's edge, its peace soothing my irritation. Majestic peaks rose above me, goat kids sounded their raucous bleats, and bees murmured as they journeyed among the dizzying, sun-warmed aromatics of thyme and sage.

How long until Father commissioned each of the hopefuls with the Challenge? Would the Oracle come in her black-hooded robe, intoning what had now become legend?

"One Truth, one truth only can save Kalliste. This truth has been hidden, covered up to the destruction of the people. It must be retrieved before the Time of the End."

Somewhere in the Green Mountains, along the eastern ridge of Kalliste, this Horn of Truth had been hidden in one of the thousand shadowy caverns bored into the fir-covered hills. Not only hidden, the Oracle said. Guarded. By a beast too terrible to describe, though some said it was half-man, half-bull and had lived there since ages past remembering.

In truth, I thanked this beast for hoarding his secret, for it meant that one after another of the loutish hopefuls disappeared into the hills. They did not return—proven worthy to co-rule Kalliste. They did not return at all.

A crab scratched along the sand toward the water. I stopped to watch, to trace its crooked tracks into the sea, erased a moment later as if it had never existed. The fleeting nature of all of life.

"The crab runs faster, even, than the king's daughter."

I whirled to the amused voice at my back, found a tallish stranger in a simple white tunic, belted with a red woven sash. I shrugged. "Perhaps he also has good reason."

The stranger smiled, still amused at my expense, and I lifted my chin to meet his mockery. He was well built and agreeable looking, a bit older than myself, I guessed. Something stirred in my chest, a warmth that came from more than the sun.

"Did you come with the suitors for my sister's hand?"

He dipped his head briefly. "I have just arrived, yes. But for what reason, this I have yet to determine."

I turned back to the sea. His presence disturbed my island peace, and the tremor that ran along my nerves confused my senses. "Perhaps when you hear what is required, you will determine you have come for the sea breezes and the Kallistan olives and wine alone."

He did not answer for a long moment.

I could feel him at my back, gazing over the water with me.

"Or possibly I will discover I have come for something I did not expect to find."

Something in his voice, the intimate way it played over my shoulder, as if his words were meant for me, raised the flesh on my arms in spite of the warmth. I licked my lips, breathed in the salty air, said nothing.

"Will you show me your island?" His voice faded a bit, as he must have turned his head to take in the wild beauty. "I would see it all. To know what it is I seek."

I glanced upward to the palace. Did Mother stand at the topmost terrace, frowning down on the impropriety of my receiving a suitor on the strand? Or was the stranger only a servant, a sailor, or keeper of horses, attached to a wealthy merchant who even now begged favors from Melayna?

"I will show you."

And so we walked, along the western rim of Kalliste, with the warm breath of Egypt whispering across the sea, caressing our faces. I showed him the dark jaws of caves and the fleeting shadows of wild boars, the scurry of scorpions and vipers through the maquis scrub, and we walked along forests of fruited olive trees and cypress and down hills of pale-pink convolvulus and dark-blue petromarula. Ravens cawed from their craggy nests in lofty ravines, and we spoke of the history of Kalliste, and of Athens, the city of his birth. And I learned that his name was Andreas, and that he was a good man.

The gold disc of the sun sank lower in the cobalt sky and still we walked and talked. He listened with interest to all I had described, as no one ever had. He laughed at my wry observations of palace life and frowned when I spoke of my days spent alone. And when the reds and golds and bronze of sunset tinged the western sky, we sat on the palace hill watching dying light tremble across the water and turn waves to molten silver. It was then I knew I did not wish him to be a suitor. For suitors must always leave.

The sun still hovered at the edge of sea, as if she conspired to lengthen this moment between us. Andreas lay across the grass at my side, propped on one elbow, a blade of grass between his fingers. "It is well known, even across the sea, what is required to win the hand of the king of Kalliste's daughter."

I closed my eyes against the beauty and against the pain.

"You would venture to gain the Horn of Truth, to win my sister?"

He laughed and lay back in the grass, his hands behind his head. "It has only been one glorious day, Chloe, but you know my heart better than that already, I am certain."

I did. By the Great Goddess, somehow I did.

I turned on him, pierced him with my sternest look. "You must not go. You must not."

"What choice do I have? To watch you from afar? To sail back to Athens empty-hearted?" The grass around him rippled in the evening breeze and a coolness rose from the water as the sun died.

In one day I had found him, and I would lose him. Lose him to the labyrinthine caverns of the Green Mountains. It was like tasting the tiniest drop of sweet honey on one's tongue, only to have it chased away by bitter herbs. I shivered and Andreas sat upright, wrapped a warm arm around my shoulders, pulled me to himself.

Long I had blessed the beast who kept me safe, but today I cursed him. In the half darkness, a goat bleated, a sad, discordant cry that echoed my own sense of loss.

As the first stars appeared, they shone their cold light down on my cold tears and I buried my head in his neck and wept.

> 6 <

Kallie reached the museum early Monday morning, even before Judith, and sank into her office chair with the sigh of one who had finally arrived home. Friday night had been a disaster, but the new week offered fresh opportunities and the chance for redemption. The certainty of what she must do was as solid as the heavy rhyton vase reproduction on her desk. In fact, dozens of reminders of her sure calling jumbled in her overcrowded office. She worked best here, surrounded by what little security she had created. She was not some sort of quest leader. She was an academic.

She stared at the wall-mounted clock beside her closed door, the second hand stuttering around its face. How long until Judith stalked the office halls? The clock—a silly imitation of a stone sundial—had been given to her by a guy she dated as an undergrad. One of her few relationships. She kept it more as a reminder that she could actually *have* a relationship than as a memento of him. Red mosaic stones rimmed the gray rock face, marking the hours. Would Judith show before nine o'clock?

She'd keep one ear tuned to the hall, alert for Judith's arrival so she could begin reparations. Time to focus on getting this periodical article finished. The submission deadline loomed only two weeks away. She would use every impressive writing skill she possessed to secure the needed funding for the *Minoan Collective*. Better than tramping through seedy neighborhoods in foreign countries looking for an ancient relic—that may not even exist—with a cobbled-together team in tow.

Besides, she was qualified to write this article. What was Dimitri thinking when he asked her to lead his team? She'd paid her dues to earn her position here in the museum. She'd done nothing to earn a plane ticket to Upper Egypt.

So. The paper. Much more logical. She sucked in a deep breath of office air, saturated with that wonderful dust-and-mildew smell of an old library, and dove into her next goal. Laser-like focus, all else blocked out, until this paper was outlined and the direction of her argument clear.

The ticking of the clock kept time with her fingers on the keyboard over the next hour, reminding her that her time ran down toward zero. With breaks only to gulp from a mug of strong coffee, she pushed forward, cross-checking facts, inserting well-supported opinions, and carefully citing sources. She kept pushing aside the prickling fear she was missing some-thing—something that tried to insert itself into her conscious mind like a worm wriggling through solid earth. A gap in her research? Or a gap in her life? Whatever it was, it wasn't worth stopping momentum for.

The sundial marked nearly nine thirty before voices in the hall pulled her back to the present, lifted her fingers from the keyboard and her nose from a ponderous text on early Crete. Judith's voice. And another.

Two quick knocks, followed by her door swinging open. Kallie jumped to her feet, startled and heart racing, prepared for the onslaught. In truth, she'd been surprised Judith hadn't called over the weekend, but she'd been grateful for the respite. Given all that had happened with Dr. Newsom, her strange bridge incident, the intense meeting with Dimitri, and the day of penning strange tales—an angry call from Judith might have shattered her completely.

Judith stood framed by the doorway, all five feet of her, with hair especially spiky today and red lipstick a slash across tight lips.

But a strange kind of relief flooded Kallie's tight muscles, for behind Judith stood Dimitri. He'd come to the museum again.

"Look who I found wandering the halls." Judith's eyes glittered like cold blue stones, telegraphing an angry message: *You've got another chance, maybe, if you can manage to act like a professional.*

Kallie forced a smile to cover the twitch of eyes and facial muscles. "Good morning, Judith. And Mr. Andreas, nice to see you again."

Dimitri nodded. "And you, Ms. Andreas." His politeness was forced, artificial. He bowed to Judith, still blocking the door like a tiny stone sentry. "Judith, could you possibly carve out some time for me after I've finished speaking with Ms. Andreas?"

Judith beamed and touched a hand against his chest. "Of course, of course."

He smiled and clasped her hand as though she'd granted him a momentous favor. "I'll stop by your office, then?"

"Yes, I'll be expecting you." With another sunny look at Dimitri, Judith disappeared toward her office.

Kallie cleared her throat to hide her amusement at Judith's flirtatiousness. Dimitri had a masterful ability to handle the woman. Unrivaled, as far as Kallie had seen. He'd somehow managed to both flatter and dismiss.

He nudged the door until it closed with a soft *click*.

She fiddled with a yellow highlighter on her desk. "Judith—likes you." The word choice seemed odd, though true.

Dimitri shrugged, a teasing smile playing about his lips. "Doesn't everyone?"

Yes, I'll bet they do. In his short-sleeved white shirt, showing off his European-tanned biceps, he looked like Adonis, god of beauty. His presence filled up her already-overfull office until there was no room left to breathe.

Kallie extended a hand toward a folding chair against a bare spot of wall, the best she could offer by way of accommodations. "What can I do for you this morning?"

But he ignored the chair and crossed to the bookshelves instead, tilting his head to read spines, picking up a Black-Figure period bowl, painted with familiar gold silhouettes chasing across the black glaze.

"You said you'd think about my proposal." His back was to her, hands and eyes still roaming her shelves.

She couldn't speak. Instead, she studied the casual set of his shoulders, the squared-off cut of his dark hair against his tanned neck.

He picked up a mottled-green faience pendant. "You didn't say how long you'd be thinking."

"Yes. Well. I want to thank you for the—intriguing—offer, Dimitri."

He replaced the pendant, did a slow turn to face her, took a step closer. His mouth flattened in disappointment.

He obviously heard the refusal in her tone. His voice was low, intense, as he moved behind her desk. "You must see you are the best person for this project, Kallie. The world needs your special talents."

He was much too close. She felt boxed in. Would he reach for her? Shake her into agreement? She straightened, tried to lean away discreetly. That heady mix of wood smoke and spice filled her senses again. Everything about Dimitri Andreas was intense.

As she had the other night, she glimpsed that elusive quality that made him so powerful, that ability to command simply with his presence, to inspire others with his vision. To win an audience.

She cleared her throat. "You flatter me, but I assure you the world can get along fine without me. I am much better suited to serving Minoan interests through my research and writing." She pointed to the latest copy of *The Curator Review*. "In fact, I've been working on an important article for the *Review* this morning. I'm hoping it will bring the Collective the attention it deserves—"

"So that's it?" He pushed even closer, trapping her between her chair and his chest. His dark eyes roamed her face.

She froze. He could grab her hands with his own, the space between them was so narrow. She glanced around the room for an escape.

"You are going to hide away in this crypt of an office until you're as old as Judith? Penning pleas for money to fund second-rate projects while the answers are out there, within your grasp?"

Kallie tossed her hair behind her shoulder. How dare he dismiss her life's work as though it were nothing more than paper pushing? She glared at him. "This is where I belong, Dimitri. The museum is my *home*."

"I don't believe that." He glanced around the windowless space, at the cluttered shelves and stacked papers, then back to her eyes. "Someone like you should not be buried alive, Kallista Andreas. Hidden behind closed doors and false names." His voice was gentle, nearly impossible to resist. He carefully came back to her, lifted her chin up to look at him, hesitated briefly while her eyes widened, then traced a finger along her jaw. "You cannot see what is true about yourself."

His touch on her face burned and she kicked her chair backward to give herself space, braced a hand on her desk, then straightened a stack of papers. "You're looking for someone else." Every instinct told her to run. Now. But she couldn't move.

"No. I know exactly what I'm looking for."

She held unnaturally still, frozen in time, and the ticking clock echoed. Finally, she lowered herself into her chair—*her* chair, *her* desk, *her* office. She touched her keyboard lightly. "I should get back to my work."

He said nothing, only exited her office with a suddenness that seemed to suck the air out with him, leaving her deflated at her desk, fingers slack and mouth dry.

His interest lay in only her research skills, his desire that she do his black-market bidding across the ocean. She knew nothing about him, and she didn't like secrets.

The encounter left her shaky, unsure. She rolled her shoulders back, stretched the anxiety from her neck muscles, and took a deep breath. The paper. She got up and closed her door. Firmly.

An hour later she'd made little progress. Her

mind was in a whirl. Judith had not breached her office. Did Dimitri go to her, complaining about Kallie's uncooperativeness? Would he tell Judith of his crazy quest?

Her office phone rang. The reprieve must have ended.

"Kallista Andreas."

"Yes, Ms. Andreas, this is Jennifer Shaw, Mr. Suarez's assistant."

Kallie stopped breathing as though the head curator had walked into her office rather than instructed his assistant to call. "Yes, Jennifer. What can I do for you?"

"Mr. Suarez would like to see you, as soon as you are able to come."

Kallie bit her lip, closed her eyes. A tremble began in her legs. "Of course. I'll come right away."

File Menu, Save, Minimize, Sleep. She performed the mouse functions numbly, her thoughts frantic.

Roberto Suarez had always seemed a kind man, if a bit austere. Did he hear about Friday night's speech? Intend to chastise her lack of finesse? Perhaps she'd be skipping Judith's rant altogether with a reprimand issued directly from the top.

With slick palms and pounding blood, she crossed the sunlit Lewis Gallery, half stumbled through the shadowy Andreas Hall, and reached the central wing. As the elevator pitched upward, her heart lurched to her feet.

She formulated explanations, apologies, regrets. Steeled herself for anger or animosity.

Jennifer rose when Kallie arrived and ushered her to Suarez's office. The first time in her two years of working at the museum. She nodded her thanks at Jennifer, unable to speak.

She cautiously entered his office. Spacious, elegant, and intimidating. A huge mahogany desk commanded the center of the room, with a massive antique globe on a metal stand in front, like the rudder of a ship. Pale collectibles stood at attention on black shelves and the wall of windows. She scanned the sea of open space between herself and the curator, who stood when she entered.

"Ms. Andreas. Thank you for coming so promptly."

She left the obvious unsaid—she could no more ignore his summons than she could continue working through a fire alarm.

"Please, sit."

The chair he indicated faced his desk but sat at an unnatural distance, almost in the center of the room. She lowered herself into it, and gripped the armrests with white knuckles, stranded in the center of the sea in the uncomfortable chair.

Suarez was a middle-aged, medium-height man with an average build and an ordinary demeanor. Such blandness should have put her at ease. It did not. She focused on his red power tie, the only bright spot of color in the room.

He let the silence stretch a few beats too long for comfort, then cleared his throat. "Ms. Andreas, I have been hearing—reports—about Friday night's important fund-raising event." His voice was mild, smooth, like a medium-roast coffee poured slowly.

She swallowed, met his eyes, and waited for the appropriate moment to speak.

"It seems all did not go as we had hoped."

"I'm afraid I was unprepared—"

He held up a palm, just above the level of his desk. A small movement but effective. "The cause matters little, I'm afraid. It's the effect that concerns us today."

Her legs were crossed, her foot bouncing. She worked to keep it still, while her thoughts careened and crashed.

"We have had several patrons express doubts about your department's research. About you. The museum operates on a shoestring, as you know, and any funding that is pulled is disastrous."

"I can assure you, Mr. Suarez—"

Again, the slight motion of the hand. She had been braced for anger but found him to be only formal . . . and, oddly, sad.

"It seems best that you leave us for a while, Ms. Andreas. Perhaps some additional schooling? Make certain that a career in the museum is truly what you want—"

"It *is* what I want! It's all I've ever wanted." She fought down the note of hysteria, turmoil in her belly.

"Is it? Since you were a little girl?" His brows were raised, the subtext obvious.

Judith must have told him of her lack of a past. The rescue from the unknown. Kallie ran a hand through her hair, tucked it behind her ear. What answer could she give?

"Perhaps, Ms. Andreas, the museum has been a necessary, and logical, part of your journey. A haven for you, I believe. Needed for a time, but only a stepping stone on the way to something else."

"No!" She was gripping the chair's arms again. *Calm down, Kallie.* "No. I love it here, love my work. And I can learn the rest—interacting with the public, winning over the patrons. Minoan and Greek research is my *life,* Mr. Suarez." She was begging now.

"Yes, I believe you. I admire your passion. But I also hope you find something else."

Something else? What else was there?

He was standing. "Ms. Shaw has a package for you on your way out, just the usual forms and such, along with an explanation of severance . . ."

The rest of his canned speech floated into the atmosphere. Kallie heard none of it.

He walked her to the door, guiding her with a hand on her elbow.

She walked on marble legs, cold, lifeless. She accepted the packet from Jennifer, then walked through heavy fog to reach her office.

Fired. She'd been fired. One bad speech and she was out. Adrift in the world.

She collapsed into her desk chair, laid her head on the scattered papers on her desk, tried to hold back the tears and stop the spinning chaos in the center of her soul.

What did she have without this job? Judith had found her huddled on the museum floor all those years ago, cleaned her up, taken her to doctors for treatment and government offices for paperwork, located scholarships, coached her through undergrad and graduate school, and finally gotten her this position—the culmination of a seven-year struggle to create a life. What was there beyond this place?

Could she really have been fired simply because of Friday night's flub? Or was something else at work? Did Judith want to push her out of the nest? The other possibility—that Dimitri had shoved his weight around—settled on her with uncomfortable pressure.

The *Minoan Collective*. The paper. She lifted her head. There was still a chance to continue with her research, to be involved in Minoan studies. And now she'd have plenty of time to write an excellent article before the deadline.

Perfectionism drove her to pick up the periodical

and flip to the submission guidelines for perhaps the tenth time, to recheck the deadline. She scanned the page. She'd need to mail it a few days before—

Her glance stopped short, anchored by a sentence she'd glossed over every time she read the guidelines.

Periodical contributors must be employed full-time by an approved institution . . .

Everything solid dropped away. The museum, her research, her office. Her life.

She fought the salty thickness of emotion at the back of her throat, gripped the edge of her desk at the panicked hurricane of her thoughts and the physical upheaval of her body.

Imagination beckoned, inviting her into its safe delusions, its grand and lovely mirage. She couldn't —not now. She shook her head against it, battled to stay in the present, no matter how dreadful.

The life she'd created in the past seven years was slipping from her grasp. But there was more to her than the museum and the research. There had to be. She had to find it.

The ticking false sundial mocked her now, reminding her of days and months and years gone by, irretrievable time, shrouded and unknown. The past was an empty hole, the present evaporating.

And what terrors did the future hold?

She reached for Judith's journal, hidden in her

purse, needing the escape in a physical, desperate way.

She would just record a few thoughts, just to calm her mind and body down before . . . before packing up her beloved office. Digging around for a pen, she hurriedly opened to a clean page.

➥ 7 ⬿

All I love will soon be lost.

Andreas and I found stolen hours together, on the misty hillsides under the morning sun, or hidden deep in the palace—away from servants, from my ever-watchful parents, and from Melayna, who clearly had chosen Andreas as her own from the fresh crop of suitors arriving from Athens.

He had made his fortune as a merchant but cared little for money and longed for influence, for a place to make a difference. This longing launched him across wind and wave in exploration. To sail the seas to unknown worlds was his heart's desire. It led him finally to the island of Kalliste, where rumor had it that a man could become king if he earned the hand of the princess through feats of glory.

"But you did not know how many had failed?" I whispered the words, though we were far from listening ears. I had led Andreas through our palace maze, into storage chambers lodged deep in the hill, and we sat upon a blanket of gold and red, sharing a meal of sweet grapes with pungent olives and cheeses and a cask of new wine.

He laughed, and the sound echoed against the silent walls of the chamber, as if we were the only creatures that existed. "No, somehow those facts never reached Athens."

I tossed a grape at him and it plunked against his solid chest. "How can you laugh? As if the danger was not real?"

He retrieved the grape from the blanket and bit down on it, still smiling.

I straightened. "You have changed your mind? You will not go?"

I had been pestering him with this argument. "Forget the Challenge, forget the Horn of Truth. Take me away to Athens."

Andreas sobered. "Chloe, I must go. There is no honor in cheating destiny. You know this." He took my hand in his, a warm clasp of belonging and security. "You must think of your people. The Truth must be found, to save them from destruction. And then there is your prophecy."

"Bah." I pulled my hand from his grasp, unwilling to admit the prick of guilt his words brought. Why had I told him of the priestess's words spoken at my birth? "Oracles have been predicting doom since the beginning of time. It is their way."

He tilted a chin to the frescoed walls. "Tell me of the paintings."

He thought to distract me from my distress. I did not answer, only traced the outline of his strong brow and cheek and jaw with my eyes, constraining my desire to touch his face.

"Never have I seen storage rooms decorated thus. Certainly you Kallistans have an unrivaled love of beauty."

"Is not Athens a beautiful city?"

"It is becoming such. But I fear we are interested more in war and philosophy than art."

My gaze played over the frescoes of our chamber, half revealed in the flickering light of our single oil lamp. "Our art is about mystery as much as beauty. The whirls and spirals, they draw you in, invite you to feel the pang of longing, the desire to understand secrets of the unknown, to go deeper and deeper still."

He followed my gaze, and I could see he chased the red lines swirling against the black backdrop. "And where do they lead, all of these secrets?"

"Everywhere. And nowhere."

He brought his look to me, to my eyes, my face, my lips. Smiled at what he saw. "An enigmatic answer, as is fitting. And perhaps Athens and Kalliste are not so far apart. Perhaps the mysteries of our philosophy and your art are one and the same."

I smiled and he drew me to himself and wrapped fierce arms around me until it seemed we were more one person than two. The musky scent of the chamber mingled with the scent of him, and he whispered against my ear, the words muffled and grave. "And you are the jewel of Kalliste, Chloe. The brightest bit of beauty I have yet seen."

I dissolved into the comfort of his embrace, let it saturate every part me, even while I fought against my desire to cling to him, to keep him from the quest. Already I felt the cords between us stretching taut, the connection near to breaking.

How long we remained thus and what we exchanged I shall not say. But when the day was long spent and we retraced our path through the darkened palace hand in hand, I knew that if Andreas must leave me the next morning, he would not leave unaided. Somehow I would find a way to ensure his safe return—to the palace and to my arms.

"Meet me before the sun has risen," I whispered as we parted at the terraced steps of the palace.

Andreas cupped my head with both hands, kissed me gently. "You shall not be far from me until then."

With one last grasp, born of desperation, I pressed my head against his chest. "We can leave now. Sail out for Athens with the sun, before—"

"No, Chloe."

His words were tender, though unyielding.

"One day you will be the good and passionate leader of your people. I would not rob them, nor you, of that brilliant destiny." He lifted my chin, kissed me again, with a passion of his own. "Until the morning. Sleep in peace."

And then he was gone, taking the palace steps two at a time, disappearing into the gloom of night. Even the moon hid behind clouds of sorrow.

I had a destination of my own, and it was not my bedchamber.

But before I could escape down the palace steps and into the city, my name echoed through the portico, sharp and accusing.

"Chloe!"

I turned to my mother's wrath.

"Where have you been?"

Even in the gloom, her face was purpled with rage. This was about more than the hidden hours of a wayward daughter.

"What is it, Mother? What has happened?"

In answer, she grabbed my arm painfully and dragged me to the throne room.

We found my father there, pacing, a tablet clutched in his hand. He turned on us and raised the tablet. "This is your doing?"

I trembled under his wrath. "I—I do not know—"

"From the king of Mycenae, who would like nothing more than to swallow our people."

My belly thudded. It had been months. I had regretted my hasty winter actions as the spring neared, but when no harm had come, I had nearly forgotten.

"My royal seal? You used my royal seal to write such a letter—insulting the king and his offer of a treaty marriage with his son—pretending to be me—"

"Father, I cannot—"

"Silence!" His eyes were like dagger points and spittle flecked the corners of his mouth. "Had you no thought for tomorrow? For your people?"

Mother spoke quietly from behind me. "For your father?"

I glanced at the tablet. "What has happened? What does he say?"

"What *could* he say, my foolish and arrogant daughter? He has honor to preserve. They are already sending armies to destroy us." He held up the letter. "And before the armies arrive—a single attacker will infiltrate, one who will ensure I am not alive to see our people destroyed."

I exhaled in a rush, the air sucked from my lungs.

The Destruction of our People.

Long had it been prophesied. And the *cause* of this destruction would be my own hasty actions?

My mother stepped to my side. "Leave us,

child. There is nothing more for you to do here."

I stumbled from the throne room. Recalled my earlier errand. It had become all-important now.

At the base of our palace hill, the city housed the residents of Kalliste, the island's capital. Along with squares and streets of markets and shops, dyers and fullers and tanners, and all that a glorious city needed, one central building offered hope to a desperate woman tonight.

I crept through the murky streets, past lamp-lit windows and dark doorways to reach the temple.

Andreas had told me strange tales of the gods of warring Sparta and Athens—it seemed the people worshipped *male* gods in those rocky cities, and many of them. Here in Kalliste, we knew only the goddess, and in her temple the priestesses served night and day. Here, I hoped, I would find the Oracle, and here I would find answers.

What would my parents say to my night journey through the city? Would they even care? The unfamiliar scents and sounds reached me through the darkness—cook fires and roasting meat, noisy taverns with men swilling strong beer, back alleys with cats scrounging for scraps of the day's fish. I pushed forward to the hallowed glow of the temple on a slight rise in the city center. Its white lime-stone walls reflected torchlight within and spilled a pale luminosity onto the surrounding streets.

I hesitated at the temple's columned portico,

scanned the stone antechamber for a familiar face, listened to the airy intonations of the priestesses within attending to their duties.

The antechamber was empty, so I strode forward into the main chamber, reverently scanning the engravings etched on pillars around me and the central altar rising from a marble pedestal. Each side of this chamber was without walls, the roof held aloft by gold-painted columns alone, and the evening breeze blew through the space, whispering along the stones and catching at my robes. The sharp odor of incense floated on the breeze and filled my nose and throat with its smoky scent.

I stood within the circle of torches, the only penitent at this hour. Where to search?

But she found me. Grabbed my arm from behind. I startled, yelped my surprise, pulled my arm from the grasp of the bony hand extended from black robes.

"You seek enlightenment from the goddess?"

Her voice grated, and I could barely see her eyes under the black hood. They were bright, I knew, like the sea. That much I remembered, though I could not see her clearly. Gray streaked her dark hair and the years rested more heavily on her face than they once had. Had I thought her ageless?

I found my voice. "Yes. Enlightenment. About the Horn of Truth. And about the beast."

She nodded once, then drifted past me.

I followed. Was this acquiescence or refusal? Only the Horn of Truth could redeem my mistake, save my father.

She approached the altar, stepped up to its platform. "Your sister's suitors leave tomorrow."

I bit my lip. How much to tell her? As the elder, the rule of Kalliste naturally fell to my sister, and any suitor willing to risk his life would do so for the prize of marriage to Melayna. But my parents' stipulations had been clear—no man would marry a royal daughter before the beast was conquered and the Truth discovered.

"I—there is someone—a man who undertakes the quest for the sake of . . . me."

She turned, and beneath the hood that dipped so low it covered nearly all her face, a slight smile tugged at her lips. "You speak as though this would be a strange thing. Are you not beautiful? Are you not royal? And will you not rule?"

"Tell me how to save him. None have yet returned. But this one—he must not be lost." My voice caught on the last word, all my determination to remain unemotional fleeing with thoughts of Andreas confronting the beast. It was not only my future that rested on him now, but the future of our people.

Her eyes cast upward. Did she consult the goddess?

"The beast is a formidable foe, it is true. But courage and truth can defeat it." She lifted her hood briefly and pierced me with her bright, bright eyes. "It is the labyrinth that destroys a man, long before he ever confronts the beast itself."

"The labyrinth?" The many-chambered caverns like underground cities beneath our hillsides were legendary.

As if she read my thoughts, the Oracle nodded. "Part cavern, yes. But the labyrinth is vast and wide and deep and dark. Many have wandered there for years, unknowing from whence they came or toward what destiny they drifted."

Thoughts of Andreas, lost and alone, wandering, pressed against my chest, stifling breath.

"How can one traverse this labyrinth safely?"

She laughed. "Oh, there is no 'safe' my child. There is only hardship and suffering and the pain of darkness and brokenness."

The pressure in my chest became pain. "Then we send men to their doom? There is no way out?"

She turned away again, ran her fingers along the altar's surface, tracing the engraved plant tendrils. "I did not say there was no way out. Only that it would involve suffering."

I joined her on the altar platform and plucked at her sleeve until she faced me again with those fathomless eyes. "Tell me how he can return."

"He must return the way that he came."

Infuriating. I shook my head. "Do not speak to me in riddles. What is the secret to the labyrinth?"

Her hands clasped mine, and in the way of mystery, our souls connected through this touch and I knew that she would give me the knowledge I sought.

"This *is* the secret, my child." Her voice was low, the words quick and light, as though she feared to be overheard. "If one should be brave enough to find and face the beast, and if one should find truth enough to defeat it, then he must return the way that he entered. There will be other paths to trod, other courses that may seem simpler, easier. But those will lead to death. Only the way of suffering can lead back out of the labyrinth."

I thanked her for the wisdom, promised to bring an offering soon, and fled back through the city to the palace, my mind whirring with the best way to use the knowledge the Oracle had granted. By the time I reached the columned entryway, I had a plan.

I grabbed a small torch from a wall socket and trotted through the silent east corridors, past the airy workshops where the best of our jewelers and smiths and potters crafted objects for palace use, finally to the central courtyard, all shadowy with starlit fronds and fountains.

Across the courtyard, down a short flight of steps, a small chamber housed my sister's supplies for painting. I fumbled at the latched door, its narrow lintel only at my shoulder, then ducked through the tiny opening into the dirt-walled room. My torch played on the walls, a body's-breadth apart, lined with shelves of paints and brushes and unglazed pottery.

There. An amphora of paint, its lip stained a bright red that well-reflected the light of my torch. I snatched it up, then looked for a brush small enough to conceal yet wide enough for a noticeable stroke on a cavern wall.

A shuffle at the door drew my attention. I lifted the torch to its source.

"Melayna!"

Her eyes were storm-dark and cold. She glanced at the stolen supplies, then curled a lip. "What are you doing with those?"

"I—I need them—for—" I broke off. I had told her nothing of my hours with Andreas, for she clearly had preferred him from the start.

"For *him?* What does he need with paints and brushes?"

"Melayna, I am sorry."

She shook her head, her hands tight at her sides. "You are never satisfied, are you, Chloe? Though I am the elder, you would have all the attention of our parents, the love of the man I choose, the very *kingdom* for yourself. You are a selfish, selfish girl."

"No, I do not want—"

"Do not want Andreas? Do you think I am a fool?"

I lowered the torch, my arm as weary as my heart, weary of her jealousy and suspicion and dark thoughts.

"You shall not have everything, Chloe. There must be something left for me."

With that, the tiny door swung closed and I heard the latch *clunk* into place.

"Melayna, no!" I was at the door in one stride, and my palm made a hollow sound against the wood, a sound that seemed swallowed by the damp earth around me. "Melayna!"

She was gone.

I did not fear for myself. Someone would be along eventually. Would hear my cries or my beating against the wood.

I feared for Andreas, for my father, and for our people.

At sunrise, all of Kalliste would assemble before the palace, to twirl colorful pennants and throw flower petals and cheer for those who rode out to risk their lives. The suitors would wave at the crowds and lift triumphant fists in the air, their horses stomping and bucking at the heavy loads of weapons and gear, anxious to be off. I had seen it all a dozen times.

There would be no one about the palace courtyard outside my prison until well after the men had departed.

What would Andreas think when I did not appear at our appointed time? And how would he ever return to me without the secret I had wrenched from the Oracle?

Sometime in the night, the torchlight died. And with it, my hope. Did I truly think that a trail of red paint could lead Andreas back to me? There were forces at work deeper than my naiveté had imagined, forces that would keep Kalliste bound for destruction and carry my father to his death.

Forces that would keep me from my throne.

I sensed, rather than saw, when morning arrived. What little light filtered under the threshold was barely a muted glimmer. I took up my frantic beating upon the door once more, but it took far too long to be rewarded by the astonished face of a palace servant peering into the tiny chamber.

"My lady—"

I did not wait for questions.

Still holding the paint jar and brush, I raced across the courtyard, through the corridors, and out to the palace steps.

The sun was well up in the sky, a burnished disc of gold that stabbed at my eyes. I held a hand to my brow, still clutching the brush, and looked over a dispersing crowd. Flower petals lay crushed underfoot. Pennants wilted from drooped arms. And far in the distance, a puff of dust on the horizon was the only sign of the hunting party.

It was like a swift falling, his departure. Like the bottom of the sea falling away under my feet and not being able to swim.

"Do not fear, Sister." Melayna's smooth and arrogant voice was at my back. "I gave him your message."

I did not turn. "And what message was that?"

"Why, only what you gave me to pass along. That if he would not give up this foolish quest for you, he must not love you, and therefore he was not worthy of you. You would have nothing more to do with him."

I should have slapped her. I would have, had my parents not stepped beside us, all tight smiles and insincere warmth.

My father scowled. "You should have been here to see them off, Chloe. It was not proper to let them leave without the entire family here to give our blessing and our thanks. Especially now, when they are our only hope."

The rest of his words were lost to me. I retreated from the palace steps, found my bedchamber, and laid upon my mattress to wait for Andreas's return.

The Green Mountain was a two-day journey from Kalliste's palace. Two days to arrive, a day or two to find the beast and defeat it, two days to return.

On the morning of the fifth day, I began to watch the horizon.

I gazed upon five more sunrises before I gave up hope.

While I watched the southern lip of the island for their return, my parents kept a wary eye on the western sea, from whence Mycenaean ships would arrive. Guards were placed around my father at all times, for protection against the insidious threat of assassination.

On the evening of the twelfth day, I ascended the High Place, a holy realm to our people, found the Oracle facing the setting sun, and stood in the salty wind, letting it tear at my hair and my robes, waiting to be acknowledged.

"What will you do?" She asked without turning.

Waves dashed themselves against breakers far below, an angry roar that reached to our high, rock-strewn cliff. "What can I do?"

"What you must."

I tasted salt on my lips and knew not whether it came from my tears or from the sea.

"How can I go after him? How can I find him and bring him back?"

"Because you will not go only for him. Nor for yourself."

Could this be true? In the twelve days I had waited for Andreas to return, the longing for him had somehow merged with the longing for my father and my people to be free and safe, and for the words of the Oracle's prophecy to be fulfilled.

I was no leader. Did not have the qualities that a leader required.

And yet, the longing had become a call, like a great horn sounding for a battle to begin, with high, clear notes that stirred the blood's passion and turned the heart to bronze and the sword arm to hardened muscle. And although there was a great and terrible fear, I felt this battle call in my body and in my blood.

Only one question remained.

Would I answer the call?

⇥ **8** ⇤

Kallie paced, holding her stomach with shaking hands.

She paced across the large and sparsely furnished office of Dr. John Newsom, M.D., keenly aware of each page he turned, of the occasional murmur of something—surprise? concern?—that reverberated from somewhere in his chest.

The gray and drizzly weather seemed to reach clammy fingers through the office, dampening even the primary colors of his décor and smothering her with musty, cave-like odors of a long, wet city winter. She heard the low groan of the heating system engaging, and she shivered.

Her feet were heavy and her pace slow, but she

couldn't sit in that chair and simply watch him read her journal. She had bled onto those pages, a strange and vulnerable opening of herself that was somehow more intimate than *anything* they had discussed in a year of therapy. She turned in her circuit of the office and glanced at him for the hundredth time since he began, trying to decipher his reaction. She felt empty, hollow, void of identity.

But no, hollow was not quite true. Or if hollow, something was at the center of the deflated thing that had been her heart, like the tiniest spark of a fire in the midst of a vast, dark cavern. She paced the other direction, paused to study the framed maze on the wall, only half conscious of the way her eyes forever traced possibilities through its channels.

What were her possibilities? Everything she'd worked for had been ripped from her. She could start over, try to find another job, perhaps in another city. The thought threatened to extinguish whatever small spark remained. Outside New York, the museum, Judith, she had nothing. *Was* no one. Perhaps if she left this world, she would even cease to exist.

Dr. Newsom cleared his throat.

She whirled, sped to the overstuffed chair, and sat. "Well? Crazy?"

Newsom's lips twitched into a half smile. "How many times have I told you, Kallie—"

"I know, I know. We don't use *crazy*. I didn't mean *me,* I meant the story."

"What do *you* think about the story?"

She huffed, sat back against the cushions. "It just sort of—flowed out of me. I don't know."

"And how did that make you feel, having it flow out of you so naturally?"

The question was typical shrink-talk, but she considered her answer anyway. "It felt right, I guess. You had asked me to journal my dreams and—and hallucinations—and the story wasn't either of those. I didn't dream it or see it. It was more like—like—" the last word emerged as a cautious whisper, "memory."

Newsom cocked his head, studying her. "Do you think it is a memory?"

Kallie rubbed her fingers against the arm of the chair. "Not *literally.* Obviously." Or maybe it wasn't obvious, and he truly did think her crazy? "But perhaps on some level." She wasn't sure anymore.

Newsom was nodding. "I agree. The first-person nature of the story is very telling." He smiled. "This is good work, Kallie. You are getting somewhere, or perhaps I should say allowing your subconscious to *lead* you some-where, and you are following. Though I will admit surprise at the religious direction your story has taken. Are you feeling a need for religion in your life?"

Was she? She had found herself in a church pew a few times over the past year.

Her frustration burst out. "I only want to know if the myths point to something within us or something without, something Other." Which direction did the maze lead? Did it lead outward from the center, or was the center where it ended? "All people, of all times, have yearned for the divine and sought to know it, and I *feel* it sometimes—this overwhelming reality and presence—"

"You are searching. And this is a good beginning."

"Beginning?" He didn't understand. At all. She withdrew inside and shivered again. Why was his office so cold?

"We've talked about the possibility of some kind of false guilt. Now it has manifested in your story, with your character feeling responsible for the coming destruction of her people." He clasped his hands above the desk and leaned over them. "Clearly you've been called to an adventure of discovery, Kallie. You should continue writing the story. Listen to your mentor and begin the journey, see what happens next."

She felt her face flatten into something expressionless. The writing had been difficult—perhaps the most difficult she'd ever done. He wanted her to continue? She reached for a handful of chocolate mints, but they tasted flat, lifeless.

"This island—Kalliste—it's where Judith got your name?"

"It's the old Minoan name for the Greek island of Santorini, yes. Very close to Crete, in the South Aegean. The Greeks actually refer to it as Thera. *Santorini* came from Saint Irene—a thirteenth-century cathedral there."

"I looked it up when we first began together. Atlantis, and all that."

She shrugged. "It was a very advanced civilization, and the island was largely wiped out when a massive volcano erupted and left the center a sea-filled crater. It may have been the source for Plato's legendary tale."

"And the labyrinth? Minos and the Minotaur?"

"Also Minoan."

"I see. Kallie, tell me what you've been doing for two days since you lost your job."

She shrugged, sighed. "I don't know. Nothing."

His eyebrows knit together. "Lost time again? Like at the bridge?"

"No. No, just wandering. Sleeping. Nothing much."

"There's a heaviness about you this morning, as though your job loss weighs on you physically. Do you feel that?"

"Yes."

"And how do you think you can lift that heaviness?"

There was only one way she could think of,

only one way to gain credibility. Secure research funding, perhaps even recoup her job.

"I think . . . I should go to Egypt."

His lips parted and he leaned forward, his usual playful smile replaced by astonishment. She'd told him nothing of Dimitri. "Egypt?"

She laid it out—Dimitri's crazy plan, the team he wanted her to lead, the fabulous knowledge that finding this key to the lost Minoan language could unlock. The little spark in the center of the cave seemed to brighten as she spoke.

"So you're going to run away?"

The question set her back against the chair. She frowned. "No, I'm not running away. I haven't even made the decision to do it. I was only telling you about it."

"So you're backing down because I disapprove?"

Inwardly, she cursed the man. Visibly, she only stood, crossed her arms. "What do you want from me?"

Newsom stood as well, uncharacteristically confrontational. "I want you to take charge of your own healing, Kallie."

She turned away. "I don't know how." She felt the pressure again, that caving-in feeling.

"Tell me about Dimitri Andreas."

Kallie closed her eyes at the subject-switch. "He's a good man. I think. Very passionate about research."

"So he is the Andreas in your story?"

"What? No!"

Newsom sat again, so she lowered herself heavily in her chair, bracing her forehead against the heel of her hand. "I don't know."

"Listen. This story—it's like all of our other conversations." He chuckled. "You are so saturated with the archetypal images that interpretation could be done by any first-year psychology student."

"Lovely. Perhaps I should be talking to one of them."

"This labyrinth you've been summoned to enter, Kallie, it's your own psyche. The enemies within, they are the enemies that represent something that truly happened in your past and they must be faced."

Face her past? Why couldn't she just move forward? Wasn't therapy supposed to be about finding a better way to live? Did she constantly have to look backward?

"You are seeking love at the center of the labyrinth, but not romantic love—that's not what you need right now. It is self-love. Is it wonderful or terrible? It is both. It is you, and you are both, Self and Shadow, trying to reconcile the two halves of yourself and find a way to love yourself, all you truly are, and even all that has happened in your life. This conflict with the sister in the story—it is also your Shadow self that must be faced." He paused, as though delivering a maxim. "Only when you confront and defeat whatever evil is at the center of the labyrinth will you be truly healed."

"You should stitch that onto a throw pillow or something."

He narrowed his eyes. "Your sarcasm is telling."

"Yeah. Defense mechanism, right?"

"Are you sure you're not the first-year psychology student?"

"Seems like I should be able to skip the first year, after all this time in therapy."

He laughed. "Don't go to Egypt, Kallie. We're on the verge of something here. Something important. You'd be running away."

Running away sounded good. Very good. "I still don't know why I must churn up a past that's better left forgotten."

"Because it's *not* better left forgotten. It's better *healed.*"

Everything in her resisted. The coldness that weighted her limbs, the shaky, suffocating pressure against her chest. An acidic taste in her throat, rancid half memories of her first moments in the museum, half dead. She rubbed the pink scars at her wrist and took an unsteady breath.

"I think—I think I should go to Egypt."

Dr. Newsom flopped back in his chair with a heavy exhale.

Psychiatrists were all about fixing people. She'd been a constant disappointment in that department.

"You're stalling, Kallie. And it's dangerous. Remember the bridge?"

I'd prefer to forget. Actually, none of this was helping. Maybe she *should* go to Egypt. But first appease the doctor—just in case she needed him in the future. "Perhaps we could keep up our sessions by phone?"

He nudged the journal across his desk, toward the children on the seesaw. "And your story?"

"I don't want to write a story."

"You don't want to face the past."

She closed her eyes, fatigue stealing over her along with a desperate desire to escape. His arguments were weights around her ankles, sinking her into a dark lake. How was it possible the back alleys of Egypt seemed less threatening than her own history? "That's not true! I'm trying to *figure out* my past. How can I face something I can't even find?"

Newsom stood and crossed his office to the far wall, then took the framed maze print from its hook. "I want you to have this."

She stood, knowing their time was ended.

He handed the black frame to her. It measured only about ten inches wide and was not heavy. "If you decide to go, take it with you. A reminder you have a puzzle of your own to solve, a labyrinth of your own to traverse. Find your way in, and then find your way out. It's the only answer."

She accepted the print and nodded. "Thank you. I will take good care of it."

"Take good care of yourself." His voice caught with some tremor of emotion.

She was afraid he might try to hug her, some sort of friendly good-bye. But he only nodded and returned to his chair. She smiled a farewell and escaped to the street, carrying the framed maze and her journal. Blinking back inexplicable tears.

ᚕ

The Café Muse catered mostly to the staff of the area museums, along with a few tourists who couldn't get through the day without their double shot of espresso. Judith had called this morning, asking to meet at the coffee shop around the corner at noon. She'd sounded worried, asking general questions that Kallie knew masked a deeper concern.

Kallie entered at 12:05 and searched the lunch crowd for Judith's spiked hair. The woman was always punctual.

There. At a small table along the honey-colored wall, tapping short fingers and shooting cold looks at the bubbly customers who sat too close or talked too loudly. Judith jutted her chin toward Kallie as she approached.

"I'm sorry I'm a bit late—"

"You look like crap. You been sleeping?"

Kallie bit her lip, placed the frame on the table, and slid into the wooden chair. "It's been a tough couple of days."

"What's with the maze?"

"A parting gift from my therapist."

Judith raised her eyebrows but didn't comment. Instead, she pushed a plate of cheesecake and a cup of coffee toward Kallie. "I had plenty of time to order for you."

Kallie looked down at the plate and sighed. The little dig about her punctuality was classic Judith. She had probably spent the remaining three minutes advising the manager on how to better run the place. "Thanks." She bit into the cheesecake, tart and sweet at once. Delicious. Nearby, a gas fireplace warmed patrons who sat in supple leather chairs. The shop smelled of coffee and pastries, and the gold and terra-cotta walls echoed the warmth. She started to feel almost normal again.

"So you're quitting therapy?"

Kallie swallowed the cake and took a sip of coffee. "I'm thinking about taking a trip. To Egypt."

"So he got to you, then."

Kallie swept a gaze over Judith's features, but the woman was hard to read. "You know about Dimitri's . . . job offer?"

"I told you Friday night he had information about the Key."

"Do you really think it can be found?"

Judith shrugged. "Every great find is lost at some point."

Kallie focused on her cheesecake. "Do you think I can find it?"

Judith was silent so long, Kallie finally raised her eyes to find her staring intently, curiously. "Do *you* think you can?"

Judith was starting to sound like Dr. Newsom.

"I think I have to find it."

The corner of Judith's mouth twitched upward. "Then do it."

Kallie stared at the fire in the woman's eyes. Judith believed in her. She tried to let her mentor's confidence seep into her insecure places, to see the mission through Judith's eyes. "Well, if I'm successful, it would mean everything to Minoan research." The flame she'd felt in Newsom's office flickered again and expanded. "And it would be a huge boon for the museum since Dimitri plans to donate—"

"Is that why you're going? To oblige Suarez? Get your job back?"

Her face flushed and Kallie lowered her gaze to her plate. "No. I don't know. Maybe." She laid the fork down, twisted her fingers together, and leaned over the table. "What's wrong with that? The museum is my life."

Judith slapped the table with an open palm.

Kallie jumped, startled, and sat back.

"The museum is *not* your life, Kallie. You don't know what your life is. The museum is your hiding place."

Kallie exhaled and flung her arms up. "Dr. Newsom says I'm running away if I go to Egypt. You say I'm hiding if I stay."

"So say something for yourself."

Why was everyone pushing her so hard? Her eyes burned. She pressed at the inner corners, trying to relieve the unvarying pressure of the damp weather. The deserts of Egypt would be dry and warm and expansive.

"I say that finding the Linear A Key is worth whatever it takes." She opened her eyes to find Judith's eyes narrowing.

"It can be a dangerous place over there." There was a challenge in her tone.

Should she laugh or cry? "I know."

"You can't be stupid. Naïve. Too much could go wrong."

"So now I'm incapable—"

"I just want you to be smart."

She loved this woman. Judith's concern often played out like antagonism. It was part of her charm, though Kallie might be the only one who saw it. "I will be. I promise."

"And don't drink the water."

"No water. Got it. Anything else?"

Judith shot a hand across the table, grabbed Kallie's fingers. "Stay safe."

Kallie nodded, another unexpected swell of emotion grabbing at her throat. Two good-byes in one morning, from two important people. Her lifelines. Who would she cling to in that vast desert country?

"And let me know immediately when you have details about your departure."

Kallie grinned. "I will."

When she and Judith finally parted on the sidewalk outside the coffee shop, Kallie paused to watch her mentor striding away toward the museum for an afternoon of work. Was the flutter in her chest jealousy? Or was it excitement at the next turn her life might take?

Regardless, she didn't want to give herself time to change her mind. Juggling her bulky purse on one shoulder and the framed maze under the other arm, she retrieved her phone, scrolled through the list of recent calls, and found the one unknown number that had called her last Saturday. Pressed the green button before her nerve failed her.

"Dimitri Andreas."

She had expected a secretary. "Oh. Hi, Dimitri. It's Kallie. Kallie Andreas."

No response. Had the call dropped? She pulled the phone away from her ear and glanced at the screen. "Dimitri?"

"Yes?"

She blinked, bit her lip, surveyed the cars and taxis fighting for dominance in the street.

"What can I do for you, Kallie?"

She took a deep breath of car exhaust and city air, held it for a moment in a chest tight with anxiety, then released it in a rush, with only three words.

"I'll do it."

Another pause, a long one. She was too busy trying to regulate her heartbeat to care.

"I'm pleased, Kallie."

Well, that's what it was all about, right?

"I'll have my assistant call you with travel details. Can you leave Monday?"

"*This* Monday? As in five days?"

"Is that a problem?"

She was beginning to be a hindrance to pedestrians so she scooted to the outer wall of the Café Muse and leaned against it. "No, I guess not. Will I—will I see you before I leave?" She rolled her eyes at her own comment. "To get all the information I need, I mean."

"You'll have everything you need."

Thanks for clearing that up.

A car honked three times, its driver gesturing rudely.

"Okay. So, then, I'll just wait for your assistant—"

"Jill."

"I'll wait for Jill to call me?"

"She'll be in touch very soon."

"Good. Great. Okay."

Another pause. There had to be more to talk about, didn't there?

"Kallie?" His voice was quieter. Less formal.

"Yes?"

"I'm very pleased."

→ 9 ←

In seven years, the closest thing to flying Kallie had experienced was the Wonder Wheel at Coney Island. She had nearly lost her lunch.

In the five-day rush to learn all she could of Egypt, pack for the journey, make arrangements with her landlord, and say good-bye to Judith, Kallie had refused to even look skyward. Thoughts of elevation in the thousands of feet were too terrifying to deal with.

Now, leaning against traffic in a reeking cab, biting her lip to keep from urging the driver faster, she still refused to think of the moment of liftoff.

A tour bus ahead slowed, belching white smoke from its tailpipe. Or was it on fire? If so, drivers paid little heed in their rush to get into the city. Her driver honked, yelled, raised a hand, said something unintelligible. Passed the bus.

Kallie forced herself backward against the

cushions, then sniffed again and thought better of it. "How close are we?"

He shrugged one shoulder, as if flight times were inconsequential, especially with the meter running. "Ten? Fifteen?"

She breathed through her mouth and watched the steady New York skyline, a black silhouette against a hazy white sky. The 10:05 from JFK to Cairo wouldn't wait for her. Would her team members? Doubtful.

She rehearsed their names and bios for the hundredth time. If she was to be the team leader, a focused and competent first impression was crucial.

Erik Gunnarson. Ex-military, ex-bodybuilder, Scandinavian Mormon from Utah. Her protection.

Caroline Austin. Her assistant, who Dimitri explained would free her from worrying about travel details. Caroline hailed from the Bible Belt of West Texas and had once been some sort of pageant queen.

And Yoshi Nakahara. Perhaps the only one of them she'd connect with. The linguist specializing in ancient languages, who would help decipher anything they came across. He had wealthy parents, multiple degrees, and was apparently a Buddhist who preferred not to discuss religion.

Interesting that Dimitri had considered it important to mention their religious affiliations.

Sounds like a bad joke. A Mormon, a Buddhist,

and a Southern Baptist walk into an airport . . .

And where did that leave her?

She glanced at the dashboard clock. Late. She flexed her ankle against the floor of the backseat, as if she could accelerate the cab.

They slid to the curb at last, she stuffed the bills into the driver's hand, shot out of the cab, and circled to the trunk. The driver took his time.

Inside, she paused, scanned the signage, remembered Judith's brief instructions. *"Check your luggage, then get through security."* As though any idiot could manage a transcontinental flight.

The airport did have a familiar feel. But was it movies and television . . . or memory?

Forty minutes later, she was positioned in Terminal 4, a straight shot to Gate B27. Her heels clicked a steady rhythm against the polished floor, and her purse and laptop bag bounced against her side. She could do this.

One quick stop at a kiosk to purchase a container of strawberry yogurt from a tired-looking elderly woman in a green polo. There'd been no time for breakfast this morning. She slipped the yogurt into her laptop case and kept moving.

Deep breaths. Team leader.

She saw them at the gate before they saw her, grouped in a familiar little knot beside a row of blue plastic chairs, talking quietly. She slowed, approached confidently with chin lifted.

Erik's red hair and massive build was more Norse god than bodyguard, but perhaps that was the point. He was grinning down on Caroline, not much shorter than he. She was all pink and white, Gucci and Prada and long blond hair. She laughed, a little-girl giggle, and leaned forward to touch Erik's arm in appreciation of his undoubtedly clever wit.

Yoshi stood a bit apart, perhaps, but was still included in the conversation. Had she expected a pocket protector and tape-wrapped glasses? He wasn't quite so stereotypical, but the steady tapping of mechanical pencil on spiral notebook spoke volumes.

She cleared her throat. They turned as one.

"Hello." She jostled her purse and bag against her body and thrust out a hand, first to Yoshi. "I'm Kallista Andreas. Kallie." She smiled at all three but addressed the one who took her hand. "Yoshi, right?"

His hand was cool and dry, and his forehead creased. "You are late. The airline recommends all passengers arrive for international flights at least—"

"Yes, yes, I know. Traffic." She tried to grin. "But I'm here now!" Shifted her outstretched hand to the Norse god. "And you must be Erik."

He jumped toward her, and his paw swallowed her hand and nearly crushed the bones.

"Looking forward to working for you, Kallie."

A lopsided smile followed his enthusiasm, but when his glance slid to Caroline's disapproving pout, the smile faded.

Stupid, Kallie. She should have greeted Caroline first. Women could be strange that way.

"And, Caroline, I'm so glad to meet you. Dimitri tells me you are a wizard with details and we'll all be in good hands."

Caroline's blue eyes flashed on Kallie, as though measuring and assessing the competition. "Well, I will certainly try my best." The southern drawl was unmistakable. It was easy to picture Caroline on the pageant runway, gushing about her passion for world peace.

"So what's the plan?" Erik actually pounded a fist into his palm, as if ready to take on back-alley black-market dealers immediately.

"Plan?" Kallie blinked. "Well, we've got a contact from Dimitri in Luxor. We'll start there. Ask some questions—"

Erik folded beefy arms across his chest. "No, I'm talking strategy. Who's doing recon? How are we going in? What's our exit strategy?"

Yoshi sighed, an exasperated little huff. "It is not a military operation."

Erik glared down on the slightly built Yoshi and lowered his voice. "Yeah, well, some of those folks over there aren't exactly lovin' on Americans, you get my meaning?"

Caroline sucked in a petite gasp and touched

Erik's arm again. "Do you think we'll be attacked by terrorists?"

Kallie opened her mouth to reassure, but Yoshi cut her off. "Egypt is one of the more liberal of Muslim countries, and in spite of recent events, we should be able to remain in zones of safety. However," his attention shifted to Kallie, "my greater concern addresses the inconclusive evidence on which this quest is founded and the odds against our success, which are extremely high."

Erik nodded. "Especially with no strategy."

The ground under her feet felt a bit unsteady and the determination she'd brought with her started to blur into a watery vapor. "I'm sure Dimitri would not be funding this trip, or sending us to Egypt, if he did not believe there was a good chance—"

"Men with money send other people to do what they will not." Yoshi's grim pronouncement weighted the air, silenced them all.

Kallie searched for a response. Already she had failed to lead, to provide vision and inspiration. Was her team slipping from her so soon?

The voice behind her was like a wall of protection. "Or perhaps to do what they *cannot*."

She turned, knowing Dimitri's voice, his face, his cologne, better than she would have thought possible.

"Dimitri!" It was Caroline who trilled out his

name, who bounced over to him and hugged him in glee. "You came to see us off!"

Interesting. Caroline's attention to Erik wasn't exclusive. Dimitri would suffice. Kallie glanced at Erik, but the man's face was blank. Perhaps he didn't even realize.

Dimitri patted Caroline's back and broke free. "Of course. I couldn't let my team leave without telling you all how important you are to me and how confident I am of your success."

His eyes were on Kallie as he spoke, and she warmed to the words, but still the fear, the wavering gray doubts born of her lack of qualifications and her lack of history clouded her mind and heart. Dimitri's confidence in her was misplaced, of that, at least, she was certain.

There was a static electronic crackle and a woman's voice blared, drowning everyone out. "Attention EgyptAir passengers of Flight 986 non-stop to Cairo, we are about to begin boarding."

She continued, but her words were lost on Kallie. Dimitri had taken her arm and was speaking into her ear. "Can I talk with you privately?"

They stepped apart from the other three who were gathering carry-on luggage.

Dimitri looked into her eyes, as though searching out the truth. "It's not too late to change your mind, Kallie. You're sure you want to do this?"

She readjusted the straps of her laptop bag cutting into her shoulder. "It *is* too late, Dimitri. What other choice do I have?"

"There are always choices."

"Not for me. I have to find a way back into Minoan research. This is the best way."

Dimitri sighed, looked over her shoulder toward the glass wall and the waiting plane. "I wish—I don't—"

"What?"

He brought his eyes back to hers, took her arms in his hands, and gripped her elbows. "If anything happened to you—"

This was dangerous. Newsom would not be happy. A man with as many secrets as Dimitri Andreas was not the right man for a woman with no past and no future. She needed to get herself straight before she could let herself believe the emotion she saw in those dark eyes.

She tilted her head toward the team he'd provided. "With Erik the Red there, how could I not be safe?"

"He's not invincible. None of you are."

"I'm afraid . . . they don't feel I'm qualified."

"You are." He squeezed her arms. "You can find it. I believe in you. Let that be enough for now."

Kallie closed her eyes, absorbing his passion for the project, adding it to her own passion for the Key.

"I'll do my best, Dimitri."

He leaned in to kiss her cheek, quickly. The kiss of an old friend or affectionate uncle. Her face grew hot all the same.

"I know you will."

Yoshi leaned stiffly into their private meeting, his face pinched. "They have called for first class boarding twice now."

First class. Of course. She smiled a good-bye at Dimitri, a little pang of regret beating against her chest. When would she see him again?

He ran his hand down the length of her arm, squeezed her fingers, and nodded.

And then she and Yoshi strode through the boarding door, down the Jetway, and into the plane. The first-class compartment welcomed them into oversized luxury, and Kallie settled into an aisle seat. Erik and Caroline sat across from her, and Yoshi climbed past her to the window seat.

Her yogurt still waited in her laptop bag, but her stomach spun with anticipation and accelerating fear. A cute, ponytailed flight attendant bent at the waist in the aisle, her eye shadow heavy and dramatic, teeth beaming in a bright, enameled smile. "Can I get you anything to drink?"

"Coke. Please." Perhaps it would settle her stomach. "In the can." Despite Judith's frequent jabs at her lack of sophistication, she hated soda poured over ice in a cup.

Moments later, fingers wrapped around the icy red Coke, she tried to relax and gave Yoshi a half smile. "It's my first time flying."

He frowned and launched into a statistical analysis of the safety of trans-Atlantic flight. It should have been reassuring. It wasn't.

Instead, she let his voice fade, turned her mind inward, and examined different strategies to win this mismatched team's loyalty.

Newsom would have a field day with the living, breathing archetypes in Row 3 of EgyptAir Flight 986. The Olympian, with his magnificently built body and his principled patriotism. The seductive Siren beside him, luring unwary sailors to their doom. And the wise Wizard, who had moved on from flight safety to explain the aeronautical industry at large. Or perhaps they were her three-headed Cerberus, guarding the threshold to the Underworld, snapping its mighty jaws and with a penchant for live meat.

But the ever-present question. Who was Kallista Andreas? Maybe the answers would come to her on this trip.

Regardless, it was as if she stood poised at the edge of the dark forest, the lip of the vast sea, the portal to a new and dangerous world.

She sipped at her Coke, letting the sweet coolness settle into her belly. She sighed and closed her eyes. Time to relax.

But a minute later, the canned overhead music ceased. There was a rush of forced air through the tiny vent above and the kick of an engine that reverberated in her chest, and then they were rolling, rolling over the tarmac, picking up speed, the pulse of the asphalt pounding up through the wheels, through the floor, into her feet.

Her breath shallowed and she clenched the armrest with her free hand.

So fast. The plane moved so quickly, a skimming of the sword-bridge across the Great Chasm of the Abyss, and all inside her was hollow and insubstantial, without breath, without life.

There came a *whoosh* that eclipsed all other sound and the gravity of all the Earth dragging her back to itself, reclaiming her, denying man the ability to defeat its mighty pull. It was an elemental, cosmic battle. It was as if she warred against the very element of Air.

Her soul seemed to flatten to emptiness. There was no turning back. She smelled a burning. Bridges, perhaps? And a burnt taste in her throat.

The unbearable weight dragged and dragged and then suddenly there was a moment of simple weightlessness, of silence suspended between heaven and earth, between life and death, and in that fraction of time she could have floated into the ether and disappeared. The elemental struggle against the Air had ended.

She was committed now. She would make a

place for herself in the present by unlocking the past.

Sunlight stabbed through the window beside Yoshi, assaulted her eyes, swallowed the jet as New York City dropped away and blue sky claimed them. Her stomach flipped, and she quickly leaned back and closed her eyes. *Concentrate, Kallie! Breathe in. Breathe out. Breathe in. Breathe out.*

She should pull out her laptop and get the preparatory work done while they traveled. Even with Caroline's planning and Yoshi's expertise, the "strategy" clearly fell to her.

But her laptop remained at her feet, and it was her purse she retrieved. She grasped and closed tight fingers around her journal and the pen from Judith.

There was only one antidote for the agitation that had wrapped itself around her heart, and she was tired of fighting.

It was time to escape.

❯ 10 ❮

By the time I descended from the holy High Place above the sea, from my wind-battered meeting with the Oracle, I had chosen my future.

The Oracle had reached her bony fingers from her dark cloak, wrapped them around my trembling wrists, and spoken words of instruction into my heart.

"Cross the ridge. Endure the Cypress Forest. Find the village at the base of the Green Mountains. They will lead you to the mouth of the cavern, to the throat of the labyrinth."

I found my parents beside the pool in the lower terrace of the eastern wing, two palace staff guarding the entrance. They nodded to me as I passed, both awkward in their new roles. In this unwalled and peaceful city, we had little use for guards. Until I interfered.

The hot springs that fed the pool kept the water steaming, making it a favorite spot for my father and his oft-aching joints. The columned terrace was partially roofed, trapping the moist air until the muted reds and blues and yellows of the wall paintings dripped with condensation. Andreas had marveled and declared all of our plumbing a wonder, but we had always lived in such luxury.

When my parents both opened sleepy eyes and focused upon me, I announced my intent, with words much firmer than my courage.

"Never!" My father the king roused his bulky frame from the pool's edge and wrapped a crimson robe around himself. He was at my side in three long strides, his dark eyebrows drawn together like the *V* of the summer geese's wings against the sky. "You shall not follow where others have failed—"

"It is ordained, Galenus." My mother's soft words fluttered from behind my father. Did she support me? Did she so willingly see me leave on what must be a fool's mission?

"Ordained, bah!" He waved a jeweled hand at Mother. "What need have we of priestesses and their prophecies? We are a mighty people without the interference of the gods."

I faced him with stony resolve, my hands clenched at my sides. "I go to find the Horn of Truth, Father. I go to save our people."

"Horn of Truth!" Father often repeated phrases when agitated. "You do not deceive me—you go to find that Athenian!"

"To save *you*, Father!"

Mother's eyes were gentle on me, but her hand on Father's arm was firm. "Galenus, it is all part of one thing. Of the Call on Chloe."

"Call." He turned away, subdued. "You speak again of prophecies. Of ignoring tradition."

"She speaks the truth, Father." My voice hardened. "I will not be dissuaded. I will heed my destiny, whatever it brings."

His back was to me, his head bent in sorrow. I would go to him, embrace him and assure him that all would be well. But I did not have this confidence.

"Go, then." He held up a hand in seeming blessing but did not turn. "Do what you must."

The weighted air felt like a heavy mantle on

my shoulders, and I looked to Mother for a sharing of the burden. But she only lowered her eyes, in grief or in resignation, I could not say.

It took only a day to pack provisions, ready my mount, and say my good-byes, but in that day my sister did not cease her harassment or her accusations.

"The prophecy is not enough, is it, Chloe?" Melayna's acidic voice followed me into the grain storeroom, where a bare-chested slave drew a week's measure from a pithos jar that reached my waist, in line with others of its kind along the crumbling wall.

I nodded to the slave, approving the quantity, and he funneled the grain into a skin pouch.

Melayna hissed into my ear. "You must find a way to draw attention, to win even more approval, to be seen as a champion. I am surprised you have not taken to bull-leaping at the festivals!"

"I should think you would be glad to see me go, Melayna. No one has returned. Perhaps my going will guarantee the Oracle's prophecy bears no fruit."

Her cold eyes looked toward the door, as if she could see beyond the ridge, past the Cypress Forest, to the Green Mountains. "With my luck, you shall return with the Horn of Truth, and your lover, besides."

I lifted the pouch strap over my head and

secured it against my body. "I want what is best for our people, Melayna. Have you no understanding of that desire?"

She followed me from the storage room. "Do not speak to me as if you do not serve your own ambition!" Her voice was harsh, hateful.

What had I done to incur such wrath? Were not sisters supposed to be close? To share secrets and dreams and laughter? Melayna had resented my very birth and every breath I'd taken since.

At sunrise of the next day, I embraced my parents at the base of the palace steps and mounted my horse, Herakles. Mother was uncharacteristically teary eyed and gripped my ankle where it hung alongside the horse's flank. I could smell her delicate perfume, a reminder of all I was about to forsake.

"Take care for yourself, Chloe. Do nothing rash, nothing foolish. Remember your people—your family—await your safe return." The morning sun, lifting only a crescent above the horizon, sparkled in the tears in her lashes.

I nodded, emotion choking my words, and reached to pat her hand. What good would my safe return be to any of us if I did not bring back the Horn?

Father said nothing, only pierced me with a sad but certain look and gave a single nod.

"I shall make you proud, Father." Would I see

him again? Would assassins take him from me before I had a chance to return and make things right?

"Go in peace, Chloe."

That was all.

A kick to Herakles, a leaning into the rising sun, and we raced together toward our destiny.

Down, down the slopes of Kalliste's highest peak we sailed, down toward the Blade Path—the ridge crest that connected the palace hill with the rest of the island. The ground on either side of the path dropped away steeply to verdant valleys, lush with orchards both domestic and wild, and the path was like a corridor to the sun itself, its rocks a blinding white with the blue, blue sea beyond. I rode with exultation in my heart and mind and lungs.

The fear of the unknown was eclipsed by the gladness that came of taking action, of doing something rather than waiting, of following what seemed to be the call on my life. I smiled into the sun, let it pull me toward itself the way the tide was pulled into the sands.

I rode hard, long enough to be away, to separate myself from home and people, and then slowed and took the Blade Path with care, feeling the overwhelming strangeness of leaving behind all I had known and venturing into the void. Away from the secure ordinariness of palace life, entering the true world of my people. It was like the shedding of an old skin, with a new and shining self emerging. Ah, the lightness and glory of it!

After some time, the Blade Path sloped downward, angling toward the edge of the Cypress Forest, and eventually flattening to a plain. I stopped to water my horse at a stream's edge and swallow a bit of dried meat and cheese, then pushed onward. By late afternoon I reached a small town at the border of the forest.

This was not the village of which the Oracle spoke. I would find those people on the other side of the forest, at the base of the mountains. But here would be a fine place to rest for the night, if they would have me.

I cantered past cultivated fields to the edge of the town, eyes scanning the small stone houses, the narrow streets, the curl of smoke that rose from scattered chimneys. Several children played near a central fountain and they raised their heads to me, then shaded their eyes from the sun at my back.

"Greetings." I smiled at two little boys. "I am looking for a place to spend the night."

They scampered away, and I dismounted, led Herakles to the lip of the fountain pool, and waited. Would they return with hospitable parents?

Soon enough, two women and a tall, thin man emerged from an alley, led by the two boys.

I lifted my head in greeting.

As one, the three adults slowed, then glanced between themselves, their eyes wide.

I had been recognized.

The man stepped forward, staring over a beak-like nose. "What is your business here?"

I bristled at the hostile tone. "I am on a journey. To the Green Mountains. I need a place to stay until morning."

"And will you take the rest of our young men when you leave?"

"The rest—? No, I travel alone." I led Herakles from the fountain, feeling suddenly presumptuous and unwelcome.

"Many have come from the palace, through our town. Headed for the Green Mountains."

Ah, now I understood. Each contingent of suitors that set out from the palace passed this way. Did they gain more hopefuls as they passed, drawn from this town?

The older of the two women spoke, a harsh edge to her voice and to her countenance. "We have little left to give. You have already taken our best."

I dropped my head. "I am sorry for the grief you have known. It has not been my doing. I go myself, now, to find the beast, to retrieve the Horn of Truth."

The younger woman wiped at her eyes. "What use do we have for the Horn of Truth? We want our brothers returned. Those whose bodies we have not already found."

A jolt of coldness passed through me. "Bodies?"

"We have sent out searchers." The man stepped forward, took my horse's lead, and turned toward the alley.

I followed, unsure if it was an invitation but unwilling to relinquish Herakles.

"We have found some. Not all. On the slopes of the Green Mountains. Their bodies mangled by some dread beast."

If I had expected sorrow in his voice, I heard none of it. Only anger, white-hot.

"These bodies—they have all been known to you?"

The women followed behind me along the narrow alley between stone houses, and I saw eyes peer from tiny windows as we passed.

Only the man would speak now. "Not all. Some were those who came from distant lands, no doubt. Greedy for the hand of a princess." This last word he spat as if it were distasteful.

"I—I am looking for a certain man—" I fumbled over the request. Did I truly wish to see any bodies they had recovered?

He slowed and turned his slitted eyes on me. "So that is why you pass this way. You say it is for the Horn of Truth, for the people. But it is for yourself alone."

"No!" A flame of anger lit in my chest. His

words echoed Melayna's. I pierced him with a scornful gaze. "No, I am only hoping to also find him."

He stopped at a narrow enclosure, where another horse and a goat were tied. "Your horse will overnight in our stable." He jutted his chin toward the attached house. "And you may stay."

"Thank you."

"The bodies of those unknown to us, we bury in a central grave. There is nothing left to see. But I will send a priestess to attend you. Perhaps she can give you the answers you seek."

I thanked him again, then ducked into the small house, following the blessed scent of cooking meat into the central room, where two young girls tended a blackened pot over a tiny fire at the wall.

Indeed, he did send a priestess. Older than the island itself, I guessed, her eyes glassy with a filmy blindness. She took me from the hearth, from the family that had sheltered me, and led me through the darkening streets. Did she lead me to the mass grave to look for Andreas? My palms grew damp and my throat dry.

At the far edge of the town, where the torch-lit streets ended and the moon gave only a watery light to the fields, she continued on, wordless. I picked my way carefully over the rock-strewn path that seemed illuminated to her, so sure were her steps.

"Where are you taking me?"

"To knowledge."

I shuddered.

A moment later, she was gone. Vanished into the darkness, as though a veil had fallen between us. I waved my hands before me, searching for her form.

"Come!" The word was a hiss, issuing from the wall of blackness before me.

A cave. The mouth of a cave, with the priestess just inside. The moonlight caught the translucent skin of her hand, waving me into its depths.

I followed, hands and feet growing numb with dread.

"If you would enter the labyrinth, slay the beast," she hissed again, "then understand what you will face."

I tracked the sound of her voice, tried to keep step with her as she pushed into the darkness. My left hand I held in front of me and my right hand trailed the slimy sides of the cavern wall, sometimes grasping at empty air as we passed tunnels we did not take. We wound downward, into the depths of one of Kalliste's many caverns, with the cold drip of water in our ears and down our backs and the skittering sounds of creatures unaccustomed to having company. My fingers passed through a sticky muck, and I swallowed against the bile in my throat.

Finally, finally the shuffling sound of the priestess's feet ceased. I stopped, hearing her wheezing breath. Eerie shapes dripped like solid water from the cavern roof.

She turned to me, touched my face with both hands, just below my ears, her fingers icy. "You are seeking after many things."

I held my breath, for she spoke with the tone of prophecy.

"For Truth. Love. Destiny."

I nodded, a slight motion, knowing she could feel my assent under her cold fingers.

There was only the sound of her breathing for a few moments. Did she look into my future?

"The Love you seek has passed beyond the realm of knowing."

My own breath caught in my throat. "Andreas?"

"I cannot see him. He is lost to my sight."

I closed my eyes, though in this place it made little change.

"Many others are lost as well. Was this one man so special?"

"He was to me."

Her hands dropped away. "Then you should turn back."

I felt her push past me, back the way we had come, but I did not move. I needed a moment to collect my frantic thoughts, to tamp down on the grief that would tear me apart.

When I turned, her shuffling gait was fearfully distant.

"Priestess, wait." I traced the stony wall, pushed

forward with hand outstretched. She did not answer.

I hurried forward as fast as I dared. The smooth flow of rock led into so many unused tunnels, empty chambers, tiny slits. How would I know which one led to the surface?

"Priestess!" There was no answer. Either she'd gone deaf as well as blind, or she had intentionally left me behind to be lost forever in the belly of the earth. I gave up calling after her and concentrated on the placement of my feet, on the search for a gleam of light ahead, on the remembering of our downward journey.

My sense of time became tilted and slanted with the twisting tunnels, but surely it had been too long. I tripped over rocks that had fallen eons ago to form bridges, scratched my face against the sharp fingers of rock that clawed at me from the roof. No surface light, no shuffling of footsteps, nothing beckoned me forward.

I was lost.

⇥ 11 ⇤

Kallie looked up from her furious scribbling to find Yoshi asleep beside her, and Caroline and Erik watching the same movie on the small screens mounted in the backs of the seat-row ahead. She stretched her neck, wriggled tense fingers. How long had they been in flight? The writing had taken on a time of its own, wrapping her in its spell, insensible to the real world.

She secreted the journal and pen in her bag. What would Dr. Newsom say when she sent these pages? She had given up the idea of suppressing the story. Newsom could be right—maybe there was some truth for her life here, some parallel lesson waiting to be discovered through the wanderings of her imagination. Her Wicked Witch of the West was really the nasty neighbor, Miss Gulch. Or something like that.

Besides, over the years she'd tried everything else, wringing her mind for memory and searching official and family-generated data-bases for any trace of a lost girl fitting her description. Milk cartons, Walmart boards, anywhere lost persons were advertised. Whoever she was, no one was missing her, no one was looking for her. This story might be the only way she'd ever uncover the truth.

Caroline and Erik both removed earphones simultaneously. The movie must have ended. As though he sensed the shift in activity, Yoshi lifted his head, yawned, and stretched his arms.

Caroline leaned into the aisle, her southern twang conspiratorial. "You sure have a lot to journal about there, Kallie. And we haven't even landed yet!"

Kallie attempted a polite nod and smile. "I have

a lot to write." Let Caroline think she was working on research or work.

A meal was served minutes later, and Kallie chose the bow-tie pasta with marinara sauce, a crunchy slice of garlic bread on the side.

As they dug in, Yoshi spoke, loud enough to include them all. "I still have not been apprised as to why we are going to Egypt, when it is the pre-Greek civilization of the Cretan Minoans that . . . holds our interest." This last was spoken hesitantly, as though conscious of the rest of the compartment's passengers and the delicate nature of their mission.

Kallie swallowed a hunk of garlic bread a bit too quickly and nodded. Finally, a topic where her expertise could shine.

"The Minoan civilization was centered in Crete, you're correct. Although they spread to neighboring islands like Kalliste as well, or what we now call the island of Santorini. They wrote in the Linear A script, which we haven't yet been able to decipher. They were eventually displaced by the Mycenaeans, who used Linear B and then later the Greeks, with their own adaptation into the Greek language. The—information—we seek seems to have been taken to Egypt at some point. Perhaps around 1450 BCE when the volcano on Santorini erupted."

"Volcano!" Erik grinned and bobbed his head. "Cool."

Caroline giggled. "More like *hot*."

Erik responded with the hoped-for guffaw.

Kallie tried not to roll her eyes. "It was actually one of the largest eruptions the planet has ever known. Left about half of Santorini submerged and the effects were felt all the way to Egypt. Some historians believe it spawned the legend of Atlantis."

Yoshi was taking notes. "And there is reason to believe our—information—survived this disaster and traveled to Egypt?"

"Yes, it's fascinating, really. Around 1870, there was a very successful family of tomb robbers in Egypt: the el-Rassuls. They stumbled across a shaft in the cliffs that led to a series of corridors, deep underground. In these corridors they found the mummies of many of Egypt's New Kingdom kings and queens. It's believed the mummies were originally buried in the Valley of the Kings, then moved to Deir el-Bahri later to discourage tomb robbing. The el-Rassuls kept their discovery secret for ten years, methodically selling off pieces they'd found in the cache before the Antiquities Service closed in on them."

Kallie paused to take a quick bite of her pasta.

Erik leaned forward to speak past Caroline. "I still don't get what this has to do with the Minoans."

She swallowed. "Two things, really. One of the kings reburied in this royal cache of mummies was Tuthmosis III, who was most likely Pharaoh when the Santorini eruption may have driven Minoans to Egypt. And second, our information is rumored to have been one of the items the el-Rassuls sold off before they were caught."

She sat back, feeling a bit vindicated in her role. Until she saw the splash of red marinara on her light-blue shirt. She suppressed a groan and tried to remove as much as possible with her napkin.

The team seemed to have had enough of a history lesson. Caroline and Erik chose another movie. Yoshi opened a book.

Kallie went to the restroom to work on the marinara stain.

Sometime later she tried to sleep. Because they were flying east, the surreal night lasted only about four hours before sunlight breeched the gaps around the pulled shades and the perky flight assistants announced it was time for breakfast. An hour later, the plane descended into Cairo. Through the window beside Yoshi spread the enormous metropolis, home to nearly eighteen million people in the city and its environs, growing larger and more real with each passing mile.

The jolt of landing stole her breath and she gripped her armrests, shaking with a fatigued excitement. When the plane finally stopped at the gate, Kallie exhaled deeply. The worst was over. Now the real adventure was about to begin.

The next few hours were a blur. Somehow Caroline managed to maintain her cheery smile as she herded the other three through the Cairo airport, dirty and colorful and noisy, to the plastic chairs where they waited for the commuter plane that would take them one hour south to Luxor. The gate area was more like a bus station than an airport, with a musty, outworn smell to match. Exhausted as she was, Kallie still drank in the sights and sounds—foreign women wrapped in bright reds and yellows, Arabic spoken over loudspeakers.

As for her team, Erik spent the wait staring at a water stain on the wall, Yoshi scribbled in his spiral notebook, and Caroline sat delicately on the edge of her chair, eyes darting as though expecting to be attacked at any moment.

After the quick flight, they landed in Luxor in midmorning, collected their luggage, and headed outside the small airport. As soon as their feet touched the ground, they were accosted by several men calling in heavy accents, "Taxi? Taxi?"

Caroline whispered to Erik, "Tell them there are four of us, plus our luggage. We need a van."

Some scurrying and gesturing occurred. It appeared the men both competed *and* cooperated when it came to foreign tourists. A dingy white van pulled up within minutes, its driver short and solidly built, with a wide, nodding smile that revealed one gold tooth. "Americans, yes?" More nodding. "Welcome. Welcome to Egypt." He bustled around their luggage, tossing it into the back of the van with ease.

The ride to the hotel was like a trip back in time, and Kallie absorbed everything. The sounds of the city pressed in on them through the rolled-out van windows. In the street, taxis, cars, donkey carts, and rickety horse-drawn carriages competed for right-of-way with blaring horns and raised voices. At a traffic light, the midday call to prayer boomed from a mosque's loudspeaker. Kallie eyed the mosque as they passed. Despite the ever-present antagonism, Islam shared more with its monotheistic cousins of Judaism and Christianity than it did with Egypt's original pantheon. So many choices. If the myths *could* be trusted, which one was true?

On the sidewalk she saw a boy beating a donkey with a stick. A family of four, perched on a motorbike, raced past. Finally, like some dusty painting from an earlier century, the palm-lined Nile, wide and green, rose up from the rocky desert.

Caroline seemed to take the appearance of the Nile as her cue to begin a tour-guide routine. "The Nile River is generally regarded as the longest river in the world and runs through eleven African countries, ending in the northern Delta region of Egypt, where it meets the Mediterranean."

The driver's eyes shifted in the rearview mirror.

Caroline continued. "In ancient times it flooded every year, causing the soil on each side to become rich with nutrients and very fertile. In modern times, the flooding is controlled by dams and farmers use irrigation."

They turned onto the street that ran alongside the Nile, crowded with tourists and hawkers. At the docks along the river were innumerable bobbing boats, from tiny feluccas to cruise ships.

"This is the Corniche El Nile." Caroline extended a hand in true tour-guide fashion. "Basically, 'Street of the Nile.' It's in French because Egypt was once occupied by the French."

Kallie smiled. Caroline must have memorized the Frommer's Guide to Egypt in her preparation. Perhaps Dimitri was right. She did seem to have their details well in hand.

They approached the Karnak Temple on the left, which Caroline pointed out—with no history lesson, thankfully. Kallie would definitely make time to explore the sprawling temple complex.

"We will be staying at the Winter Palace hotel." Caroline smiled. "You'll like this, Kallie, since you like to write. It seems the great mystery author Agatha Christie stayed at the Winter Palace while she was writing *Death on the Nile.*"

"Hmmm." Kallie smiled. She'd never heard of Agatha Christie. Yoshi and Erik seemed impressed.

"Oh, and also Lord Carnarvon, who funded

162

Howard Carter's expeditions in Egypt when he found the tomb of King Tut, he stayed here, too."

Now these men, she'd heard of. "Sounds great, Caroline."

"Yes, it's a grand old hotel. You'll love it."

Mostly she loved the idea of a hot shower and a comfortable bed.

A few minutes later she discovered the interior of the hotel was indeed delightful, from the massive atrium topped with gold-leaf moldings to the reds and blacks of the vast tapestries spanning the tiled floor. She was eyeing the huge crystal chandelier overhead when the old-fashioned ring of the desk bell brought her attention back to Caroline making arrangements. The desk clerk confirmed four rooms, and Kallie sighed with relief. No sharing rooms on Dimitri's dime.

The clerk needed to see passports, and she unlatched and reached into her laptop bag to retrieve hers. Instead of finding the passport, her hand sank into a gooey mess.

"What—?" The yogurt she'd purchased at JFK had exploded. Apparently cabin pressure was too much for the foil-sealed carton. Pink goop coated everything inside the bag.

⇒ 12 ⇐

Kallie's face flamed. Why, why did everything seem to conspire to make her look foolish? She pulled the dairy-coated passport from her bag with a sigh.

The desk clerk, a tall Egyptian man with gorgeous eyes and a bright smile, reached under the desk for a stack of napkins, as though yogurt-covered passports were an ordinary occurrence. "I am so sorry, Ms. Andreas, for your disaster." He took the passport between two fingers and began to wipe it down. "But we will take good care of you here at the Winter Palace. Please"— he extended a hand for her bag—"you will allow us to have it cleaned for you?"

The genuine warmth of the man, so indicative of his country's gift for hospitality, melted the rock of embarrassment in her chest. "Thank you, no. I can take care of it. But I appreciate it."

He nodded and bowed a wide smile in her direction, then copied her passport information and returned the damp booklet.

One steaming-hot shower later, Kallie sank with sheer joy into her sumptuous white bedding. Egyptian cotton. Lovely.

She'd barely drifted off when an insistent melody interfered with her dreams. She propped herself on two elbows, blinked around the room. Ah, it was one of the new cell phones Caroline had handed out to the team when they arrived. Preprogrammed with all their numbers, as well as Dimitri's, and able to call internationally. She scrambled out of the bed and retrieved the phone from her bag, then glanced at the display. Dimitri.

She punched the green button. "Kallista Andreas." She answered automatically, still half-asleep.

Dimitri laughed. "Glad to hear you're all business even after the long trip."

"Yes. Sorry. How are you, Dimitri?" She sank onto the bed again. Hearing his voice was rather like sinking into a comfortable bed after an exhausting day. The tension of the trip seemed to drain from her. She fluffed the pillows behind her back and relaxed.

"Worried."

"Really? About?"

"You."

Kallie grinned, grateful that he couldn't see her face from across the Atlantic. "What has you worried? Between Caroline's Day-Timer and Erik's muscle, what could go wrong?"

His answer was too long in coming. "I don't know. I just—I wish now I had come with you. It doesn't seem right, having you over there doing my—"

"Dimitri. You know the Linear A Key is as important to me as it is to you." Perhaps more important. "We'll be fine."

"Okay. Tell me about Luxor."

"Well, it grew out of the ruins of Thebes, the capital of Egypt's New Kingdom, about 1,500 years before the common era."

"Very funny. Tell me about *you* in Thebes."

Kallie settled back into the pillows and spun out her first impressions of Egypt, of Luxor, of the Nile, and the Winter Palace hotel, and everything she'd seen and felt thus far. How did it become so comfortable, talking with Dimitri? He didn't feel an ocean away. More like he was in the room. Perhaps she was also wishing he'd come to Egypt.

When she'd finished, Dimitri chuckled. "After all that, I'm surprised you're not asleep."

"I was, when you called."

Dimitri sighed. "Sorry, I—"

"Don't be sorry! I'm—glad—you called. I mean, it's good to hear your voice."

The phone went silent for a moment. "It's good to hear your voice, too, Kallie."

She searched for a topic to continue the conversation. "How is it going, settling your father's estate?"

"Hmmm. It's a complicated process. Harder than I imagined." He went on with more details, which Kallie only half-absorbed. The other half of her mind wandered. She still had questions. Why had Dimitri disappeared to Europe for so long? Any why return only after the last of his family was gone? Despite her aversion to secrets, she didn't have the guts to ask again. Not yet.

"I should let you sleep," Dimitri said.

"What? No, that's okay—" She could have talked to him forever, as long as they didn't talk about the past.

"No, I want you to stay healthy and alert. Get some rest. Do you have plans for tonight?"

She glanced at the bedside clock. "We're supposed to meet for dinner in a couple of hours. We're going to wait until tomorrow to contact Tarik Rashid."

"Well, enjoy your evening. And Kallie?"

"Yes?"

"Be safe."

She said good-bye, tossed the phone onto the bed, curled up into the sheets, and fell asleep smiling.

ಬಃ

She awoke with a jolt, fighting through that hazy feeling of displaced confusion. The morning sun edged a hard line down the center of the heavy hotel drapes.

Today was the true beginning of her adventure. Last night the team had met for an elegant dinner in the hotel's dining room and a sunset stroll along the Nile, but today, out there in the city of

167

Luxor, she would start tracking the pinnacle piece of the *Minoan Collective.*

She sank back into the bed and indulged a bit of daydreaming. Would there be a published memoir one day? Would it begin with this morning, with waking at the lip of the Nile, nervous excitement fluttering in her stomach, alternating with solid confidence in herself and her work?

Regardless of what the future held, in this moment she resolved to be the person Dimitri believed her to be. She had crossed the globe to pursue a dream for the good of the world, and she would not back down. The old, fearful Kallie had been left in New York. Here in Egypt she was the bold explorer, ready to take on back alleys and black markets.

She met Erik in the luxurious lobby at their agreed-upon time. No need for Caroline or Yoshi yet, as they were only going to ask a few discreet questions to track down Dimitri's contact who dealt in less-than-scrupulous artifact sales.

"Ready?" Erik's big grin matched his body, and his red hair was spiky and disheveled, as if he'd jumped from his bed and run to the lobby.

Kallie inhaled, feeling the excitement in her chest. "Definitely."

She led him out to the Corniche El Nile and at the curb glanced both directions. "Do you think one of them will simply stop for us?"

Caroline had informed them last night the

horse-drawn carriages that trekked through the city were not only the most economical way to get around, they were the least conspicuous. A far cry from their expensive cousins who paraded elegant couples through Central Park, these *calèches* were rickety and worn and cheaper than a taxi.

Erik followed her gaze. "From what I've seen, anyone with room for tourists will have us in their sights—"

"Ride to temple, lady?" A child's loud voice interrupted Erik's prediction.

Kallie turned to see a calèche slowing beside them, a boy of about eight sitting on the red-and-white-striped cushion, waving at them, beside his father who held the reins.

The boy grinned, revealing missing teeth. His dark eyes sparkled with the innocence of youth. "We take you to temple, very cheap."

Kallie smiled. "We want to go to Old Market Street."

The father nodded, his dark skin glowing against his gleaming white robe. "Market Street, yes. Very cheap."

"How much?" Erik's voice sounded wary and suspicious. Did he believe the boy and his father would cheat them? They had plenty of Dimitri's money to fund their travels, but then it was probably best if others were not aware of their cash supply.

It was the boy who answered, as though in training to take over his father's business. "Only ten pounds."

Kallie narrowed her eyes. "For ten pounds, you will stay with us while we shop and bring us back."

"Yes, yes. And we know best places in market. Very nice places."

Run by their family, no doubt. It was the Arab way—a complicated system of kickbacks and payoffs to help each other take the most from tourists. But in truth, the ten Egyptian pounds they requested converted to less than two American dollars. It was almost embarrassing to be haggling.

"Good." Erik was already climbing aboard. "I'm hungry."

Kallie followed, and Erik extended his hand to pull her into the black-hooded carriage. The vehicle was obviously a source of pride to both father and son. From the rim above their heads, an assortment of jingling silver charms hung from five-fingered metal hands—tiny horses and horseshoes, birds and bells. The interior cushions were covered with a plush, though worn, azure blanket.

"You have camera?" The boy reached out his dark hand. "I take picture of pretty lady and big husband."

Erik shook his head, laughing. "No camera."

170

The boy shrugged, turned back to face the road, and they were off. They quickly left the main tourist street along the Nile and turned to narrower side streets.

Kallie breathed in the sights and scents, only half-aware she searched within all of it for something familiar. It was a habit of the past seven years, as if everywhere she traveled her mind kept asking, *"Here? Is this place where you belong?"* In the ancient land of Isis, the Great Mother, would she find answers to her own origins? Oddly, today, she didn't feel a sense of belonging, but she did feel a sense of the familiar. As though she'd gazed on the Nile, the Theban necropolis on the other side, and even the alleys of Luxor at some time in her past.

The horse clopped its way through noisy, sunlit streets. The first streets were residential, with timeworn doors presenting crumbled tan faces to the street. Garbage-lined alleys jutted off like spokes, and red and yellow pennants crisscrossed above the street, flapping in the hot breeze. They passed through to other streets, with doors opening to struggling businesses and low-slung, dirty banners above iron-barred shops.

The calèche competed for right-of-way with taxis, with donkeys and their carts, with harried pedestrians. They were inundated with the incessant honking of horns and the overpowering stench of garbage and manure and poverty. Was there no Public Works department to clean up the astonishing amount of trash?

Stray cats watched them pass with greedy eyes, and it wasn't long before stray children ran alongside, their hands outstretched. For what? Money? Kallie watched them with a deep sadness. Their junior driver shooed them off with harsh Arabic. Apparently Kallie and Erik belonged to him for now.

At last they turned onto a wider street, still crammed with blaring traffic, crowded with makeshift vendor stalls set against the buildings. Tables slid by, piled with white onions, with yellow lemons, with huge bulbs of fragrant garlic. A young man tended some kind of oven, a pyramid of tan and wrinkled baked potatoes beside him for sale. The odor of the streets mingled with the more palatable smell of spiced meat, and the bright colors of fresh fruits and vegetables drew the eye from the garbage at their feet.

The calèche slowed, then stopped at the narrow door to a rug shop. Their driver turned, pointed to the dark interior. "Very nice rugs here. Very cheap. They ship to you."

Kallie eyed the shop. It was as good a place as any to disembark and start their search. She pointed behind them. "We'll shop for a while, then meet you at the end of the street." She fished five pounds from her pocket. "Five now. Five when you pick us up."

The boy snatched the note from her hand with a grin. "Okay, okay, good."

They jumped to the street, and with a smile Kallie waved to the boy.

Erik scanned both directions. "How are we supposed to find the right shop?"

"There can't be too many butchers on one street, can there?" She shaded her eyes from the sun and peered down an alley, overhung with clotheslines crammed with woven blankets and lined with tables of T-shirts, scarves, and embroidered tunics. "Come on."

She led the way past jewelry, leather bags, shops of souvenir sphinxes and temples and pyramids, spice stands with shallow bowls of golds and browns. With every step they were loudly encouraged to stop and look. "No charge for looking," Kallie heard more than once. She smiled and shook her head at each eager salesman, but it only seemed to encourage them further so she began to ignore them, rude as it felt.

Soon the obviously tourist-targeted stalls and shops thinned, and the local market revealed itself, with household goods like utensils. And meat.

She looked at Erik and sighed. A sea of fish and meat stalls stretched into the dusty distance.

Erik shrugged. "But he said *butcher*, not just meat vendor, right?"

"True."

They pushed farther but needn't have worried. There was no missing the three men struggling to hang an entire cow's carcass from a hook outside a shop. The flesh dripped into a bright-red puddle on the sidewalk, then ran toward the street as though still pulsing from the cow.

Kallie slowed and put a hand to her stomach, then continued toward the shop, Erik on her heels.

The scene worsened. An alley shot off from the main street just before they reached the shop, and Kallie's quick look revealed a dozen or so sheep and goats meandering, waiting their turn for slaughter, and a big Arab with his knee on one's neck and a blade gleaming in his hand. The alley pooled with blood, and they had to step over the stream that ran toward the street.

The three men finished with the cow and turned as one, with wary eyes, toward Kallie and Erik.

They probably didn't get many American tourists coming for a closer look.

Kallie picked one of the men at random, about her age with a blood-smeared yellow T-shirt, and made eye contact. "We're looking for Tarik Rashid."

The man wiped sweat from his forehead with the back of his arm. He glanced between her and Erik, as if surprised she had spoken. "Who looks for him?"

"My name is Kallista Andreas. A—friend—of mine told Rashid to expect us."

They glanced between themselves, then one of the three, an older man, waved them toward himself. "Come. Wait in here."

They followed him into the unlit butcher shop, and Kallie blinked furiously, her sun-blind eyes leaving her in the dark.

She had only time to think, *Step one accomplished,* before an angry bark from Erik and a loud shuffling behind startled her. Two powerful hands grabbed her arms from behind and dragged her deeper into the shop. She lifted frantic eyes to the front door. Erik's form was outlined in the sunlight, held back by the other two men.

"Get your hands off me!" Erik thrashed in their grip.

Kallie screamed something of the same, peppered with a few rougher words. She wriggled against her captor's hands. He pulled her backward, half dragging as she lost her balance against him.

On the other side of a narrow doorway, he kicked a wooden door closed, pushed her against it with one arm against her throat, and used the other hand to slide a rusty lock.

Kidnapped or murdered, either way—*Step one, failed.*

→ 13 ←

The back room of the butcher shop had no windows, but even in the dark, with the Egyptian's hairy arm pressed against her throat, the black holes of missing teeth and jagged pink scar of a half-torn ear leaped out in horrifying detail.

Kallie's stomach rebelled at the sights and sounds. She gouged at his arm with her fingernails, instinct kicking in, mind and body on fire.

Her throat seized, breath choking. She managed a gurgling sort of shriek.

"No scream!" Her attacker pushed her flat against the door. "I am not stupid. I know why you come." His voice was rough, hoarse—as though the smoke of a thousand hookah pipes had worn tracks in his throat.

Kallie stilled. Did he think she was someone else? She licked her lips, managed a whisper. "Dimitri Andreas."

The pressure against her neck lessened, slightly. She sucked in a notched and ragged breath, then nearly gagged at the stench of his body, his breath, and the bloody shop. With all her strength, she tried again.

"Dimitri Andreas sent me. He said you could help."

His brow furrowed. Flies buzzed around the

dark shapes on hooks along the wall, and muffled curses filtered through the door at her back.

That's right. Now you know who you're dealing with, friend.

Her attacker smiled. She should have given Dimitri's name from the start—

"Ah yes, a man who can pay."

Kallie shifted on her feet and her shoes sucked noisily away from the floor, from some unspeakable stickiness. "Yes, he's willing to pay for the right information."

He grinned again, leaned in to brush her cheek with his own. She swallowed, closed her eyes, and turned her head.

"And how much more would he pay for *you,* lady?"

Hope deflated. So, name-dropping wasn't always the best recourse in Egypt. "I assure you, he has no interest in me—"

"You said your name is Andreas, too."

Kallie stifled a curse.

"He sends his wife, yes? His sister?"

He was still so close, and Kallie fought to focus her eyes over his shoulder, past the split ear. The dark hole of the butcher shop felt like the pit of the earth.

He grinned his half-toothed grin again. "What kind of man does this?"

Behind her, behind the door, a thunderous crash shook the walls. Her attacker's dark eyes flicked to the door, the whites large and bright in the dim light.

Kallie's hope reignited. She seized the moment of distraction, shoved him hard, ducked under his arm, and spun. She faced his surprise with feet planted at shoulder-width and arms held aloft, loose and ready.

Where had that come from? The move had been automatic and smooth, like the steps of a dance she'd known all her life. Something flooded her arms, her legs, a hardening courage that came from confidence in her own body.

She slid forward, her eyes cold and focused on his. *Go ahead. I dare you.*

He stood against the blackened wooden door, his turn to be pressed into its roughened splinters and rusty hinges.

And then the door crashed open. Tossed him forward, onto the sticky floor at her feet. His forehead bounced, he twitched once, like a yellow fish flopping on shore, and stilled.

Light at the door outlined Erik's massive form. "You okay?"

She nudged her abductor's shoulder with her foot.

Erik crossed to her. "What are you doing? Let's get out of here!"

"We didn't get what we came for."

The man on the floor groaned and shifted.

"We're looking for Tarik Rashid." She kicked

at his shoulder again, and that surge of something flowed through her again. "Where can we find him?"

He blinked once, twice, but said nothing.

A deep and frightening anger gripped her insides. She should kick him harder. In the stomach. It would feel good to hear the *woof* of air pushed from his lungs.

Erik saved her the trouble. He put a huge foot on the man's neck and pushed against his windpipe. His eyes bulged and he scrabbled in futility at Erik's ankle.

"Karnak Temple." Scraped from his throat. He gasped. "Meets people in the square outside. Like a guide."

Erik paused a moment longer, then lifted his foot. "We'll tell him you said hello." He grabbed Kallie's hand and they shot out of the back room, past the other two friends, unconscious on the floor of the shop.

In the street, they looked both ways, then ran toward the end of the Old Market, past loaded tables and flapping fabrics, toward the calèche that should be waiting for them.

"That was amazing!" Kallie panted alongside Erik, who still clutched her hand. "Did you see the way he looked at you? Like he was sure you were going to kill him!"

Erik said nothing and she glanced up to see his face set, his jaw tight.

Their driver and his boy were indeed still waiting for their additional five pounds, and Erik pushed Kallie into the calèche, then jumped in beside her and barked at the driver to return them to the Winter Palace hotel. He leaned past Kallie to watch behind them, through the crowded market street.

She followed his gaze. "Do you think they'll follow us?"

Erik said nothing, just watched the street. His military training seemed to be in play, all grim focus and tensed muscles.

They reached the hotel without incident and without speaking. Kallie paid the sweet boy, smiled her thanks at his proud father, and followed Erik.

His eyes still flicked left and right, but he seemed to relax once they were inside.

Caroline and Yoshi met them in the lobby. Caroline was fishing something from her over-large bag and sweet floral perfume followed her.

Yoshi stepped away from the cloud of scent, eyes bright and pen twirling between his fingers. "And what was the result of your excursion? Did you learn the whereabouts of the black-market antiquities dealer?" His voice was loud, sharp.

Erik stomped toward him like a boulder rolling downhill.

Yoshi's eyes went wide and his hands flew upward, even the pen ceased its twirling.

Erik stopped short of the smaller man, his hands in fists at his sides. "What's wrong with you? Why don't you just get one of those street loudspeakers and announce us to the whole city?"

Kallie touched Erik's arm and turned sympathetic eyes on Yoshi. He looked like he was about to bolt. "Erik's a little tense. We had some—trouble."

Yoshi and Caroline listened with wide eyes and dropped jaws, and then Caroline finally succeeded in retrieving her phone from her bag. She speed dialed and was relating the story to Dimitri in her whispery southern-belle voice before Kallie knew what had happened.

A moment later she held the phone to Kallie. "He wants to speak to you."

She took the phone with a strange flutter in her stomach. Must be a lingering reaction from the incident in the market. "Yes?"

"Kallie." With only that one word, his voice was warm and worried, concerned and reassuring all at once.

She pressed the phone against her ear, as if it were the man himself. "I'm fine, Dimitri."

He said nothing, but she could hear his breathing, could picture him rubbing at his forehead, his eyes closed.

"Really, Dimitri. We're both fine."

"I should never have—"

"Yes, you should have. I can handle this. We'll find it."

"I don't care about the Key, Kallie!"

The storm of emotion reached across the ocean, wrapped around her, and silenced her defensive-ness. He cared. The warmth she'd felt at hearing his voice spread to her face.

"Let me talk to Caroline."

Kallie inhaled at the abrupt demand. Was he angry? She returned the phone to the girl, who took it with a saccharine smile, listened a moment, then flicked her gaze toward Kallie.

She could only guess what he was saying about her. Incompetent? Never should have trusted a girl who couldn't even keep a job?

Caroline turned her back to the three of them with a little laugh, then sauntered across the lobby to the red-and-gold-flowered couches and sank into one, all smiles.

What were they talking about now?

Caroline slid one sandaled foot under herself and tucked her hair behind her ear, a flirtatious gesture that felt like a needle-stick in Kallie's gut.

When Caroline's gaze strayed to her again, as though Kallie were the topic of conversation, she forcibly pulled her attention away from the girl and faced the men. "So what do you think? On to the Karnak Temple?"

Yoshi frowned. "Does that seem wise?"

Erik shook his head. "Enough for one day. At least for you. I'm going to do some surveillance there before we all go. If everything seems clear, we'll go in the morning."

Kallie bit her lip. She'd felt confident in her leadership when they left this morning, but obviously it was Erik who had saved the day. She nodded. "Fine."

With a last glance at Caroline, still absorbed in her conversation with Dimitri, Kallie headed for her room, to shower off the events of the morning.

After her shower, she eyed the books she'd brought covering Egypt's Eighteenth through Twentieth Dynasties. She should be reading up on the Karnak Temple and the famous valleys on the opposite bank of the Nile, where the Theban kings tried to foil tomb robbers by mummifying themselves into the hills far from their mortuary temples. So many of the famous Pharaohs, from King Tut to Hatshepsut—Egypt's only female Pharaoh—had been found in the Valley of the Kings.

Instead, the anxiety still tensing her muscles led her to the journal, with a powerful urge to write a story she *could* control . . .

→ 14 ←

In the depths of the cavern, abandoned by the priestess, my lungs felt near to bursting. I tried to breathe, to gather courage and fight back the panic of the stone pressure all around me. My body throbbed in rhythm with the echoing drip of water, and my skin was clammy and cold.

Was this the Truth of the labyrinth? There was no way out, that it was only a portal to death, to the Underworld? That one could pass into the earth, but not out, never out?

I trudged ahead, mindful that I seemed to be in little danger for now, except from the imaginings of my mind, which could truly leave me ranting mad.

How long did I wander? Minutes? Hours? Long enough for my mind to grow numb.

But the eyes, the eyes always saw even when the mind was past seeing, and when my light-starved gaze detected a soft glow ahead, I left off my fearful touch of the cavern wall and stumbled toward the light like a parched traveler reaches for water.

Yes, yes it was moonlight, streaming against the wall of the cavern, welcoming me into the field, reminding me that resurrection was possible. I lurched through the cavern's mouth, reborn from the earth's belly into the world of the living. I raised my hands in joyous thanks to the sky, the moon, the very air, and breathed deep of its starlit chill.

I saw no priestess on my return to the town. I slunk through the streets, into the home where I had taken a meal, and retrieved my pack from among the sleeping inhabitants. Then slipped to the adjoining stable and untethered my horse with soft words of reassurance.

"We are away, Herakles. There is more welcome for us in the Cypress Forest than we have found in this place."

But perhaps it was justified, the cold hatred I had felt from the townspeople. The royal family had taken their youths and sacrificed them to an unknown horror. And for what?

I mounted Herakles and clucked him out of the alley to the edge of the town, where we made a wide circle, keeping to the moonlit fields with the forest ahead.

Yes, still the forest.

I had thought much of my next actions while wandering the dark cavern. The priestess had given me to know that Andreas was dead, and I believed her, despite her trickery. One could tell when a true thing was spoken, and her unseeing eyes had seen that Andreas had passed into the Underworld.

So I must decide whether the accusations were

true. Did I ride to the Green Mountains for the love of Andreas alone? If so, I may as well turn back.

But if I rode also for Truth and Destiny, as the priestess had said, then these were still to be found ahead of me, not behind.

And so I turned Herakles toward the Cypress Forest, dug my heels into his flanks, and lowered my head for the run.

For Truth. For my people.

For redemption.

කැ

Brambles snagged at my legs as I breached the narrow path threading into the Cypress Forest. Had many travelers come before me? The path looked unused, not well-trodden as it should have if each party of suitors had crossed its threshold. Curious.

I had left the town and its enigmatic priestess behind in the moonlight. The sun had risen hours ago. Now the coolness of the forest came as a relief from the morning sun that glared hard and clear on my shoulders.

I gave Herakles his head, for the undergrowth was thick and there was little choice but to follow what clearing the track afforded. But soon trees thickened overhead, their trunks grew longer and thinner as they gasped for open air, and ground brush grew sparse, flattening to a carpet of mossy ferns and rotting limbs.

We lost our sense of time, Herakles and I, as we picked our way through fallen logs. I would have given much for a trot, but the littered forest floor prevented speed and required circuitous detours.

How long would this journey through half-light last? I thought back to the Oracle's words. *"Endure the Cypress Forest."* The words boded ill, implied suffering. Thus far, the intermittent shafts of sunlight falling across my eyes and the cool relief of shade brought only pleasure.

Hours later, I had no such confidence. I had seen no alternate tracks, and yet suspected my path did not lead straight through the forest, as would be expected. Had it been hewn here by troublesome spirits, to misguide and trap unwary travelers? The variable light above had fallen low in the sky, below the tree line. I should have been able to sense its rays from the west, reaching through the cypress trunks. But the forest lay shrouded in twilight, giving me no message of direction, no assurance of release.

In a tiny clearing, I pulled up on Herakles's reins and circled around once, twice, peering into the half shadows. The oppression of the forest closed around me. A chill born of both forest and fear burrowed beneath my cloak and into my bones. I patted Herakles's head with a comfort I did not feel. It would soon be night. It would be best to give up on finding the far edge of the forest and instead bed myself down in safety.

The clearing seemed as fit a place as any, and I slid from my horse's back with a whispered word of explanation. "It is neither warm nor secure, Herakles, but it is the best we have."

Night fell hard, a heavy tide of darkness sweeping the forest, settling over trees and moss and decay with a sibilant whisper of unknown dangers. I huddled close to Herakles's body, willing some heat from his legs to leech into my own limbs. In the darkness I heard every wet snap of branches under animal feet, flicked away the scuttling tickles of unfamiliar insects, inhaled the suffocating scent of decay around me, close and thick.

In the late watches of night, I thought of Andreas and longed for the safety of his warm arms. I whispered questions to the sky, questions with no answers, and tried to still the trembling of my limbs.

Morning came, but it was a weak awakening, a barren lightening of the sky from black to slate, barely visible through the cypress. I broke my fast on what little bread I retained, saved the dried fish for later, and washed down the crust with a few sips of wine. Before I finished, a great drop of rain plopped onto my cheek, an insult from the sky. I wiped the water from my face, glared upward, then mounted my horse.

The rain did not fall steady and even, not

beneath these trees. It collected on patchworks of leaves and ran down limbs. Too weighted to remain upright, the leaves released heavy beads to pelt my head and arms as I rode, soaking me to the skin and leaving me shivering. All was green and brown and gray, and more than once I felt a shadowy presence slipping along beside us, as though tracking our progress.

If it *was* progress we made, and not a futile, circular journey leading nowhere.

"We have no sun to guide us today, Herakles." I tightened numb fingers on the reins. "And I have lost my sense. Would you could speak and tell me what you know. Can you smell the sea to guide us? Hear the call of the Green Mountains?"

But Herakles remained my silent ally, and we pushed forward. I tried to focus on the trees we passed, tried to form a picture in my mind's eye of each bend in the path, each cluster of trees, so I would know if our path looped. But my eyes were as heavy as my limbs, an aching, shuddering fatigue that left me sweating and clammy. Did I grow feverish?

How long had we journeyed in that dark place? Was it the Underworld itself, some trickery of the goddess to lead unsuspecting travelers beyond the world of men? The last of my food disappeared, the rain did not abate. I met hunger and illness, fear and hopelessness along that path.

I clung to the consolation that if this were the

road to the Underworld, I would soon be reunited with my beloved, if indeed Andreas were already dead. My moments of grief were deep and dreadful, as though my mind remained trapped in the caverns, abandoned by the priestess.

Was it only my mind that whispered to me out of that wet and dripping wandering? Voices mocked and reproached, accused and ridiculed. *Go back, fool. The journey is too hard for you. There is no redemption to be found.* And later, when still I pushed on, *You are not worthy, little girl. You shall never reach the Green Mountains. Never grasp the Horn of Truth.*

Whether foul spirit or fevered delirium, I did not know.

I only know I went on.

For days? Perhaps. Certainly I saw daylight fade, darkness descend, morning return. I remained on the back of Herakles, and at times we both slept, him standing with head and ears drooping and me, splayed across his back, my cheek against his coarse mane.

If it had been a mortal enemy, I could have stood, could have put my lengthy training in the fighting arts to bold use, both sword and body. But this was no mortal that came against me. Mind and body shrieked at me to renounce my destiny, to lay down, to rest, to die.

But I would not. The memory of my father and my people, betrayed by my foolish arrogance and in Mycenaean danger even now, would not give me release. Exhausted, lost, and feverish, I pushed on, certain the foothills of the Green Mountains lay beyond the next bend in the trees.

I would not be deterred, not by pain nor by sacrifice.

And then, as though my determination alone had created this widening of the path, this brightening of the way, I sensed the forest had changed, that it opened before me with permission to leave. That it finally released me to pursue my journey, my destiny.

Nearly senseless, I nudged Herakles toward light and freedom. He seemed to intuit the opportunity as well and began a trot, a trot that soon brought us to the place I feared I would never see. The edge of the Cypress Forest.

At the last row of trees, I pulled up on his reins and looked back into the murky depths, then ahead to the sun-dappled hills, the white walls and reddened roofs of a grand village nestled at their feet.

Emerging from the forest was like leaping over the edge of a cliff. I had passed the halfway point. There was no going back. The Cypress Forest had been endured.

The sun broke through to warm my face and dry my sodden clothing, and we stepped into it fully, Herakles and I. Stepped forward to meet the villagers who would lead us to the mouth of the cavern, where I would find the Horn of Truth to save my father.

The labyrinth where I hoped, against reason, to find Andreas.

→ 15 ←

"It's a relatively safe place to meet."

The team stood in the hotel lobby, hearing Erik's advance scouting report of the Karnak Temple complex.

Kallie eyed the street outside the lobby window, then her team. Would having Yoshi and Caroline come along with them give her more protection than Erik alone? Would there be more safety in numbers? Tarik Rashid should be expecting them, and there was no reason to think their attackers from the day before would have put him off, not when he would be expecting payment.

Yoshi fidgeted with a camera around his neck, as though making certain the settings were correct. He seemed to feel Kallie's eyes on him. "We must appear as ordinary sightseers, not attract undue attention."

Erik clapped him on the shoulder, knocking him forward a bit. "No worries, Yosh. The place is overrun with folks. We'll blend right in."

Kallie smiled. Their team was as unlikely a

foursome as she could imagine. Hopefully Erik was right.

A taxi was cheaper for four people, and they reached the large parking area, teeming with tour buses and lined with souvenir stalls as the gold disc of the sun climbed overhead to bake the cracked pavement.

Kallie stepped from the backseat of the aging taxi and surveyed the area. Massive tan stone pylons towered at the far end of the parking area, their slanted walls still splendid after three thousand years. What would the ancient Pharaohs have thought of the commercial value of their temples and chapels, erected for worship of the gods? Would they have been proud of their descendants, finding ways to increase Egypt's wealth through tourism? Or horrified to see hordes tramping through sacred spaces, gawking at the ancient relics without understanding?

The thought of the sacred drew her toward the temple entrance. Such an ancient civilization. If any would know of the origins of humanity, would it not be the Egyptians? Could their creation myths be believed, even in part?

Kallie led the others across the pavement, doling out a bit of history as they walked. "The complex was built up over hundreds of years, by over thirty Egyptian kings. Only the Precinct of Amun-Ra is open to the public, but even that area is spread over sixty acres."

Caroline huffed. "Well, I certainly hope we are *not* expected to wander around that entire place looking for this guy!"

Erik pointed ahead. "The so-called tour guides are allowed to roam around outside the entrance, offering their services. We should find Rashid there."

Caroline took care of ticket purchasing, Erik kept watch, and Yoshi took pictures. She should be rehearsing her questions for Rashid, but Kallie's mind and heart had already pushed past the avenue of ram-headed sphinxes that led to the first pylon, beyond the Hypostyle Hall, to the Sacred Lake and the myriad obelisks. She imagined it intact, with colorful pennants flapping on poles high above, and guards peering down from slits in the pylons. It felt right, to be here. As though she'd been here before. Was it possible?

"You would like a tour?" Their first salesman had approached. "I can show you many wonderful things, all temples and hieroglyphs." He was a short, balding man with a pleasant smile.

Erik held up a hand. "We're looking for a particular guide today, I'm afraid. Would you know Tarik Rashid?"

The Egyptian frowned. "I can give you good tour. Tarik does not love Egypt like Qeb loves Egypt." He poked his own chest.

Caroline returned with their tickets and Kallie stepped forward. "I'm sure your tour would be wonderful, Qeb. But we promised a friend we'd seek out Tarik." She fished a few pounds from her bag. "Perhaps we could give you something to help us find him?"

At this, Qeb's shoulders dropped in resignation, and he thrust a thumb over his shoulder. "Come." They followed to the steps that led to the short avenue of sphinxes and waited while he approached another Egyptian loitering in the area.

Tarik Rashid brought a slight chill of foreboding to Kallie's arms even under the hot sun, even before he spoke. He was an attractive man, tall and thin with carefully styled full hair and a pencil-thin mustache, but it was the eyes—shifting and narrowed—that troubled her. They were introduced by Qeb, Kallie thanked him with generous *baksheesh,* and the four were alone with their target.

Rashid eyed Qeb's retreating figure, then looked at Erik, suspicious and perhaps a bit hostile. "You ask for me?"

Kallie answered, drawing his attention to her. "Dimitri Andreas sent us. He believes you have information that could help us in our search for a particular—item."

Rashid flicked a glance left and right, then from Kallie's head to shoes, a look that somehow

195

seemed both angry and interested at once. "Keep your voice lower, lady, if you do not want trouble."

Caroline slipped behind Erik, and Yoshi's pen was twirling again, but Kallie took a step closer.

Rashid's eyebrows rose at her approach, and a leering smile tugged at his lips.

She spoke quietly. "We don't want trouble."

"I told Andreas—it is not safe to speak about such things casually."

"That's why we are here. To speak formally."

Again, the amusement, and the attention all on Kallie. "I will speak to only you. Alone. We will tour the temple. There are eyes on me, always."

Erik shoved her aside. "No way."

"Take it easy, Erik." Kallie gripped his arm hard.

The huge Scandinavian glared down at her. "If you think I'm letting you—"

"Quiet, quiet." Rashid held his palms to them, but his gaze was roaming the crowd that pressed around them. Did he fear for his job as a tour guide, or was it something more? "I will take you both. But you must look like couple."

Erik frowned. "A couple of what?"

Kallie sighed. "A couple, Erik. Husband and wife."

"Oh."

She would have laughed at the color that crept

up his neck, but the tension was too high. Instead, she took his arm and glanced back to Yoshi and Caroline. "You two find your own guide, keep an eye on us."

Yoshi appeared horrified at this prospect, even more so when Caroline followed Kallie's lead and hooked her arm through his.

She and Erik followed Rashid down the steps, along the Processional Way of facing ram-headed sphinxes, and between the entryway of the first pylon. She tilted her head back to see the lofty top as they passed, and a shiver ran through her. The Temple of Karnak complex was the largest ancient religious site in the world, and tourists had been arriving here since the Greco-Roman era. One couldn't help but be awed.

They entered the forecourt, with its dozens of sculpted Pharaohs staring down, arms crossed over their chests, with the crook and flail clutched in each hand. Kallie dragged her attention from the chapels and alcoves around the perimeter, tried to ignore the tunnel-like double row of massive, fluted columns that loomed ahead. She focused on the guide who led them. "What can you tell us of the piece?"

Rashid didn't answer, only pushed farther into the courtyard until they reached the corridor between the ten fluted columns, their mottled stone dwarfing the tourists and yet still inscribed with hieroglyphs all the way to their capitals.

Rashid turned, waited for them to approach, then glared down at Kallie. "I can tell you of the great Hypostyle Hall, which we will enter."

Okay, if that's the way they had to play it. In truth, she didn't mind the facade of the tour. She was in one of the most remarkable places on the planet. Might as well enjoy it.

He led them through the corridor. "The Precinct of Amun-Ra was built as you see it here in the Eighteenth Dynasty, when Thebes became capital of unified Egypt."

She listened to Rashid, soaked up the smell of ancient sand and the buzz of tourists and the pale blue desert sky, then followed him into the hall, which defied description.

Rashid let them wander the hall, tossing out facts as they tried to absorb the 134 massive columns in sixteen rows. The largest of them were over ten feet wide, large enough for a crowd of fifty people to stand upon their capitals, and sixty feet high. Every one of them was carved from top to bottom in reliefs, both hieroglyphic and pictorial. Rashid pointed out specific designs —a double ankh, royal cartouches, scenes of kings interacting with gods—and Kallie ran her fingers lightly over the reliefs, some shallow, carved hurriedly, and others deeper to last through the ages. She felt a strange desire to wrap her arms around the column, but if there had been ten of her, she barely could have embraced it.

They must have known something, these Egyptians. To build with such majesty and beauty, they must have had some truth. But if there were one or more divine beings out there somewhere, would they have allowed the extinction of their worship? Would a real god stop revealing himself or herself?

She was vaguely aware of Yoshi and Caroline also wandering the hall with their guide, but the spell of the forest of columns absorbed her so completely she forgot why they came.

Rashid directed their attention upward to the architraves that still topped some of the columns, their painted undersides still vivid with reds, blues, and yellows in cartouches filled with ancient scenes. "It is witness to great power of time that temples such as these can be buried and lost for many hundred years, then unearthed and remain still as beautiful."

The guide came alongside her as she gazed up at the paintings that still spoke through the centuries. "Egypt is still full of treasures. We can learn much from those that still exist." His voice was low, intimate.

Kallie answered in kind, like some sort of scripted code. "I would love to see more of such treasures."

"You must only know where to look."

This was all she was to get until they had seen the Hatshepsut Obelisk, passed beyond the sixth pylon, and detoured to see the perfect stillness of the Sacred Lake, its dark green water shining in the sunlight.

On the far side of the lake, Rashid surveyed the ruins around them, seemed satisfied that no one watched or listened, and at last spoke plainly. "There has been talk for a few months." He smoothed his thin mustache. "Something brought by the Minoans, linked to the tomb of Rekhmire, vizier to Thutmosis III. Something important to their language."

Kallie's heart tripped a few beats in her chest. This was it. To be in this place was awe inspiring, to be sure. But to be so close to the Linear A Key sent a flood of heat to her extremities and left her nearly unable to breathe. "Where can we purchase it?"

Rashid barked out a little laugh. "That is not the way it works in Egypt, lady."

Kallie flushed. How close were they, really?

Rashid pulled a small, white card from his pocket and handed it to her. A business card, printed in English. *Nigel Pendleworth, Research,* and a phone number.

"He is Egyptologist. But one that does not always wait for the Western funds."

Kallie nodded. Funding for digs could be scarce. Nigel Pendleworth, whoever he was, must have found some less-than-legal ways to pay for his work.

"Do not give my name. If you give names, he will tell nothing."

She pocketed the card. "And he knows where the Lin—where the item is?"

Rashid shrugged. "I know very little. He knows more."

Thanks for the details. Kallie looked to Erik. "Shall we finish our tour?"

They followed Rashid out through the Hypostyle Hall, into the forecourt, and finally beyond the first pylon to the sphinxes. So much more they would not see—the Botanic Gardens, the Great Festival Temple. Perhaps another time.

Rashid let Kallie pass him as they exited and whispered harshly against her ear, "They watch now. You must look like couple, nothing else." He spoke loudly, as though conscious of listeners. "I hope you enjoyed tour of Karnak. Very delightful, my tour?"

Kallie wrapped an arm tightly around Erik's, then clasped his hand with hers and leaned her head against his bicep. "It was wonderful, just wonderful. Wasn't it, honey?" She blinked up into Erik's wide eyes. "Doesn't he know so much about Egyptian history?"

Did she sound properly tourist-like? Her flattery of Rashid's knowledge was barely an act, even if the fawning tone and romantic clinging were fake. He truly had given them a delightful tour.

201

Erik grinned. "Uh, yeah. I guess."

"Thank you so much. I believe you said fifty pounds?"

Rashid's eyes narrowed. It was a fair price for his tour, but not his information.

Kallie pressed some bills into his hand and communicated more with her eyes.

He glanced down at the money, nearly two hundred pounds, and nodded. "Thank you, nice lady." He bowed his head toward Erik. "And nice man. I hope you enjoy Egypt."

Kallie was still clutching Erik as Tarik Rashid walked away, and her eyes followed the departing guide up the steps, to where Yoshi and Caroline stood waiting.

They were not alone.

Next to Caroline stood Dimitri Andreas.

⇝ 16 ⇜

At the sight of Dimitri standing beside Caroline, Kallie's fingers tightened involuntarily, squeezing Erik until he wiggled his hand within her grip.

Neither Caroline nor Dimitri looked pleased to see she and Erik locked together.

Kallie extricated herself from Erik and took a few uncertain steps toward Dimitri.

After that first shock, her body seemed to react

in the opposite way, with an unbinding of all that had been stretched taut over the past few days, a settled feeling like coming home. She was happy to see him, happier than she would have expected. It was good and right that he was here. She needed him here.

She exhaled as though she'd been holding her breath for days. "Dimitri. What are you doing in Luxor?"

He jogged down the steps to meet them, Caroline and Yoshi following. "I changed my mind about staying in the States."

She shook her head, a bit dazed. "But you got here so quickly."

He smiled. "No faster than you, I'm afraid. After we spoke yesterday I had Caroline make arrangements for me to fly out immediately. I left New York yesterday afternoon and arrived here this morning."

Caroline held up her phone. "He's been texting me since you two went in there." There was a tiny stress on the word *two* and a flick of her eyes toward Erik. Subtle, but an obvious message embedded.

Dimitri took her hands, looked into her eyes. "Are you okay? After yesterday, I mean—"

She pulled away. Everyone was watching. "Yes. I told you yesterday. I'm fine. We're both fine." She retrieved the card Rashid had given her from her bag. "And we've made some progress."

She explained what Rashid had told them. "Shall we call him now?"

Dimitri checked his watch, a heavy, expensive-looking thing. "It's been a long twenty-four hours for me, I'm afraid. Let's wait until tomorrow, see if we can track him down."

She nodded but ran her finger along the edge of the card. Perhaps she could find Pendleworth while Dimitri was sleeping off his jet lag. She didn't really need a partner, did she?

But Dimitri hailed a taxi for the other three and insisted that he and Kallie take a calèche back to the hotel. Along the way, he couldn't take his eyes off the Nile.

Kallie followed his gaze to their right. "You like the water?"

"Hmm? Oh. No, it's the boats. I love the boats."

She laughed. "Take a walk along the Corniche and you'll hear a dozen offers to board one of them—'good price, very cheap.' "

He turned smiling eyes on her. "If you'll go with me."

"What? I wasn't serious—"

"Take a boat ride with me tonight. When the sun starts to go down."

A sunset boat ride on the Nile with Dimitri Andreas. A flutter of fear—that same foreboding she'd had when they said good-bye at the airport—flicked through her veins. "All right. But you should rest first."

He smiled, as if amused at her mothering tone.

Kallie focused on the clopping horse ahead and the far-reaching temple complex sliding by on their left. Dangerous territory, once more.

Several hours later, as Kallie predicted, it took only a short stroll along the water's edge to receive enough offers for a month's worth of sunsets. Dimitri kept walking, as though looking for something particular. Did he have high standards when it came to feluccas?

Finally he slowed on the quay, almost directly across from the Luxor Temple.

Kallie eyed the temple's columns across the street. They hadn't visited this one yet, only its larger cousin farther north. Oddly, it looked as though the minaret of a mosque jutted up from within it. What was that about?

"She's beautiful," Kallie heard him say. She turned back. Who had caught his eye?

A young Egyptian man, about her age and eager, smiled broadly. "You like to sail tonight? See the sunset? I give you best price in Luxor." Behind him, his felucca waited, sails lowered.

Dimitri laughed. "Yes, I'm sure you will. How much?"

Kallie let them haggle and drifted to the water's edge, to the small boat that bobbed against the dock, its sails wrapped around poles. The white hull was painted with a yellow and black logo— a sun inscribed with *Sandra in the Sun*. That the logo was designed in English, not Arabic, made the intended passengers clear.

"She is named for my mother." The sailor stepped up behind Kallie, his voice filled with pride.

Dimitri touched her elbow with a smile, guided her toward the boat with his eyes on her. "All beautiful women should have vessels named for them."

Kallie resisted rolling her eyes at the line and boarded the boat, nodding to another man who stood at the bow.

They were adrift in minutes, the sails unfurled and the craft pointed west, across the river. Kallie sat along the boat's starboard side, on a low bench covered with orange- and rust-colored cushions. The felucca could hold about ten people, but tonight she and Dimitri were its only passengers. They neared the western bank of the river and then pointed south, against the current. Dimitri sat alongside her and they watched the end of the Luxor day slip past them, docks lined with cruise ships and cargo boats and water dotted with feluccas. Above the lip of the water, the Luxor Temple rose majestically, then restaurants and hotels, then their old Winter Palace hotel, its yellow walls glowing in the dying sun.

Their two hosts chatted with them a bit but soon retreated to their posts fore and aft, leaving

Kallie and Dimitri in comfortable silence under the purpling sky. A white sliver of moon glowed to the south and the watery green of the river darkened. The river danced against the hull of the boat, rocking them gently. It was a dreamlike landscape, with children waving from the muddy shore of the western bank and the call to prayer sounding from the city. An elderly man at the shore unrolled a ragged carpet and bent over it, facing upriver.

Kallie shivered a bit against the evening breeze and Dimitri wrapped an arm around her shoulders. She inhaled against the pressure of his arm, wanting him to remove it, hoping he would not. They fit together, but the pull was frightening.

He spoke quietly, as though distracted by deeper thoughts. "I'm glad I came."

She closed her eyes. "What about your business at home?"

"I don't have a home." The words seemed more confession than argument.

Kallie angled her head to look at him, but his eyes were on the river. "I thought you chose the Long Island estate—"

He shrugged and forced a laugh, shaking his head. "Ignore me. I'm feeling melancholy tonight. Something about the water, the boats. I don't know."

It was there again, one of those tiny windows

into the real Dimitri. She didn't take her eyes from his. "Did you do much sailing in Europe?"

He glanced down, his eyes only inches from hers, lips parted as if to answer. But then looked away again, back to the eastern bank of the river and the city of Luxor, its lights coming to life in the darkening twilight. "That was a long time ago."

Something in his tone made her shiver once more.

Dimitri looked at her arms, folded in front of her. He pulled them apart, then with his finger traced a slow line from her elbow to her wrist, stopping at the band of scars. She could feel the skin burning under his touch.

"Tell me about these."

He'd noticed them before, that much was obvious. Had he been wanting to ask, the way she'd been curious about his time outside the States? The lure of sharing confidences was powerful, but it was like falling into a pit, like losing her bearings. Like losing herself.

She pulled her arm away, braced it against her body once more. "It was a long time ago." Secrets could go both ways.

They spoke little for the rest of the boat ride. Though he didn't remove his arm, the distance between them had grown. Their sailors no doubt thought them the most unromantic couple to ever take a sunset cruise. When the felucca at last nosed back into an open spot along the dock, Kallie escaped with relief.

Back at the hotel, Dimitri grabbed her hand before she reached the elevator. "Thank you for sailing with me tonight."

She smiled, a bit of sadness clinging to her. "It was beautiful."

He reached across and tucked a strand of hair behind her ear. "Kallista. Most Beautiful One."

She fought a flush of pleasure. The words were meaningless. Of course he would know Santorini was once called Kalliste. That the meaning "most beautiful" applied to the island. Not to her.

His gaze was still on her. "That's what I would name my boat, if I had one."

She shrugged one shoulder. "I have a feeling you could get one."

"Perhaps I will. But only if you promise to sail with me again."

Oh, he was charming. That was certain. Charming and seductive and most of all, guarded.

"I concern myself with the present, Dimitri. Not the future."

"Nor the past."

She nodded, felt the unspoken words between them, about themselves, their lives, their secrets. "Nor the past."

He gripped her upper arms, kissed her lightly on the cheek, then whispered into her ear, "Good night, most beautiful."

And then he was gone, leaving her at the elevator doors. Off on some mysterious business, no doubt.

She intended to sleep as soon as she returned to her room. But sleep would not come, and the early morning hours found her scribbling in her journal, a new vista opening before her on her beloved island, a new battle for her alter ego to wage. When at last she ran out of whatever was driving her and laid the pen aside, a desperation to understand what it meant swept her. She collapsed against the back of the desk chair where she'd been writing and leafed through the filled pages.

She'd promised Dr. Newsom that if she wrote anything more she would send it to him. But somehow composing on her laptop felt wrong, as if only the leather journal could call the story forth.

But that didn't mean she couldn't type it up now.

An hour later, the scenes she'd written on the plane, last night, and tonight's ramblings were in a document. She hovered over the Send button. E-mailing the scenes to Newsom felt akin to sending pictures of herself naked. Exposed. And yet, she didn't know what any of it meant. *Send.*

The morning came too soon, and after a hurried shower, a quick decision on khakis, a pink button-down shirt, and a skipped breakfast, she rushed to the lobby to meet Dimitri at eight o'clock. Yesterday he had taken the business card Rashid had given them and promised that by this morning he'd have a plan.

She saw him before he saw her, standing at a front window, looking over the street, to the Nile. He wore a light jacket and jeans, as if ready for sightseeing, not a business meeting. She slowed her approach, watching as he lifted his hand to touch the window.

"Dimitri."

He dropped his hand, turned, and smiled. "Ready?"

"I don't know." She laughed. "Ready for what?" She scanned the lobby. No sign of Yoshi, Caroline, or Erik.

"We're going to TT100."

She sucked in a breath. "The tomb of Rekhmire? Seriously?" Any Minoan scholar worth anything knew that the Eighteenth Dynasty vizier's mortuary chapel held one of the most important paintings linking the Minoan civilization to Thebes—a frieze of visitors from Crete bringing tribute to the Pharaoh.

Dimitri smiled. "Seriously." He extended an arm toward the door.

"What about the others?"

"This one's just for us. I've tracked down Pendleworth—it appears he's doing some work in the tomb. We'll just go and have a chat with him."

"I feel bad having all the fun."

He laughed. "I think you overestimate your teammates. Yoshi's holed up in his room, working on some kind of paper or dissertation or something. Caroline and Erik were happy for a day to spend poolside."

"Well, their loss."

She followed Dimitri outside and glanced up the street for oncoming taxis.

"Over here." He walked toward the curb, to a parked motorbike with two helmets perched on its seat.

She raised her eyebrows. "You're kidding."

Dimitri laughed. "Having trouble keeping up this morning, are we?" He tossed her a helmet. "Put that on. I can't make any promises about being able to drive this thing safely."

She strapped the helmet under her chin, then awkwardly straddled the bike behind him. It wasn't his potential lack of skill that terrified her as much as the insane traffic patterns of Egypt.

But then they were off, weaving through cars and taxis, calèches and donkeys, crossing the bridge over the Nile, where craggy summits of the desert mountains loomed against the pale sky. They reached the west bank and raced along the road between sugar cane fields worked by turbaned men and banana plantations like deep-green jungles. Dimitri honked his horn with the best of them.

Kallie wrapped arms tight around his waist and

smiled with the sheer joy of it. They flew past the Colossi of Memnon—the pair of sixty-foot seated statues that once guarded the entrance of the now-absent Temple of Amenhotep. Kallie stared at their disfigured faces as they passed. She would never get used to the extravagant number of ancient monuments adorning the Egyptian land-scape.

Ten minutes later, Dimitri detoured off the main road onto a path more gravel than asphalt.

The dust kicked up and Kallie bent her head against his back.

He turned slightly to shout at her. "Are you up for going off-road? A shortcut to the valley."

Kallie lifted her mouth to his ear. "I'm up for anything."

Dimitri patted her hand at his waist and nodded.

The taupe-colored limestone cliffs loomed ahead, unchanged in the three thousand-plus years since the Eighteenth Dynasty kings had chosen their deep recesses as the safest place to begin their immortal journeys into the afterlife. The Valley of the Kings was not the only burial cache. Queens and nobles were interred within the cliffs as well. Temples built by Hatshepsut, by Ramesses II, and others embellished its rocky landscape.

Ahead, she could see the pyramidal shape of the Sheikh Abd el-Qurna, the mountain that some said inspired the kings to move their burials from the pyramids in Lower Egypt to the cliffs of Thebes. Dimitri seemed to have aimed their motorbike directly at the mountain far in the distance, heedless that they followed little more than a windswept desert track now.

They continued on for some time, the dust and wind grabbing at her hair, stinging her eyes, the desert silence that somehow could be heard under the roar of the motorbike's engine pulling them deeper into the valley.

And then the engine died.

→ 17 ←

Just like that. No warning cough, no worrisome sputter. The motorbike engine simply cut out.

Kallie eyed the desolate surroundings as they drifted to a stop. They were in trouble. She hopped off the bike, followed by Dimitri, and both removed their helmets.

He fiddled with a few things on the bike but clearly had no idea what he was doing.

He glanced at her, eyebrows raised. "I don't suppose you know anything about motorbikes?"

"I don't even know anything about bicycles."

Dimitri sighed, looked left and right.

There was nothing in either direction, nothing but the monotonous brown of everything and the narrow track they had followed.

Kallie tried optimism. "Someone will surely come along. It's clearly a road of some kind."

"When's the last time you saw another vehicle?"

Okay, so her optimism wasn't shared. "Should we walk?"

"Which direction?"

Good question. She shielded her hand against the sun and looked across the river, then toward the cliffs. "How far do you think we are from the Tombs of the Nobles?"

He followed her gaze. "Not far, I don't think. I actually thought we would have reached it by now."

She narrowed her eyes at him. "You didn't run out of gas, did you?"

He grinned. "Not that stupid. No."

She studied the traitorous bike. "Will we just leave it here? On the side of the road?"

Dimitri shrugged, as if it were disposable. But then he could probably buy the thing ten times over with the cash in his pocket.

He pulled out his cell phone but shook his head. "No signal out here. Not surprising."

"Well, standing here in the sun isn't going to solve anything." She started down the track. "Although I do wish we weren't traveling to the west."

Dimitri caught up with her. "What's wrong with heading west?"

She laughed. "You know your Greek history better than Egyptian, I see. The Egyptians believed the afterlife was located in the west, where the sun died every night. 'Traveling to the west' was a euphemism for death."

"Great. And what do we do when we get there?"

"Nothing too difficult. Answer questions posed by forty-two gods in the Hall of Judgment. Have your heart weighed to make sure it's lighter than a feather. That sort of thing."

"Easy."

She glanced sideways at him. "So you think you'd be judged by Osiris to be 'True of Voice'?"

The familiar mask dropped over his expression, and he did not answer.

An hour later, the idea of walking to the tomb had played itself out, and Dimitri admitted that perhaps he *was* the world's biggest idiot.

Kallie eyed the sun's position and tried to laugh. "Come on, we've still got another hour or so before Sekhmet kills us."

"I find it disturbing how much you know about death in Egypt."

They needed distraction, so she called up her museum-guide voice. "Egypt's version of the destruction of mankind. Men got too arrogant, weren't paying enough attention to the gods. So Ra decided to send his daughter Sekhmet. She was a lion-headed goddess who represented the sun at midday. In this land the midday sun was pretty much the personification of evil. She came to earth and started slaughtering everyone, getting an unquenchable thirst for blood."

"Terrific."

"The gods were appalled and saw that mankind would become extinct if they didn't stop her, so they filled a field with a red drink that looked like blood, but they mixed it with beer. She gorged herself until she collapsed in a drunken stupor. By the time she awoke, mankind had learned his lesson."

"I think I prefer the creation stories."

Conversation dwindled as the sun rose higher and the cliffs ahead seemed to grow only slightly closer. Kallie's throat was so parched it might seize up if she tried to speak.

She licked cracking lips, wanting to push away the empty and detached feeling that was growing inside her. "You definitely know how to show a girl a good time, Dimitri."

"Yeah, you should see what I have planned for our next date."

She smiled at the word, then pursed her dry lips against the pain. "Not sure I'm interested."

"Come on." He lightly punched her arm. "I'm *rich*. No woman ever says no to the rich guy."

She glanced sideways at him. The tone was playful. The words were not. "Is that what you think? That women are only interested in you because of your money?"

He shrugged. "Pathetically cliché, I know." His voice took on a dramatic tenor. "Wealthy, isolated bachelor. Never trusting any woman to love him for himself. Pushing them all away—"

"Okay, I get it." She laughed. "It's your curse."

"Yeah, well, I'll bet you've got some curses for me right now."

She nodded. "Not aloud, though. You know— because you're so rich."

"Right."

She let it go, the opening he'd given her. For all the jokes, perhaps he really did believe that his money cursed him to loneliness. He had love to give, that much she'd seen.

But with Sekhmet's killing sun burning their heads and sucking moisture from their bodies, perhaps he'd never get that chance.

The sun blurred the sand ahead of them, or perhaps it was only her eyes. A small rock tripped her. Not lifting her feet high enough.

Dimitri caught her, clutched her to himself. Then pointed. Ahead, a cloud of dust moved toward them on the track.

She would have cried if her tears hadn't dried up long ago.

They waited and she fought the urge to wave her arms wildly like a stranded survivor signaling a helicopter from a jungle island. There was no way they'd be missed.

Another motorbike pulled alongside and slowed.

Thankfully, the driver appeared local and not another idiot tourist out for a jaunt under the murderous sun. He wore no helmet, only an orange-checkered keffiyeh to protect his head from the elements.

"You are walking?" His eyebrows drew together and he shook his head.

Dimitri pointed behind them. "We were riding. Our motorbike broke down."

"Where do you go?"

"Valley of the Nobles. Tomb of Rekhmire."

He tilted his head to the back of his bike. "I will take you."

With effusive thanks, they both managed to climb onto the back of the bike. Kallie had seen dozens of these motorbikes around Luxor, often piled with two, three, even four people. They would manage.

The tomb proved to be only a ten-minute ride, midway between the Valley of the Kings and that of the Queens, but they might have perished on the side of the road before reaching it. Dimitri insisted on paying their savior, even though he at first declined.

He left them at the entrance to the tomb complex, but they didn't have far to find Nigel Pendleworth, sweating on a bench outside TT100, the mortuary chapel of Rekhmire.

"Ah, there you are at last." Pendleworth mopped his forehead with a dingy rag, took a swig from a metal water bottle, and nodded toward them.

Kallie hadn't realized he was British until he spoke, though the name should have given it away. He wore the khaki jumpsuit and pith helmet of an early twentieth-century archaeologist—Howard Carter and Sir William Flinders-Petrie rolled into one stereotypical gentleman.

"I was expecting you some time earlier. I was about to quit for the day."

Dimitri pointed to the bottle. "Would you have any more of that? We've been stranded in the desert for a bit."

"Is that right?" His dubious look at the two of them implied they were either idiots or liars. "Here, then." He pointed to a larger thermos, and Dimitri grabbed it up and handed it to Kallie.

Water never tasted so sweet.

Pendleworth gave them a moment but then straightened and cleared his throat. "So you said you were interested in making a donation to the work here?"

Kallie hid a smile. Money made the world go 'round, after all.

Dimitri pointed to the tomb entrance, a narrow wooden door set into the rock. The yellow sign, inked in black Arabic and English identified it as Rekhmire's tomb chapel. "We'd love to see what you're working on."

"Yes, yes, of course."

He led the way, and Dimitri stepped aside to allow Kallie to enter next. She ducked under the low lintel and blinked in the semidarkness. Only a few bare bulbs had been strung to illuminate the chapel, which was shaped in a reverse T, with corridors extending left and right, a longer hall disappearing to perhaps one hundred feet ahead of them, and a ceiling sloping upward into darkness. The musty damp so typical of tombs tickled her nose, and the grit of desert sand still in her mouth made her feel like one of the first intrepid academics opening a new tomb. The silence wrapped around them, beautiful and deep, until Pendleworth interrupted it.

"No mummies here, I'm afraid." He smiled condescendingly, as though they were curiosity seekers and nothing more.

Kallie drifted to the wall opposite the entrance. "It's not even a burial tomb. Rekhmire was probably buried with the kings. Why would there be a mummy?"

"Quite right, quite right. The lady knows her history."

She also knew exactly where to find the section she sought. The chapel walls were covered, floor to ceiling, with intricate and detailed paintings of every scene imaginable—wine production and law courts, potters and metal smelting, statue building, funeral processions and feasts—the colors fresh as if they'd been painted in the last century, with very few lost sections. Carefully lettered prayers and incantations accompanied the pictures.

But here, here was the portion of wall she'd come to see, almost in the corner. The painting of tribute brought from various foreign lands, depicted in five registers. The people of Punt brought monkeys and baboons and incense trees. Below that, the people of Crete. The Minoans.

Kallie ignored the Nubians with their giraffes and leopards and ivory, the Syrians with their elephant, the last group of miscellaneous foreigners. It was the Minoans she came to see, the Minoans for whom her hands seemed to rise of their own accord, drawn to touch the paintings in spite of herself. Pendleworth was kind enough to simply clear his throat, and she dropped her hands, feeling her fingers burn and a breathless pressure in her chest. She traced the treasures with her eyes alone, the silver ingots and rings, the baskets of lapis lazuli, the myriad pitchers and bowls and amphorae. And the rhytons—the drinking vessels in the shape of the heads of lions and bulls and ibexes. So fascinating.

This feeling of connection to the painting, finally seeing it in person—it was the weepy feeling like the end of a sappy movie.

"Beautiful." She spoke the word as a whisper, and it echoed reverently in the chapel. Dimitri drew up behind her, and she could feel his emotion almost as clearly as she felt her own.

"It's the Mycenaeans you'll be interested in, then?" Pendleworth called from the entrance.

"The Minoans." Kallie's voice sounded harsh, defensive. "The Mycenaean garb was painted over the people long after the original painting was finished. To show they had taken over Kalliste by that time."

"Kalliste?"

She held out a palm. "Thera." She used the Greek name for the island. "And Crete, of course."

"Ah, well, it's all Greek to me." Pendleworth guffawed at his own joke.

Dimitri drew her away from the painting and faced Pendleworth. "We were hoping you had some knowledge of a piece particularly important to Minoan language research."

"Eh? What's that?" Pendleworth was sweating again.

"Perhaps a piece that traveled through the hands of the el-Rassuls before anyone realized its potential? Something with the Linear A script?"

Pendleworth's eyes narrowed. "And what makes you think I'd know—"

Kallie stepped toward Pendleworth, her eyes fixed on his. "We were told you've found some—creative—ways to fund your work. Activities that give you special insight into lost pieces."

They were speaking in code, all of them. She would have preferred to rake him over the coals for his illegal activities that hurt the scholarship of all antiquities, but now wasn't the time.

Pendleworth grunted. "Can't say I remember the particular piece you're looking for."

Dimitri smiled, pouring on his trademark charm. "I have significant resources, Pendleworth, to use in locating this very special piece." He extended a hand around the chapel. "Resources that could perhaps be well spent here, on your work."

Pendleworth's chin quivered and he removed his helmet to scratch at his balding head.

"What would it take, Pendleworth, to finance your work for, say, one year?"

At this, Pendleworth's eyes shot open for an instant before he masked his excitement. "I should think with that generous donation I could spare some time to help with your endeavor."

Dimitri nodded, apparently satisfied. He handed Pendleworth a business card. "My private cell number is on there. You can reach me here in Egypt. Give me a call the moment you have some information."

Dimitri headed for the entrance.

Couldn't they see the rest of the chapel? Perhaps he was going for the dramatic exit. Probably best if she followed.

But Dimitri turned before ducking under the door. "Oh, and one more thing."

Pendleworth's eyes narrowed in suspicion.

"We need a ride."

⇒ 18 ⇐

An hour later, Kallie lingered under the cool water of her hotel shower, washing off desert sand and drinking in the water through every pore. Oddly, Judith's warning before Kallie had left popped into her mind. *"Don't drink the water."* Did this count?

She gave herself a few minutes to think about how close they'd come to serious trouble. For all their casual banter during the ordeal, it had been real and it had been dangerous. The second time her life had been in danger in three days.

Today's battle hadn't been against bad guys, but it was no less real. In fact, just as she had battled the element of Air to survive the trans-Atlantic flight, today had been a struggle against the very Earth.

Was she up for this?

She let the cool water soothe her skin, run through her hair, and felt the comfort of it. There was nothing wrong with wanting to avoid pain, with wanting to be safe. Nothing to be ashamed of. Perhaps she should get back to the academic life. Leave the adventures to others.

Others—like the scholarly Yoshi? The flirtatious Caroline? Wasn't she as qualified?

Kallie shut down the water, toweled off,

wrapped herself in the fluffy robe provided by the hotel, and crawled under the jacquard spread.

The temptation to quit was heavy on her, like the irresistible desire to fall asleep when one is overcome with fatigue. The thought of safety enveloped her like the warm robe around her body. Should she let it all go? It would take more than physical strength to survive the possible danger. It would take a spiritual sort of strength she wasn't sure she possessed.

Thoughts of the spiritual reminded her of the scenes she'd sent to Dr. Newsom in the early morning hours, about seven o'clock last night, his time. Would he have responded yet?

She fought the pull of sleep and tossed the blanket aside, then went to her laptop to check her e-mail.

Yes, there it was. A message from Newsom. She scanned it quickly, then sat back against the desk chair, taking in his assessment of her ramblings, trying to fit his shrink-talk into the living, breathing scenes she'd sent. But they were fuzzy to her already, written in a sort of haze last night. Perhaps if she reread what she had written . . .

I left the Cypress Forest behind, grateful to be rid of it, grateful for its lessons. I was stronger for it, I had no doubt.

The city of Lycoris was a bright jewel at the

foot of the verdant Green Mountains. While other cities of Kalliste had succeeded through their shipping exploits on the sea, largely trading in the products of other peoples, Lycoris produced its own unique product, and with such, it had amassed a great wealth.

I had arrived at the perfect time of year to see Lycoris's glory. The springtime fields of crocus blooms on the breeze-swept, sunlit slopes, their pale lavender and deeper mauve petals shielding tiny offerings of golden saffron, threads so carefully harvested by the people of Lycoris. The spice prized throughout the far-flung islands for its flavor and its golden-yellow dye was cultivated here by man, woman, and child and splashed a backdrop of color behind the wealthy city.

Herakles and I approached slowly, and I debated the wisdom of declaring myself or remaining simply a traveler in need of shelter. But it was the people of Lycoris, the Oracle had said, who would lead me to the mouth of the cavern. Would they do so without knowing why I sought such danger?

We cantered beyond the edge of the city, its welcoming streets a relief after the forest. I had heard in my studies that other kingdoms, other cities beyond Kalliste, required walls to protect their people from enemies. Kalliste had no enemies and no such walls.

It seemed a pity to think of a people forced to hide behind walls.

I dismounted and led Herakles through the narrow, winding streets that twisted around larger buildings. The facades of the two- and three-story houses were of rectangular dressed stone, polished and perfect. I found the central fountain, searched for someone to offer a pail for Herakles. I would not risk offending villagers by allowing him to drink directly. My last sojourn in a village had not been a safe haven. Would Lycoris prove so hostile?

A young girl approached shyly, a green-and-blue-glazed faience pot on her hip. "Are you in need?"

I smiled. "Water for Herakles here would be most appreciated." I took the pot from her proffered hand. "Do you know of a place for me to rest?"

She smiled, the expression lighting her face. "You may certainly stay with us."

I watered my horse but shrugged. "Perhaps you should ask your parents first."

"It is only my father and me. But I will ask."

With that, she ran off, without her pot, without my name. I took some water myself, then sat on the lip of the fountain to wait.

She returned quickly, her father in tow, just as the children in the first village had done. It was only one man, though, tall and well-muscled, with a dark and striking look about him. From his clothing, he was clearly wealthy, and I stood to greet him.

His hands extended in greeting. "Selene tells me you—"

The words broke off as he studied my face. My appearance after the Cypress Forest must be dreadful.

But then he was on a bent knee, pulling Selene down with him. "My lady."

I sucked in a little gasp. Here? So far from the palace, still to be recognized? "You know me?"

He rose, head still lowered in respect. "I have made many trips to the center of the island, my lady. To bring saffron to the palace."

Of course.

"You would do me great honor to be my guest. Whatever way I can serve you."

I lifted my chin, grateful for the warmer reception and not wishing to interact too casually. "What is your name?"

"Isandros, my lady."

"Well, then, Isandros, for now, I am in need of only hot food, hotter water, and a bed. After that, we will talk more of what the people of Lycoris can do for me."

He bowed, smiling, then extended an arm toward a wide street off the central courtyard, with a quick look at his daughter and flick of his eyes toward the horse.

The girl stepped forward and took the reins from my hand. "I shall take good care of Herakles, my lady."

I smiled and touched her chin with my fingertips. "I am certain you shall."

Isandros's home did justice to the man who sold his saffron to the palace. The ground floor, with its small windows to retain the dry coolness, held his workshop, storerooms for food, and a mill for grinding grain. He led me up the stone stairs to the dwelling rooms, these with large, airy windows to capture the mountain breezes, plastered with fine limestone and frescoed with deep pinks and yellows and whites, much like the palace. I wandered the largest room, examining the wall paintings. Many were quite fine. Melayna would have approved.

I rested until Isandros brought me baked barley, grapes and olives, and goat cheese, and Selene came with hot water for washing and clean clothing, soft and elegant. Had it been her mother's? She showed me the private room, and I stripped my soiled garments and scrubbed the Cypress Forest from my skin, relishing the scratch of the cloth and the sting of the heat. The plumbing of Isandros's house was as fine as any in the palace—clay-pipe drains built into walls and floors that carried effluence underground and away.

By evening I was clean, fed, and well rested. I descended the stairs once more to speak with

Isandros, to plan my foray to the cavern and ask for his assistance.

I found them both in the workshop, bent over crocus petals.

Isandros lifted his head, looked me over appreciatively, and smiled. I forced away a blush. It was not the glance of a commoner for a king's daughter, but the approval of a man for a woman. Inappropriate, no matter how gratifying.

He set aside his work and stepped toward me. "Tell me how I can be of service."

"You can show me the mouth of the Great Cavern, where the beast is said to live."

His smile vanished. With a stern look, he shooed Selene from the shop. She ran past, her eyes on my face, wide with awe.

"Please, shall we sit, my lady." He indicated a low bench along the wall.

I sat first, holding myself erect, then slid farther from him when he joined me.

"What you are asking, it is very dangerous."

There was nothing to do but explain it all—how I came seeking the Horn of Truth after the failure of so many others.

"Is this not something your sister should have done?"

His question, direct and honest, surprised me.

"I—she is uninterested. Unwilling, I suppose."

"Unwilling to do what she ought for her people."

I disliked hearing it put in such a cold manner but could not disagree, so I said nothing. Nothing, even, of my own guilt in the matter.

"My lady"—he took a deep breath, as though fearful of his own words—"I have been to the palace many times. Watched the king and queen, your sister and yourself, in your interactions with each other and your subjects."

"I regret I do not remember you—"

He held up a hand and shook his head. "No, nor should you. But in my unseen role I have seen much. Others have seen the same. Your sister, she is not—she is not good, my lady. The city of Lycoris does not believe that Melayna should next rule Kalliste." His eyes were on his work-worn hands clenched in his lap.

My lips parted. "What are you saying?"

"We believe the younger should rule the elder."

I sucked in my breath, then remembered my station and held my chin aloft. His words, the Oracle's words, seemed written in the stars. "I appreciate your approval, Isandros. But that is not for me to decide. I only seek the Horn of Truth."

He looked into my eyes, his own filled with admiration. "And that is why we believe you should be queen."

I breathed in the praise, let it settle my fears.

He placed a hand on my own, a too-familiar and yet comforting gesture. "Let us not speak of the

Great Cavern, or of the beast, until tomorrow. It will soon be night and nothing can be done today."

I removed my hand from his clasp but nodded my agreement.

I stayed the night, but on the following day a succession of the city's most prominent citizens came to call on me at Isandros's home, meeting me on the roof, where Isandros had installed me in cushioned comfort beneath soothing shade. One after another they came, each one expressing their delight that I had come to their fair city, each one concurring with Isandros's opinion that I ought to hold sway in Kalliste over my sister, that they would prefer to submit to my rule, my command.

The heady stream of flatterers did not cease until late in the afternoon, when Isandros brought me a cup of cool wine, smiling as he approached. "You are greatly loved here already, my lady."

I took the proffered cup and gave him a serene smile. "They are a good people, the people of Lycoris."

"And for you, they would gladly fight."

I frowned over the lip of the cup. "What are you saying?"

He sat at my feet. "That you have no need of the labyrinth, of the beast. No need to prove your worth. Already your worth is well known, and you will be supported."

His words had a mighty pull, wrapped in relief. "But what of the Horn of Truth?"

He shrugged. "We have the sea and the fields and the mountains. What need have we for any Horn of Truth?"

It was a good question. I had only the Oracle's word that this Truth was needed. If I had a people to fight for me, could not all remain just as it was on the Most Beautiful Island?

"There is a festival planned in your honor this night." Isandros got to his feet. "You must come and see, see the authority you have over a people who love you."

His eyes on mine were bright, and I felt again that warm flash of what passes between men and women, not royal and subject.

I bowed my head in formal consent. "I will come."

The festivals of a wealthy people are something to behold. Wine and music flowed through the city streets and through the flower-strewn central square. Laughter and dancing, abundant food, the glorious setting sun, the torches lit when the horizon purpled—it was exhilarating and even more so because it was done in my honor.

When the torches smoked in the night air and the jubilation began to settle, Isandros placed me on the edge of the fountain in the square and called out to the people.

"Citizens of Lycoris, your future queen!"

A mighty shout went up from the crowd, fists uplifted. As if I had raised an army to storm the palace and claim the throne. A tremor of uncertainty jolted from my heart, through my arms to my fingers. I closed them into fists to stop the trembling.

Isandros stepped up beside me, whispered in my ear. "We are rich, and we are many, and we have influence, my lady. And we shall make you queen." To the people, he shouted, "Good health to Queen Chloe!"

The crowd roared in response, "Good health to Queen Chloe!"

The trembling in my fingers spread to my limbs. This praise, this acclaim, it was like cheers for a winner at the annual games. A winner who had cheated to earn his prize. This I knew.

I had not earned this. I had never sought power, nor acclamation. It was a trick of vanity, a giving in to something born of self. An attack aimed at my latent belief that I was better than my sister.

I heard their cheers, saw their upraised faces, glowing with admiration, and all became suspended in a sea—a moment of timelessness and weightlessness, no breath, no blood—only my decision, my choice.

To choose honesty, humility, or to accept this mask, out of pride and arrogance.

To have the admiration and acclaim of the people, without having suffered the trial.

The moment stretched taut, and I felt the pain of it, as though my very body were pulled in both directions and could not last. I must free myself from one obligation or the other. I must.

"No!" It was a shout over their voices, over their heads, and it came from my lips. A deep silence rippled over the crowd, out to its edges.

"I am not the queen. I am not even the eldest daughter. And what I do, I do for the people of Kalliste. I must find the Horn of Truth. For the salvation of our people!"

The silence continued, and in it I could hear the final echoes of music and laughter and dance, drifting away like smoke in the wind.

Nothing more need be said. I was not their leader, and they were not mine to command. I stepped from the fountain wall, turned my eyes to Isandros, and gripped his arm.

"It is time."

☞ 19 ☜

Kallie set aside the journal, exhausted. How could simply reading take such a toll?

She grabbed her laptop and climbed back into the hotel bed, then propped pillows behind her, bracing the laptop against her bent knees. She checked the time at the bottom corner of the display. Three o'clock here. Nine in the morning in New York. She reread Dr. Newsom's e-mail. His first appointment was at ten, and she could call any time before. She grabbed her cell phone from the nightstand and dialed.

He picked up on the second ring. "Good to hear your voice."

He truly did sound glad, and Kallie smiled. It was nice to know he cared.

"Any more hallucinations? Lapses in time?"

"No crazy stuff. Sorry—I mean—no, no problems like that."

"Good. And your writings are good, too, Kallie. Really productive. I'm pleased with the progress you're making."

"Progress? What progress?"

"I should think you would have analyzed yourself quite thoroughly by now."

Kallie picked at a loose thread on the bed-spread. "I haven't had the time to analyze anything. Dimitri came over, too, and we've been busy trying to make headway with tracking down the piece."

"Hmm." The sound was quiet, concerned even.

She frowned. "What does that mean?"

"Let's talk about the scenes you sent. It's quite an epic, isn't it?"

She chuckled. "Yeah, I'm a regular Tolkien."

"Kallie, I'm not talking about the quality of the writing. I'm talking about the themes, the meta-phors. You're really opening up, do you see that?"

"How about if you tell me." She had a sudden craving for his chocolate mints. Anything to crunch on, to distract.

"Well, when you left off last, you were still deciding whether to undertake this journey of the soul, whether or not you wanted to seek the truth. But in these scenes, you've made the leap. You've listened to the Mentor, defied anyone who might discourage you—mother, father, sister, everyone around you—and crossed the threshold of your ordinary world into the realm of the adventure."

"Quite the hero, aren't I?"

Dr. Newsom cleared his throat disapprovingly. "Don't sell yourself short. You are indeed the hero of this story, and you have performed heroically. You've descended into the belly of the whale, so to speak, in that first cavern and encountered the first real danger of the journey —the winnowing away of false motives."

"False motives?"

"This idea that you have undertaken this journey in some quest for romance. We've talked about this. When the priestess informs you that Andreas is dead, it's your subconscious telling you that it's not romantic love you're after, it's self-love."

He paused, seemed to hesitate over his next words.

"Kallie, this is why I'm concerned about this

Dimitri guy. The way you described him in your e-mail—you need to understand that it's the unknown of your own psyche that is calling out to be discovered, not the secrets of a rich, mysterious philanthropist."

"You don't need to worry—"

"Your first priority must be your own healing. Don't derail your progress now by getting distracted with a relationship that is a substitute for understanding yourself."

"Got it."

"Okay. So you survived the first brush with danger, the first test of your motives. But this chapter in the Cypress Forest, this is really interesting."

Kallie repositioned on the bed, shifted her laptop to the nightstand.

"Now we're getting to the meat of the journey, don't you see?"

She could hear the excitement in his voice, like an English professor unpacking the symbolism of Shakespeare. She had given him a fascinating case study. Great.

"The Cypress Forest is the true beginning of your trials. Like Odysseus's journey. Or the Twelve Labors of Hercules. Interesting name for the horse, by the way."

"Thanks." The name had just popped out. Had there been some subconscious choice to name the horse after Hercules?

"So, you're committed now to the journey, to the trials. The danger is great, but you are choosing to survive, to pursue. You won't succumb to what is comfortable or easy, no matter the threat."

Kallie's eyes strayed to the window, the view of the Nile and the deadly desert beyond. "Wow."

"Yes, wow. I'm proud of you, Kallie."

"But it doesn't feel like I'm really *getting* anywhere. No closer to the truth."

"Exactly! You fear you are wandering the forest in circles. Like all of this might lead nowhere. But what have you already learned? What do you already know?"

She lifted her chin, inhaled. "That if I keep pushing forward, past the pain or sacrifice or whatever, that I'll find the edge of the forest. Find my way out."

"Yes!"

Kallie laughed. Was he thrusting a victory fist in the air? After more than a year of therapy, it must be gratifying for him to feel some progress. She wished she felt it, too.

"And think of other lessons you've learned. You are not alone, you've made allies. But the journey is not about romance or approval. You could shortcut the journey and remain comfortable, but you won't choose to do that—you'll push forward to find the truth."

"The Horn of Truth?"

"Yes, fascinating. The horn—a battle cry, a declaration, the start of a new thing. It's all there." He paused, as though letting her absorb. "Keep going, Kallie. This myth you're creating, it's your true self—guiding you. You already know the answers. Let it guide you onto the next leg of your journey."

"Out of the village at the base of the Green Mountains?"

"Out of the village, to the mountains, to the labyrinth. To wherever the journey takes you. It's the only way to heal."

That's what she was afraid of.

Newsom's words stuck. Even after they disconnected.

"It's the unknown of your own psyche that is calling out to be discovered, not the secrets of a rich, mysterious philanthropist."

She closed her eyes and wriggled deeper into the bedding.

"Your own healing . . . Don't derail your progress by getting distracted with a relationship."

Apparently she'd telegraphed more than she intended in mentioning her relationship with Dimitri. Newsom sounded frustrated. Perhaps even angry. Jealous? No, that wouldn't be professional.

He was right. She'd come far in these past weeks, writing a story that felt like it was truly leading somewhere, that connected powerfully with her soul. A story that could lead to answers. And until she had answers, she had no business getting involved with anyone.

Not that Dimitri had given her reason to think—

Her phone rang. She snatched it up, saw Dimitri's number, forced herself to pause before answering.

"Hey, Dimitri. Feeling better?"

"Feeling great." His voice was low, as if the conversation was for them alone, wherever he was. "You?"

"It's amazing what a shower and a little rest can do." She closed her eyes again and relaxed against the pillows.

"Have dinner with me."

She rubbed the back of her neck. "Will everyone else be there? I haven't even seen them today—"

"Just us. Something a bit more—upscale—than the hotel restaurant."

The Winter Palace's restaurant was not exactly fast food. Was there really a better place in Luxor?

She ran a hand through her damp hair. "I'll need a little time."

"Call me when you're ready. Take all the time you need."

Dimitri's words replayed in her mind as she dried her hair, put on her makeup, shook out the only nice dress she'd brought: a red silk, knee-length, with a flouncy skirt. *"Take all the time you need."* Did his words apply to more than dinner?

When she found him in the lobby, he was staring out at the water again. He had a fascination with the water, didn't he? She edged up to the picture window at his right and looked out over the river, running dark under the blackening desert sky.

He inhaled slowly, as though filling his lungs with the view. She could trace the sadness in his profile, the longing. Like the first time she'd seen him, staring into the glass case in the museum, as though *he* were Odysseus, looking over the water toward home.

Suddenly aware of her presence, he straightened, turned, and smiled. He wore a dark suit tonight, with a red shirt the exact color of her dress, open at the collar.

Kallie laughed and pointed to the matching shirt. "We're a bit too cute, I think." She looked down at herself. "But this is the only dress I brought. Do you want to change?"

He lifted her hand to his lips, kissed it lightly, and let it drop. "I'd rather make sure everyone knows I'm with the prettiest girl in the place."

She forced a smile.

"What's wrong? You don't want me to tell you—"

"I don't want you to be a stereotype. I want you to be real."

Dimitri's playful grin faded, replaced by a look so somber it almost broke her heart.

She reached up to touch his cheek. "It's okay to be real."

He grasped her hand, smiled, and pulled her toward the front doors. "Let's go. I think you'll like this place."

And she did. Somehow Dimitri had gotten them outdoor-restaurant seating on a cruise ship docked in Luxor overnight. She saw more than a few bills exchanged as they boarded and wound their way through the elegant tables. Strings of tiny lights crisscrossed the deck, turning the restaurant into a floating oasis under a sea of stars. They were seated at a table along the rail, with a view of the river.

Kallie placed her clutch on the table and draped the white linen napkin across her thighs. "So you didn't get enough Nile last night?"

"I didn't get enough of *something*."

She glanced up, found his eyes on hers, and flushed. She should have put Dr. Newsom's number on the phone Caroline had given her. She was going to need him to get through this night without losing herself to Dimitri's magnetic field. Time to change the subject. "We've run out on our colleagues again. Is Yoshi still working on his paper?"

"No, I think Caroline is playing tour guide for both the guys tonight. She has a company credit card and a determination to see all of Luxor. They'll be fine."

She let concerns about the others fade as they talked and laughed through oyster appetizers, through bowls of creamy lobster bisque, through savory grilled lamb and fluffy couscous. But the conversation grew serious over pastries and coffee.

Kallie wrapped cold fingers around the tiny white cup of espresso and considered her response to the question he'd asked.

"You can back out if you want to, Kallie. I won't hold it against you. Won't think less of you." Dimitri lowered his hands to the table, let his fingers brush her own where they still clutched her cup. "You've already encountered more trouble than I expected, and who knows where Pendleworth will send us next. I—I don't want you to be in danger."

She nodded. "I've given it some thought, I'll admit. I've always believed I belonged in a little office, tucked away in the back halls of a museum. This Indiana Jones thing isn't really my style."

"I could get you a bullwhip."

She laughed and looked over the rail toward the river. The water lapped the boat, the strings of lights reflecting off tiny ripples in the water.

"No bullwhip. But if I'm going to do this, maybe a fedora."

Dimitri caught her fingers in his own. "You're sure?"

She brought her gaze back to his. "This is my life, Dimitri. Research, uncovering the truth. It's who I am and who I want to be." She felt her voice and her blood warm to the truth. "If the Linear A Key exists, it *must* be part of the *Minoan Collective*. The chance to unravel the language— it's an overpowering and undeniable call on me I can't ignore. I won't ignore."

He was watching her, smiling on her, a strange light in his eyes, almost as though he were proud of her, of her passionate declaration. He drew her hands toward himself, then stood. "Dance with me?"

She'd barely noticed the live band while they ate, she was so engrossed in the conversation. The piano, double bass, and small bass drum had been playing jazz throughout the meal. No disco, no belly dancing on this cruise, apparently. But Dimitri had probably known that.

She'd not had much practice with dancing. He guided her smoothly toward the dance floor, and she imagined him dancing his way across Europe, a different girl in his arms every week.

But tonight it was her. Only her.

He turned when they reached the other couples, and she expected him to reach for her, but he stood motionless for a moment, his face frozen into that serious expression again. No, this time it looked more like fear. He lifted his hands, hesitated, dropped them.

Did he sense the shift in the atmosphere between them, as she did? What caused that fear in his eyes?

Well, she was not going to be stranded on the floor. She stepped close, took his hand in hers, and rested the other lightly on his shoulder.

There was an awkward pause, and then he yielded, letting go of whatever had held them apart. He drew her in, his hand pressed against the arch of her back.

They fit together again, just as they had been on the felucca last night.

The band had no vocals, but the words to the song they played lit a trail of fire across Kallie's soul as she melted against Dimitri.

Unforgettable. That's what you are.

His cheek was against her hair, the slightest whisper of a touch. He pulled back, his head just above hers, and searched her eyes. The music played on, soft and subtle.

Kallie swayed with him, returned his gaze, hardly conscious of their steps. She felt her skin flush under his touch, her heart rippling over the notes. The slow beat of the snare drum and the deep pluck of the bass strings matched the rhythm of Dimitri's movements—in turn pulling away to study her face, then returning his cheek to her hair.

He drew her close again, and his lips grazed her cheek, her ear. He released their handclasp, spread both his palms across her shoulder blades, and buried his face in the bend of her neck.

The piano trilled over the high notes, and Kallie's hands wrapped around his neck until it was more embrace than dance, their feet hardly moving. She closed her eyes against his shoulder, felt herself at the crest of the hill, just before the descent, her heart racing. Terrifying. Thrilling. Inevitable.

He reached to unclasp her fingers behind his head, then drew her hand down until her palm cradled his cheek.

And then he kissed her wrist.

Heaven help her, with closed eyes and warm lips, again and again Dimitri kissed the angry pink scars that had followed her from the dark pit of the past.

And she felt herself weeping, weeping until she had to reclaim her hand and bury her head against his chest.

When she lifted her eyes, it was to lay her wet cheek against his, and to whisper frightened words against his ear. Words that would change everything.

Her secret. Her curse. Her truth.

"Dimitri. I don't know who I am."

➤ 20 ⬅

The music stopped a moment after her confession. Couples pulled apart, returned to tables.

Dimitri stood in the center of the dance floor, staring at his shoes.

A hard knot of regret formed in her chest. What had she done?

"Dimitri, let's sit down." She tugged on his sleeve, then hurried to her seat. He joined her a moment later, still not looking at her.

"I—you probably want a bit more explanation—"

"Yes." His voice was like lead.

His reaction puzzled her. Curiosity, she would have expected. Surprise, maybe. But he was acting as if she'd admitted she was married or a paroled felon.

"I know Judith told you I ran into some trouble a few years back, and, uh, that's when I changed my name."

He met her eyes at last, and it wasn't anger. It was shock. "Yes."

Any thoughts she'd had about telling him everything evaporated in panic over his response. "Well, that was the trouble I had . . . I lost my memory."

"Lost your memory." The repetition was dull, monotone.

"I know, it sounds like some kind of Victorian novel or something." She shrugged nonchalantly to hide her fear, even though her heart was beating erratically and she felt trapped, terrified. "But, there you have it."

"And the scars?"

She swallowed and drew her arms protectively to her chest. "I don't know."

"Something terrible happened, then. To cause it." His gaze was on his hands, folded on the table.

"It would appear so, yes." Her voice was now a whisper.

"How long ago?"

"Seven years."

At this, he sucked in a ragged breath and closed his eyes.

What was he thinking? Was he realizing how damaged she truly was and rethinking this whole romantic thing?

"I—I've learned to deal with it, though." She tried to sound competent, grown up . . . not a scared little girl.

"Yes, yes, I can see you have." He stood. "I'm going to find the server to pay the check."

Just like that. Dinner was over.

She nodded, then wiped away unstoppable tears when he wandered away. The hollowness of her past was a gaping hole in her chest, an emptiness somehow larger than her body itself. She was an incomplete person, a broken person. Why did she ever let her guard down?

They were both silent on the way back to the hotel. She couldn't guess his thoughts. She knew her own. She never should have opened up, never should have tried to connect. Tonight was the perfect reason she'd kept her distance from relationships. When you put your heart out there and the other person didn't accept you, didn't understand you, it was too painful to even be with him anymore.

Dimitri gave her the obligatory kiss on the cheek at the elevator again, as he had last night. Then he hurried away. Nothing like he had last night.

In her room, she let the tears flow. It felt good to cry into her pillow, to embrace her loneliness, to remind herself of who she was. Or who she wasn't. Her story journal lay on the nightstand beside her head, and it made her think of Dr. Newsom. He knew her whole story and still seemed to like her.

She curled up into a ball and wept over Dimitri, until she finally surrendered to the heavy oblivion of sleep.

୭୬

Sometime in the early light of morning, her phone shrilled, jerking her upright from sleep. A dull headache from the night's tears throbbed behind her eyes. She fumbled for the phone, disoriented.

Mid-April. Egypt. She glanced at the clock. Ugh. Five thirty in the morning.

"Yes?" She rolled to her side, cradling the phone between her ear and the pillow.

"Good morning, Kallie. This is Caroline. How are you this morning?"

The girl's sugary morning voice was enough to make Kallie want to slap her.

"It's five thirty."

"Well, I know, silly. But this is your wake-up call. We're on the move!"

Kallie propped herself on an elbow. "What are you talking about, Caroline?"

"I don't know the details—that's your department, I suppose—but apparently Dimitri got some information that y'all were waiting for last night. He had me arrange our flight out for this morning. We need to leave for the Luxor airport in about one hour."

Kallie sighed and rubbed her temples with one hand. "Where are we going?"

"Back to Cairo. We're going to see the pyramids!"

Despite the early hour, a thrill ran across Kallie's weary nerves.

"Kallie, I hope you can be ready in an hour," Caroline said. "I didn't think you'd need more time than that, you know, since you don't really . . ."

The words trailed off, but Kallie got her meaning. Caroline's preparation for the day, between hair and makeup, clothing and accessory choices, probably took far longer than an hour. "I can be ready in ten minutes."

The team, now numbering five, met in the lobby in an hour and took two taxis to the airport. Dimitri had nodded pleasantly and promised to explain about Cairo on the plane.

When they boarded the flight, she found they were seated together. Had he arranged that or was it chance?

She settled herself against the window and turned to him as he buckled his seat belt. She would act like nothing happened. And not let down her walls again with him.

"So, Cairo. Tell me."

He seemed relieved at her choice of subject, dodging the awkwardness of last night by focusing on the work.

"I heard from Nigel Pendleworth last night. He tracked down some sources who indicated that a piece with a still-undeciphered language, plus hieroglyphs and another language, was indeed part of the el-Rassul take from the royal cache."

"Hieroglyphs!" She had expected Linear B and Greek.

Dimitri shrugged. "I know, but it has to be our piece, don't you think?"

"So what happened to it?"

"The last his source knew was that it had found its way to Cairo. But there's a guy there, working for CPAC, who has been tracking many of the el-Rassul pieces. We're going to talk to him."

Kallie nodded. The Cultural Property Advisory Committee worked to implement UNESCO's 1970 Convention to halt black market trafficking of antiquities. If anyone would know where the piece had ended up, it would be one of them.

It seemed like he had more to say, so she waited.

"Kallie, about last night—"

She held up a hand. "Not necessary, Dimitri. Obviously I have a lot of 'baggage,' as they say. Right now I really need to focus on my therapy, on figuring out my past and getting emotionally healthy, you know?" Was she rambling? "It's not a good time for me to get—distracted—by other relationships."

He was staring at the in-flight magazine in the pocket in front of him. He'd been so hard to read since last night.

"I understand."

"Why don't we talk about you instead." She smiled, hopefully a friendly, interested smile. "You've spent so much time in Europe. Where was your favorite place?"

"I have many."

"So, you were in Europe for what, seventeen years?"

He glanced sideways at her, a sharp, narrow-eyed glance. "How did you know that?"

She flushed and looked away. "A little online searching, I guess." Or stalking.

"Yes. Seventeen years. First attending university in London, but then I decided to stay in Europe, do some traveling, that sort of thing."

Was she getting the standard interview answers? He seemed less than candid.

"And in all that time, you never wanted to go home? See your family? Your father?"

"Kallie, perhaps you are comfortable with analyzing the past. I am not." With that, he grabbed the magazine he'd been eyeing and opened it to a random page.

Conversation over. Got it.

ಚಿ

Pendleworth's contact would be found on the Giza plateau where the three iconic pyramids stood in a line and pierced the Egyptian sky.

But when they emerged from the Cairo International Airport, Dimitri announced they would spend the rest of the day in Cairo before heading to their Giza hotel for the night. He shrugged at the surprised glances. "Can't be here without seeing a bit of the city."

The view of the streets from the windows of

their hired van produced a nervous twinge. There had been so many aerial news photos of Tahrir Square during the protests and demonstrations of the Arab Spring. The chaotic traffic, bad enough in Luxor, was multiplied tenfold here. Compared to Cairo, Luxor had been small-town. Would they be caught up in violence?

But Tahrir Square, the center of the Egyptian Revolution such a short time ago, buzzed with tourists and natives around its plazas and statues and huge traffic circle, and only the burned-out headquarters of the National Democratic Party attested to the end of Hosni Mubarak's presidency.

The pinkish stone of the nearly-two-hundred-year-old Egyptian Museum rose above the north end of Tahrir Square and beckoned to Kallie with its legendary collection of treasures, including the prized display of King Tutankhamun's tomb artifacts. All of it was to be moved to the state-of-the-art Grand Egyptian Museum being built some ten miles away, near the pyramids. But today they would see it all. A thrill ran through her as the van skimmed to the curb near the museum's courtyard.

Dimitri led them for hours through the dizzying maze of galleries, halls, and corridors stuffed with vessels and sarcophagi, statues and steles, until Kallie was ready to weep from sensory overload. They staggered back into the waning sunlight, her stomach growling audibly.

Beside her, Caroline laughed. "I think it's time for Kallie to eat."

Erik grunted his agreement. He'd spent half their museum time sitting near the exit.

Dimitri remained quiet during their dinner at a street-side café near the museum. The others ate and drank in high spirits as the sun sank beyond the Nile.

She should never have told Dimitri about her vacant memory. It had affected everything between them.

Their van was ready after dinner to take them to their hotel in Giza, and Kallie breathed out her relief when Dimitri claimed the front seat beside the driver. She climbed toward the back and was joined by Yoshi, who said little as they traveled out of the city, along the river.

From the standard postcards of Egypt, those unfamiliar with the country would believe the three pyramids of Khufu, Khafre, and Menkaure, stark against the desert sky, would be reached only by a trek through the remote and desolate sand. But as their van honked and lurched through the nighttime city of Giza, a glimpse of a purple-lit pyramid jumped into her view, looming at the end of a street of shops and restaurants. She jerked away from her seat cushion, forehead pressed against the glass.

"Was that—?"

The driver nodded. "Yes, one of our pyramids.

It is the Sound and Light Show now. You will see it tomorrow night?"

Dimitri answered for the group. "Perhaps."

Even after the day of travel and sightseeing, none of the team seemed ready for bed when they reached the hotel. Kallie settled her luggage in her room, then wandered down to the hotel bar, a wide space with clusters of intimate round tables and a gleaming grand piano at the far end.

She was the last of the team to arrive. Caroline and Erik were knee-to-knee at one of the small tables, and Yoshi was talking at the bar with two strangers. Dimitri sat at the piano, playing softly.

Kallie held back, biting her lip. Should she join him?

He answered her unspoken question by raising his eyes and giving her a quick smile of welcome. She slipped toward the piano and sat at the closest table.

Dimitri's attention was on the keys again, a slow rendition of jazz pianist Bill Evans's "We Will Meet Again."

Her heart felt overfull, a river cresting its banks, at the music and the sight of Dimitri creating it. The haunting refrain lingered in the air after the quiet final notes drifted up the scale.

Dimitri lifted his eyes to hers for only the briefest moment, then inclined his head toward the bar, where Yoshi sat on one side of an attractive girl and another man sat on the other side. "Have you seen that?" His voice was low and amused.

Kallie stepped to the piano to get an unobtrusive look at the threesome. Yoshi's body language was telegraphing his interest in the girl, and the other guy didn't look pleased. "What's going on?"

Dimitri shrugged, the corners of his mouth twitching. "All I know is that Yoshi was there first. He had her laughing and touching his arm before the competition showed up."

Kallie raised her eyebrows and laughed. "I didn't know he had it in him."

"Better keep your eye on them. Who knows what kind of damage Helen of Troy there could do to our poor Paris."

She leaned against the piano and studied his hands, hovering over the keys. "So, are you taking requests?"

In answer, Dimitri pushed away and stood. "Not this evening, I'm afraid. Need to get some sleep before the big day tomorrow." He stepped to her side and kissed her lightly on the cheek. "You should get some rest, too. You look tired."

Thanks.

He was gone a moment later, leaving her standing in awkward isolation at the piano. She could interrupt Caroline and Erik's cozy conversation, join Yoshi's epic battle for the love of a woman, or be seen following Dimitri from the lounge.

Instead, she wandered to the wall of windows and studied the hotel parking lot for a few minutes.

Yes, everything had changed between them since her confession. It had been a stupid impulse.

Although, if this relationship was to develop into anything more, the truth would have to come out sometime. Perhaps sooner was better.

"Don't get distracted . . ." Newsom's voice in her head again. She should be thinking about the forgotten past and the present pursuits, not the impossible future.

Somewhere beyond the parking lot, at the edge of Giza, lay some of the oldest structures on the face of the earth, likely built to ensure passage to the afterlife, to the future. Would entering such a sacred space help bring together her own dead memory and the life she had yet to live, like the Egyptian goddess Isis reassembling the scattered pieces of her husband, Osiris?

⇒ 21 ⇐

Giza was a miniature of its larger sister Cairo, with traffic that bumped and jostled their cab ride from the hotel to the plateau's gated entrance. Camels and donkeys competed with taxis, cars, and motorbikes, and their cab driver tried to divert them to a friend who would give them a good tour of the pyramids. Dimitri and Yoshi were in the car behind, but in the backseat of Kallie's cab, Caroline was all southern charm over steely insistence that they be taken *directly* to the entrance.

Beyond the squat building that sold tickets, the five breached the gates at the top of the plateau, near the pyramid built by the Pharaoh Khufu, the largest of the three, and stopped to take it all in. A haze hung over Giza, which sprawled to the left and below and merged imperceptibly with Cairo to the east along the green belt of the Nile. But to the west and south there was nothing but treacherous desert, out of reach of the Nile's ancient yearly inundations and stretching four hundred miles to the Valley of the Kings. That barren land was where she and Dimitri had been stranded. It was nearly noon and the sun scorched Kallie's head and shoulders. She shuddered and vowed not to ever go out in that desert again.

Dimitri led the way toward Khufu's pyramid. "Michaels is supposedly working in one of the mastaba tombs on the east side."

Kallie tilted her head to scan the tips of the three main pyramids of the plateau—built by father, son, and grandson—with their southeast corners on a perfect diagonal and their sides aligned with true north. It was difficult to get a sense of their size with only the vast skies behind them, until she noticed the people small as ants wandering around the base of the first pyramid. She couldn't even make out the miniscule human figures near the others.

The team followed Dimitri like children on a school tour. Kallie lagged behind, soaking up the moment. With the city indistinct in the haze below, it was easy to imagine tens of thousands of workers hauling quarried and trimmed limestone up from the harbor that had long since disappeared. She leaned her head back to scan the rubbled side of the pyramid, reaching up and up toward the cloudless sky. What would it have looked like with its white limestone facing intact, its gold capstone catching the light of the rising Egyptian sun?

Dimitri left them at the base of the pyramid to ask a few unobtrusive questions. They waited below the two entrances into the Great Pyramid —the higher original, hidden entrance and the other lower, hacked-away opening made by

262

robbers working for Caliph al-Ma'mun in the ninth century.

Below, the city stretched into the unseen distance and wrapped around their position on the plateau. A mournful sound drifted up from the crowded streets and tenements, first from one place, then another and another, nearly simultaneous broadcasts.

Caroline cooed. "How beautiful. What are they singing?"

Kallie lowered herself to sit on a rocky ledge. "It is the *Dhuhr*. The second of the five daily prayers. The muezzins are calling it from loudspeakers on the minarets of mosques all over the city."

"Oh." Caroline's nose wrinkled.

Kallie straightened, fought down the annoyance in her voice. "So now it is not beautiful because it is Islamic?"

"No, it's not that—it's just—oh, I don't know." Caroline waved a hand. "It just scares me a little, I guess. Who knows what they're chanting?"

Kallie sighed. "I do. The prayers reinforce their basic faith. There is no deity but Allah, and Muhammad is his messenger."

Caroline shrugged. "Not what I believe."

Kallie flicked a pebble from her ledge. "Islam and Christianity have more in common than you might think, Caroline." She jabbed a thumb behind her. "Even the ancient Egyptians believed many of the same things you do, with their developed theology of the afterlife. The only one who truly stands in disagreement with everything around us is Yoshi."

Too late, she glanced at Yoshi for permission. They had never spoken of his Buddhist faith, and it was only Dimitri who had told her of it.

But Yoshi was nodding. "You are always trying to find God outside of yourselves, all of you." He took in Erik with a sweep of his hand, though the big man was staring absently across the plateau. "You will not find the divine until you stop putting a mask over it and see that it resides all around and within you."

Caroline held up her palms and shook her head. "Oh no. You're not going to pull me into your crazy nature-worship stuff. Not this girl." She fixed a sweet smile on her lips for Yoshi. "No offense."

"But that *is* offensive."

Kallie snorted a laugh, then covered it with a hand. Yoshi's bluntness seemed lost on Caroline.

"Well, I don't believe in all that pantheistic-animals-are-gods-can't-eat-beef stuff, and I'm no mystic. I'm from the South."

Yoshi opened his mouth as though to correct or explain but then closed it again and looked away.

But Kallie couldn't be silent. "Caroline, your faith is either very mystical, or it is not true. The incarnation of God into man, the death and resurrection of Jesus that satisfied the debt incurred by sin and broke the power of death, the breaking in of the supernatural into the natural world—what is all of that, if it is not a great mystery?"

Caroline's eyes widened. "Well, if I didn't know better, Kallie Andreas, I'd take you for a Baptist!"

Kallie laughed. "I'm not taking sides. Just making a point."

Dimitri returned, thankfully cutting the conversation short. He sighed and shook his head. "Jack Michaels is not here, as far as I can tell. I asked around, but no one knew of him. Somebody mentioned a dig at Dashur—he might be there."

Kallie stood. "So let's go to Dashur."

"What?" Caroline's pink lips formed a pout. "What about the pyramids?"

Kallie was ready to set off, the possibility of actual information on the Linear A Key burning in her gut. "The Bent Pyramid and the Red Pyramid are both at Dashur." She pointed to the Great Pyramid. "Built by this guy's father, so they're even older."

"But I want to see the *famous* pyramids."

"You've seen them."

Dimitri shrugged. "Caroline's right, Kallie." He held up a handful of tickets. "This is a once-in-a-lifetime opportunity, probably." He glanced at his watch. "But we can't linger too long. If Michaels is at Dashur, he'll be clearing out long before sunset. That place isn't very safe."

Nods bobbed all around, and Kallie sighed, outnumbered. Though it wouldn't be all bad to see the inside of the most famous pyramid in the world.

They climbed the short distance to the medieval entrance used by tourists and slipped into the shadowed interior, a small chamber that snaked around to the beginning of an upward-leading shaft, laid with wooden boards. Metal frets extended across the planks for support as they climbed. How had the ancients made their way up this shaft without the assistance of these wooden planks?

Dimitri led the way, with Kallie following and the others behind. A touch of claustrophobia tightened her chest as they pushed up into the Ascending Passage, narrow enough to touch both sides and forcing them to bend at the waist as they climbed. Hemmed in on every side by people and stone, Kallie determinedly focused on her breathing and tried not to think about the nearly six million metric tons of stone pressing down on her.

The shaft opened to a higher-ceilinged slope at about the halfway point, the Grand Gallery, and her breathing eased, even though the steep climb was beginning to take its toll.

They reached the level of the burial chamber

sweating and silent and had to stoop once again to make their way into the chamber itself.

In the dim light provided by a few fluorescents, the black granite walls glowed with a dull sheen, and the chipped and open sarcophagus yawned toward the back of the chamber. Despite her impatience to get to Michaels, Kallie sucked in a breath of awe. "It's larger than I expected." The ceiling must have been twenty feet high, and the chamber held a humidity that seemed odd in the desert.

The others stood at her side in silence. Somehow the idea of standing in the tomb of a five-thousand-year-old Pharaoh left little to say.

The climb down the shaft was accomplished more quickly. She and Dimitri emerged onto the side of the pyramid, taking deep breaths of the open air. Caroline pushed up behind them, but Yoshi and Erik lagged, caught behind some slower-moving tourists descending the shaft.

Three black-garbed men snapped to attention outside the entrance and stepped toward them. "You are the man looking for Jack Michaels?"

Kallie noted the pistols at their waists, and the assault rifles slung over their shoulders. Tourist Police.

Dimitri narrowed his eyes and hesitated. "Yes. Do you know—?"

"You will come with us." The first of them wrapped a tight hand around Dimitri's arm, and the other two reached for Kallie and Caroline.

"Hey!" Caroline struggled to wrench her arm free. "Nobody grabs me without an engagement ring in his pocket!"

"What is this?" Dimitri planted his feet on the narrow pyramid ledge. "What's the problem?"

"Some questions, only. You will come with us."

⇢ 22 ⇠

Yoshi and Erik emerged a moment later, and Erik jumped toward the black-uniformed men.

Dimitri held up a hand. "Tourist Police, guys. They want to talk with us."

The team was forced down the stepped side of the pyramid and led to a modern building slightly west of the Great Pyramid.

Inside, the front room was dark and dusty, with a choking, low-hanging haze of cigarette smoke.

Their captors reassembled, splitting them into three different groups. One pushed Yoshi and Erik down a narrow hall, another shoved Dimitri through a wooden door at the back, and the third forced Kallie and Caroline into metal folding chairs in the front room, some kind of police station.

A bead of sweat rolled down Kallie's spine. Detainment in a foreign country was never a good thing.

The well-built and heavily mustached police officer glared at them with piercing eyes, leaning against an aging desk. "What is your business with Jack Michaels?"

Caroline looked to Kallie, clearly giving her the lead.

"We are researchers. We have a few questions of history for him, that's all." Did she sound defensive? She forced her hands to relax in her lap.

"He is historian, then? Respected historian of Egypt?"

"Yes—"

"No!" He kicked a heel backward against the desk. "He is agitator!"

Adrenaline kicked her heart in a panic, her palms sweating. *Dimitri, what have you gotten us into?*

"We don't know anything about that. We're only looking for some information—"

"You are *spies* for America." He spit out—spittle actually landing on Kallie's shoe. She dared not move. "You will help Jack Michaels speak against the Freedom and Justice Party."

Was Dimitri insane? Asking questions about someone suspected of anti-Muslim sentiments, someone in public opposition to the current president and the FJP that had gotten him elected after the revolution?

Caroline leaned forward, her eyes wide. "But

we *love* freedom and justice! We're Americans!"

Kallie nearly clamped a hand over the girl's mouth.

But it appeared that her ignorance of Egyptian politics played well here. The police officer turned to look at her, gave her beauty-pageant body the once-over, and grinned lecherously. "You do not look like spy."

Caroline burst out, shocked—placing a fluttery, manicured hand over her chest. "Spy? What do I know about spies? I'm only a secretary."

The officer's glance shifted to Kallie, and the grin dropped away. "You do not look like secretary."

What did that mean?

"I'm a researcher, I told you." She was shaking and clasped her hands tightly, trying not to hyperventilate.

Furious sounds reverberated from the back room where Dimitri had disappeared. Angry Arabic.

Their captor seemed to take the shout as an indication the two women were also guilty. His face darkened. "You would not like jail here in Egypt. You must tell how you are working with Jack Michaels or you will see our jail."

Shouldn't they be allowed some sort of phone call to an embassy or something?

Kallie huffed. "But we're not working with Michaels. We don't even know him."

He leaned toward Kallie to study her expression and stroked his full mustache. The gesture was so stereotypically villainous, Kallie should have found it funny, but the situation was growing more hostile, and jolts of electric tension were firing along her nerves. They could not lose the only lead they had to the Linear A Key. And a night in an Egyptian jail cell would be terrifying.

The door in the back was yanked open and Dimitri's captor strode out with a nod to his goon.

Dimitri followed, a furrow between his brow as he took in their officer, leaning over Kallie. "We are leaving."

Kallie blinked but then got to her feet and pulled Caroline up to stand with her.

Dimitri jerked his head toward the hallway and spoke to the men. "Bring the other two."

The officer who had guarded the women opened his mouth as if to object, but the other who had questioned Dimitri nodded.

Yoshi and Erik appeared in the hallway, their faces set with wary optimism. Yoshi had no pen to spin and looked ready to crack apart.

Erik's hands were fisted at his sides, the veins in his arms and forehead bulging. "Everything cleared up?" His voice was a low growl. He looked ready to clear up anything himself.

In answer, Dimitri inclined his head toward the door. The group of five fled to the exit.

At the door Caroline turned, gripped the door

frame, and yelled over her shoulder, "For people who supposedly support freedom and justice, y'all certainly have bad manners!"

Kallie grabbed her arm and yanked her from the doorway. The girl could really be an idiot.

Dimitri was setting a rapid pace across the plateau, toward the entrance, and the rest followed.

Kallie caught up with him, her legs wobbling. "What was *that* all about?"

"I'm not sure. It seems Michaels has been confrontational about the new regime's lax attitude toward looters. He hasn't been making many friends here."

"How did you convince them—?"

"Money convinced them. That's all they wanted, really. A payoff."

Money again. It seemed to solve all of Dimitri's problems. And yet she heard the resentment in his voice, as though he hated being nothing more than a cash flow.

Kallie exhaled and willed her body to calm down. They needed to get out of here. "To Dashur, then?" The sun was already sinking toward the desert.

"It's about thirty miles. I don't know if we can make it before he leaves."

They passed the Great Pyramid and headed upward toward the parking lot. Kallie grabbed his sleeve. "We have to try."

Dimitri glanced at her, thought for a second, then nodded. "We have to try."

In a hired van, the group seemed to relax, though only slightly. They traded stories of their impromptu confinement, and Kallie had them laughing with her impression of Caroline conquering their captor. A tense undercurrent ran underneath the banter, but it was good to laugh, and Kallie felt a sense of belonging to this team for the first time.

It was nearly four o'clock by the time they reached the more remote desert location of Dashur and its two famous pyramids.

The tension in the van had remained high since they left Giza, so she left off the history lesson about the reason the Bent Pyramid was bent, with its upper portion sloping at a gentler angle than the bottom. The pyramid builders were still perfecting their craft.

Inside the dig-site entrance, few tourists were left. They wandered the area leading up to the Bent Pyramid, with the Red in the distance, looking for signs of Michaels's work.

"There." Yoshi spotted a few keffiyeh-covered heads bent near a narrow fenced-in area, and one baseball cap on a man who seemed to be directing the others as they worked in the sand.

Dimitri strode toward the site.

The American-looking man's attention shot to

their group, and he straightened and spoke a sharp word to the men in his employ.

Like djinns appearing by magic, three more Arab men materialized. The unmistakable sound of rifles cocked into readiness reverberated across the sand.

The team slowed, drawing up behind Dimitri.

He shaded his eyes from the sun hovering at the horizon. "Jack Michaels?"

The man scowled. "Who's asking?"

"Name's Dimitri Andreas. Nigel Pendleworth sent me. Said you might be able to help us."

Michaels waved an impatient hand. "I've got work to do. The sun's almost gone."

"We won't be long."

Michaels turned away. "Come on, then."

They entered through a gap in the orange-plastic fencing. Kallie stayed close to Erik, eyeing the rifle-carrying men in white robes, who seemed even more threatening than the police they'd just escaped.

"You're well-armed for an archaeologist."

Michaels huffed at Dimitri. "You wouldn't think so if you saw the other guys." His back was to the group, bent over a trough of pebbles and sand. Ahead of him, a large hole yawned in the ground.

"Other guys?" Kallie glanced around the dig site and beyond, to the lonesome and darkening desert.

Michaels suddenly turned and focused his attention on Kallie. He was under forty, with the lean but hardened build of a man who spent time with a shovel. "Looters. They'll start showing up soon. There's no stopping them these days. God knows the government doesn't care anymore."

She traded a look with Dimitri. It hadn't taken Michaels long to start spewing his rhetoric. No wonder he'd aroused the attention of local police.

"What's your business with Pendleworth?" Again, the question seemed directed at Kallie. He took off the baseball cap, smoothed his blond hair, and replaced it.

She answered. "No business with him, really. We're just doing some research here and ran into him in the valley. He said you might be able to help us with the information we're looking for."

Michaels grunted. "I took you for rich donors on a holiday to see what your money was funding."

She shrugged. "Sorry to disappoint."

Michaels gave her a long look and a lopsided smile. "Honey, you're not disappointing."

Dimitri stepped to her side. "We're searching for a specific piece, something that might have been part of the el-Rassul cache."

"Boss?" One of the robed men—a gun in his hands—drew close. He spoke in heavily accented English. "It is almost dark."

The obvious fact, so forebodingly uttered,

seemed to disconcert Michaels. "We've got to get this last section sorted out." He glanced at Dimitri with some resentment. "You picked a rotten time to show up with questions."

Dimitri shrugged. "Can we help? Then take you to dinner perhaps—"

The man's gaze slid toward Kallie. "Deal." He pointed toward the large trough. "Need to sift through the last of today's haul for anything of interest."

Caroline uttered a little cry of protest at the filthy task he'd assigned them.

Michaels frowned. "What's the matter, sweetheart? Afraid you'll break a fingernail?"

Dimitri moved toward the trough. "There's not room for all of us to work. Kallie, can you help? The rest of you can wait over there."

He hadn't released Kallie from duty, and she would not have wanted him to. She stepped to his side and plunged her hands into the sandy dirt. "What are you excavating?"

Michaels pointed to the large hole. "Underground entrance to a thirteenth-dynasty pyramid, long gone. But the burial chamber is under there somewhere. We're tunneling through."

"Boss!"

All attention snapped to the Arab guard. He had pivoted to shield Michaels with his body and raised his rifle, the butt wedged against his shoulder.

Kallie followed the sight line of the gun out into the desert. A swarm of figures was spilling over the dunes, as though Pandora's jar had just been opened. Impossible to make out details at this distance, but Michaels and his crew launched into frantic action.

Michaels yelled instructions in Arabic, grabbed up guns, and tossed them to the other workers. He hesitated with another rifle, then pushed it into Dimitri's hand.

Erik was already grabbing one for himself.

Dimitri pointed the rifle toward the ground, cocked it, and put Kallie behind him. "We need to get the women out of here!"

⇒ 23 ⇐

Kallie should have been annoyed at Dimitri's reference to "the women," but she was only too grateful to leave the gun-wielding to the men.

Michaels jerked the barrel of his gun toward the hole. "In there. The tunnel's big enough for a dozen people."

The armed guards helped lower Caroline, then Kallie into the hole, braced with a narrow ladder of very few rungs. Her hands were already slick with perspiration, and her legs felt wobbly under her. Both girls were shaking when they grabbed each other's hands at the bottom.

Yoshi hesitated above her head, squinting down into the cavern. "I have never picked up a gun in my life."

"Then get down here!" Caroline's voice was shrill.

His pale face hovered in the opening, then with an emotion-charged glance at Caroline, Yoshi pulled back. "Give me a gun."

Caroline whimpered her surprise, and she and Kallie clung to each other.

Darkness fell quickly in the desert, and very little light penetrated into their small cavern. The two pushed back into the depths, away from the hole.

This was insane. Erik might be okay, but Dimitri and Yoshi, armed with rifles and facing down looters in the middle of an Egyptian desert? Had they stepped onto a movie set? Kallie breathed through her mouth and tried not to scream for Dimitri to get down into the hole.

Caroline returned to the bottom of the opening, peered up toward the waning light.

"Caroline, get away from there." They would be trapped if any looters glanced down into the chamber.

"I'm not going any deeper." Caroline's voice was whispery but harsh. "It's filthy!"

She'd rather face death than dirt? Or was something else drawing her to the surface?

The sound of yelling, all in Arabic, erupted from the ground level.

No shooting. Not yet.

Kallie did a quick count. Four Americans, at least six locals in Michaels's employ. Did they outnumber the raiders?

One shot. Deafening in the stillness of the desert.

Kallie grabbed Caroline's arm and sucked in a breath.

Caroline put a hand over Kallie's and squeezed.

More yelling.

Then silence. Long and tense.

Was it a standoff? Two groups facing each other, rifles pointed like rival street gangs in a showdown? Or twitchy fingers ready to grab pistols and fire at each other, like the climactic scene of an old Western?

The suspenseful silence stretched on and on.

Kallie couldn't hold the tension in her body anymore. Her legs were shaking with it. She slid down to the rocky floor.

Caroline stood near the ladder, though not so near as before, arms wrapped around her slight frame.

The sound of conversation, strained and low, filtered down into their chamber. Kallie could pick out Dimitri's voice, and the other seemed to be Michaels's.

Moments later, the two men descended the

ladder with flashlights, Erik trailing, followed by Yoshi. All four were still armed.

Kallie jumped to her feet.

When they were all in the hole, Michaels surveyed the group with his flashlight. "Turns out you picked a good time to come."

Yeah.

Caroline slapped Yoshi's arm, and not playfully. "What were you thinking?" Her voice quivered on the edge of tears.

He looked down at her upturned face. "I wasn't thinking. For once."

Kallie observed the exchange between them, surprised. In the past few days a sincere affection seemed to be growing between Yoshi and Carolyn. She had not expected that.

Michaels shrugged. "The geek held his own up there, beauty queen. Didn't hurt having three more armed Americans, either. These locals are a little less likely to bring international wrath down on themselves."

Kallie stepped toward Michaels. "They're gone, then?"

"Ha!" His laugh held no humor. "They're never gone." He glanced up the hole. "No, they're waiting out there in the darkness now. Waiting for us to leave, so they can pick off my guards and get what they came for."

"But there's nothing here but dirt!"

Michaels didn't acknowledge that Caroline had

spoken. Instead, he pushed toward the back of the chamber and fumbled around in the darkness. A moment later, a red camping lantern blinked to life, throwing long shadows over the group.

In response, a sliding sound came from the hole above, and what little light still filtered from the night sky disappeared. Their guards had covered the hole with planks. Sealed them in.

Michaels grabbed some thick and dusty mats from a rickety crate and tossed them to the floor near the crumbling wall. He looked at Kallie and pointed to one of the mats. "I'm afraid we'll have to wait it out. They'll be gone when the sun comes up."

Caroline's voice took on its no-nonsense tone. "You expect us to stay here all night?"

"It's not the Cairo Marriott, I'll admit." He gave Kallie a half smile. "But we try to be of service."

"Marriott?" Caroline snorted. "It's not even the Motel Six."

The group of six assembled on the floor of the chamber, with Michaels placing himself near Kallie with obvious intention. Dimitri sat across from them, legs bent and forearms resting on his knees.

Kallie's gaze drifted toward the sealed exit. "What are they after?"

"Anything. Everything." Michaels shrugged. "They wait until significant activity seems to be happening at a dig, then swoop and grab what they can."

Erik grunted from his position against a wall. "Where's the police, the military? Why don't they put a stop to it?"

"They don't care. Not like they should." His voice hardened. "They would see all of Egypt's ancient history discarded."

Dimitri raked a hand through his dark hair. "How can that be? Don't they see the value—?"

"How could the medieval Christians have pulled down ancient temples to build forts and castles? Same thing. The Islamists see anything before Mohammed as pagan. Has no value to them."

Kallie studied his creased forehead, dropped chin. "Well, Mr. Michaels, it seems you are doing all you can to rectify that."

He glanced sideways at her. "Jack. Please."

She smiled. "Kallie."

Dimitri cleared his throat. "So, how often do you spend your nights in holes?"

Jack shrugged. "Beats the alternative." He pulled his collar away from his throat and turned in the lantern light to bare his neck to Kallie. "See that? Bullet grazed me one night in El Hibeh."

Caroline gasped. "What if they shoot your guards and come down here?"

"It's a possibility."

Dimitri got to his feet and paced. "No one's getting shot, Caroline. Not tonight."

Kallie squinted at him. "You can't know that."

He signaled frustration with his eyes, sending a message meant to shut her up.

Fine. If he wanted to offer meaningless reassurances, she wouldn't stop him. She glanced at Jack who shook his head slightly, as if half amused by the naiveté.

In the end, it was Yoshi who reassured them all, quoting statistics about the number of Americans killed in foreign countries as a result of "international incidents." Very few, as it turned out. Statistically speaking. Though Jack's story of armed gangs systematically looting important sites stole the comfort from Yoshi's numbers.

They spent the night dozing in fits. Jack dimmed the lantern, but still Kallie woke multiple times with chilled limbs and numb fingers. Sometime in the small hours of the morning, she took to blowing on her hands to warm them.

In the half-light, Jack slid closer and wrapped his large hand around both of hers, transferring warmth.

She glanced at Dimitri, but his head was tilted back against the dirt wall, his mouth slack.

Later, she stirred to consciousness again, head leaning against Jack's shoulder. His hand still covered hers, as though they had been close acquaintances for years, if not more.

She pulled away, and the movement nudged him awake.

He blinked, smiled down on her, and released her hands. "Look there." He jutted his chin toward the opening above the lantern. A bit of light edged the cracks around the planking. "We made it."

Kallie stood with him, stretching the stiffness out of her legs.

The others came to life as well, Caroline leaning against Yoshi, Dimitri and Erik both propped against the opposite wall.

"We're still alive." Caroline's voice held incredulity.

Kallie tapped her lips with a finger. "What are the odds?"

They all glanced at Yoshi, who opened his mouth, then snapped it closed at the laughter that followed. A self-conscious grin lit his features.

Jack headed for the ladder.

Dimitri held him back, one hand wrapped around the archaeologist's arm. "Hold on. We helped you up there last night. It's time to return the favor."

Jack turned, eyebrows raised at the hand on his arm.

Dimitri released his grip. "We are looking for something."

"Right. The el-Rassul cache, you said."

"Yes. Some kind of piece small enough to move easily. An inscription in several languages. Hieroglyphs, perhaps."

Jack's eyes narrowed. "Why all the attention for this piece suddenly?"

"Suddenly? We've been searching for years."

"Not you. Someone else. You're not the first I've heard asking questions."

Kallie slid toward Jack. "Who? Who's been asking?"

He shook his head. "Don't know. Just word on the street. A woman asking questions. Supposed to be a bit ruthless."

Dimitri crossed his arms. "Tell us what you know, Michaels."

They all huddled around Jack in rapt attention. Whatever clue Jack would give them, it would be the only lead they had.

"Venice."

Dimitri glanced, puzzled, at Kallie. "Venice?"

She scanned her fuzzy brain. The Venetian Republic had spanned over a thousand years of European history, from the seventh century to nearly eighteen hundred, growing fabulously wealthy on sea trade in the Middle Ages. Was there a connection to the Minoans she had missed? The two cultures never overlapped, though the Venetians *had* ruled Crete and Santorini for nearly four hundred years . . . She could think of no connection to Egypt.

Jack wrapped a hand around the ladder. "Rumor has it that it was acquired here in Egpyt, in Thebes, in the early twentieth century by Louis Manin."

Kallie shook her head at Dimitri's quizzical look. "Don't know him."

"He was the great-grandson of the last doge of Venice, Ludovico Manin."

She edged closer to Dimitri. "Fascinating." The Republic of Venice had been ruled by its doges, or dukes, for its thousand-year history. "Why would he want it?"

"He was a collector and apparently obsessed with obtaining artifacts from all the cultures the Venetians once ruled."

"So the piece is in Venice?"

"I have no idea."

Caroline leaned in. "This woman—the dangerous one—does she know about Venice?"

Jack shook his head and shrugged. Apparently they'd reached the limit of his inside information.

Dimitri pointed upward. "All right, then. We're even. Let's get out of here."

Jack turned to Kallie. "I still feel a bit indebted. Perhaps that dinner could be breakfast—"

Dimitri crossed the dirt floor between the two of them, forcing them both to take a step backward. "I'm afraid we'll be on an early flight to Italy, Michaels. Maybe some other time."

→ 24 ←

Kallie kept to herself on the plane that lifted off from Cairo, sat with an empty seat between herself and the rest of the team. The incident with the tourist police, the ordeal with Michaels, even his obvious interest in her—it was all exhausting. Now their global treasure hunt had them on a plane again, with Dimitri just as distant and silent as ever. Kallie simply didn't want to think about any of it for a while.

She just wanted to *escape* . . . to somewhere safe, comfortable, known . . . She closed her eyes.

When I stepped from the lip of the fountain, to the dismay of Isandros and the rest of the city of Lycoris, the night air blew suddenly cold. I shivered against it, and Isandros threw his cloak over my shoulders.

"Come." He led me with one arm wrapped around my waist. "It is not time tonight. Not now, while the moon is not yet reborn and the mountain sleeps in darkness."

I let him lead me, weary from the festival and from the emotion of my choice.

"I will take you in the morning, my lady. I will take you to the mountains and the Great Cavern, and may the goddess preserve you."

The night wind carried us back to Isandros's home, pulling at my robes with greedy hands. The taste of moisture was on my tongue and a threatening rumble rolled in the distance. I fell into the bed on Isandros's second floor and slept well, barely mindful of the storm that slashed at the stone house through the night.

In the morning, the city and the world had been washed clean, a freshness sparkling on stones and flowers and faces of children. All was gladness again, save the heart of Isandros.

"I know I promised, my lady."

He was pleading with me as Selene helped me pack provisions for the journey.

"But how can I be the one to escort you to destruction?"

I smiled down on Selene. Such frightful words for her young ears. "Have hope, Isandros."

But his downcast face showed no hope, and in truth, I did not have overmuch myself. From the palace I had brought with me a midsize dagger, two coils of rope, a small vial of strong poison— for what purpose I had no idea, but it seemed a good idea at the time—and my hard-won skill in close-quarter fighting. Nothing more. If the beast were as fearful as Kalliste lore made it out to be, it would take all of this and cunning besides. Now that the battle was so close upon me, doubt weighted me down like massive bricks chained to my heart.

I forced a royal smile—I hoped. "I promise you, Isandros, if I should be successful, I shall pass this way again, so you who have shared in my fear will also share in the joy."

The oath did little to cheer him, I could see. But he kept his word. By midmorning we were ready. I gave Selene a kiss on the head, extracted a tearful promise from her to take good care of Herakles, and received the pouch she had packed.

And then we were off, climbing grassy slopes along a narrow trail used by flower harvesters. I ran my fingers over soft crocus petals and gloried in the smell of the wet grass and feel of wind in my hair. The day was glorious, with a cerulean sky and voluminous clouds like sheep's wool. The mountain was peaceful, a paradise.

And yet such horrors lurked beneath. What would I find within the mouth of the cavern? A pile of picked-over bones—all that remained of the suitors who'd hoped for the hand of the king's daughter? I shuddered.

"Isandros?"

He slowed on the path ahead and turned.

"Tell me of the others who have come this far. Who has led them to the cavern?"

Isandros continued on, silent for a few moments. When he answered, I could barely hear the words. "No one, my lady. Those few who have emerged from the Cypress Forest, these we have merely pointed in the right direction. No one has been willing to take them there."

I pulled up, watched his strong back as it moved away from me. "Thank you for your care, Isandros. And for your courage."

I did not bother to ask about Andreas. Isandros would not know the names of the men who had climbed this hill ahead of me.

We climbed until midday, leaving behind the cultivated crocus fields for wild oleander and eucalyptus and making our own path through the flora. I saw no evidence that others had preceded me.

The grasses and flowers merged into scattered trees, no more than spiky scrubs poking from the mountainside. The trees began to play tricks with my eyes, and more than once I mistook their spines for human form. But each time I jerked my head toward the illusion, it disappeared like a spirit melting into the trees. Only the trees, I told myself, but the sensation of being followed haunted me.

When the sun had dropped deep in the sky, I called ahead to Isandros to halt his steady march up the mountain. "You must return. I will not have you stranded on the mountainside after the sun has died."

He shielded his eyes and glanced toward the sun's position, then farther up the mountain, and turned back to me with a sigh.

"You know I am right, Isandros. Come, point me in the right direction and say good-bye. It is time."

I must keep to this angle, he said reluctantly, all the way to the top. He pointed upward, to a copse of trees that stood higher than the rest along the ridge. "There, just to the right, you will find the entrance to the Great Cavern. You will see it—a great opening like the open maw of a lion."

Somewhere beneath my feet, in the water-eaten depths of this mountain, did the beast wander even now, awaiting my arrival with hungry jaws?

I readjusted Isandros's pouch over my shoulder and clasped his hands. "Thank you for everything, Isandros."

He returned my grip, pulled my hands to his chest, and held them there. His eyes were misty. "May you be protected and find success, my lady." He lifted my fingers to his lips and kissed them gently. "And remember, should you change your mind and return to us, we are ready to fight for you and for your throne."

The mists of emotion had clouded my own eyes and thickened my throat as well. If the world had been different, there could have been something more between this saffron grower and myself. But the world was as it was. I was a princess, and I still had not given up on Andreas. Even in this parting, I felt my eyes drawn toward the ridge, excitement building along my veins.

We parted, and I watched him pick his way down the hillside, traveling much faster with the aid of the downward slope.

And I was alone. I turned my head toward the stand of high trees on the ridge and, with a deep breath, continued my upward journey.

It would be dark, or nearly so, before I reached the ridge. Did I have the courage to enter in the darkness? Remembering the cavern where I had been abandoned by the priestess, I realized day or night made no difference. But the day had been long and the climb arduous. I should at least rest before undertaking the final part of my journey.

Final. Did I not expect to return? I realized in that moment I did not. Somehow, though I had chosen to pursue this path for Truth and for my people, I did not, in my heart, believe I would succeed. Why then, did I persist? I could not say.

I reached a small clearing as the first star ignited in the violet sky. I would bed down here, a small distance from the cavern, but perhaps safer. Who could know if the beast ever emerged, scenting human flesh?

I pulled a thin blanket from my pouch, the weightiest I'd been willing to carry, and spread it across the rutted clearing. Tree limbs screeched against each other in the twilight breeze, like the cry of a wounded animal, and sent a chill across my skin. I wished for a fire, but it was too dark to gather wood, and the light would have left me exposed.

So, cold and weary, I stretched across my blanket, propped my pouch under my head, and whispered good night to the stars.

The grove of trees continued its nighttime sighing around me, with the occasional snap of a twig to remind me I shared the hillside with wildlife. But when a footfall too large for a harmless forest creature fell to my right, I shot up from the blanket and peered into the night.

Before I had time to think, a figure flew at me from the trees.

Wild and white, its robes flapped and its hair streamed backward and it screamed—a throaty cry of fury. I caught the glint of silver reflected from the stars and instinctively dove aside as it passed.

"Melayna!" I was on my feet in an instant. I had grabbed my pouch and withdrew the dagger as I jumped, dropped the pouch, and faced my sister.

She whirled, saw the dagger, and slowed.

"What are you doing?" I backed away. Had she tried to kill me? Surely there was some predator about and she had swooped in for my protection. I dared not take my eyes from her to search for the danger.

"I am taking what is mine." The words were a snarl.

She had not come for my protection.

"Not like this, Melayna! You would kill your own sister?"

She circled me, bent slightly at the waist, knife held out, its wicked point aimed at my belly. "For the throne? Who would not?"

"I would not!"

She laughed, guttural and mocking. "Ah yes, because you are the righteous one. The perfect one. The *chosen* one."

Grief tore at my heart even as anger surged in my blood. It was unfair, all of it. The Oracle's prediction. Melayna's betrayal. Unfair.

"Melayna, please. Let us talk. This is not the way—"

"Talk then, Sister. Say what you would say."

Even in the dark I could see her red, red lips and the feverish spots of color high on her pale cheeks. But her clothes were spotless and whole, and she did not look as though she had traveled the same path as I.

"How did you get here, Melayna? Did you follow me through the Cypress Forest?"

"Ha!" She straightened, lowered the knife to her side. "You and that Oracle. You have always been her little slave, doing her bidding. Too foolish to know she plays with you, makes sport of you."

I focused on the words, even though my heart was breaking into pieces over Melayna's betrayal. "How does she make sport of me?"

"Did you not know there was an easier way to

reach the Great Cavern? I have ridden only one day, across sunlit plains and shallow streams. No hostile villagers or Cypress Forest for me."

Could it be true? Would the Oracle have sent me on such a difficult journey when it was not necessary? But the proof stood before me. Melayna had not been in the Cypress Forest. The palace wealth, even the palace scent, still clung fresh to her. But I must cast aside the question of the Oracle's wisdom to address later.

"Nor did I stop to rally people to my cause, in some fruitless quest for revolution."

"How—how did you know that I—?"

"That fool who brought you here. I heard him pledge his undying allegiance to the younger sister. You've duped him and his entire city, I assume."

"No! No, I never wanted—"

"Yes, you never wanted the throne, never wanted my suitors, never, never, never!" Her voice rose to a hysterical pitch and she jabbed with the knife to emphasize each word.

I rose to my full height, dropped my dagger to my side, and spoke with clarity. "All of that is true. I have never sought anything but the good of our people."

"Well, I am here now so you can go home."

I frowned, studied her petulant expression. "You are here to defeat the beast? To retrieve the Horn of Truth?"

She flung her dark hair over her shoulder. "That is right. Did you believe yourself to be the only hero of Kalliste?"

"I am no hero, Melayna. But are you certain this is what you wish to do? There is great danger—"

"So I am not good enough to fight your beast now?"

I sighed and closed my eyes. Only briefly, for I still did not trust that knife in her hand. "Why now? Why, after all this time, have you decided to think first of our people?"

Her lip curled and her eyes bore into mine. "Because now *our people* think first of only *you!*"

I inclined my head and studied her face, thinking on her words until understanding dawned. "They have heard of my departure to retrieve the Truth and have pledged allegiance to me, even in the capital city."

"That's right, little sister. Even in your absence you win support."

"Then let us do it together. We will defeat the beast and bring back the Truth to the people, together. Save them, save Father, together. I shall make them understand you are as devoted to them as I."

"And you think this will sway them? No, I must come back with the Horn of Truth myself. And you," Melayna took a step nearer, "you must not come back at all."

I did not want to fight my sister. It would likely end with one of our deaths, and both prospects chilled me. How could I cause my own sister's death? But how could I let her kill me?

"There must be some way to have what you want without this awful deed."

Melayna hesitated. "I can think of only one. Leave now. Go home in defeat. Tell the city you were too fearful to proceed. You left it to me to save them."

I considered her words. Only last night I had learned how my pride could lead me astray. Was this humility, this humiliation, what was required of me now?

She seemed to gain confidence from my hesitation. "Think of your future, Sister." Her tone had become needling, fawning even. "You do not wish to be queen. Think of your studies— when would you have time to pursue such things with all the matters of the kingdom to attend? But if I were queen—if I were queen I would ensure the works of the finest scholars and priests from all the world would be brought to your feet. Tablets from Punt, from Egypt and Nubia, from the other islands across our sea, and the lands to the east." She smiled, an almost-benevolent smile befitting a queen. "All that knowledge, all at your feet for you to study."

I swayed a bit, thinking of such a thing. My parents had never regarded my studies as important. To be afforded all the knowledge of the world and all the time needed to absorb it . . .

Was all of life to be a series of choices like this? I had chosen destiny over my physical comforts and over the acclaim of my people. Was I now to choose it over even my heart's desire—the knowledge of the ages? I felt as though everything important had been stripped from me, shed like old skin, and yet I had no confidence that new skin lay underneath. Perhaps I would be as a shell that when cracked open is found to be empty. No pearl, no life.

Could I not retain this one thing, could it not still be used for the good of my people?

"And you will fight for the Horn of Truth? You promise me this?"

Her eyes gleamed. "Whatever it takes."

The temptation was powerful on me. But in that moment, with those three words, the truth opened as I had not yet seen it. Melayna did not love our people. She did not come here to fight for them, for their salvation. She came for herself alone, to satisfy her lust for power. She would use our people, let them come to harm, if it suited her desires.

She would not make a good queen. She was not fit to rule Kalliste.

I had made my decision. But I knew she was right. If I pursued the Horn of Truth, if I retrieved it, I would be made queen. And my studies would be lost to me. This loss was the greatest I had yet endured, save the loss of Andreas. I felt as though my lifeblood drained from me and I wanted to weep.

Melayna mistook my sorrow. "Do not be saddened, Sister. They will still welcome you, even if you—"

"I am not going home, Melayna."

Her eyes sharpened.

Righteous anger boiled through my veins, and my fingers tightened around my dagger. "I am going into the Great Cavern."

"Aaarrrrr!" She ran at me, knife extended.

I feinted left, slipped right.

Her knife sliced the air. She spun and came again, hair streaming.

Oh, how I wished not to kill my sister.

She had not practiced as I had. I waited, counted. She fell toward me and I cracked my forearm down upon hers. The knife held, but she screamed out in pain.

Still unwilling to use my own dagger, I grabbed at her knife arm and pushed it upward, above our heads. Our bodies locked together, faces almost touching. I felt the firm muscle of her under the soft clothing, smelled the fresh scent of palace perfume on her skin. She was so beautiful.

She twisted in my grasp. I swept a leg under her foot and she lost balance.

One shove and she fell. I realigned, ready for

her next attack, but she hit the ground with a strange *crack* and lay still.

Fear and dread and paralyzing grief surged through me. I dropped to the ground. "Melayna!"

I felt around her head. She had hit a tree root when she fell. In the darkness I could not see if there was blood, but I felt no sticky warmth.

She moaned once.

I did not have long.

I snatched the knife from her hand, ran to my pouch, still lying open on the blanket, retrieved the shorter of my two lengths of rope, and returned.

Before she grew alert I had her arms tied behind, and her body secured to a tree.

When she moaned again and lifted her head, she found me seated on the ground before her, knees drawn up to my chin and arms wrapped round my legs, with both our weapons in my hands.

She licked her lips, then spit. "Go then, little sister. Go and meet your destiny."

And although I had planned to spend the night regaining my strength on the thin blanket in the tiny clearing, I knew it was not to be. My time had come.

I gathered my pouch, heavier now with Melayna's knife, took a last look at the sister I had once loved, and headed for the mouth of the Great Cavern.

After a quick layover in Rome, the short flight to Venice deposited the team at the Aeroporto di Venezia Marco Polo on the Italian mainland, just north of Venice, by five o'clock in the evening.

Their motorboat driver was an older Italian man who looked as though he'd spent his life on the water under the Venetian sun. He and the guys loaded their bags onto the large boat while the women boarded, and they were off—shooting toward the horizon, where the city's buildings were lit in gold by the sun setting across the water.

Caroline had somehow arranged a private motorboat for them, more like a small yacht, rather than the slower public ferry or tourist bus across the long bridge to the lagoon-city. She really was a wonder.

Kallie stood alone at the rail and reveled in the beautiful moment.

Dimitri's online research yielded only the fact that Louis Manin, great-grandson of the last doge, died in 1950 with no legitimate children. It would be a puzzle to pursue. But right now, all that mattered was Venice, city of floating palaces.

Minutes later, their boat navigated into the mouth of Venice's Grand Canal. Caroline assumed her tour-guide role, gathering everyone up into a little group. Yoshi and Erik seemed especially eager to hear her patter.

"Venice sits in a lagoon—a calm section of the Adriatic protected by a breakwater. The city is shaped like a fish, with the S-shaped Grand Canal running through the middle of the fish, starting at its mouth." She pointed ahead, to the narrow opening ahead of their boat. "Four hundred bridges and two thousand alleys in this tiny city! No cars, of course. Everything is brought by boat and transported through the streets to its destination. We'll be staying at the Hotel Danieli tonight, thanks to Dimitri's generosity." She gave him an eyelash-fluttering smile. "We'll have to travel the entire length of the Grand Canal, so we'll get to see all the best sights tonight as we pass them!"

Kallie grinned. Caroline's excitement was contagious.

"The Rialto Bridge, St. Mark's Basilica . . ." She was ticking off the highlights on her fingers now, but Kallie just wanted to watch the city slide by. She pulled away from the team and found her spot at the rail again.

It was like floating through a luxury neighborhood. The city of palaces was built when Venice was the world's richest city, and the three-story buildings lined the wide canal on both sides in pinks and tans and corals, their front doors opening to the water. Long, thin windows with flower boxes trailed pink flowers, and green vines dotted each mansion. They passed gorgeous hotels, outdoor restaurants with red awnings, glass-fronted shops. And everywhere, the look and smell of a city that was elegantly decaying against the water. It was the most sensual city she'd ever seen, and she drank in all of it— golden lights flickering to life and reflecting across the canal, soft music from hotel bars, and everywhere the smells and swish of water.

They passed under the Rialto Bridge, its white span like a picture postcard, and curved around the lagoon until the spire of St. Mark's Basilica appeared above the famous square.

Dimitri joined her at the rail. "Almost there. We'll see all of it much better when we walk the city."

Kallie sighed dreamily. "I've already seen almost more than I can bear." The remnants of the Venetian trading empire of the Middle Ages were still so steeped in luxury, it was unimaginable what it must have looked like at the height of its glory, before time faded its vibrant color to faded pastels.

He smiled, looking over the water. "I know what you mean."

The pink-stuccoed Hotel Danieli proved to be as elegant as the rest of the city. How much would someplace like this cost per night? The lobby looked like a palace, everything gold and marble.

Caroline checked them in, then handed keys to each of them. "I'm sure y'all are just as tuckered out as I am." She smiled around the group, letting her smile linger on Erik. "Why don't we all go to our rooms and rest up a bit, then meet down here for dinner. Say, eight o'clock?"

Dimitri nodded. "Sounds good. You four go ahead. I have a few arrangements to make."

Kallie's room could have housed them all. Furnished in period pieces, with a balcony view of the water, it looked like Queen Elizabeth's sitting room. The *first* Queen Elizabeth. She wandered the room appreciatively, touching the smooth woods and soft drapes, then gazed out the window at the water lit up with lights of a dozen boats. Did Dimitri give the others as nice a room as he assigned to her? At that thought, she quickly looked at the time and decided on a hot shower.

Thirty minutes later, she stepped from the shower, wrapped herself in a towel, and froze. Was that the door to her room she'd heard open? Strange time for housekeeping to enter. Still dripping, she peeked her head around the door frame.

"Dimitri!" She stepped into the room and called his name before she'd considered what she was wearing.

He whirled, eyes wide. "What—?" His glance went to her towel. Did he actually blush? "Why are you—showering—in my room?"

Kallie pulled back into the bathroom. "This is my room!"

He huffed but seemed at a loss for words.

She'd brought no clothes into the bathroom. Ah, but there was a robe on a hook. Hurriedly, she put it on, tied the sash around her waist, and ran a hand through her dripping hair. He was still standing near the door.

She crossed the room to a desk beside the door, passing uncomfortably close to him, and picked up the white folder with her key card. "408."

He lifted his hand, a matching white folder in his fingers. "408."

Seriously? It was like something from an old movie. Now they'd call the front desk about the mix-up, learn the entire hotel was booked, and have to spend the night with a blanket hung between them, right? *Not* going to happen.

He stood so close, not speaking. Why wasn't he speaking?

He touched her wet hair. "Destiny, maybe?"

Something in the way he said the word set off a moment of such deep longing in her heart, like being offered a feast after seven years of starvation. Heat surged in her chest, flamed out to her fingertips, and the intensity was terrifying. She backed against the door, braced her hands against it, feeling her heart pounding, shaking her head.

Dimitri watched her retreat with sorrowful eyes. Then nodded once and turned away.

"I'll take care of it."

ಌ

The hotel staff was all apologies. Apparently, their matching last names had caused confusion, leading a desk clerk to believe they were a couple and booking them into the same room.

"I'm simply mortified." Caroline stood at the door to Room 408, eyes flashing. "I should have explained there is no *personal* connection between you and Dimitri."

Kallie bit the inside of her cheek. "Yes, well. How about I just room with you instead?"

Caroline's eyes widened.

Dimitri rounded the corner.

"It's all settled, Dimitri." Kallie smiled at Caroline and squeezed her hand—hard. "We two girls are going to get to know each other better."

Thankfully, Caroline took the cue and turned to storm off to her room . . . leaving the door open a crack.

Kallie was obviously intruding on Caroline, but it was safer, not having a private room. The disaster on the cruise ship combined with Dr. Newsom's advice had convinced her—no relationships until she'd figured out who she was. Dimitri stepped out while she got dressed and gathered her belongings to move to Caroline's room. Well, that answered her question—Dimitri had the gorgeous room, not her.

Later, they all had dinner together in the hotel, with Yoshi expounding on the history of Venetian-Greek relations until even Kallie's eyes were glazing over. Everyone agreed they were too tired for sightseeing tonight, and they retired early.

Kallie gave Caroline the bathroom first and wandered to the balcony overlooking the lagoon, cell phone in hand. She was overdue for a promised phone call to update Judith.

A moment after the speed dial, the connection spanned the ocean and the older woman answered.

"Hey, it's Kallista."

"I was beginning to worry."

Kallie smiled at the sharp disapproval in the woman's voice. What would Judith say if she knew about the desert stranding, police detention, and dig-site looters? She'd probably fly out and personally escort Kallie back to the safe museum.

"All is well. We're in Venice."

"Find anything?'

"We're on the trail. Some encouraging tidbits."

"Hmph." Judith's snort spoke volumes. "Tidbits."

"We'll get there."

"I heard your benefactor decided to join you."

"How—?"

"Are you certain you're not simply wandering Europe for the romance?"

Kallie frowned across the lagoon. The lights of

the island of Murano, with its glass-making factories, shone a sparkling path across the water. "You know that's not why I came."

"Just checking. I figured if he's there, why does he need you?"

"Good question. I'll ask him."

Judith laughed—an unusual but welcome sound.

They chatted for a few more minutes, and after a promise to call again soon, Kallie disconnected and returned inside the room. Caroline emerged from the bathroom in a hotel robe, wringing out her hair.

Minutes later, the day's exhaustion overcame her and she fell asleep.

The next morning, she met Dimitri as arranged, inside the front doors of the hotel.

Was she simply an extra cog in the machinery? Perhaps they all were—all but Caroline. If they found the piece and its second language was hieroglyphic, Yoshi would be of no help. Erik's muscle seemed superfluous in this peaceful city. And what use was it for Dimitri to continue including her?

He looked great, as usual, his black Windbreaker contrasting against a white buttoned shirt. He smiled when she approached, but it was still a sad smile. "Ready to see Venice?"

"More than ready. But I'm not sure why you need a partner at this point. You'd do fine searching for the piece on your own." Even as she said it, she prayed he wouldn't agree. She was dying to see Venice and hated the thought of missing out on finding the key to Linear A.

He guided her through the front doors with a light touch on her elbow. His voice was low behind her. "Oh, I need a partner more than you know."

He was doing it again—suave, smooth words that left her a bit breathless and extremely annoyed with herself for falling for it.

"So, where are we headed?"

"San Marcos Square. The Doge's Palace. There's an expert on Venetian history there. We should be able to see him."

Dimitri's money and contacts opened every necessary door, reinforcing that she was only along for the ride. But, no matter—she was *here*—and she was going to absorb every bit of it!

Kallie tried to take in all of the city's architectural jumble. Traditional Gothic with its pointed arches combined with Byzantine Gothic's narrow arches on thin columns, all filled in with the frills of the Islamic period. One could study here for years.

Tourists and locals and pigeons crowded the wide-open Piazza San Marco, bordered on three sides by restaurants and shops and on the fourth by the famous basilica. Kallie craned her neck to see the top of the spired brick bell tower in the courtyard, and then the four bronze prancing horses on the front of the magnificent church. Adjoining the church, running out toward the water, was the fabulous multistoried palace, with its two lowest levels of Gothic arches and walls of white limestone and pink marble rising up to a crenellated roof poking into the blue sky.

Dimitri led her to the tourist entrance and bought the standard tour tickets. Kallie noticed a price for the *Itinerari Segreti*, the "Secret Itineraries" tour on the wall above the counter.

He noticed her interest. "There are all sorts of hidden passageways and concealed doors in this place, where the administrative offices of medieval Venice operated. There's a separate tour of those parts of the palace."

But right now they were taking the standard tour, fascinating as the other seemed.

Inside, they ascended the wide marble stairs under a vaulted ceiling, and Kallie gaped at the opulence. Clearly, the palace had been built to show off the might and wealth of the Venetians. Every inch of space was a celebration of Venetian Gothic architecture with such vibrant colors and elaborate gilding she tried to memorize every detail. They joined their tour group and followed the smiling female guide, who spoke nearly flawless English.

"The Most Serene Republic of Venice, *La Serenissima*, was one of the most powerful cities in Europe for over four hundred years." She led them to a massive room, covered floor-to-ceiling —and even *across* the ceiling—with enormous oil paintings, separated by thick gilt frames. "In this aristocratic republic, the Doge was like an elected king, and here in the Hall of the Great Council is where the government ruled."

She let them wander the hall, taking in the paintings. Their group numbered about twenty, a variety of ages and nationalities, but one woman caught Kallie's eye. Long dark hair, serious eyes. She examined a painting closely but glanced at Kallie more than once.

Kallie watched her from the corner of her eye. Something was so—familiar—about her. The way she moved, the way she tossed her hair back over her shoulder as she leaned in for a closer look at a painting. Again, her eyes shifted to Kallie.

A surge of excitement flashed through her. For seven years she had wondered if she would ever encounter someone who knew her, knew her before the museum. Someone who could tell her who she was. She started toward the woman, but then that suspicious stare was back, an almost hostile look that gave Kallie pause. She seemed to sense that Kallie meant to approach, turned her back, and moved away.

Kallie sighed. Had she imagined the flicker of recognition in the woman's eyes?

Their guide was pointing out the colossal painting at the end of the room. "Our famous Venetian painter, Tintoretto, here completed his crowning work: *Paradise*, the largest oil painting in the world."

The work was awe inspiring—some seventy-five feet wide and thirty feet high, covered in the Renaissance conception of a sprawling, chaotic heaven, with more writhing figures than one could count—angels and men, bodiless heads, and nameless beasts. Kallie tilted her head to try to take in the whole of it. The medieval view of the divine was so different than the ancient. All of the god-becoming-man of the Christian church's foundational premise entwined the human and divine in new ways, suggesting closer contact, interaction, and even interdependence. But she felt an uncomfortable twist in her gut at the thought of a frenzied heaven like this.

When they exited the Hall of the Great Council, Dimitri led her down a side stairwell, away from the tour group.

"What are we doing?" She looked over her shoulder, expecting to be slapped into cuffs by tourist police.

"There are offices down here. We have a meeting."

Down a long, narrow hallway they found a pinch-faced, middle-aged man sitting at a desk in a cramped office. His sallow skin looked as if it never emerged from his buried station, and he stood when they arrived, as though feeling some relief at having visitors.

"Mr. Andreas?"

"Yes, Mr. Vegliantino, thank you for meeting us."

Roberto Vegliantino extended a hand to two wrought-iron chairs at an angle in front of his desk. "Please."

Dimitri introduced her as his associate, then wasted no time. "What can you tell us about the pieces in Louis Manin's collection?"

Vegliantino lifted a pair of reading glasses from a string around his neck. "Hmm. Yes. Interesting. I've been doing some checking since your phone call." He looked up and smiled, a patronizing smile that seemed meant to engender gratitude. "Anything I can do for a man such as yourself—"

"Yes, thank you. What did you learn?"

Vegliantino's smile disappeared. He cleared his throat and checked his notes. "Well, of course Louis Leonardo Manin, the last doge's great-grandson, never knew the doge. The elder Manin had died about fifty years prior to Louis's birth. But in later life, Louis became quite a collector, rounding up pieces from around the world, attempting to obtain something significant from every corner of Venetian conquest. Quite impressive, really."

"And the piece we spoke of?"

"Yes, well, Manin had no legitimate children, only two sons by a widow whom he never married. His estate passed largely into the hands of the Venetian government, and many of the pieces were sold. I was able, with some difficulty, of course, to locate a catalog of some of the—"

"Something with an unknown script? And perhaps another language? Hieroglyphs?" Dimitri's excitement was bleeding into his voice.

Kallie tried to appear less enthusiastic. The little man had already pegged Dimitri as a walking bank account, willing to pay.

"Yes. Something like that. Sold in 1975, to a Greek collector, originally from Santorini."

Kallie gasped. Crete would have been logical, as the largest island of the Minoan culture. But Santorini, her Santorini, was tiny in comparison. What were the odds of the piece having been purchased by someone who had lived there?

Dimitri placed his hand over hers and tightened his fingers. She felt a mutual thrill run through both of them.

"His name?"

"That, I am afraid, I do not have. The information, you understand, can be very difficult to obtain. The work of a historian is never ending, but we live to be of service—"

But Dimitri had pulled a checkbook from his inner jacket pocket and Vegliantino's words trailed away with a pleased smile.

Outside the man's office, Dimitri grinned at her. "One step closer. And we're all the way up to 1975."

Kallie grabbed his arm. "And Santorini! But how can we find out who the collector was?"

Dimitri's gaze traveled over her shoulder, a quick frown creasing his forehead.

Kallie turned, followed his gaze. "What is it?"

"Nothing. I just thought I saw someone watching us. But she's gone."

"She?" A flutter of foreboding left Kallie cold.

"Probably just someone who works here. Anyway, I think I can track down a friend who lives here in Venice, who might know something about the Greek collector. I'll do some checking around. Why don't you do a bit more sightseeing?"

Kallie smiled. "The *Itinerari Segreti*?"

He laughed. "You're really into the secret passageway thing, aren't you?"

"Come on, it's fascinating, you have to admit. This whole city is like smoke and mirrors, all masks and illusion. It's fitting there'd be a secret underbelly to the palace."

He led the way back toward the main entrance. "Take the tour, then. You'll like it. You'll even get to see the prison where Casanova was held."

They arranged to meet in two hours in the square, and Dimitri left her with a new ticket in hand. He headed back into the *piazzetta*, the smaller square outside the palace. Should she have told him of her other reason for staying? The hope she'd see the woman from the Great Hall again? Was she the same woman Dimitri had seen watching them in the corridor?

She joined the tour, but it was only her and four other tourists, all French. They followed the guide through the private offices of the doge's assistant and the Keeper of the Secret Archives, then to a room clad in mirrors with the coats of arms of the Republic's chancellors mounted along the wall.

They descended into a stone corridor with barred windows and reached the Torture Room and the adjoining cells, where political prisoners were held or those awaiting trial. It was here that Casanova escaped The Leads and his trial for various controversial seductions and "public outrages against the holy religion" in 1753.

After the prison, they reached a gorgeous room, the ceiling again painted lavishly by their famous Tintoretto, but the guide's explanation of the room's function ruined the beauty for her. Here, with no accountability to the Venetian public, the Inquisitors for the Maintenance of State Secrets interrogated and tortured prisoners.

The group moved on, but Kallie hung back, getting a closer look at the paintings above her. There was so much art in this palace, it could put many museums to shame. Judith would love to see this.

A voice from behind, hissing in her ear, chilled her blood.

"What are you doing here?"

Kallie half turned.

It was her. The woman from the hall, standing behind her. She wore a clingy black dress and carried a small handbag.

She took a breath. "Who are you?"

It was the second question she wished to ask. The first was "Who am I?"—but that seemed a strange opening.

The woman jabbed Kallie in the side with her index finger and scowled.

Kallie backed toward the door.

The woman circled to block her exit. Her dark eyes traveled up and down Kallie's body. "I told you to stay away."

"What?" Kallie's memory rocked and lurched, searching for a foothold. So familiar, this woman, even her words.

The phone call. Weeks ago, the night of that horrible fund-raising gala, when she'd gotten that strange, warning phone call. *"Stay away from what is not yours."*

"I—I don't know what you're talking about—" There was more here, more than the phone call. Something farther back, farther back than even seven years. "Please"—she held her hands out to the woman—"please tell me who you are, what you know about me."

The woman's eyes darkened, like black fire. "You really don't remember, do you?" She took a few menacing steps toward Kallie, gripped her small purse in both hands.

"No. I'm sorry. Have we met?" Kallie spoke the phrase like a lame one-line opening at a bar, not like the bottomless void of unknown fears that it was. She pressed damp palms against her jeans.

The woman laughed, a short, cynical laugh with a curled lip. "You could say that." She opened the bag and a small gun slipped out, a tiny thing in the palm of her hand, like a child's toy.

Kallie knew nothing about guns, but that was probably not a toy.

"What—what are you doing?" Kallie looked over the woman's shoulder, toward the door, toward the long-departed tour group. It had been idiotic to let herself be left alone. The woman from the phone call, the woman Pendleworth had told Dimitri was also searching for the Linear A Key—suddenly it all came together and Kallie realized she'd been foolish, naïve.

And somehow, somehow there was even more—for this woman knew Kallie before she knew herself.

In answer to Kallie's question, the woman half smiled, cold and frightening. "What I should have done years ago."

⇒ 26 ⇐

A panicked heat shot through Kallie's body. Wouldn't a gunshot echo in this wood-paneled room? But what difference would that make? She'd be dead.

"Hold on." She put her hands in front of her, as if they could stop a bullet. "You must have me confused with someone else."

And yet, mind racing, Kallie knew that was untrue. She *knew* this woman. What had Kallie done to warrant being murdered? She slid two steps to the right, trying not to look at the only door in the room.

The woman's lips tightened along with her fingers on the gun. "Stop."

Would it be like a movie, with the bad guy explaining all his dark motives before the fatal shot, giving the hero time to escape? Doubtful.

Instead, almost without thought, Kallie kicked her leg high and wide. Connected with the gun-holding hand with a dull *thwump.*

Hand and gun jerked left, the woman screamed a curse, but she did not let go. Her black-ice eyes turned deadly. She brought the gun back to center and pulled the trigger.

Kallie dove right, heard the slight *pop* of the gun.

Don't be fooled. Tiny but deadly.

She hit the parquet floor, rolled and jumped to her feet, aimed toward the door. Blood pounded in her ears and heat singed her fingertips, but her movements felt natural, automatic. Like muscle memory.

First bullet missed. Next one might get lucky.

She had no weapons but her body, no match for bullets. Better to evade than attack.

The woman got off another shot, but Kallie was already through the door, careening down a long corridor, toward the front entrance, hopefully.

She had a stray thought about the beautiful medieval paintings marred by bullet holes, but now was not the time for preservationist concerns. Not when a bullet to the back of the head seemed likely.

Somehow, she found her way out of the complicated palace, to the front tourist entrance. She grabbed a security guard and pointed behind her. "There's a woman with a gun!"

It was enough to set the ticket line screaming and diving, and in the chaos, Kallie took to the piazzetta, aiming for the thickest part of the crowd. Tourists and pigeons parted at her approach, and when she reached the *campanile*, the bell tower, she slowed and tried to appear casual.

On the far side of Piazza San Marco, she entered a narrow alley of shops where the walls of the buildings blocked the sun, pulled out her phone, and texted Dimitri.

Need to meet you immediately. Someone just attacked me.

She kept to a brisk pace down the alley, barely noticing the window displays of jewelry, of colorful scarves, and rainbow-hued candy, of masses of ceramic masks with sequined eyes and velvet and feathers. She kept moving, heedless of direction. The city was an absolute maze of alleyways and streets, many ending at narrow canals. Water everywhere. Occasionally a bridge gave passage to the next street, but often she had to backtrack. More than once she glanced over her shoulder, searching the window-shoppers for a familiar dark head and angry eyes.

Her phone buzzed in her hand, and she jumped. A call, not a text.

"Dimitri?"

"Are you okay?" His voice was all-out panic and it warmed her.

"For now. Where are you?"

"At a café on the Campo San Polo. In the center of the city. But it would be easier for me to find you. Where are you?"

She swept a gaze up and down the dark corridor. "I have no idea. In one of the million little alleyways of this city."

"Keep walking until you hit a corner. Then tell me what the sign says on the wall."

Her present narrow confine opened up to a wide square with several outdoor restaurants and a crowd of people dining at metal tables with umbrellas. She searched for the gray stone wall-engraved sign she'd seen in other squares. "Campo San Angelo."

"Perfect. Stay there. I'll be there soon." He paused, still connected. "Kallie, are you sure you're okay?"

"I'm shaken up but not hurt. I'll be fine waiting for you here."

"I'm on my way!"

Oddly, the little incident in the palace, far from freaking her out, had felt more like waking up. As if she'd been asleep for the past seven years and had suddenly become her true self. Like using muscles that had atrophied. Where did she learn those bullet-dodging maneuvers? Had she been some kind of spy? The idea made her smile. Was it so far-fetched?

Perhaps she'd been here before, in this eternally dying city, just as Dimitri had. And Luxor, too. The Karnak Temple, the valleys of tombs in the western bank. They'd seemed familiar, hadn't they?

Her fingers itched for her pen and journal. If she could just start writing, something would flow, some kind of truth, of memory.

Where was Dimitri? It seemed like an hour already. Probably only ten minutes. She scanned the square. In the center of the square was the white stone circle of a closed-up fountain. Above the far end, she could see a brick bell tower, but it couldn't be the one from St. Mark's. It was leaning slightly. Strange.

"Kallie!"

She jumped and turned.

Dimitri was striding across the campo, jacket flapping.

"Not so loud!"

He glanced around. "Were you followed?"

Yes, it was all spy-movie stuff now. Very cool. "No, I kept checking. But she *knew* me, Dimitri."

"Who knew you?" He led her to a pastry-shop window, filled with pastel-iced treats, and they huddled there, backs to the campo.

She told it from the beginning, from seeing the woman in the Hall of the Great Council, to her suspicion they'd been followed to Vegliantino's office, and then the attack in the Hall of the Inquisitors.

"She *shot* you?" His voice pitched an octave high.

"Shh, Dimitri." They were attracting stares. "Shot *at* me. Twice, actually. She missed."

She'd barely gotten the words out when Dimitri pulled her roughly to his chest, smashed her face into his jacket, and held her head there with one hand. She could feel his heart pounding, his breath heavy.

"This is crazy, Kallie. I'm sending you home."

She yanked away. "You most definitely are not!"

He still held her arms and stared into her eyes. "What's gotten into you?"

"I have no idea." She laughed. "But something's happening in me, I can feel it. I think I might be close to remembering."

A flinch, like sudden pain, passed over his features and his fingers tightened on her arms. "That's wonderful." His tone said anything but.

Confused, but not about to push him, Kallie changed the subject. "Did you find your friend?"

He turned back to the window display. "Not yet. But we should be able to meet her in a few hours. We'll stay out of sight until then."

"Her?" The pronoun stabbed her oddly.

"Stella Ferraro. An old friend who's—helped me—in the past."

His hesitance didn't ease her concern.

"You hungry?"

Kallie looked over the pink- and lavender-iced sugar cookies. "Starving."

She would have enjoyed eating outdoors, but Dimitri thought it best they stay inside, somewhere private, and she agreed. He made a quick phone call to Caroline and asked her to let Yoshi and Erik know they'd meet at the hotel later.

The afternoon passed strangely, hours of clandestine sightseeing, slipping from quaint alleys, across picture-perfect miniature bridges that spanned murky blue-green canals. They stopped on more than one bridge to watch gondoliers navigate their boats through the tiny waterways, delighted tourists waving up at them.

Dimitri was clearly anxious to be away from the city, given the morning's events, but Kallie loved every minute of their afternoon and wished for more time to get to know Venice.

When the sun had set and they'd eaten dinner at an out-of-the-way café along a tiny canal, they followed the series of yellow signs on every street corner, lettered with opposing arrows for "Per Rialto" and "Per S. Marcos"—indicating the Rialto Bridge and the Piazza San Marcos, the city's two main tourist destinations. They pushed along the *Merceria*, the city's main shopping and foot traffic thoroughfare. Stella would be meeting them near the bridge.

"I wish it weren't so public." Dimitri kept his hand on her arm as they wound through the crowds. The Rialto Bridge spanned the Grand Canal, with restaurants lining each side of the water, their lights just now coming on. Patrons dined al fresco in spite of the cool weather, and many of the tables had propane heaters in the center to warm the customers. Gondolas traveled back and forth across the canal, and a *vaporetto*, one of the city's water buses, churned past, filled with passengers. The vaporetto driver yelled a curse at the gondolier blocking his passage.

The Rialto's white stone steps led up one side and down the other, with a short span across the top. Dimitri led her to the base of the steps and they waited. He didn't take his hand from her arm, as if afraid she'd topple into the water or be snatched away. She could feel his tension through his fingers.

A young Italian in a low-slung hat passed too close and brushed Kallie's shoulder. She pulled back, and the man's gaze shot to hers, narrow-eyed under the hat.

He slowed, and Dimitri stepped between her and the man.

"You are looking for a friend?" His English was heavily accented and his voice low.

Dimitri looked left and right. "Where is she?"

"Not here. She does not trust you are alone." Again, his glance traveled along Kallie.

"She knows I would bring no one I did not trust myself."

Kallie turned her head, as though she could not hear their conversation. Lamplight glittered in the gentle lapping of the canal water, and somewhere a violinist began to play.

"You were not followed?"

Dimitri's voice was agitated. "Why would I have been followed? No one even knows I have contacted her."

Kallie shifted to take in the young man again,

from his thick eyebrows to his glossy shoes. He had an air of money about him, but perhaps ill-gotten.

"Very well. Come."

Dimitri gripped her elbow as they pushed through the alleys crowded with evening shoppers and tourists looking for cafés and restaurants.

Along a cobbled street, their escort suddenly disappeared into a shadowed doorway.

Dimitri pushed through first, and Kallie followed.

It was a souvenir shop, though unlit and smelling of neglect. Light from the alley filtered through dusty windows to reveal shelves of Venice trinkets, from porcelain masks to Murano glass to plaster replicas of St. Mark's and the Rialto.

The Italian vanished once more, through a door in the back of the shop.

They followed, into a dark hallway.

Kallie pushed away a stab of concern. There was no one here who would want to hurt them, was there?

The hall twisted and bent twice, like the alleys of the city in miniature. Kallie lost her sense of direction. Wouldn't they have crossed a block of shops and emerged into another alley by now?

A rectangle of light glowed ahead, from the cracks of a closed door. The man from the bridge pushed the door open, and a room opulent enough to rival their hotel spilled soft light into the hall.

The walls and furniture were draped in fabrics, jewel-toned and gauzy, and sprawled across one of the two couches was a woman in a silk robe.

"Ah, there you are, my *sweet* man!" The sultry female voice, heavily accented, called from the couch.

Dimitri turned immediately, pushed Kallie toward the voice, and then toward the woman herself.

Her garishly made-up eyes widened at the sight of Kallie. She sat forward, the robe falling open. "I expected you to come alone."

Why did that not surprise Kallie? The woman was in her mid-thirties, perhaps. Extremely attractive, with a clingy, low-cut dress under the robe that left little to the imagination.

If Kallie had been hoping that Dimitri's "friend" was a matronly older woman, she'd been disappointed.

"Stella, this is my associate, Kallista Andreas."

Stella stood, her smile tight. "Associate? Do *not* tell me you have gotten married, Dimitri. You will absolutely break my heart."

He shook his head. "Just a coincidence on the last name."

"Well, then." She crossed the room and embraced Dimitri, kissing both cheeks. "What can Stella do for you?"

"We're looking for a specific piece." He smiled.

"I knew you were the woman in Venice to ask."

"You are not so bad at acquiring—information —yourself, Dimitri."

Kallie had taken a quick inventory of the front room. The shelves were stuffed with all manner of souvenirs that tourists in Italy would gobble up. Perfect cover for someone dealing in illegal antiquities. But that meant Dimitri was also involved.

He shifted, as though to block her from Stella's view. "Kallie was shot at this afternoon, by someone who may be searching for the same piece that interests us."

Stella's artificially perfect eyebrows rose. "You surprise me, my love. You are usually more careful with your—purchases."

Stella kept glancing over Kallie's shoulder to the doorway. Was she worried they'd been followed? Did Stella have enemies that might show up at any moment?

Dimitri explained roughly what they were after, the information they'd uncovered thus far.

"Santorini, you say?"

He glanced at Kallie. "Stella knows more about the private antiquities trade in the past century than anyone in Italy."

And by "private," you mean illegal. Kallie kept her mouth shut but hoped her expression conveyed disgust.

Stella patted Dimitri's cheek. "Always the

flatterer, this one." Her eyes flicked to Kallie's, with an unspoken territorial message women always understood. "But so sweet, no?"

Kallie said nothing.

"Can you help us, Stella?"

"Of course, of course. Let me check something."

She went to a filing cabinet, pulled out a few manila folders, and began rifling through papers.

Amusing, the picture of a black-market dealer with her office files. Kallie shifted on her feet, jittery with apprehension or annoyance, she wasn't certain which.

"She's always been really helpful," Dimitri whispered. As if he needed to explain.

"Ah, here it is." Stella slid the cabinet drawer shut and returned to his side. "Just as I thought. Nicolaos Papadakis from Santorini. Purchased several of Manin's pieces."

"Nicolaos Papadakis. Thank you, Stella." Dimitri leaned in to kiss her cheek, but she turned and gave him her lips instead, reaching up to slide her fingers through his hair and hold him there.

After too long a moment, he pulled away and exhaled, with a glance at Kallie.

"Oh, do not mind me, my dear." Stella's smile was on Dimitri, but her words were for Kallie. "This one is a lover, but he always leaves. The one that got away, as they say. No?"

She reached for Dimitri again, but he stepped back.

"Again, Stella, my gratitude. Please, let me know if there is anything I can do for you. You have my number."

She laughed with a sly look at Kallie. "Yes, I have your number."

He practically pushed Kallie back through the front of the shop, out into the cobbled street, then away from the Rialto Bridge.

"So that was great, right?" Kallie watched his profile as he hurried them along. "We got a name."

Dimitri didn't answer. He was angry.

She had no idea why.

⇒ 27 ⇐

Kallie jogged to catch up with Dimitri. He'd already turned a corner without her. She'd lose him in the crowd—or in the dark—if he didn't slow down.

"Hey." She grabbed his jacket sleeve. "What's going on?"

He stopped beside a mask shop display, its window exploding with color, and looked over her shoulder. "Just being careful."

"It's more than that. You're angry."

He tugged his sleeve from her fingers and continued down the alley. "Don't worry about it."

"Are we headed back to the hotel? Maybe Caroline can still get us a flight to Santorini tomorrow."

"Can you forget about the Key for one night, Kallie? We don't even know if Papadakis went back to Santorini."

She got a better grip on his arm and dug in her heels. "Dimitri, what is wrong?"

He exhaled and turned back to her, but his glance went over her shoulder again, and this time his eyes darkened and his chin lifted. "Don't turn around." He slid her hand into the bend of his arm. "Keep walking with me. Look like a tourist."

She fell into step beside him, staring into shop windows without seeing. "Is it a woman? Dark hair?"

"No. Two men."

Was she relieved or more concerned at this?

"You think they're following us?"

In answer, Dimitri took a sharp cut across the alley, into a wider street, then pulled her hurriedly along, away from the huge palaces that lined the upper portion of the Grand Canal. They pushed through against crowds for several minutes before he looked backward.

She felt the muscles of his arm tense under her hand. "Still there?"

"Yes."

The crowds were thinning now, farther from the

tourist sections. Dimitri walked faster, and Kallie's hand slid from the bend of his arm to grasp his hand until they were nearly jogging through alleys, across wrought-iron bridges spanning canals, along precipitous walkways that crumbled into the murky water.

Footsteps matched their own and shadows leaped across buildings like special effects on a movie set.

"We should get back toward the tourist area." Dimitri pulled her along a canal, then slowed at a corner to glance at the ubiquitous mounted street sign pointing toward the Rialto Bridge. They followed its arrow in that direction.

They rounded a corner and came upon the Grand Canal and a vaporetto slid past, still full of commuters at this hour, but there was no stop nearby for them to hop aboard. It glided away, lights blinking. The Rialto Bridge was still too far away for them to quickly get across the canal, and this side was beginning to feel unsafe.

Another boat chugged to the wooden planking along the canal, this one a wooden motorboat. Its driver, who looked like he should still be in school, inclined his head toward Dimitri. "Private taxi?"

Dimitri pushed her aboard without a word, then jumped in after her.

"Where to, then, sir?"

"Away. Just away."

The boy guided the boat away toward the center of the canal, picked up some speed, and shot past the vaporetto.

Dimitri and Kallie stood in the center of the boat, watching behind.

Another boat was pulling away in their wake. Were they still being followed?

"What do they want?" Kallie gripped Dimitri's arm for support on the rocking water taxi. "We don't have anything."

Dimitri turned to the boy. "Can you make this thing go faster?"

He glanced behind, then toward Dimitri, eyebrows raised. "In a bit of trouble, sir?"

"You could say that."

"Hang on, then."

Kallie took his instruction as reason to stumble into a seat.

Dimitri joined her, eyes still trained backward. "They're keeping up."

"Not for long, sir."

A sudden jolt to the right nearly flung Kallie from her perch. They shot into a side canal, narrow and dark. The boat righted and jammed her shoulder into the rail. She gasped with the shock of pain, then bit her lip.

The motorboat skimmed through alleys that seemed too narrow to accommodate it, but their driver was like the Italian cousin of a New York City bike messenger, finding openings where

there were none and never slowing at inter-
sections that would have terrified a lesser man.
The canal system of Venice was like Dr.
Newsom's maze drawing, still packed in her
suitcase in the hotel. She was no more certain
there was a safe way out.

"I think we're okay." Dimitri clapped the boy
on the shoulder and nodded toward the empty
canal behind them. They were still near the
Grand Canal but behind one of the mansions that
ran along it. "Good work, man."

"You want me to take you somewhere else,
then?"

Dimitri hesitated, then shook his head. "Let us
out here. We'll wait awhile and find our way
home."

Kallie climbed out of the boat while Dimitri
rewarded the boy with more cash than necessary.

"Ask for Luciano if you need a driver." His
grin was conspiratorial. "I get you anywhere."

"Yes, I'll bet you could."

The water taxi disappeared with a lurch and a
belch of smoke, leaving the two of them standing
along a cobbled walkway outside a building
with lights on in its upper floors but darkness at
ground level.

Dimitri tried the first door they came to and
found it unlocked. "Come."

She followed him inside.

"Watch your step. All of these old palaces are flooded on their ground floors now."

Only a narrow ledge of crumbling flooring hugged the perimeter of the wall. The light coming from the Grand Canal's lampposts illuminated just enough of the interior to see crystal chandeliers and larger-than-life wall portraits, all hanging on mossy walls and ceilings above a watery floor.

"It's like something from the *Titanic*." Kallie's whisper echoed through the empty chamber.

"I think the *Titanic* is more flooded than this."

She half laughed. "I guess so. It's just all this elegance, combined with all the water. So strange."

"We'll wait here awhile, in case they're still searching."

She leaned against the wall, then at the dampness and pulled away again. "I don't understand why everyone is suddenly so interested in the Linear A Key."

"It may not even be the Key. If I had to guess, I would say those men were more about Stella than us."

"You have some dangerous friends, Dimitri."

He said nothing, and she saw the anger from the street outside Stella's shop return to his expression.

"I'm sorry—"

"No. No, you are right. I never should have brought you here."

"Is that what's bothering you? Because you know I want to be here."

He looked away, his jawline tightening again.

They waited in near silence, until Dimitri poked his head out of the building and searched the alley in both directions.

"I think we're safe to head back to the hotel."

But Kallie wasn't ready for the night to end. "Why don't we get something to eat, some coffee?"

"Fine."

They walked for a while, wandering the city, knowing a café would present itself eventually.

In spite of the crazy water chase and Dimitri's mood, the spell of the Venice night worked its magic on Kallie. A light mist began to fall, and in the golden-hued lamplight, the rain-slicked cobbled streets reflected the colors from the shop windows, soft and muted as everything was in this incredibly romantic city.

The crowds thinned as they reached the deeper districts. An occasional couple strolled past, heads together, smiling into each other's eyes, trading secrets. Kallie watched them all, watched the way they seemed to know each other.

Dimitri led her across a lacy white bridge as a gilt-edged black gondola slid under them in near silence, the man and woman sharing a kiss in the rain. Ahead, a green-and-white-striped awning beckoned, the rain collecting between its stripes and falling in rhythmic drips to the stones.

Dimitri opened the door for her, and she ducked inside, shaking droplets from her hair.

Soft music played inside the café, something sad and soulful and Italian, and the smell of espresso and pastry was like a welcoming embrace. They went to the counter and chose cannoli covered in chocolate shavings and several cream puffs.

"Do you think that's enough?" Dimitri glanced at her sideways with a half grin.

Kallie laughed. Was it over, whatever had been troubling him? "I think I can make do with that. Although, I could really go for some hot chocolate."

Dimitri nodded to the boy and held up two fingers. *"Due cioccolato caldo, per favore."*

He led her to a table in the corner, covered in a soft green-and-white fabric that matched the awning. They were nearly alone in the shop.

"You surprise me tonight, Dimitri." She settled herself in the chair across from him. Even though his mood had improved, she wasn't ready to let it go. "We've had a very successful day in tracking the piece, and yet you seem more discouraged than ever. Is it just those men in the canal?"

"And someone taking a shot at you?"

"Besides that, yes."

He sighed, folded his hands on the table, and studied them. "Stella."

"Stella? She seemed very—nice."

He laughed, more of a snort. "You are gracious."

"I got the feeling she was a friend."

"She is." He sighed again. "It's just—I—she—"

"Talk to me, Dimitri."

He met her eyes. "I can only imagine what you must be thinking." He dropped his voice. "Between the black-market stuff and Stella's innuendo—"

"I think you're a man who knows how to get things done."

"No matter the method."

She exhaled. "I know we don't agree on everything you are involved in, but I believe you feel you are doing the right thing."

"The right thing." The words were repeated in disgust, and he rubbed his temples with two fingers.

"What is it? Sometimes I believe you are—eaten up—by something. Guilt, regret, I don't know. I wish you would tell me."

He seemed to wage an internal debate, then inhaled and raised his head. "Kallie, I want you to know the truth."

"Oh?" He had so many secrets that the declaration was unexpected.

He spread his hands on the table. "Well, some of the truth, at least."

"Ah." That was more like it.

"I don't want you to think that I'm some kind of con artist or a crook or—"

She placed her hands over his. "Dimitri, I don't think that. I know you."

He looked up at her, and she saw pain in his eyes.

"Don't ask me how, but somehow I know you. I know you are a man of integrity. Nothing that has happened tonight has changed that."

He clung to her hands. "Integrity."

"Yes."

He shook his head and muttered something. Something like, "If you knew . . ."

The server brought their pastries and hot chocolate, and they pulled apart to give him space on the table.

When he left, Dimitri ignored his food, but Kallie sipped the hot chocolate, thick as a melted candy bar.

"I've been traveling the world, buying black-market antiquities for some time now."

She chose a luscious-looking cannoli and took a bite. "I see."

"I find pieces I believe unlikely to ever see a museum, pieces whose provenance is already unknown, and I buy them. Then I donate them anonymously to museums around the world."

His words spilled out like a confession, but Kallie set her pastry down to take his hands again. "That's—that's incredible, Dimitri."

"I know how strongly you feel about illegal trade, but somehow finding things with lost

340

histories and giving them a home has given my life purpose."

Giving a home to things with lost histories. Did that include women? The thought should have made her feel like a project. Instead the word *home* echoed in her heart.

"You're too hard on yourself." She smiled at him. "You're a good man, Dimitri Andreas."

His shoulders dropped, and she felt the tension leave his hands. But that wasn't all of it, not all of his confession. There had to be more.

Instead of continuing though, he grinned. "I was worried you'd think the worst of me."

She picked up a cream puff and held it to his lips. "Well, I don't. I think the best of you. Have a cream puff."

He laughed and took the pastry, licking powdered sugar from his lips. "And don't tell me that I'm too hard on myself. What about you?"

"Yes? What about me?"

"When we first met you had me convinced you belonged in an office. And yet here you are, fighting off kidnappers, getting stranded in the desert, getting *shot* at—and still not giving up!"

She reached for her hot chocolate, and he grabbed her hand, turned it outward to reveal the inside of her arm. His voice was low and soft. "You're like these wrists, Kallie. Damaged somehow, but still so incredibly strong. Smart and passionate *and* strong. As I knew you were the moment we met."

She pulled her hand from his and cradled the cup, staring into the chocolate depths. "Thank you."

The silence lengthened between them, but it was not an awkward silence. It was a silence in which something was built, a connection that could not be ignored, building until she could hardly bear it.

"Kallie—" He reached for her once more, his voice so raw with emotion it terrified her, but she pulled her arms back, tucked her hands under the table, kept her eyes on its stripes.

He was still hiding things. And her past was still a blank. Until those two things were resolved, nothing more could be between them. She would have no more secrets, no unknowns.

He reached again, this time for her cheek.

She shook her head and turned away.

He leaned in and shoved aside the plate of pastries, as if he read her thoughts. "Why not?" He flattened a palm against the table, rattling the cups and saucers. "Why not?"

She raised her eyes, let him feel the depth of her conviction. "Because I will not live with secrets and questions. Secrets and questions are all I can remember. I will not add to them."

His jaw tightened, the muscles bulging. "And you think I have secrets."

"I know you do."

"Ask, then." He sat back in his chair, braced his palms against the edge of the table. "Ask whatever you want."

She inhaled. Really?

"Why did you not return from Europe until your father, your entire family, was gone? What were you doing all those years, besides buying antiquities? Why are you so fascinated with the Minoan culture—so desperate to find the Linear A Key?" She stopped, breathless.

"Are you finished?" His lips were drawn into a scowl.

"For now."

She expected glib answers. She expected evasion. She did not expect him to deflate, to drop his head into his hands—hands that were now rigid with tension.

He was muttering again. "I can't do this. I can't do this any longer."

"Dimitri, I'm sorry—"

"No." He looked up, grabbed her arms just below the elbows.

She clasped her hands around his forearms, as well. Something was about to change.

His voice was so soft she had to lean in to hear him.

"There is no one alive who knows what I'm about to tell you, Kallie. All these years I have never trusted anyone enough to admit the truth."

She kept silent, letting him say it, willing him to say it.

"I am not Dimitri Andreas."

She rocked backward, but he did not release her arms. "Wh—what? Who are you?"

He looked into her eyes, deeper than anyone ever had. "I have no idea."

⇢ 28 ⇠

The café spun, the street, all of Venice—the world spun around Kallie's head until a blackness grabbed at the edges of her vision, and still Dimitri gripped her arms.

Her vision cleared, and she focused on his face, his beautiful, deceitful face.

"I'm sorry, Kallie. I'm sorry I couldn't tell you sooner. I have trouble . . . trouble trusting people."

His hands were warm but firm on her arms, and she couldn't wiggle free. "With a secret like that? Who could you trust?"

"Do you see now? Do you see we are connected, somehow?"

She breathed through her mouth. When would she regain her balance? "It is a wild coincidence, but—"

"Seven years."

"What?"

"Seven years ago I woke up in a museum in Prague, naked and with no memory."

Her breath left her in a *whoosh*. All the air from her lungs was sucked out by this revelation.

She yanked her arms away now, covered her face with her hands. Was she rocking? "What does it mean, Dimitri? What does it mean?"

He pulled his chair around the table, turned her until their knees were interlocked and his hands were on her shoulders. "I don't know. I only know we share a past somehow, we share this crazy passion for ancient Greek, and that from the first moment I met you, I felt as if we belonged together. I felt as if I had come home."

She lurched into his arms. What wondrous words. *Belong. Home.* She could not remember ever belonging to anyone. She felt as if she could fall into him and never emerge.

But she must be strong. She must stay on her own journey, see it through. Dr. Newsom would not approve. But neither would he believe the connection between them.

She pulled away. "How—how did you become Dimitri Andreas?"

"He was my first friend in Prague. He'd already been traveling Europe for ten years by then, estranged from his father and with no other family. When he heard my story, he began telling people we were brothers. We resembled each other, and it was believable. I took his last name since I had none. It just seemed right. And then—then he got sick." The hoarseness of emotion returned to Dimitri's voice. "I begged him to go back to the States, get good medical care, reconcile with his father. But he wouldn't. And when he died—when he died, there was some mix-up and some people thought I was him, and it seemed the easiest thing to simply *become* him."

He swiped at his eyes. "Now you will surely think me a cheat. To come back and take all that money." He ran a hand through his hair. "So much money."

She touched his face with her fingertips. "You're giving it all away, aren't you?"

He shrugged. "Does it matter? It's not charity if you've stolen it first."

"It matters." She smiled. "You're a good man. Whoever you are."

He reached up to take her fingers and brought them to his lips. "And you're an amazing woman. Whoever you are."

They walked back to the hotel, arm in arm, and Kallie let her head drop to Dimitri's shoulder, let herself have this one night to believe that everything would work out.

When they reached the street where their hotel fronted the Grand Canal, Dimitri pulled her into the lamplight, lifted her chin, and kissed her.

She returned the kiss, let it linger, pulled away, and searched his eyes.

He stroked her cheek and wrapped a strong arm around her shoulders.

The walk to the hotel had felt like a blissful, magical dream.

Abruptly, Kallie shook her mind free. No, this wasn't right. He might be thinking it was a beginning, but to her, it was an end. She would not let him get this close again, not until she had pushed through. She was so close to remembering, to understanding, she could feel it. Understanding for both of them. Even on separate continents, something unknown had forged a link between them. An almost mythic, supernatural link. And she had to figure it out before she could continue playing the role of someone she was not. She was too unsettled, too confused . . . now even more so.

In this city of masks, they had both found a way to remove their own. She would not pretend again.

She stopped him from taking her upstairs, still outside the doors, and kissed him again. This time on the cheek. "Good night, Dimitri."

And she left him there, outside the Hotel Danieli. A quick look back from inside the lobby revealed him under the streetlamp, staring out at the Grand Canal.

She turned and fled to her room.

⇴ 29 ⇷

The sun rose behind the spires of St. Mark's Basilica and cast slender shadow-fingers down the length of the piazza, reaching the shaded portico along the south side where Kallie sat at a small table outside the Caffé Florian.

Elbows propped on the marble tabletop, she adjusted her sunglasses and studied the early crowds that half filled the square, intent on their morning coffee or a full day of sightseeing. She wore a wide-brimmed hat above the glasses. Ridiculous, with the sun barely risen and her table in the shade. But Dimitri had insisted on the "disguise" since she refused to remain hidden in the hotel. After last night's rebuff, she didn't have the heart to argue.

A waiter emerged from the arched entrance to the café's murky interior. Dark pants, crisp white jacket over a white shirt, black bow tie. The impeccable uniform confirmed the pricey nature of the establishment.

Dimitri said he would meet her here, a favorite spot of his. They had all but abandoned Caroline, Yoshi, and Erik to sightseeing in Venice. Somehow the further this adventure took the two of them, the more it seemed meant for only them.

"Caffè, *signorina*?"

Kallie nodded. *"Sì, per favore."* The tantalizing aroma drifted as he poured, mingling with the smells of Venice into something wonderfully European.

She searched the crowds again, but not for Dimitri's face. Did a crazed woman with a tiny silver pistol still roam the city, looking for her?

Her journal and pen lay at the edge of the table, beside the steaming coffee. She rubbed a chilled finger over the embossed cover.

Everything seemed so close now, so . . . *inevitable.* Dimitri would surely return with news of Stella's Greek collector and his whereabouts. And the writing—her story—it was poised on the brink of a breakthrough, she could feel it.

The morning breeze brushed her hair across her neck and the campanile bells rang out the top of the hour, echoing across the piazza. The crowd seemed to pause as one, with a breathless glance at the bell tower, then continue its mission.

Her phone rang.

She checked the number before answering. "Dr. Newsom!"

"Hello, Kallie. Or should I say, *'Ciao'*?"

She smiled. "Ciao. Isn't it the middle of the night there?"

"I'm working late, yes. I wanted to catch you before your day got started."

"You got my e-mail?"

"I did. You have time to talk?"

Kallie scanned the square once more, looking beyond her perfect grid of white tables and sunny yellow chairs, past the flower carts that lined the square. No sign of Dimitri or her attacker. "I hope you didn't stay up late just for me."

"There is some pretty interesting stuff here in this chapter."

Her waiter set down a silver platter loaded with ceramic dishes of olives, cheeses, and nuts. Kallie paused until the waiter moved on. "I'm getting somewhere, you think?"

"Indeed. This last one is quite revealing. Leaving the village. Facing your enemy. How do you feel about it?"

She sipped the bold coffee, still scalding. "Not sure what the deal is with the sister."

"No? It seems your earlier antagonist, who was more of a nuisance, has become your nemesis."

"It also seems a little sick that it's my *sister,* don't you think?" A flock of pigeons fluttered to the gray stone of the piazza, pecking and searching.

"No, not sick. Informative. Things are heating up, Kallie. You're getting so close now, and your Shadow self, who has *literally* shadowed you to the Great Cavern, is trying to keep you from learning the truth, trying to tempt you into taking the easy way out."

She leaned her shoulder against the outer wall

of the café, brushing the quaintly peeling paint merging past and present. "Perhaps it's a warning I should heed."

"You know better."

"Do I? I can't escape this sense of guilt, Doctor. What if I suddenly remember and it's not some horrible thing that was done to me, but it's some-thing I did to someone else?"

"Perhaps you had no choice."

"Like a soldier traumatized by his actions in war?"

"You won't know unless you enter the cavern. Face the beast."

Her fingers ached from her tight grip on the phone. "I'm not sure I have the strength."

"Are you kidding? Look at how strong you've already been, fighting off your Shadow. You've disarmed her, tied her up, left her behind. You're ready, Kallie. Ready to find the truth."

She fought the constriction in her chest, flexed her tight fingers. "I'm terrified."

"So embrace the terror. Focus on it. Let it build like water behind a dam until it's unbearable. Then open the floodgates and see where it takes you."

Her gaze wandered along the brown-and-white diamond pattern of the tiled floor, advancing toward the basilica and, to its right, the Doge's Palace. "You would think after being chased and shot at, writing a story would seem like a pleasure cruise."

"What?" Newsom's shock reached across the ocean. "You were *shot* at?"

She chuckled, bent her head to hide beneath the hat's brim, and gave him the brief details of yesterday's incident. "We'll be leaving Venice soon, though, so we'll be fine."

"Kallie—"

Something about his tone chilled her, something more than worry for her safety.

"Did—did anyone else see this woman who attacked you?"

"See her? Well, Dimitri might have seen her—well, no. Not exactly."

"Has it occurred to you how similar this event seems to the story you've been writing?"

Kallie placed her palm flat against the cool marble of the table. From the entrance to the café's interior her white-jacketed server stood with three of his coworkers. He watched her with dark eyes. Waiting. For the lunch crowd, or a signal for more coffee, or some gesture of need. Perhaps for her to panic at the implications of her overseas shrink.

Yes, she had thought about it. Tried not to think about it. Events in her life were starting to *mimic* her story, instead of the story leading her forward. It was very unsettling.

"Have you been having any other hallucinations?"

"Any other *hallucinations?* No! No, this was *real,* Doctor!"

Wait—was it? They had been alone in the Hall of the Inquisitors. She had fled before the woman might have been apprehended by security guards. Had she imagined the attack?

A flush began at her chest and bloomed across her throat and face. What would Dimitri think?

Was she was alone on a precipice, balanced over the abyss of insanity?

"Kallie, I don't want you to worry. But I think it's best if you stick close to your team until this thing is over."

Until this thing is over. Again, the sense of the inevitable, of the tide of memory pulling her out to sea, of the fated future waiting to claim her. She pulled the sunglasses from her face and rubbed her eyes. "I'll try."

"And don't stop writing."

She disconnected and dropped the phone to the table. The pigeons scattered with noisy squawks and wing-flapping, drawing her eyes to the basilica.

The domes and spires and round-arched portals of the massive thousand-year-old church seemed to promise peace with God inside its medieval depths, despite the Last Judgment mosaic above the central arch. Kallie followed the lavish gilt ornamentation with her eyes. Did the architects and artists believe their promise?

She checked the time. How much longer until Dimitri joined her? The other café patrons seemed to watch her and whisper with heads together, and the horns of boats on the Grand Canal signaled danger.

Paranoia started to rise within her—but perhaps unfounded, if Newsom was correct. Nothing and no one chased her except her own shrouded past.

She found the pen in her hand, the coffee and silver platter pushed aside.

"Let it build like water behind a dam."

Or like leaning over a bridge, waiting to fall.

She teetered there, at the edge of the bridge, hand on the floodgates. Felt the fear build and hold.

Breathless, dizzy, hands slick with perspiration, she opened the journal. Her heart pounded and pulse fluttered, yet it seemed as though the blood in her veins had ceased to flow as well, building up, expanding in her chest, unbearable with the suspended breath before an inescapable plunge.

The instant her pen touched the paper, the dam broke and the blood rushed through her veins into her arms, her hand, her fingers, and onto the page, with words surging from her like one possessed.

Somewhere along the San Marcos Piazza, musicians began to play, a swell of music that built and peaked and released, underscoring the words that poured forth . . .

⇥ 30 ⇤

My anger at Melayna's betrayal, at her hatred toward me, fueled my entrance into the Great Cavern. I stopped only to prepare a torch, soak it with oil, and strike it aflame with a flint, then passed into the cavern's dark mouth with a certainty I had not felt since riding from the royal palace. This labor, this challenge, it was *my* destiny, not Melayna's. It was *my* role to earn redemption, not hers—she who had done nothing to harm our people, and nothing to save, either.

The celebrated entrance was no more than an opening in a knoll, crumbling and matted with roots. I passed through, the blackness blotting out the moon overhead. Blood *whooshed* against my eardrums in a pulsing rhythm, and my pouch dug sharp edges into my shoulder's flesh. I hesitated at the lip of the cavern, listening beyond the whisper of trees outside, beyond the blood in my ears, into the depths of the entrance. Listening for small creatures or one large beast. I heard nothing.

An arc of the torch revealed a single tunnel, its roof high enough at its beginning for me to walk upright. I stepped forward, torch thrust ahead, hardening my resolve with reminders of destiny. My hand shook with fear and fury. But deep in my heart, a confidence was growing. I had surmounted many challenges to reach this cavern. Why should I not also retrieve the Horn and save my people?

The walls of the tunnel brushed my elbows, slimy with the dripping accumulation of centuries. The torch popped and sizzled with moisture and gave me light enough to see a pebble's throw ahead, to note the downward slope of the tunnel floor. Within minutes, I had no backward view of the entrance. I had been swallowed by the mountain.

The air was heavy with a bone-needling chill. I shivered and kept the torch as close as I dared, but then pushed it forward again when the tunnel disappeared into darkness. The orange-yellow flames reflected from the walls, hideous shadows flickering across frozen waterfalls of stone that had hardened into columns. My footfalls should have echoed, but they were absorbed by clammy air. The tunnel smelled of decay and animal stink. I kept my eyes wide for signs of the living things that made that stink.

Ahead, the tunnel split. Diverged into three paths, presenting me with an impossible choice. I aimed the torch at each tunnel in turn, its flames vibrating in my trembling hand.

The labyrinth begins.

How many more branches would be presented? If I found the beast and retrieved the Horn of

Truth, would I then wander forever, lost in the cavern's depths?

I fished out my second length of rope, a narrow red twine still coiled in my pouch. The paint I had planned to give Andreas would do no good if the torch failed, so I had devised this second plan.

Not yet. I would not begin to mark my path yet—not until I was convinced I could remember no more branches behind.

How much time passed as I ventured deeper in the cavern? With no sun or moon to mark the hours and every step an eternity, I could not say. The floor, slick and smooth, continued its downward plunge into blackness, and I fought to retain my footing, and my composure. Water had eroded paths like tree roots through the mountain, and whenever the tunnel branched I kept to the left, so that returning would be a simple matter of choosing the right. I came upon a crossroads that joined at least six tunnels, the leftmost one a dead end at a blank wall. I retreated, unwound my twine, and secured one end around the largest rock I could find. A flutter of claustrophobia at the thought of coming to the end of my lead somewhere deeper in the mountain shook my fingers and burned in my throat. I tied off the rope and moved into the next tunnel, carefully playing it out behind me.

The gradual awareness of sound stole over me like night falling—nearly imperceptible as it advanced but then erupted full upon me. The sound of scraping. Footsteps perhaps. And another sound, its tenor low and urgent, like the mutterings of a madman.

I drew myself up, torch wobbling, and listened.

Yes, muttering. Human speech. More than one human. Advancing toward me.

Heat rushed through my limbs and dampened my forehead and neck. A nausea born of both fear and hope churned in my belly. Should I call out or should I take cover?

But there could be no hiding without extinguishing my torch, and this I would not do. Instead, I held it aloft, faced the sound, and waited.

The murmurs grew no louder, and from the sound of them they seemed to be echoing in a larger space than where I stood. I shuffled forward, gripping my torch. The tunnel opened into a larger cavern, lifting some of my oppression. Yet at the same time, I could still hear the echoes of speech mingled with a low moaning. The hair on my arms tingled. I gulped in a breath of stale air and ventured a question.

"Who is there?"

My voice had the effect of a heavy blanket thrown over the voices. Silence met my inquiry, complete and hollow.

And then I saw them. Eyes squinting and blinking against the torchlight and pale, pale faces half turned and frightened. Five, no six men—with tattered clothing and jerky movements, huddled together and eyeing me with suspicion.

Their muttering began again, all of them at once, with lips barely moving. *Who is she? What is she? Why has she come? Does she know?*

I took a step forward, waved the torch, and they shrank back as one. "Who are you?" I studied each for a familiar face.

"Who are you?" One of them had spoken, as if for the group. Did he merely parrot my words as a lunatic might?

"Chloe. Daughter of King Galenus and Queen Harmonia."

He gasped—they all did—and leaned toward me. Several lifted bony hands as if to touch me for reassurance, but we were separated by the cavern.

I turned to the one who had spoken. "Are you —are you looking for the beast?"

He nodded slowly. "The Horn of Truth. We are finding the Horn of Truth. For the hand of the princess."

I blinked. The words were delivered in a tone both empty and distant, as if he had been repeating them so long he'd forgotten their meaning.

"How long have you been searching?"

"We are finding the Horn of Truth. For the hand of the princess."

I advanced on the group slowly, keeping contact with my gaze. "Have you not given up? Are you lost?"

None answered, and I suspected if they had, it would be with the same empty phrase.

How had they survived this long? The waxiness of skin and revulsion toward light spoke of weeks underground, yet I saw no supplies, no food or water.

Remembering they had spoken to each other with some clarity when I first arrived, I tried again. "I have come to find the beast myself, and to retrieve the Horn of Truth. There is no need for you to continue." I held up the coil of twine, pointed to its stretched-out length behind me. "Take hold here, and follow the rope until you reach the end. Then take each right-hand tunnel and you will find the open air."

"We are finding the Horn of Truth. For the hand—"

"Yes, yes, I know. But it is over now."

At this declaration, their mouths went slack and eyes blank. Perhaps I should not have spoken harshly.

"It is never over."

The simple phrase, uttered by their spokesman, ran a chill through me—a foreboding as of a prophecy—and I believed him. Somehow, in some inhuman way, they were trapped here, existing beyond the requirements of the living,

360

yet not dead. Doomed to wander endlessly, ever-believing they would find what they sought. Unending torture, like Sisyphus, cursed by the gods to each day push his boulder up the hill and each night watch it roll down.

"You—you can still escape . . ." And yet, I knew the words were futile.

Instead, I must push past, continue with my own quest, with the hope that my success might somehow benefit these lost ones.

I moved toward them, toward the large tunnel where they huddled, but they did not move, even when my torch grew near.

Then one of them, a tallish man with flesh hanging in folds where there had once been fat and muscle, grabbed the torch from me. Two others circled my arms with bony fingers.

"You will help us." This from several, as though they had become one mind.

"No." I tried to wriggle free. "No, I must continue on my own."

They would not release me. I looked into the empty eyes of each. "You are getting nowhere. You are wandering in circles!"

No response. I had been gentle with my resistance, treating their mental weakness as though it were physical. But I could not allow them to pull me into their delusion.

I kicked and clawed and twisted from their weakened grasp, snatched my torch, retrieved my rope from the cavern floor, and backed into the largest of the branching tunnels, holding the flame between myself and the men. "Follow the rope to the outside!" I yelled again, even though they would surely ignore my entreaty.

I continued walking backward until the fear of the unknown behind me outpaced my fear of the lost suitors, and I turned to face the tunnels.

Too soon my length of twine came to its end. I suppressed the panic that threatened to well up and overflow my courage and searched for a rock to weight its end, then several more large stones to build a low barrier across the tunnel, high enough to trip over. If I should chance to return, and without a torch, I did not want to miss the end of the rope and wander into the wrong branch.

This accomplished, I pressed forward with as much focus as I could bring to my surroundings, memorizing each step.

The sound of men came again on the heavy air, from ahead. Had they taken a different route and advanced past me? But these sounds were different, not fretful muttering but low moans of despair and hopelessness.

Shaking with a premonition of evil, I breached the large cavern, brandished the torch in a frantic arc, and took in all I could at once.

The ceiling was high—too high for the light to illuminate—the stone room vast, black, and musty. To my left, a narrow channel of brackish water gushed. Opposite my position, on the right, a small tunnel opened and an orange glow emanated, an evil shade of orange with nothing of firelight's usual warmth.

And against the back wall, another group of men, as shocked to see me as the first.

I advanced, squaring shoulders and narrowing my eyes. These would not lay hands on me as the previous group had done.

But their faces did not have the empty, staring looks of heedless wandering, the self-deception I had seen in the others who still believed they would someday find the Horn of Truth.

Instead, a snarling anger twisted their features into masks of half-men, half-animal. They paced and stared, like large cats with eyes on an enemy. Like starving beasts surprised by the sudden appearance of prey.

A weakness throbbed through my limbs, a trembling sort of frailty. I lowered the torch, backed against the cavern's entrance, thought to go another way.

But that far tunnel and its orange glow . . . This was no random cavern where these men had amassed. Something existed beyond, and to go back would be to give up.

"Is it—is the beast there?" I pointed, watching for signs of humanity in the men. There were perhaps a dozen, all with twisted expressions of fear and hate and anger. And despair. Above all, it was despair that tinged their skin with the pallor of hopelessness and clouded their eyes with vice.

My voice broke through their surprise. They leaned toward me, held by invisible bonds, then stretched and sprang, hands outstretched like claws, teeth bared, gurgling with deep-throated growls.

I gasped, stumbled backward, thrust my torch between us. All for naught. A moment later I was at their feet. Greedy hands probed and tore my clothing, picked at my hair, snatched away my pouch. A grimy finger was thrust into my mouth and I gagged, spitting and twisting my face to the muck beneath my body.

Their moans swelled to shrieks and mingled with my own, and I felt their despair leech into my skin, into my blood, into my soul.

Hopeless, useless, cursed. Why had I come? At the edge of the beast's lair but no closer to truth. I had entered full of my own success in the forest, in the village, and against Melayna, believing I could accomplish what no one else could. Ever the foolish and arrogant child who had brought destruction to my people.

They dragged my body to the rock wall, like an animal brings its kill to its den. My torch was brought, and they waved it with grimaces of pleasure, creasing their filthy, misshapen faces, and contemplated me with intent I could not read.

How long since they had eaten? Did the beast require sacrifice? Would I become as they, my humanity lost?

This, then, was all that was left to me.

Redemption could not be earned.

There was only the self-deceptive, endless wandering of the men I'd met or the honest descent into depravity of these half-men.

Propped against the wall, I watched them circle, my muscles turning to water and my bones withered. They produced a rope from somewhere and secured me with it, then growled and hissed among themselves in a language I did not understand. I searched each face for humanity, for pity, and found none.

Beyond them, across the cavern, the fiery glow of that chasm persisted, drawing my eyes. Its heat seemed to lick my skin, its flickering fingers pulled at my flesh.

What purpose these creatures had for me, I did not know.

But somehow, somehow I knew the burning pit would be my end.

→ 31 ←

Kallie shoved the journal across the table, jostling the silver tray of nuts and olives. She reached for the coffee. Maybe it would help the unbelievable thirst. Her hand shook, rattling the cup against the tray.

What kind of sick story was she writing?

Her ramblings had taken a turn for the bizarre. Was it a sign she had grown close to the truth? Whatever lay in the burning pit beyond the dark cavern must be the awful truth her subconscious had sought to repress all these years.

And here she was, working hard to dig it out.

Could one be traitorous to one's own self? What would happen if it finally emerged?

"Caffè?" Her waiter had returned, crisp and starched, at peace with himself.

She lifted a trembling hand. "No. *Grazie.*" Enough caffeine.

The square had filled with tourists while she'd been buried in her journal. She checked the time. Where was Dimitri? The bell tower chimed another hour past, and the deep gongs shuddered in her chest in counterpoint with her heavy heartbeat. The sun beat against the gray stones of San Marcos Square, but her toes and fingers were chilled.

Uncovering the truth might drive her over the edge of sanity, but hovering here at the brink was little better.

She fished a few euros from her bag and dropped them to the silver tray, then fled into the square. Dimitri would call her if he didn't find her at their meeting place. She had to move, to do something. Anything.

The massive domes and spires of the cathedral at the end of the square beckoned again with their promise of tranquility. No one visited Venice without touring St. Mark's Basilica. Yoshi, Caroline, and Erik had visited yesterday. Would a stroll through its gilded depths offer some measure of peace for her inner turmoil?

A line meandered from the entrance. Meager, since tourist season was not yet in full swing. She hurried across the square and claimed a place at the end. Those ahead of her seemed quiet—in comparison to the flock of tourists pushing past —as though preparing for an experience of the sacred and holy. Her heart reached out for the same . . . for something to quell the distressing anxiety her writing had caused, to offer relief from the precipitous fear of terrifying revelation.

She scanned the opulent exterior of the Byzantine church, a symbol of Venetian wealth and power for over a thousand years, and recalled the tour book's bullet-pointed facts. The structure had begun more humbly, with Venetian merchants bringing back the bodily remains of the Gospel-writer Mark from Alexandria and installing them in the church. Over the centuries, a plethora of mismatched stone columns and elaborately carved friezes had been plundered from a host of ancient buildings, brought to this crossroads port of the world, and evolved into this expanding beauty. East met West in an explosion of Greek-Byzantine extravagance that rightly earned its nickname *Chiese d'Oro*— "Church of Gold." The lower register of arched portals was topped by an upper marble-faced exterior and elegant, lofty spires jutted into the sky surrounding five huge gray domes.

She reached the interior quickly. An English-speaking tour group clustered to her right, in the long atrium inside the front doors.

"Over forty-thousand square feet of mosaics cover the walls, vaults, and cupolas of the basilica." The guide gracefully waved her arm overhead. She had straight dark hair hanging down her back, flawless skin, and perfect teeth. It seemed only right that she blended into the breathtaking atmosphere. Kallie edged closer to the group, then followed the girl's upraised hand to the atrium's front line of cupolas above, each splashed with gold and bronze and encrusted with gems.

"Here in the atrium we find a series of mosaics telling the stories of the Old Testament, from

Creation through Abraham, Joseph, and Moses. When we move into the main body of the basilica, the story moves into the New Testament and beyond, recounting the Gospel."

The group of about fifteen stood with mouths agape at what their guide suggested was only a sort of "prologue" to what they were about to see. Already it staggered the imagination to take in the abundance of fantastically skilled artwork. Kallie traced the story with her eyes, from Adam and Eve, to Cain and Abel, Noah's Flood, the Tower of Babel. She knew the broad strokes of the Old Testament from her years of ancient studies.

Their guide gave a little chuckle of amusement. "It's ironic, really. These mosaics were created to relate the biblical stories to the illiterate masses. Now the masses can read, but we've largely lost our ability to understand art."

But Kallie understood it. It flowed through her in an almost physical way, this ancient story of the Judeo-Christian God reaching out to man. It carried her thoughts and emotions into the current. She followed the silent group into the cross-shaped cathedral. The long, central nave branched into left and right transepts. Chapels and altars lined the walls and multiple choir lofts perched in tiny balconies, all rising to the lofty heights of five domes, with their intricate mosaics on gold backgrounds. The grandeur stirred Kallie's heart, and she could almost hear medieval participants singing out the rest of the story begun in the atrium.

Tourists kept to carpeted runners that marked out paths on the tessellated floors, only partly covering the exquisite geometric patterns. Across the vast space of flooring, all manner of birds and animals—peacocks and eagles, doves and foxes—intertwined with the loops and spirals in a dizzying display that drew her through its puzzling paths. Kallie trailed her fingers over the red velvet rope anchored to wrought-iron stanchions that blocked the majority of the cathedral from the casual touch of years of visitors. Their guide hummed along, pointing out mosaics of Mary and Jesus, of early church fathers and of Mark the Evangelist, whose remains even now supposedly lay in the crypt under their feet.

The cathedral smelled of Venice and tourists, mingled with incense and smoke, and Kallie scuffed along the carpet, longing to feel the gold under her fingertips, to absorb some of the holy awe that lay heavy on the place. A low hum undulating through the cathedral came from visitors paying homage to this place where the divine seemed to touch the human.

It was a story that was the same, and yet so different, than the scattered and fragmented Greco-Roman mythology she'd immersed herself in for years. In this awesome place, it seemed as though there had always been this one story, this true story, and all the rest merely the lightest touch of searching fingers, a glancing brush of man's imagination against the truth, leaving the seeker stained with the colors of it, with the beauty of its essence—but not its entirety.

Did every heart yearn for God and seek to know him? Was the world, as it seemed, teeming with the overwhelming reality and presence of the divine, with a mystical significance that could not be ignored? Kallie's question was not whether the myths could be believed, but only—*which one?*

The crypt under the altar in the front apse of the building drew only a passing comment from their guide. A powerful desire to descend into the crypt, to experience the focal point and heart of the basilica, swept Kallie. Visions of the fiery cavern of her story mingled with the idea of the burial crypt and her breathing grew shallow with tension and foreboding. She must see it. She must see the crypt.

The group's eyes were trained on the guide. She scanned the cavernous cathedral. Tourists wandered on their own, keeping to assigned paths, ignoring all but the mosaics. Her shoulders tightened and her heart pounded uncontrollably. Fantasy and reality blurred, as though the convoluted designs at her feet pulled her through the labyrinth to face the beast underground. Without another glance and with little thought of risk, she slipped from the group, toward the front of the cathedral. The echoing cries of the Great Cavern's prisoners beat against her ears, and she clawed at her constricted throat.

There were steps. A small door. Unlocked. So easy? The pressure of countless tons of gold and marble bore down on Kallie, thickening her blood and slowing her heart.

She stood within a small chapel, three naves and an apse, arched stone above columns, all tan and white and brick, with a brown-and-white geometric marbled floor. Ornate by ordinary standards, its gilding paled in comparison with what lay above. Daylight filtered from an opening to the cathedral above and spilled over the altar, creating whispery corners of shadows and light, pulling Kallie into its depths.

Alone, unknown, unmissed. She drifted through the crypt, let the fear and the knowledge she had fought for seven years fill up the empty spaces within.

Just as today, no one had ever missed her. No one had ever looked for her. Whatever happened to her seven years ago, she might as well have fallen into a cavern, or into a crypt. She was unmourned, unloved, alone. She gave permission to the pain, opened herself to it, let it shout and scream and smother her with its truth. The sorrow swamped her soul, and she reached for a wall to steady her wobbling legs.

Will they throw her to the beast, deep in this crypt?

Kallie shook her head, violent and swift, to disconnect fact from fiction, reality from distortion.

Sanity from psychosis.

The two would not yield, welded together and inseparable, and she was slipping, slipping to her knees beside the wall, her fingers scratching at the rubbled brick.

Oh, God, what is happening to me?

The story was writing itself. Scribbling across her brain with an invisible pen.

The cavern, its half-human prisoners, hovering with whispered musings and malformed faces. The ropes binding her, digging at her skin.

How long? How long must I lie at their mercy?

Struggling against the bindings, frantic, the taste of metal, sharp breaths through the mouth. Did minutes pass? Hours? The ropes burned, burned like flames against her wrists, raising welts and then drawing blood.

Must get free. Must get loose before they decide.

At the base of the wall, she drew legs to chest, tightened shivering arms, bent face to knees, stifling a scream. She felt the ropes even now, raging against her wrists, but she did not look. Would the pink scars glisten with fresh blood? She rocked against the stones, fighting the shallowness of breath that threatened to steal her consciousness.

But what was this consciousness? Where did she exist in the realm between the real and the unreal? Did she exist at all?

Who am I? Who am I?

The question was the beat of her heart, the pounding in her veins, the breath in her chest. She was at once both hot and cold, both present and absent. Buried and alive.

They are dragging me now. Dragging me, screaming, kicking, toward the fire.

A sacrifice to the beast. No Horn of Truth. No redemption. Only the hungry glow of terror, the pit of the Underworld, waiting to swallow. Fear and shock mingled, driving out memory and sanity and hope. Only grief and hopelessness remained. The fearsome faces of the prisoners twisted in ugly laughter. The orange-yellow light blinding her eyes.

No! Do not push me through!

But the cavern floor dropped away, replaced by a shroud of warm air and darkness and empty floating, floating. The air grew faster, hotter, beating against skin with tongues of fire while the floating turned to falling. Falling without end.

So this is death.

But death bottomed out.

A jolt, a deadening *thump* against frozen ground that stole her breath and sent sharp stabs of pain through her limbs. The air was cool and dry and dark. Small points of light, far off, stretched to play against marble statues. Could this be the Underworld? More like palace than pit, silent as the grave but a silence born of peace, not loss.

And then she knew.

She knew. And the truth slammed against her with a force that could obliterate worlds, that indeed *had* obliterated her world.

She scrabbled to her feet, braced herself against the bricks, sucked in deep breaths of the crypt air, all the while her mind—her memory—playing over that twilight morning, seven years ago.

The prisoners of the Great Cavern, those helpless, hopeless suitors, had pushed her into the mouth of the beast.

And she had awakened on the floor of a New York City museum.

Black spots burst behind her vision. Hyperventilating.

She had to get out of here.

She ran, ran for the tiny door that had allowed her access to the crypt.

Locked.

She pounded a flat palm against the wood, heedless of the consequences. The black spots turned to silver stars, pinpricks of cold metal at the edges of her sight.

It can't be.

"Help! I'm locked down here!" She jiggled the

latch, willing it to release, unreasonable panic bursting in her chest and spreading like heat through her arms and legs.

The door sucked open a moment later, revealing the shocked face of a security guard. "Signorina! *Non potete*—"

She did not stay to hear the rest. A quick shove and she lunged up the narrow flight of steps to the cathedral floor, then fled toward the front entrance, past the entering visitors, out into the square, into the crowds.

To be lost in the crowds, to be grounded in this time, this place, before her mind splintered into a thousand shards, was all she wanted.

She stood in the blinding midday Venice sun, in the center of San Marcos Square, turning circles, unseeing, thoughts racing against the truth.

The truth.

I am Chloe. Princess of Kalliste.

No one was searching for her, this much was true.

It is I who am searching. For the Horn of Truth. And for Andreas.

She staggered against the stones beneath her feet, caught herself against a stranger.

Searching.

For Dimitri.

⇀ 32 ↽

She fixed her eyes on the bell tower, on the rise of its orange-tan bricks that remained steady while anchored to this floating, undulating city, and tried to will stability into her own shaking legs. The tourists flowed and jostled around her, a twisting, spinning chaos, and she reached out once more, needing a tether to keep her from plummeting to the stones.

Her hand found empty air, and she leaned to her right, letting that outstretched hand lead her across the square, to the first café with outdoor seating. She grasped the metal back of a bright yellow chair, dragged it across the stones, and sank into its solid embrace.

The Horn of Truth. The beast. Here? In this time?

Andreas is alive. Did Dimitri keeps secrets from her still? Or did he speak the truth of his own loss of memory?

The Linear A Key—it must be the Horn of Truth.

She propped her elbows on the table and braced her forehead against her palms. It was too much, all of this at once. She seemed to be plunging into depths too dark to navigate, then soaring, returning to take deep gulps of Venice air.

Tears dripped to the white metal table. Was she crying? She ran her palm along her cheek and it came back wet.

Relief. It was the soul-fatiguing sense of relief that brought the tears. Relief that washed over her heart and filled up the empty places. The unknown past, the hollow isolation of not belonging anywhere, to anyone—it slipped away with the tide. She wrapped her arms around herself.

She did belong. To Kalliste. To Andreas.

The dizzy sensation of tumbling did not abate, but it was like falling from a great height and being surprised by a soft landing. Like staggering through a violent storm and pushing open the door to home.

She must call Dimitri. Andreas. Her thoughts swirled into an eddy of confusion, tried to gain a foothold. She still felt more Kallie than Chloe, at least sitting here at a Venice café in San Marcos Square. And Dimitri—it seemed right to call him by the name he'd chosen here. They would not be Chloe and Andreas until they returned home with the Horn of Truth.

She pulled her phone from her bag and scrolled through her contacts to dial his number. What would he say when she explained? Would he think her explanation of their shared past insane, or would the truth awaken him, the way she had awakened in the crypt? Her thumb hesitated over the green button.

If only she could speak with the Oracle first.

Like another wave, memory slammed her backward against her chair. The phone clattered to the stones, bounced and slid, and Kallie watched it, open mouthed and unable to react.

Judith.

That last morning on the High Place, when the Oracle had challenged her to pursue the Horn of Truth for her people. Even now in her memory she could see the gray-streaked hair under the black hood, the sea-blue eyes piercing her, the craggy face etched with the wisdom of years. Judith's face.

How could this be? She had followed Andreas into the Great Cavern, where they had both fallen through to this time, this place, but the Oracle as well? Did Judith know?

A nearby café patron picked up Kallie's phone and reached across to return it to her. She nodded her thanks, then cycled back through her contacts to find Judith's number. There was only an instant of delay before the ring reached across the ocean. Amazing.

"Kallista?" Judith's shrill voice was unmistakable.

She had given no thought to what she would say if Judith answered. The words came anyway. "It's Chloe."

Judith's quick intake of breath was audible across the sea.

She knew. Judith knew.

The woman's words were both a sigh and a celebration. "At last."

"I don't understand any of this—Judith—I need you to explain." The name felt right and yet strange, but she knew no other name for the Oracle.

"There are many things that cannot be explained, child. You must know only that this test has been apportioned to you, and you must pass through it." Her tone was softer than it had ever been these seven years. How frustrated had she been to watch Kallie wander without memory? Why had she said nothing?

"You always knew? You did not—forget—as I did?"

"I did not forget. No."

The clock tower's bells clanged the hour, forcing Kallie to wait through twelve deafening gongs before speaking. Pigeons lifted from the square at the raucous noise, and tourists ducked and turned shoulders to avoid the birds.

When the chimes ended, Kallie whispered, "You followed me?"

"I followed you. But I could not intervene. This is how it must be. Part of the trial."

"But you have been protecting me." A rush of warmth for Judith, in all her crankiness, filled her heart.

"I have tried. She has not found you yet."

She?

Another wave, powerful and breath-stealing, washed its memory over her. Like ripping masks from the guests at a masquerade, one after another.

"Melayna also came through!"

The mental whirlpool began its spin again, sucking thought downward. The woman in the Doge's Palace, her tiny silver gun pointed at Kallie. That strange familiarity. Her cryptic words.

"She has found me, Judith." Injustice and betrayal were like a bitter taste in her mouth. After all these years and across time, still Melayna sought to destroy her sister for her own greed.

"When? What did she say?"

"She tried to shoot me. To kill me."

"Kallista, you must get away. You cannot allow her to find you again."

She noted Judith's use of her name in this time, even as her thoughts raced ahead into a plan.

"I will call Dimitri, tell him everything—"

"No!" The word was like a whip-crack across the miles.

"But he must—"

"Kallista, no person can see the truth for another. His awakening must happen naturally, as yours did. It is the only way."

"Why? What is all this about, Judith? Is the Horn of Truth the artifact we've been looking for? How are we to find it? To return home?"

"All will become clear, I promise. You must

only continue your quest. But first you must get away from Melayna."

"We will probably be leaving Venice soon."

"Good. Perfect. Call me when you're safely away."

With that, Judith severed the connection, leaving more questions than answers.

Kallie lifted her gaze to across the square, to the Caffé Florian where she had penned the last chapter of her story this morning, waiting for Dimitri. *Her story.* It seemed a lifetime ago, or as though the memory belonged to another person.

Dimitri did not appear to be waiting, so she left her seat and walked toward the basilica, toward the Doge's Palace, dialing his number as she walked.

He answered on the first ring, and the sound of his voice was like a warm quilt thrown around her shoulders. Why could she not tell him everything? What harm would it cause?

The words built up in her heart, threatened to spill over.

"Kallie? Are you okay?"

She was better than that. She was loved. But not here, she would not tell him on the phone, walking along the canal.

"Kallie, I'm on my way to you." He sounded winded, rushed.

She smiled. "I'm fine, Dimitri. But I—I got tired of the café, and I'm headed back to the hotel. Let's meet there. In your room." Where she could tell him what he'd been longing to know for seven years. She knew that longing.

"You're all right? You're sure?"

She laughed. "I'll see you soon."

She hurried past the palace, past the Bridge of Sighs where condemned prisoners would savor their last glimpse of Venice before the gallows, past the fruit and flower markets. On her right, vaporettos chugged along the waterline, pulling into docks to load with chattering tourists. In the few days they'd been here, she'd fallen in love with Venice, but still, it was Santorini—Kalliste —that held her heart.

But would the way back be as treacherous as the journey thus far? What dangers would they face in trying to return to their true home in Santorini's shadowy past?

Her footsteps slowed, heavy with a sudden desire to stay, to stay here in this time, with Dimitri. They could give up the search for Linear A, for the Horn of Truth. Leave it to Melayna if she wanted it so much. With Dimitri's money, they could live well and love each other for years to come, without threat or danger. Why not?

A water taxi bellowed out of the dock, and she picked up the pace. She must see Dimitri, must look into his eyes and know him for who he was. Somehow it would bring clarity. It must.

She had her eyes on the pink exterior of the

waterfront Hotel Danieli when the icy voice drilled into her ear from behind.

"You are too simple, Sister. You always were."

Kallie half spun, but Melayna was already pressed close, preventing movement. That tiny silver gun, so like a toy, was in her hand as it had been in the Doge's Palace, this time biting into Kallie's rib cage. "Melayna—"

Her sister hissed a laugh against her ear. "I knew it. I knew the innocence was an act."

"No! No, I only just remembered—" But what did it matter? Kallie tottered, that vertiginous feeling of existing between two worlds sweeping her again. Did she really stand along the docks in twenty-first century Venice with her sister?

Melayna shoved against her, rough hands moving Kallie forward along the canal.

She eyed the hotel, so close she could almost call out if any of her team had been standing outside. "Melayna, listen to me. You can have it. The Horn of Truth. If you can find it. I—I don't know where it is. I don't even know *what* it is."

"Please." Her sister's voice oozed sarcasm. "You and Andreas have been searching the globe for it. You expect me to believe you're ready to forget it all?"

Kallie had done more forgetting than remembering. "How—how have you done all this, Melayna? Found me? Taken care of yourself these seven years—"

"Seven years? What seven years?"

They had reached a tiny alley, and Melayna pushed her into its dark mouth, then along its length until they were deep in the middle, pressed against the greenish-black moss of stones slimy with moisture. The alley smelled of garbage and Melayna's perfume.

"You followed me somehow. Into the Great Cavern, past the half-men who live there and into the beast's fiery pit. And you came to this time, seven years ago. Did you not lose your memory?"

Melayna watched her through narrowed, cold eyes, her lip curled. "The journey has addled your brain, Sister. I saw no beast. No half-men. I only worked out the pitiable knots you tied and stepped into the cavern's mouth."

The stones leeched warmth from Kallie's back and she searched Melayna's sneering expression for fallacy. "And then?"

"And then, here. Now. Twenty-one days ago, to be exact."

Twenty-one days? When Kallie had wandered for seven long years? More injustice.

"It's an astonishing world, is it not?" Melayna jerked her head toward the end of the alley, as if they had separated themselves from the world at large here, as though nothing but them existed in this place-between-places, time-between-times. And how could it?

"Cell phones, Internet." Melayna was laughing.

"It took only a few days to realize the potential, to search you out."

"But how could you have known—?"

"Simple. As I said, you are always simple. A few 'keywords' as they say—*Kalliste, Andreas, the Minoan civilization.* And there you were. Though I will say I was impressed with the position you'd managed to worm yourself into, in that Temple of the Muses."

Kallie pushed away from the wall, anger firing her blood. "I have worked hard for seven years to earn that position—"

"You have been here that long? Truly?" The first sign of uncertainty flickered in Melayna's eyes.

Kallie pressed into that uncertainty, all senses alert to the position of the gun. "You know nothing of what is going on here, Sister. You think you can simply kill me and the Horn of Truth will be yours?" Her voice was like steel and she hardened her resolve to match. "This is more than simply claiming rulership of Kalliste. It is about *earning* it."

"Oh, you are so pure, are you not? As though you have nothing but our people's welfare at heart. You forget I have been watching you, seen you with him."

Kallie's chest heated and her muscles tightened. But what purpose was there in explanation? Melayna would see everything through her own

venomous point of view. All that mattered now was that gun and Melayna's determination to destroy her.

"So you are going to shoot me in this alley? Walk away as if it were nothing? And then what? How will you find the Horn of Truth? How will you return to Kalliste?"

Melayna's spiteful black eyes poured hatred. "I will concern myself with that when the time comes. Until then, I must only ensure that it falls to no one but me."

Kallie's hands formed fists at her side, but she did not take her eyes from her sister's face. "I am not so easily disposed of, Melayna." She brought her fist down, hard, on the hand that held the gun.

A yelp erupted from Melayna's lips, and the gun clinked to cobbled stones.

Kallie lunged for the end of the alley.

Melayna jumped the other direction, toward the gun on the stones.

Kallie ran. Any moment she'd feel a bullet. Or would she even feel it? If she died here, would her body fall in Kalliste?

Shadows paused at the end of the alley, outlined by blue sky. "Kallie?" Yellow hair glowed like gold in the sunlight.

"Caroline! Yoshi!" She glanced behind. Melayna's hand was at her side, but her eyes were trained on the two team members.

"Yoshi and I were going out to get something to eat—" Caroline cocked her head. "Are you okay?" Her glance darted over Kallie's shoulder, to Melayna in the alley.

"Fine. I'm fine. Let's go." Why did they have to choose today to sneak off alone, when it was Erik she really needed?

Yoshi bit his lip. "We were thinking of trying that little bistro—"

"No." Kallie took their arms, pulled them toward the hotel entrance. "No, let's go back to the hotel." She glanced over her shoulder again. Melayna followed. Should she lead her away from the hotel? But Melayna had proven her investigative skills. No doubt she'd already learned where they were staying. A heavy, locked hotel room door sounded better than the open air.

"Come on." She dragged them faster, until Caroline protested and twisted her arm from Kallie's grasp.

The hotel lobby welcomed them with a soundless, plush promise of protection, but Kallie hurried through its gold and marble décor to the wide stairs. It seemed imprudent to stand and wait for the elevator.

"Kallie, we're hungry!" Caroline stomped a little foot on the travertine floor at the base of the stairs. Yoshi, as usual, was quiet, but his eyes were narrowed in a way that questioned Kallie's sanity.

She eyed the front doors, and the waterfront beyond the windows with its striped-shirt gondoliers and loitering tourists. No sign of Melayna.

"Fine. I'll—meet you later. I'm going upstairs."

She took the heavily carpeted stairs as quickly as she could, reaching Dimitri's room within moments. She knocked lightly, then louder.

"Dimitri! Are you there?"

She was too exposed here in the hall. The thought made her slightly nauseated and dizzy again. She slapped her hand against the door.

Wait—didn't she still have the key she'd been given when assigned to Dimitri's room by mistake? She fumbled through her bag, found both key cards, tried one unsuccessfully, then the other. Green light.

On the other side of the door at last, she leaned back against the wood. Could a bullet penetrate the door? She retreated into the room, sat on the edge of a velvet chair placed under a gilded mirror, and watched the door as the minutes ticked past.

Where is he? He had said he was on his way to meet her in the square. He couldn't have been far.

She pulled out her phone again, dialed his number.

"Can't wait to see me?"

At his teasing tone, she breathed out tension. "Where are you? What's taking so long?"

"I'm almost to the hotel. I had to make a quick stop. I've got lots to tell you, though. Time to pack your bags for Santorini."

She had plenty to tell him, too. "Hurry, Dimitri."

"Kallie, are you sure you're—? What—? Hey, what are you—?"

A sharp *thwack* cut off the rest of his words.

"Dimitri?" Kallie stood, smashing the phone against her ear. "Dimitri!"

Silence met her calls, and in that space her body flooded with a heat that drained away a moment later, leaving her shaking and numb.

"Do not worry, *Kallista*." The familiar hissing voice came over the line.

The words were like stones pummeling her chest.

"You'll see him again. In fact, what better way to ensure that neither of you gets in my way?"

Hearing her sister's voice, knowing she had Dimitri—it was like being thrust back into the storm after finding yourself home. Kallie's knees buckled, and she slipped down into the chair.

Her voice scraped over the only question that mattered.

"What do you want, Melayna?"

→ 33 ←

"You know what I want."

Kallie paced Dimitri's hotel room. Did her sister have that gun pressed against Dimitri somewhere? Was he already dead? Cold bands of dread tightened around her heart, her lungs.

"Tell me. Just don't hurt him."

Melayna laughed. "That depends on you, doesn't it? On whether you're as noble as you claim."

She crossed to the window, looked down the length of the Grand Canal. "Where are you?"

"One hour." Melayna's voice was razor sharp. "Meet me behind the San Salvador Church off the Merceria."

Kallie leaned her forehead against the chilled glass of the window and stared into the brilliant Venice afternoon. A church. Perfect. "Don't hurt him, Melayna."

The connection broke but Kallie remained motionless, phone still to her ear, suspended in the moment. One hour. One hour to make this work.

First call—Judith.

She answered immediately. "What is it?"

"She has him. Melayna has—Dimitri. She wants me to sacrifice myself to free him."

She could hear Judith's breathing.

"Kallista, there's something I did not tell you."

Dread clenched at her stomach. What else?

"If the truth is forced upon him, he will not awaken."

"What are you saying?" She returned to pacing and rubbed her free hand against her damp neck.

"He must understand on his own, as I said. If you tell him—if *she* tells him—he may not be able to cross back."

"Judith, I don't understand any of this—"

"Find him before she explains, Kallista."

"And then what?"

"Save him."

The Oracle was no more forthcoming in the twenty-first century than she had been in Kalliste. Kallie disconnected with a huff.

Second call—Caroline.

"Hey there, Kallie! Did y'all change your mind about eating—?" Caroline's voice sang over the horn of a water taxi.

"Caroline, listen. We need to get out of Venice. Today. As soon as possible."

Caroline huffed, a pouty little sound of disappointment. "So soon? We've hardly—"

"Make the arrangements, okay? Get us a flight this evening. It's urgent—I've got to meet Dimitri immediately, so I can't explain." Kallie swung a glance around the room. Packing Dimitri's things seemed premature. Hopefully not unnecessary.

"Oh, fine. I'll call you with details."

"Thanks. Is Erik with you?"

"No, I think he's at the hotel—"

"Thanks." She ended the call and turned off the volume on her phone. She didn't want a ringtone to cause a problem when Caroline called back.

Now Erik.

He answered sleepily. Had she caught him taking a nap? She needed him alert.

"Erik? Time to do what you do best."

ᘛᘚ

Kallie checked the time on her phone. Fifty-three minutes since Melayna's last call. Still seven minutes before they were to meet behind the church.

She leaned her back against the wall of the tiny alley running off the main shopping street of the Merceria. Tried to slow her heartbeat. The shadowy inner recesses of Venice were getting more oppressive than romantic. She searched both ends of the narrow lane. Alone.

Melayna would not approach from this direction, not expect her to be on the east side of the building. But could Kallie's hastily conceived plan succeed? Everything depended on Erik. He'd taken her bizarre instructions like a soldier —no, like a general, his mind jumping to tactical strategy.

She glanced at the time again. The minute-digit

was unchanged. Was that possible? Had time slowed? She'd given up faith in any sort of linearity.

Faith. What did the truth of her identity mean to her questions of faith? In Kalliste, she had never questioned the way of their people, never known anything else. Now was not the time, but the questions would not wait forever.

The sharp odor of garlicky tomatoes wafted through the alley. Somewhere a pot of sauce was simmering for this evening's meal. She could almost taste the pungent flavor, the bite of pasta. She closed her eyes against the piercing stab of longing for a home and a family and peace.

But these things were not to be. Not yet. In the hour since Melayna's call, a current of thought ran behind her frantic phone calls and rushed preparations—a steadying realization that her journey could not end here, not in this time nor this place. She must find the Horn of Truth, or the Linear A Key, or perhaps they were one and the same. She must fight her way back to her people, to save them from destruction, whatever that meant. And she must take Dimitri with her, somehow bring him to the place of his own awakening.

The cold of the late-spring afternoon seeped under her skin. She wrapped her arms across her chest, tapped her heel against the stones.

As though in echo to her heel-taps, a sharp

crack exploded in the building behind her.

The sound drove breath from her lungs. She jerked her arms outward.

A gunshot.

Had Erik been armed? Did Melayna shoot Dimitri?

Her body expanded with heat, then deflated. Without thought, without pause, she ran to the side door of San Salvador, rattled the knob against its lock. Could she kick it in?

She would have to circle to the front.

Halfway down the alley, the door scraped open behind her. She swung a tight circle, arm raised.

"Kallie!"

Erik's red hair, his broad shoulder, poked from the doorway.

She sprinted back. "What happened? Is Dimitri—?"

"Get in here." His head and shoulder disappeared.

She jumped into the darkened doorway after him and blinked in the half-light, willing her eyes to adjust.

It was a back room, dusty and used for storage, with boxes and splintered benches piled against the wall. Through a cracked door, the marble mosaic of the church floor was barely visible.

Erik had one massive arm wrapped around Melayna's upper body, trapping her arms against her sides.

She bucked and growled against his grasp.

Erik shook his head, his brow creased. "She's a crazy one."

Kallie kept her eyes trained on Melayna. "Where's Dimitri?"

"I'm here." His voice swept out of the darkness.

Kallie spun toward him, in the shadows against the wall. "I heard a gunshot."

Dimitri bent to the floor, then stood with Melayna's silver gun in his hand. "She missed." He glanced at his shoulder, to a jagged hole in his jacket. "Mostly."

Kallie gasped. "Let me see!" She reached for the jacket, pulled it from his shoulder.

"I'm fine." The bullet had grazed his skin. It drew blood but barely penetrated.

He pushed her hand away, then waved the gun toward Melayna. "You wanna tell me what's going on?"

Kallie turned on Melayna. How much had her sister told Dimitri? "We need to get out of here, Dimitri."

Melayna hissed, still in Erik's grip of steel. "This isn't over, Sister. Far from it."

Erik tightened his forearm and Melayna cried out. He jerked his head toward the side door to the alley. "You two go. I'll take care of her."

She had to get Dimitri out before her sister said too much. "I'll explain later." She clutched his hand and dragged him toward the door with a nod to Erik.

Melayna's eyes spit fire.

"Don't hurt her, Erik. Just keep her away from us. I'll be in touch."

"Who is this woman, Kallie?" Dimitri was pulling from her grasp.

"Yes, tell him, Kallie." Melayna smirked in Erik's hold.

But Kallie was out the door, betting that Dimitri would stay at her side.

A moment later he joined her in the alley, his hands empty of the gun.

She started walking toward the cross street. "We should get that shoulder treated."

"I need a bandage, that's all." He was at her heels and she could feel his eyes glaring down on her. "What I really need is answers."

"Can we just get away from here first?" She scanned the length of the street they'd reached. "Somewhere quiet."

He grabbed her hand and took the lead. "I know a place."

They wound through tiny side streets, across narrow canals and forgotten bridges, until Kallie could not have found her way back to where they'd left Erik and Melayna, even with a map.

What would Erik do with her sister? She didn't know him well enough to be assured he wouldn't hurt Melayna. She barely knew herself well enough anymore to be assured of what she wanted.

Dimitri led her to the narrow door of a tiny café, one seemingly undiscovered by tourists. The interior was dimly lit, with only one shuttered window allowing in the Venice afternoon. They found a table at the back, where no patrons and barely any light intruded.

Dimitri pulled out her chair, lowered himself beside her, and propped his forearms on the table. "Now, start talking."

"Shouldn't we see about your shoulder—"

A young man approached. Dimitri waved him away with a grunt about coffee and then shook his head. "Forget the shoulder."

Kallie sucked in a deep breath. What to tell him?

"It was the woman from the Doge's Palace— the one who shot at me."

He frowned, rubbed his forehead. "She wanted *you,* Kallie. Not the Linear A Key. Not information. She said she was using me as bait to draw you."

"I know." What else did she say?

"Why?"

Kallie bit her lip, studied the woven plaid tablecloth under her fingers. "She wants to stop me from finding the Linear A Key, I suppose. So she can find it first." The answer sounded lame. Evasive.

"That makes no sense—"

Kallie's phone vibrated in her pocket and she pulled it out, holding up a finger to Dimitri. "Caroline?" She listened as the girl gave her their flight details, then instructed Caroline to gather their belongings from the hotel. "We'll meet you at the airport, then. Thanks." She laid the phone on the table.

Dimitri's eyebrows lifted. "Airport?"

"You said to pack my bags. I had Caroline make arrangements for us to get to Santorini right away. We leave in a few hours. Until then"—she glanced around the quiet café—"I suggest we stay right here. I should call Erik, though . . ."

"Erik will know what to do. He's much smarter than he lets on."

She raised her eyebrows, but she'd seen confirmation in the past few hours.

"Did you know he wants to start his own security company? He's always thinking about it, making plans in his head."

Kallie relaxed against her chair.

Dimitri covered her hands with his. "Listen, I love the idea of a private afternoon with you, but I'm not leaving here without answers. I can't let anything happen to you."

His hands were warm, and his look even warmer. She took a moment to let the past sweep over them, to revel in the knowledge he loved her now as he had loved her from that first day on the sunny hillside of Kalliste, and they were together.

"Let's not talk about any of this, Dimitri. Not for a while." The waiter brought their coffee but she didn't release her hold on his hands. "Tell me about your seven years. I want to hear everything." Everything that had happened since they parted.

He searched her eyes, ran his gaze over her face, her mouth. Then pulled her hands to his lips and kissed them both. "I will tell you. And then you will tell me of the seven years of Kallista Andreas."

She tried to smile, tried to swallow the emotion that threatened to have her crying out the truth. She nodded, not trusting herself to speak.

The afternoon waned and turned to early evening and still they talked. Dimitri told her of his adventures all over Europe, and she remembered the younger man he'd been in Kalliste, remembered that day on the hill beyond the palace when he'd shared his dreams of sailing the world, of charting the unknown.

And he drew memories from her as well, of her schooling and her work in the museum. Of her loneliness and confusion. At this, he cupped his hand against her cheek.

"You're not alone anymore, Kallista."

She closed her eyes and leaned against his hand. "I know."

He dragged his chair closer, slid a hand into her hair, and his lips on hers were warm and familiar.

She returned the kiss, with all the passion and truth she could not say in words.

He pulled away, surprised, and whispered, "Something's changed."

She sucked in a quick breath. Had he remembered? "Everything has changed."

He leaned his forehead against hers, looked into her eyes. "Tell me, Kallie. Last night—last night when I kissed you, you retreated. I feared you wouldn't return. Tonight—"

She pressed a finger against his lips. "I can't explain. You must trust me."

It was his turn to pull away. "Does that include today? Getting abducted and used for target practice?"

Kallie reached for his hands, closed her eyes. "Yes."

But he would no longer be put off. "I thought we weren't going to keep secrets any longer."

She exhaled, her chest tight and hot. How could she keep the truth from him? Yet, how could she risk speaking it? She shook her head and looked away.

Dimitri slid his chair backward, then stood and went to the window, the set of his shoulders angry and tense.

The time had come to leave Venice. They slipped from the café, into the street that had grown as dark as their afternoon hideout, and Kallie searched the canal-fronted street for anyone watching from the shadows. But the shadows were empty.

They hurried through the back streets, silent, in a weaving pattern that eventually led to the Grand Canal. Dimitri sought a water taxi and they climbed aboard to sail along the lamp-lit mansions that hovered at the water's edge, their crumbling walls valiantly defying the ravages of centuries.

Dimitri stood at her back but kept his distance.

Kallie wrapped her arms around herself, chilled, and watched the city slide past. She would never see Venice again. In spite of the coldness from Dimitri, part of the sadness was replaced by a spark, a thrill at what was to come.

Kalliste. She was going home.

Two hours later, the lights of the lagoon-city receded beneath them as their jet lifted toward the clouds. She had questioned Erik with her eyes when they'd met at the airport, but he only shook his head, and she didn't dare press him, not with Dimitri in earshot. Now the team of five relaxed in the darkened cabin. Dimitri closed his eyes without a word to her, and she said good-bye to Venice through the blurry window.

The travel by Air did little to frighten her anymore. She had survived the desert Earth in Luxor. And now the City of Water dropped away, powerless. She could see it clearly now, the three elements that had challenged her thus far in this world.

They would land in Santorini in two hours.

All that remained was a Trial by Fire.

Kallie awoke to Dimitri leaning across her.

He jutted his chin toward the airplane window. "We're landing soon. Can you see the island yet?"

She leaned against the dark window and shielded her eyes with her hands. Even without the cabin lights, the view from the plane was entirely dark. "I can't believe I've never asked you, Dimitri—have you been to Santorini? In the past seven years, I mean."

"Never. I visited Crete last year. It's when I began searching out the Key in earnest." His voice grew soft, contemplative. "It was strange. I had such a strong desire to day trip over to Santorini."

Kallie studied his profile, the way his eyes trailed away from her. "Why didn't you?"

"I don't know. I—I felt like it was the wrong time, somehow." He raised his head. "Sounds crazy, I know."

She smiled, a brief smile that had more of sadness in it. "It's the right time now."

He leaned his elbows on the armrests and laced his hands together. His mood was so somber. Was he still angry at the secrets she kept?

He leaned forward, toward the window. "Lights?"

Kallie turned back to the darkness and caught a glimmer of light at the edge of the window frame. A moment later the plane banked, revealing the island, with its ring of lights announcing each village that clung to the rim of its central black hole.

Kallie sucked in a desperate breath and her muscles tightened in horror.

"What is it?" Dimitri stared. "Kallie, are you all right?" He touched her arm. "You look like you've seen death!"

She pulled her gaze from the window, from the gaping wound in her beloved island. "The—the caldera." How had she not remembered until this moment?

He glanced from her face to the window and back to her face. "That's the crater where the volcano blew, right?"

She nodded, the motion abrupt and jerky. "I'd forgotten."

"Forgotten? That a volcano turned the round island into a doughnut?"

She eyed the window again. The pockets of light revealed a circular band of villages along the eastern side of the island, and a western rim of disconnected islands so narrow there were only a few scattered signs of life. The eruption had blown the top off the mountainous island, and seawater had rushed in to fill the void, turning the circular landmass into a ring-shape with a vast central lagoon. Kallie frantically pieced together fragments of memory of her life on the island with textbook details of the past seven years. It didn't take long.

The lagoon that brought visitors from all over the world to sit at its cliff edge and drink in the famed sunsets—that circle of seawater filled the hole where her palace once stood.

"Kallie, talk to me. What's upset you?"

She shook her head. "Nothing. It's nothing. Just excited to finally be here."

His eyes narrowed in obvious suspicion, but he let it go.

Within minutes, the team was gathering carry-on luggage and disembarking. Kallie paused at the top of the rolling stairs outside the plane door. She closed her eyes, took in a breath of the island air, and sighed.

Dimitri preceded her down the stairs. She caught up with him before the last step and reached for his hand.

He paused and studied their clasped hands. "I don't know if I can do this, Kallie. It's too late for anything less than honesty."

"Just give me time, Dimitri. A little time."

They stepped off the stairs together, onto the Santorini tarmac.

A jolt like an electric shock blew through her body.

She gasped, her fingers tightening around Dimitri's, and shot a glance at him.

He stood motionless, eyes wide and unseeing, lips parted.

Wake up, my love. Wake up.

He turned his head, slowly, slowly toward her. "Did you feel that?"

She turned to him, her eyes blurring. "Tell me."

He shook his head. "I don't know. It was like—like electricity. And music. All at once."

Like coming home.

Caroline bumped against them from behind. "Come on, you two lovebirds. Are ya'll just gonna stand there all day?"

As usual, Caroline led the way through Customs, secured transportation, and had them whisked away toward their hotel with her typical efficiency.

Dimitri followed in a haze, speaking little.

Would there be any flicker of recognition in his eyes as their cab passed along the rim? They were headed to the northernmost town of Oia, where Caroline had booked them rooms in a small hotel.

"It's a pity we didn't arrive during the day." Caroline perched on the edge of the cab's front seat, staring through the window. Yoshi and Erik were in another cab behind them, leaving Kallie and Dimitri in the backseat alone. "The drive along the coast must be magnificent in daylight." She turned to do her tour-guide thing. "Santorini is the most photographed island in Greece, you know. All those pure-white houses built into the sides of cliffs, the bright blue-domed churches, the black volcanic sand."

Dimitri still gripped Kallie's hand, silent.

She smiled at Caroline. "I'm sure we'll have some time to take our own photos."

The cliff-side town of Oia was like a white jewel set into the black cliff, its limestone houses lit from within by a thousand lamps and glowing with a bluish tinge in the night. The cab wound through several narrow streets but could only take them as far as a small parking lot at the outskirts of the town perched on the cliff. Yoshi and Erik's cab parked behind and the team alighted, forced to roll their luggage up a steep and winding lane, with only the driver's pointed, vague directions to guide them to their hotel.

Ten minutes later they stopped at the peak of the town. Even in the night darkness, the cliff's white houses glowed with the reflection of stars and moon, and churches with iconic blue domes and pink-washed walls breathed peace over the hillside and the caldera.

The town was a narrow-alleyed jumble of

apartments, shops, and cafés, all built one upon the other, with terraces of one forming roofs of another, shared walls, and hardly a way to discern which doors belonged to which establishment. They found their "hotel" at last, a six-room guest house near the famous windmills. They wearily filled the tiny place, relieved and tired. The proprietor and his wife greeted them warmly, bustled about getting them settled, then left them to say their good nights to each other in Kallie's tiny room. The team made plans to reconvene for lunch the next day, after Kallie and Dimitri had a chance to visit Nicolaos Papadakis, the collector they suspected had the Linear A Key somewhere at his cliff-top estate and vineyard.

The rest of the team drifted to their rooms.

Dimitri and Kallie walked out to her narrow balcony, leaning on the waist-high wall that overlooked the caldera. A half-moon hung crooked over the sea, pinned there by a cosmic hand, shining a path across the dark water.

Dimitri's arm brushed hers but he did not look away from the water. "I can't help feeling tomorrow will be very important, Kallie."

"Do you think he'll tell us if he has it?"

"It's not just the Linear A Key I'm talking about."

She wanted to lean her head against his shoulder but resisted. "What else?"

"Do you remember what I said in the café the

other night? That when I met you, I felt a sense of belonging, of coming home?"

She closed her eyes, filled her lungs with the Kalliste air. "I remember."

"It's here, too. It's you—and it's this place."

"I know."

"You do?"

His voice held a question, but she kept her eyes closed.

"Maybe sometime you'll tell me . . . because I don't really know why. Not yet. But I think—I think tomorrow I might understand."

She turned and smiled warmly at his serious eyes. "I hope so. Good night, Dimitri."

He leaned toward her, as though he would kiss her, then pulled away and gripped the balcony wall. "I hate these things you will not share, Kallie. There cannot be anything between us until there are no secrets between us."

"I know." She looked down and started to pull away.

He pivoted and grasped her arm, gazing deeply into her eyes, as though he could maybe decipher the secrets she wouldn't tell him. Finally, he touched her cheek and swept a strand of loose hair away from her face. "Until tomorrow, then."

Kallie watched him leave, mixed emotions on his face. She could decipher every one of those. She felt them herself.

⇥ 35 ⇤

Nicolaos Papadakis had been in his thirties in 1975 when he had acquired pieces from the last Venetian doge's great-grandson, Louis Manin. The years had apparently been kind to his bank account.

A member of his household staff led Kallie and Dimitri from the massive front door of his elegant estate through bright-white rooms to the sun-drenched piazza overlooking the crystal water. More whitewashed estates sprawled across the cliff to their right, but to the left the hillside was strewn with untrained vines—an oddity for a vineyard—and dotted with a warren of black-mouthed caves that stretched down to the dark beach and sparkling Aegean Sea.

The morning walk from their inn had given Kallie and Dimitri a chance to see Oia by daylight, a study in brilliant color. Beside the signature white limestone houses and piercing-blue church domes, bougainvillea vines spilled magenta-pink flowers over walls and roofs. Salmon-painted buildings dotted the grassy hillsides. They passed the two huge windmills whose squat, round bases had also been turned into villas for rent, then twisted through crowded alleys of shops just opening up, owners busily dragging their paintings, clothing, and souvenirs outside to draw tourists.

Now that they were inside Papadakis's private estate at the edge of town, they could see Oia as a whole, tumbling down the cliff in all its beauty. Adjoining his piazza was an oval swimming pool, with azure-blue water that matched the cloudless sky. Chaise lounges lined the pool's rim, their red-and-white-striped cushions cool and inviting.

"So here is the reclusive Dimitri Andreas."

Kallie swung toward the strong voice, to a lean, elderly man, cigar in hand, braced against the wall of the balcony. A trellised terra-cotta pot at his side overflowed with hot-pink bougainvillea spilling over the balcony's edge.

Dimitri stepped from behind her and crossed the piazza, hand extended. "Mr. Papadakis, thank you for meeting us."

But Papadakis's eyes were on her.

She smiled and joined the two men.

"Mr. Papadakis, my associate Kallista Andreas."

He lifted an eyebrow. "Is that what we're calling them these days?"

Kallie laughed. She liked him already. "The last name is a coincidence, Mr. Papadakis. No relation."

He stubbed the cigar into a ceramic dish on the balcony wall, then took her hand and tucked it into the crook of his arm. "Good. Then you're free."

She laughed again. "What did you have in mind?"

"Ah, never ask an old man such a question, my dear. We aren't afraid to tell the truth."

Dimitri cleared his throat.

Kallie grinned. Papadakis was making Dimitri amusingly uncomfortable. They'd heard the collector was a bit eccentric, but she'd never minded eccentricities.

Papadakis pulled her across the piazza to a pair of white wicker chairs under a blue umbrella. "Yes, what is it, Andreas? Why are you standing about, coughing like you've got something to say?"

"Mr. Papadakis, as I mentioned on the telephone—"

"Does your lovely—associate—here know all about your dealings?"

"Yes, of course—"

"Good. Then I'll talk to her. You find something else to do with yourself for a bit. Go visit the vineyard. Have a taste of some Papadakis wine. George will show you around."

Dimitri's face whitened.

Kallie almost laughed. The old man probably didn't get many female visitors. She could charm the information out of him just as well or perhaps better than Dimitri. "Go on, Dimitri. Mr. Papadakis and I will be fine here by ourselves."

"Nicolaos, dear. Call me Nicolaos."

She patted his hand, then turned and winked at Dimitri. "Nicolaos and I will have a nice chat while you're seeing the vines." If only Judith could see her now, charming the potential donor.

Dimitri opened his mouth, then closed it again, jaw clenched.

She looked between the two men. They were much alike. Nicolaos reminded her of Dimitri, like an older version of him. Perhaps the old man he would become if he stayed here in Santorini, in this time. The thought was sobering.

Dimitri waved a hand at them. "Fine. I'll be back in a little while." He left on the heels of George who had suddenly appeared.

They sat in the wicker chairs and a young girl brought a tray with two glasses of white wine and a plate of sweet-smelling honeyed baklava. When she disappeared, Nicolaos sighed and crossed one leg over the other. "Alone at last."

Kallie looked over at him with a smile as she scolded. "That was rather cruel to send him away. Dimitri is very anxious to speak with you about your collection."

Nicolaos grinned, shrugged one shoulder. "And I am more anxious to speak with *you*."

"We're both very hopeful you'll be able to show us the piece we're looking for."

"Linear A, is that it?"

Kallie leaned forward. "Do you have it? Did you purchase it in Venice, all those years ago?"

He sighed. "Ah, Venice. Such a beautiful, wonderful city."

"It would mean a great deal to the study of Minoan culture, having the language."

He lifted a glass of wine and indicated the other, still on the tray. "See what kind of culture we have on Thera now."

She tasted the wine and smiled. "It's lovely. But the Linear A—"

"What is it you're so eager to find?"

She frowned and set the glass on the tray. "The language has not yet been—"

He waved away her words. "Besides that. Besides." He stared her down. "I see the longing in your eyes, my dear. For something far greater than a piece of clay."

"It's a tablet, then?" A thrill ran through her.

Nicolaos sat back in his chair and scowled. "I ask again—what is it you are really searching for?"

"Truth." The word spilled out, uninvited.

He lifted his chin. "Ah. Now we are getting somewhere. But what is truth?"

She said nothing and turned away. How had he evaded her one-and-only direct question so easily? And what would he say now? Would he even talk about Linear A? She waited tensely, listening to the sound of waves tossing themselves against the rocky coastline below, the scent of wine and flowers in her nose.

"Did you know Pontius Pilate asked those very words of Jesus, just before handing him over to his death?"

It was such a strange, unexpected question. Kallie glanced at him in surprise. At his intense gaze into her eyes, she turned back and stared over the water, watching the jewel-like ripples in the sun. Did she know that from her study of history? She couldn't remember. Why would Pilate ask that of Jesus right before executing him?

"The right question. And perhaps the right person to ask, don't you think?" When she remained deep in thought, he followed her gaze out to the sea-filled caldera. "Such beauty from such destruction."

The words pained her. Made her think of the lofty palace, of her parents. Their magnificent capital city. All flung into the heavens with so much dirt and ash. The date of the eruption was controversial. She had no way of knowing how much longer they had.

"Did you know they were warned?"

She turned to him, searched his face, still watching the sea and the rocky cliffs on the other side of the vast caldera. "Warned?"

Nicolaos shrugged. "That's what the archaeological evidence suggests, especially down in Akrotiri." He pointed to the southern tip of the curved island, opposite their perch. "No human bones. They all got out." He took a bite of baklava. "How do you suppose they knew?"

Her mind raced. "There might have been earthquakes first."

He chewed and swallowed. "Most likely. But still—evacuate an entire island based on earthquakes? It was as if they had been told it was coming, wouldn't you say?"

Kallie stood, unable to remain still, and crossed to the balcony wall. The breeze played with her hair, pulling it from her eyes. She had known all of this at one time—the lack of bones, the speculation about the warning. She had thought of none of it since she emerged from the crypt of St. Mark's.

The Linear A Key, if it existed—and she was not at all sure it did—what could it say that would help her people? Could she even bring it back with her? If it was written in Linear A and later languages, and in the Theban kingdom of Egypt after the people of Kalliste fled the volcano, then in her time it had not even been created yet.

Perhaps—perhaps the Horn of Truth she had been sent here to find was *not* the Linear A Key. Perhaps it was not a physical object at all, but only a sort of trumpet-call of warning. A warning to sound for the salvation of her people.

The air grew sharp with the tang of the salt sea and Kallie could hear every wave break against the cliffs, taste every flower that grew on the mountainsides, see for miles across the island beauty. She gripped the edge of the wall as her vision darkened for a moment and the breath constricted in her chest.

This truth of their coming destruction—*this* was what she had been sent to another time to discover!

It was like having her assumptions blasted away, with a deep crater forming where certainty had been.

Nicolaos joined her at the wall. "What is truth?" he said again.

But was there more than knowledge of the eruption to bring back to her people? Greater knowledge, greater truth?

All their searching for the gods, their attempts to connect with the divine, she saw it all with new clarity now, with the sweep of history before and after her precious community of Kalliste, and all the reaching of man throughout the ages to understand God. The natural, physical beauty her people worshipped—could it be loved and adored, but as only a marker for truth?

Nicolaos's voice was quiet, slipping out over the caldera. "We all have a deep hunger, Kallie. For beauty, for wonder and awe. Something beyond our physical senses, waiting to be discovered. The physical world, including all its myth, points us to a world more real than this one."

"What is truth?" Pilate had asked Jesus. Had the answer to his question stood before him, and he did not see it? If so, then the reasoned theology of the hard-backed wooden pews she had experienced missed the momentous. Missed all the breathtaking mystery wrapped up in the pinprick of time when fantasy and reality had somehow touched.

Yes, a deep cavern had been dug into the center of her assumptions. What sort of water would flow into its hollow spaces?

Nicolaos touched her hand on the wall with his own.

She turned to him with tear-stained cheeks.

"Forgive an old man. Some days I talk more philosophy than archaeology, I fear." He patted her hand. "It is only that I see a woman still resisting the gifts she has been given, still fearing to embrace all the purpose assigned to her. Running from her strengths and from the life she has been called to live."

Kallie swiped a hand at her cheeks. "Who are you? Are you—do you—do you know Judith? You sound like her." Well, not like *Judith* exactly. It was a foolish question, but she could not put any other thoughts into words.

"She sounds like a woman I would enjoy meeting." He smiled toward the sea. "Come back tonight. Come back and have dinner and watch the sun set over the caldera with me. You and

Dimitri. We will build a fire and watch the island grow dark together."

She nodded and swiped again at her damp face. "Yes. Thank you."

Behind them, Dimitri cleared his throat again. He was back.

Kallie kissed Nicolaos on the cheek and crossed the piazza. "Come, Dimitri. Nicolaos has invited us to return this evening. We can talk more then."

He was open mouthed with surprise again, but she sailed past him, through the house and out to the winding lane that led back along the ridge of the town.

Dimitri questioned her on the walk back to the hotel, but she quickly admitted she'd gotten no information about the Linear A Key. She lapsed into silence, her mind and heart too full to speak.

If the Horn of Truth were only knowledge—knowledge she already had—then all that remained was to return.

Without Dimitri?

And what of Melayna? She'd questioned Erik about her sister this morning, before she and Dimitri had left for Nicolaos's estate. Erik had complained she'd not given him enough information for the operation in Venice. Without a better alternative, he had left Melayna secured in the abandoned building and simply walked away. Kallie would not believe she had seen the last of her sister.

Time was running out. She needed something drastic.

At the door to the inn, she turned to Dimitri. "I want to see Akrotiri."

He squinted and frowned. "Now?" At her silence, he looked toward the south end of the island. "I'll call for a cab."

On impulse, she grabbed his arm. "No. Let's rent one of those motorbike things. I saw shops at the bottom of town."

"A four-wheeler?" Dimitri's eyebrows rose and a little of his old humor returned. "Really? After Luxor?"

In answer, she started down the narrow street.

Twenty minutes later they were sailing south along the coastline, the wind pulling at her hair and her arms wrapped around Dimitri's waist. At least they would not die of thirst if their bike broke down.

In spite of the friendly ride, the strain between them was mounting. Her refusal to speak of her time with Nicolaos had infuriated Dimitri. The rigid tension of his body was evident under her embrace, and they rode the twelve miles in silence.

The dig site at Akrotiri was still active, covered by roofing. They paid the entry fee, refused the guided tour, and started into the site, which would be the closest thing to home either of them had seen in seven years.

Time to wake up, Dimitri.

⇢ 36 ⇠

Dimitri and Kallie entered the dig site, the remains of a town under a vast, newly constructed roof to protect the finds. A wall-mounted map of the site, along with its location on the island, stopped Kallie in her tracks.

How had she not realized? She'd given little thought to the dig site's location since the name was unfamiliar. But this was Lycoris! Her village of Lycoris, where Isandros and his daughter had sheltered her, before this life began.

Wooden decking, like a seaside boardwalk, ran the perimeter of the roofed area and crisscrossed over the excavated town in places. Half-crumbled walls, only the lower levels, marked off houses. Terra-cotta pots, wells, fire pits—they were all there.

"What is it?" Dimitri's voice broke into her trance.

"Oh, uh, just thinking about the past." She moved forward before he could say more.

They wandered the remnants of the village, wordless.

It was so real, all of it. A tangible piece of the past. The tourists who followed guides and peered over the walkways believed they were seeing the true village.

And yet—it was not a real representation at all. Not the Lycoris village where she had danced and celebrated, where fountains had splashed and children had played.

It was somehow like these last seven years.

She had believed New York City was real, and the tale in her journal only fiction, a shadow of something that had happened to her that she couldn't remember.

But it was the twenty-first century that was the shadow, a parallel to her real life in Kalliste. It was the myth that was fact, more real than anything else.

She thought again of Nicolaos's question of truth. Was it possible all of the myth and longing of the human mind had become distilled into a single, historical moment in time, when myth became fact?

It was like waking from a dream, then finding it was the *dream* that was real and everything since waking untrue.

"Seen enough?" Dimitri's voice seemed to come from a faraway and cold place.

She inhaled and took a last look at Lycoris. Not Lycoris. And it had done nothing for Dimitri. She sighed from her soul. "Yes."

They were back in the upper part of Oia within an hour and spotted Yoshi, Caroline, and Erik out sightseeing.

Caroline waved and trotted over, her heels

clicking dangerously along the stone alley. "Where have you two been?" Her smile faded as she took them both in. "What's wrong? What's happened?"

Did they look that unhappy?

"Nothing." She nodded to Yoshi and Erik. "We've been to a dig site on the other end of the island, that's all. Are you three having fun?"

Yoshi frowned. "I'm not sure what 'fun' we are to be having. It's a town built on a cliff. And Caroline insists on hanging over every precipice." It was his usual sour observation, but there was a bit of teasing in his voice and a sideways glance at Caroline, as though he were baiting her.

He'd changed since that moment in the Egyptian desert. And anxious Caroline? Hanging over cliffs?

Caroline rolled her eyes at Yoshi. "Hopeless." She turned to Dimitri. "Did you find out anything from the old man?"

Dimitri circled Caroline and headed toward their inn. "You'll have to ask Kallie about that."

"Hmm." Caroline cocked her head. "It looks like Mommy and Daddy are fighting."

Kallie ignored the pain in her chest and gave the team a quick explanation of their lack of findings and the plan to return to Nicolaos's estate that night. They invited her to join their sightseeing, but she claimed the need for a walk alone and ignored Erik's look of concern as she took to the cliff-side steps that switchbacked downward toward the beach.

Halfway down, she saw a figure ascending toward her and watched as the shape grew more familiar.

"Judith?" She shielded her eyes and stared.

The woman took the steps quickly. "You didn't call."

Kallie huffed, a strangled half laugh. "So you flew over here to scold me?"

"Don't be ridiculous. I booked a flight as soon as we spoke yesterday."

"How did you know——?"

Judith's look of derision stopped her questions. The woman knew everything. Of course she did.

"I still do not understand how Melayna has fit so comfortably into this world. How *you* stepped in with your memories intact and a place of prominence."

Judith looked out over the sea. "There are questions for which even I do not have answers. But I can tell you that Melayna's success is a curse, not a gift."

Kallie sat on the step, suddenly too confused and fatigued to hold herself upright. "Does it even exist, Judith? The Linear A Key?"

Judith leaned against the wall and folded her arms, looking down on Kallie. "Does it matter?"

"I suppose not. Not if I don't need to find it."

"What *have* you found, then?"

"I think I've found the Horn of Truth. A horn that sounds with two messages. One for their bodies and one for their souls." She lifted her eyes to Judith.

The woman's face was unreadable. As it always had been. "So what will you do?"

"I must get home. But I do not know how." She clutched at Judith's dark pant leg. "Tell me how, Judith. Tell me how to get home."

"You fought through forest, village, and mountain to get here. You faced your sister. You fell through the fires of the beast's mouth."

"Yes." The memory could have brought her pride, but it only left her sad.

"You have fought through New York City, through Luxor, and through Venice to get back. It is time now to step through fire once again."

"And Melayna?"

Judith shook her head. "This I do not know. We must wait and see. But I can tell you this—you were born into this world in ignorance and not by your own will. But you will be born again into your true home with knowledge, and by your own choice. This I know."

Kallie nodded, tried to take it in. It was still not an answer. Not a plan.

"You will know the time when the time comes, my girl. I promise you this."

Kallie stood, continued her steps downward, heedless of Judith behind her. Whatever was to come, Judith would not be there. Kallie needed time to think.

An hour later, after a walk along the beach, she climbed again and wandered toward her room. How long until they would leave again for Nicolaos's dinner party? Perhaps she should attempt to sleep—

Her door was ajar.

Sucking in a breath, she stood with fingertips against the bright-blue slatted wood and pushed it gently toward the darkened interior, then leaned her head in.

Dimitri sat, at a chair beside the bed. He did not see her enter.

He was far too occupied with reading her journal.

⇥ 37 ⇤

He didn't see her in the doorway. He continued to read, and Kallie's breath hung suspended. Should she stop him? What was that conventional wisdom about not waking sleepwalkers? Did it apply here?

But then he was dropping his head, closing his eyes, shutting the journal. He had come to the last entry, finished the tale.

"Dimitri?"

His head jerked upright, then he stood, the

426

journal clenched in the hand at his side. "Kallie! I—I'm sorry." He lifted the leather volume. "I came in to wait for you—saw it lying there beside the bed—I'm sorry."

His eyes reflected such pain, Kallie slipped across the room to him. "It's okay, Dimitri. I don't mind." She slid the journal from his tight fingers. "Did you read it all?"

He nodded, his eyes still clouded. "You haven't finished the story."

"No."

"How does it end?"

She replaced the journal on the bedside table, her back to him. "I don't know yet."

"It's a strange story."

"Yes. Yes, it is."

He wandered over to where she stood, kissed her absently on the cheek, then drifted toward the door. "I'm going to walk. I'll come for you when it's time to leave for the Papadakis estate."

She said nothing, watched him go.

Whispered a prayer.

The sun was dropping toward the caldera when she met Dimitri outside the inn. They walked again along the rim to Nicolaos's estate. It was good neither of them was driving, for how could anyone take their eyes from the sky? Had the Kalliste sunsets been so spectacular all her life?

They arrived on Nicolaos's piazza to find the

sun's orange rays and long shadows slanting across the white stones. Nicolaos hailed them from the hillside to their left, a few steps down from the terrace.

He had changed his clothes—a dark, open-collared shirt and white dinner jacket that set off his deeply tanned skin and snow-white hair. Standing among his vines, he could have been a magazine ad for the best Santorini had to offer. From somewhere, soft music played, a tune reminiscent of an ancient time. Behind Nicolaos, a bonfire roared on the hillside. He extended a cigar-holding hand to a table set with linen and china and crystal, three wrought-iron chairs placed around it, facing the sea and the last of the sun.

"Welcome, friends."

A settled feeling, at once both premonitory and inevitable, washed over Kallie.

Here they would sit and watch the sunset. And when they left this place, things would never be the same.

Dimitri touched a hand to the back of her chair as she sat, though there was no need to pull it out for her. He lowered himself to the chair on her right, and Nicolaos sat on her left. They watched in comfortable silence as the sun lit the caldera with fire. Black volcanic cliffs spanning to the south, white houses and blue roofs, violet-blue sea and sky streaked with orange were a picture postcard too breathtaking to be described with mere words. It did not present itself as a scene to be spoken but as a beauty to be absorbed— soaking into skin with promises of joy and sorrow, of reward and of loss.

When the sky had gone purple-dark and the first stars silvered the air, Nicolaos's staff came and fed the bonfire and fed the guests.

Nicolaos regaled them with stories of his misspent youth, his accumulated treasures, his legacy. They laughed and wondered and sat spellbound through tales of travel and adventure, and through the evening the wine flowed and the food was hot and Dimitri's hand found hers on the tabletop.

Would they could remain here in this moment.

But she knew better.

And when a flicker of white at the piazza steps drew her attention, she barely felt surprise to see her sister with the firelight dancing across her stony features.

"The end of the quest?" Melayna waved a hand toward Nicolaos, but her eyes were on Kallie. She held a gun, different from the one Erik had taken from her, but just as deadly.

How did she do it? The guns. Money. A passport? Melayna had adapted and found her way through twenty-first-century life in a fraction of the time it had taken Kallie, who'd spent weeks in an institution, wrapped in shock and confusion. But she could not ask her sister her secret. Not with Dimitri able to hear.

The journal. He had read their story. How long would it take him to make connections? How much must he understand before he could no longer return home?

She lifted her chin, then stood. "There is nothing here for you." She felt rather than saw the two men stand with her.

"Hello." Nicolaos extended a hand. "Are you a friend of—?"

"I am no friend to anyone here."

Nicolaos seemed to notice the gun in her hand. His tone grew ominous. "What is this? Who are you?"

Do not answer that, Sister. Do not answer.

"I'm someone who knows what she wants. And it's something you apparently have."

Dimitri had pulled out his phone, was surreptitiously dialing.

"Do not even think about it, Andreas." Her tone was chilling. She circled them, putting the bonfire to her back, the gun still trained on all three.

The light and heat played over Kallie and threw her sister's features into shadowy darkness before the fire.

She had not noticed until now the fire had been built against the entry of a large cavern, one of many on the hillside. Its open mouth yawned behind the flames, an arc of blackness.

Nicolaos's voice was stern beside her. "What is it you want?"

"The same as them." She waggled the gun in Kallie's direction. "The Key to the lost language." Her eyes met Kallie's. "The key to everything."

Nicolaos's voice was a growl. "Even if I had it, I would not give it to you."

The old man still had guts. But her sister was capable of anything. She didn't want to see Nicolaos hurt. "He doesn't have it."

"Oh, he does." Melayna laughed. "And he's going to give it to me, and then I'm going to go home. Isn't that what we both want, *Kallista? To go home?*"

Dimitri's eyes were on her, dark and questioning. "She knows you, Kallie?"

She had to get Melayna away from him.

Dimitri's eyes narrowed. "And you—you know her!" This last was delivered with an undercurrent of pain. "You've remembered, haven't you? You remembered, and you didn't tell me."

Oh, God, what am I supposed to do?

Trial by Fire.

The time had come, hadn't it? To delay could mean Dimitri would never return home. Nicolaos could be hurt, even killed. And if Melayna carried out her threat, Kallie would never return to her people with the Truth she'd been given to deliver.

She had to leave. To leave this place, and to

take Melayna with her, before her sister could do more damage. For the salvation of her people.

She had to leave without Dimitri.

Dimitri's fingers clenched her forearm. "Who are you, Kallie? Who am I?" His voice was tortured, full of longing, of an ache for a home he did not know.

There was no moment of indecision, no suspended, agonizing choice. It was decided before it was even thought. She was princess of Kalliste. And its people, her people, were her responsibility. More vital than personal happiness. More than love.

But there was pain. Deep, soul-scorching pain at the thought of leaving him, perhaps forever—of living without him. It was like a death, this decision. To rule without him would be like giving up air.

They were connected, she and Dimitri. She was not alone, not unloved. But she would act in the best interest of her people. Now and always.

There was no time for a good-bye. Not a moment for even a flicker of hesitation. Overwhelming grief threatened to paralyze her. She must force sluggish limbs to respond.

The Great Cavern, with its fiery entrance, beckoned. She saw only that black hole and all else dropped away.

Kallie put her head down, and she ran.

Toward Melayna, toward the fire. Toward home.

Everything happened at once, and yet slowly. A gunshot pierced the night air. She felt only the wind in her hair.

Dimitri yelled her name—*Kallista!*—like a man drowning.

Melayna screamed her name—*Chloe!*—like a raging animal.

She hit Melayna, head down, and drove her backward into the flames. The heat of the bonfire blazed against her skin, danced against her pores, burrowed into her chest.

The orange light blinded, seared. Was this death? Had she been wrong about the fire? Destroyed them both?

But then it was behind them, a hungry roar at their backs. They tumbled into the cavern, unhurt. Kallie regained her footing, blinked into the darkness.

Had they crossed? Were they home?

A shadow in the back of the cavern shifted, footsteps scratching against the gritty floor. A figure emerged, pale face under a black hood. Piercing blue eyes.

She had only one thought, one question for the Oracle. "Will he awaken? Will he come home?"

Her lined face did not smile but looked on both sisters in solemn silence.

Kallie glanced at Melayna—at her hand, empty of the gun, and her face, empty of compassion.

433

The Oracle spoke at last. "It has been *your* test, Chloe. Yours and Melayna's. Not his."

A memory tickled, of her mother and the Oracle, speaking together in the throne room. Her mother, fearing for her daughters' safety. The Oracle, insisting they must be tested before they could rule.

Melayna pushed forward. "And she has failed! She did not bring back the Horn of Truth. The younger shall not rule the elder! Your prophecies are false, Oracle."

Ice-cold, those blue, blue eyes turned on Melayna. "She has passed the test, Melayna. In her sacrifice she has proven herself worthy to rule, and with her open heart she has received truth of which you know nothing. You did not pass through the trials as she did, and hence you learned nothing. You do not love, and hence you shall not rule."

Kallie sucked in a breath. Was she worthy of the Oracle's commendation? She did not feel qualified to lead her people.

And yet, in the darkness of the Great Cavern, she gave up her own will and smiled to think of the Truth she had been called to deliver. Destined to deliver. She closed her eyes against the pain of leaving love behind and readied herself to go home.

A great hissing sound filled the cavern, and shouts reached her ears. The heat at her back cooled, and the air clouded with a thick smoke, pungent and choking.

When it cleared, would she see her beloved island whole again?

Not smoke. A fire extinguisher.

Kallie turned, shielding her eyes with one hand, coughing. Beside her, Melayna moaned and began coughing as well.

The fire had been doused by a huge red extinguisher in Dimitri's hands. Beside him, Nicolaos held Melayna's gun as if he knew how to use it.

Kallie whipped her head back to the Oracle, but she was gone.

Melayna stumbled out of the cavern, still coughing.

Dimitri stood outlined by the moonlit sky. The extinguisher slipped from limp fingers and dropped to the ground at his feet.

His eyes were on hers. His eyes were on fire.

He said only one word. One whispered word.

"Chloe . . ."

Dimitri was awake.

She let Dimitri have his moment—the reeling, deafening roar of truth she well remembered. He swayed, lifted a hand toward her, lips parted.

She stumbled around smoking embers toward that outstretched hand, and their moments on the palace hill overlooking the Kalliste sea blended with dancing on the deck of a Luxor ship and heads bent together in dark Venetian cafés. It was theirs, all of it, memory and time, swirled into a heady jumble of questions and answers. And love. Above all, beneath all, saturating everything that was or ever would be, love.

He met her halfway. Hands burrowing into her hair, warm palms cocooning her head, lips finding her cheeks, her eyes, her mouth. She tasted tears. Perhaps they both wept.

He broke away, then pulled her close again. More kisses. The spicy scent of his cologne was like that first night at the Andreas estate, a scent that had wrapped her in yearning for deep mystery and unknown adventure.

His fingertips were on her face now, tracing her eyelids and the slope of her nose and the corners of her mouth like a man born blind.

"You knew." The words were a ragged whisper. "You knew before you ran through that fire."

"For only a short time, my love. And the Oracle instructed me to keep silent."

He circled her shoulders with both arms, pulled her to his chest, and the beat of his heart beneath her cheek was like the rhythm of a dance.

Over her head, he focused on Nicolaos and inclined his head toward Melayna. "Keep your eye on that one, Nicolaos. She's crafty."

Nicolaos cocked an eyebrow and nodded, the pistol still trained on Melayna.

Dimitri returned his gaze to her. "Chloe—"

"Kallie." She pulled away and held his gaze. "For now. Kallie. And Dimitri."

He nodded once. "What happens next?"

She turned to Melayna, their arms still entwined. "I thought—I thought the fire, the cavern—I don't know."

But Nicolaos had taken the decision from them, a phone at his ear. His words were a torrent of angry Greek, and Kallie caught enough. *Police.*

Nicolaos asked few questions while they waited, seemingly content with their explanation that Melayna had been following them across the globe to snatch the Linear A Key, should they find it. He waved Melayna to one of the wrought-iron chairs and took another himself. Dimitri offered to take the gun, but Nicolaos gave them a wry smile and shook his head.

"Most fun I've had in years."

A quick summary to the two law enforcement

men who arrived within minutes was sufficient. They snapped handcuffs on Melayna, instructed Nicolaos to come to the police station to make a formal complaint, and relieved him of the gun.

One of the officers pulled Melayna toward the piazza's steps, but she strained against him, her eyes turned on Kallie. Her eyes blazed like the fire they'd fallen through together.

"This is not over. You do not even have the Key. And you do not know how to return."

Dimitri started toward her.

Kallie grasped his arm and pulled him back. She looked at her sister sorrowfully. "Good-bye, Melayna." Her heart twisted in her chest. "Be well. Find peace."

But Melayna gave no response, her mouth a hard, angry slash. Even as she was forced to the steps, she kept her snake eyes fixed on Kallie. Finally, she turned and was lost in the night. The policemen's boots scuffed across the stone piazza and then faded, leaving the hillside dark and silent.

"Well, you two have brought me much excitement, I will say."

Kallie turned to Nicolaos. He reclined in the chair, but his eyes danced.

"I am sorry we put you in danger, Nicolaos."

He waved away her concern. "More wine?"

Kallie smiled gently at him. "Thank you, but we

should be leaving. Do you want us to drive you to the police—?"

"No, no, my dear. I have a driver." He rose and came to her, both hands extended. "I am thinking you are saying good-bye to Nicolaos as well. A final good-bye?"

She grasped his hands and winked. "Even before we have pried all your secrets from you."

He kissed the fingers of each of her hands. "An old man has little but his secrets. However . . . they do not always die with him."

She cocked her head at the cryptic words.

He grinned. "When the world is ready for Linear A, the world shall have it, dear girl. Do not fear."

It was all she would extract from him, but it warmed her, to think of their language, lost for millennia past, but with the promise of the future. She embraced Nicolaos quickly.

Dimitri shook his hand, still silent and dazed.

Nicolaos dipped his head in understanding.

Then Kallie and Dimitri retreated across the starlit piazza, through the gracious estate, and out to the street.

They did not speak during the short walk along the dark cliffs, but when they reached the inn, Dimitri led her to the balcony of her room, overlooking the sea.

He leaned his forearms on the half wall and studied the night. "The Horn of Truth?"

Kallie stood beside him and told him all she knew, all she had come to understand. All the questions still in her heart.

"Then we must return." He pulled her to his side, one arm around her waist.

"Yes."

They studied the sea, the inky blue of the water-filled caldera, the dark smudges of volcanic land still jutting from its center. Palea Kameni and Nea Kameni—the "old and new burnt islands"—both formed by ongoing underwater eruptions.

"We must return to the center."

Even as he said the words, Kallie knew them to be true. There would be no ruined palace there, but the two burnt islands marked the origin of the fiery blast that had destroyed her home. Active sulfur vents sent whispery-white fingers into the sea air, testifying to the inferno that still boiled under the surface. *Through the fire.*

She rested her head against his shoulder. "Caroline and Yoshi and Erik will wonder what has happened to us."

He tightened his embrace until she fit snugly against him. "We will need to tell them something. So they won't search. And the money. Dimitri Andreas's estate. I must make sure it's taken care of. I owe him that."

Strange. All of it, so strange. The other Dimitri Andreas, the real one, who had befriended him and had never known of their shared name.

Kallie sighed. "We can take care of details in the morning. Then take a boat to Nea Kameni in the afternoon."

He kissed the top of her head. "And be home by evening."

She smiled. The words were hopeful, and she shared his hope, but the future was still unknown.

She sent him back to his own room, despite his desire to stay. Not here, not in this place. They would find their way home and be married in the palace, and then they would be together.

⇥ 39 ⇤

In the morning, Kallie and Dimitri met the team for breakfast at an outdoor café down the street from the inn. White tables with white umbrellas, white paving. This town was nearly blinding.

The three already sat at a table set with a pitcher of orange juice and a set of glasses. A bowl of ripe plums completed the perfection. Kallie paused at the entrance to the patio, a wave of surprising affection for their little team washing over her.

Caroline's sharp eyes darted between the two of them. "What? Something's changed. Did you find it?"

Dimitri pulled out Kallie's chair, then sat beside

her. "No, we haven't found it. But we *have* made a decision. To stop looking."

Erik *harrumphed* and folded his arms over his massive chest. "Just like that?"

"I want to thank all three of you for your willingness to pursue this quest. You'll be well rewarded, I assure you."

Yoshi's dark eyes narrowed on the two of them. "There is something you are not telling us."

Dimitri cleared his throat, shifted in his chair.

Kallie leaned forward, reached for the pitcher, and began filling glasses with juice. "We might as well tell them, Dimitri. It doesn't need to be a secret."

She felt his startled gaze on her but kept pouring, then shifted to look at Caroline. "Dimitri and I have decided being—together—is more important than lost artifacts. We are going to sail the world." She filled the last glass and put the pitcher down in the shocked silence that followed.

Dimitri wrapped warm fingers around one of her hands. "Kallie is the woman I've been looking for all my life. I'm not going to waste time on the past."

She nearly laughed. It was all such a tangle— the past, the present. Their future.

Caroline quickly picked up her glass and sipped the juice, watching them over the rim of the glass. "Well. This is certainly a surprise. Isn't it a

442

surprise, boys?" She flicked a glance at Yoshi, who looked at her as though he'd sail the world with her if she asked. "I supposed we should have seen the signs along the way . . ." She was rambling, and the guys just stared.

Kallie slowly downed her glass of juice, letting the sharp sweetness of it waken her senses, then clinked the glass back to the table. "You know, I think we've all learned some lessons during this trip. Haven't we?" She looked around the table, waiting for the uncertain nods. "I've been so proud to be part of this team. I wish we could go on together, but now a new exciting life beckons." She turned and grinned at Dimitri.

Dimitri stood. "We have some business to take care of back at the hotel, but we'll be leaving this afternoon. Thank you all for everything you've done. It's time for you to follow your own dreams now."

Kallie stood and clasped Dimitri's hand. The other three remained frozen in their seats, their faces mystified, all of them speechless.

Dimitri extended a hand to each of the men in turn, a handshake of good-bye. He held Caroline's hand a moment longer and placed his other hand over hers. "Caroline, I trust you'll get everyone back to the States?"

She nodded, her eyes still wide.

"Feel free to extend your stay here. Enjoy the island. Your expenses will be covered." He smiled into her eyes. "See my attorney when you return, Caroline. I need someone capable to run my organization while I'm gone. He'll have all your instructions."

Caroline's ruby-tinged lips parted, but then she straightened and nodded once, the air of a CEO already infusing her.

Dimitri stepped back to Kallie's side. "Yoshi, I trust you'll keep Caroline in line?"

Yoshi curled a hand around Caroline's and grinned. "I won't let her out of my sight, boss."

"And Erik." Dimitri turned to the big man, as though bestowing his final gift. "Give Caroline a few days to get organized and then make an appointment. She'll have some funds for an investment I've been meaning to make. A private security firm run by someone I trust."

Erik exhaled in surprise. "I can't—"

"Yes, you can. You've got what it takes."

Erik nodded, surprised gratitude in his eyes.

Dimitri stepped back from the three, pulling Kallie with him. "Thank you again, all of you, for your help."

And then they were walking back to the hotel, hand in hand, leaving their team gaping in the sun.

It seemed a lifetime ago, that day in the airport when she had thought of them as the three-headed Cerberus, guarding against passage to the Underworld. The hound had turned out to be a playful puppy.

Back at the hotel, they worked through the rest of the arrangements. With no employer and no close friends besides Judith, Kallie had no one to call but her landlord. She promised him a check would be forthcoming from Dimitri's account. "Do whatever you'd like with my things," she told him, leaving him sputtering in confusion.

Dimitri already had a will in place, leaving his money in trust and the dividends of his estate distributed to various charities and museums in the event of his death. He made a phone call to his lawyer, who had power of attorney, to instruct him in Caroline's new appointment.

While Dimitri talked with the lawyer, Kallie grabbed her journal and went out to the balcony. She had one more person to whom she owed an explanation, and one more entry to pen in the myth that had become fact.

She wrote the ending of the story that had not yet ended, with faith in the promise that had been made. An ending with return, with joy, with redemption. An ending with hope.

On the back flyleaf of the journal she scrawled a message.

Dr. Newsom,
You walked through the start of this journey with me, but I must finish it alone. I have found the truth about my past, the truth about myself, and perhaps one truth that surpasses

and sustains all others. Thank you for your compassion and your guidance. I have found the center of the labyrinth at last, and there is peace.

With love, Kallista Andreas.

She took the framed print of the unsolvable maze and placed the journal on its glass. With a whispered "I'll be right back" to Dimitri, still on the phone, she took the print and journal to the hotel's tiny lobby and asked the owner for packaging. When she had wrapped and addressed the package to Dr. Newsom, she gave the owner money to ship it across the sea.

Back in the room, Dimitri had finished his calls. "There will still be loose ends." He shrugged. "But it's the best I can do."

They packed their bags, then carried them down the winding steps to the docks below. In short order, Dimitri had chartered a private boat for the day.

"The day?" Kallie bit her lip and stared over the water. "If we leave it at the island, they'll look for us."

Dimitri took her suitcase in his free hand. "He took my credit card number as security against loss. If the boat doesn't return, he'll get his money."

Then they were free, afloat in the caldera, prow pointed toward Nea Kameni, the larger of the two central islands. Dimitri worked the sails and rigging like the experienced sailor he was, albeit with more ancient technology, and Kallie sat on a vinyl deck bench, savoring the clean-swept sea air as the boat lifted and slapped against the water in an easy rhythm. The sun etched a channel across the water like a path to freedom, and the sails snapped in the wind with the exhilarating cry of *home, home, home* in her ears. She lifted her face to the sun and smiled.

After arriving at their destination, their boat joined the flow of private and tourist boats pouring into Nea Kameni's small harbor.

Kallie eyed the glut of people disembarking, milling around at water's edge, trailing upward on the black gravel path toward the crater's rim. "I hadn't expected so many people."

Dimitri took her hand. "We'll just have to wait until they're gone."

They disembarked together, then trekked up a wide path along with a large group that had descended from a pirate ship, no doubt a tourist gimmick. Families with water bottles and sun visors and cameras strapped around sweaty necks trekked alongside them until they reached the top of the island, a huge circular crater with sloping gravel sides.

Here the groups posed and re-posed to snap pictures of themselves in front of a "real volcano" with its steaming sulfur vents. Kallie and Dimitri circled the crater to the far side and scrambled downward until they were out of sight.

They found a large rock and sat, and Kallie looked backward toward the rim. "Do you really think that's it? That's where we'll cross back?"

Dimitri looked westward, over the sea. "It seems too ordinary, doesn't it?"

Kallie kicked at a few loose pebbles, porous and black. "Do you remember the day you told me your greatest desire was to sail to unknown worlds?"

He did not answer for several moments. "It would seem I have accomplished that and more. But it's time to sail for home."

They waited out the day, drifting through conversations of past and future, of reality and mystery, of the strange in-between place in which they had been stranded. Of the technology that was both a blessing and a curse, and of what their journey meant. Finally, when the sun had started its fiery descent, they crept back to the rim and found it deserted. They circled back to the eastern side and peered downward to the narrow inlet where they had arrived. Their solitary boat bobbed at the water's edge.

Dimitri sighed. "We need to let it go."

He spoke of the boat, of their luggage on board, of their life in this time and this place. Kallie nodded.

They made their way back to the sea, and Kallie

waited on the shore while Dimitri made some sort of adjustments to the boat. He jumped from deck to shore, released its moorings, and joined her, his face pained. "It's a beautiful boat."

"What will happen to it?"

He grabbed her hand and led her toward the trail without a backward glance. "It will sink."

She set her face toward the rim and breathed in the salty air. Almost there. Her heart pounded with the nearness of both hope and terror.

They had done all they could to alleviate any burden they would cause in this world. It was time to return to their own.

The sun was a sphere of burnt orange in a violet sky when they reached the top and looked over the edge once more at the slope of the crater. There was no yawning hole at the bottom, only a blackened pit with a sandy base.

Dimitri led them along the rim to the place where the largest bursts of steam escaped from a wide fissure in the rocky crater. The smell of sulfur burned Kallie's eyes and set her legs shaking. She closed her eyes against the fumes and the fear. "It is like leaping into Hades."

"Are you ready?" Dimitri's voice was low and solid, a certainty to which she could cling.

"No."

He laughed without mirth and twined his fingers into hers. "Neither am I."

She opened her eyes and stared into the depths

of his, lit by setting sun. "We must have faith."

He inhaled, then exhaled with a nod. "Faith."

They positioned themselves in the Air above the blackened crack in Earth's crust, a breach between worlds, surrounded by Water, seething with underground Fire. An elemental struggle if ever there had been one.

Hands tightly clasped, eyes only on each other, they jumped.

For Kallie, it was like death and it was like life—this leap toward destiny or destruction. All she had known in this life floated away, more like lifting than falling, like spinning away from the blue-green globe, into the void of deepest space. Her heart soared with the lift, and she stopped breathing, thinking, seeing.

Falling. Soaring. Spinning. The dark void is everything.

The chaos filled with a rush of sounds—wild water and roaring wind. A sudden and powerful jolt of heat and pain. Then a still, eerie silence more frightening than noise.

Finally, awareness came. The solid presence of cool stone underneath. Lungs slowly dragging in shaky breath. Eyes blinking open, unfocused in dim light. Thoughts distilling.

We jumped. And we survived.

⇻ 40 ↢

Newborn, I rocked on my hands and knees, calming the whirl of mind and body and soul. The slick patina of slime beneath my splayed fingers smelled of bat droppings and fetid water.

"Andreas." The word rasped from my throat as if I had not spoken in years. I swiveled left and right, squinting in the murky shadows thrown by the dull-orange glow at my back.

"Here."

I scrabbled across the slippery rock floor, reaching for the voice. Our hands met in the dark, and his arms pulled me close. I bent my head to his shoulder. Tension drained from my limbs, and I choked back a sob.

"Sshhh, do not weep, Chloe. It is over."

Was it possible? I would not believe we had conquered the labyrinth until I stood in the sunlight, but still, to have come this far—across time and against sensibility—it seemed the divine was upon us, taking us from death to life.

Thoughts of the divine lifted my head, and I peered through the darkness toward the remembered entrance to this stone vault. I had much to tell my people. Of the many tracks, the wanderings through mists of myth and legend yet to come, all failed or else wrapped up into something greater, something true.

But first we must find our way home.

A shift in the cavern's atmosphere shot fear through my body. I arched away from Andreas, senses alert. I had been here before, and it had not ended well.

Muttering voices, foul and angry, drifted like smoke across the cavern floor. More than one of the half-men who'd thrown me to the beast awaited our return.

"Who is there?" Andreas shifted to place me behind his body.

I clutched at him, the scars on my wrist burning afresh. "They do not speak. They are not human."

But Andreas stood, pulling me with him, and reached a hand of greeting across the darkened cavern. "I am Andreas of Athens. I passed this way before, many years ago."

A shuffling sound revealed a distorted face, and then another, and another into the glow. A dozen men, eyes wide and lips parted. Did our arrival shock them? The smell of burning flesh tickled my nose, twisted my stomach.

"The beast has spit them back."

This from the back of the crowd, and heads jerked toward the voice as though indeed, a dead man, had spoken.

I stepped forward. "Yes, we have returned. And with good news. With Truth, and with freedom."

They shrank fearfully from my voice and from me.

I extended my hands, suddenly overwhelmed with pity and with love for these lost and hopeless men, who in their wandering had surrendered their humanity. A desperation to make them understand. To save them. "Will you come with us? Come into the sunlight, and we will speak of Truth. There is only destruction if you remain."

The one who had spoken pushed his way to the front of the crowd, his eyes still luminous in the glimmering. His voice was whispery-harsh, a ragged thread barely tied to something mortal.

"They *shine*."

I looked to Andreas, saw only the man I had ever loved—twice.

But there was no denying the near-rapturous way some of the men looked upon us. Were we so changed? And yet it seemed only a few took notice. The rest of them averted their eyes or snarled and gnashed their teeth in our direction. Would they attempt to return us to the beast? I shifted away from the glowing pit, pulling Andreas with me.

"Who will come?" I inclined my head toward the tunnel that led away.

Glances rippled among them, some senseless and hungry, others wondering, perhaps yearning.

A throaty growl issued from the rock walls around us, as though the cavern itself conspired to keep these hopeless ones trapped. But no, the growl became a rumble in the rock beneath our feet, then a tremor that blurred the vision. *An earthquake.* Or at least a warning of impending disaster. My mouth tasted of metal, and coldness flooded into my hands. The tremor ceased, but not before loosened stones tumbled to the cavern floor.

"Come." Andreas's voice was strong, authoritative. He met their eyes with fearlessness as he took my arm and led me to the tunnel. The invitation had been extended. We could not force them to accept.

I breached the tunnel entrance ahead of Andreas, and the crushing weight of numbing darkness sucked the breath from my lungs. Head high and hands forward, I traced the blackened sides of the tunnel as I walked, until the wall fell away from my left hand and only the right kept me anchored.

But Andreas took up my empty hand with his. "I can feel the wall on this side, still. I will know if another branch leads away."

"And then what?" This was the dilemma. Coming from the outside, I may have only known one tunnel. Retracing, we might make a hundred missteps into oblivion. How far until we found the scarlet cord I left behind?

"And then we hope."

And it was hope that pushed me forward. Hope

and love for my people, who even now knew nothing of what was to come and needed a leader to show them the way.

The sound of feet dragging, scuffing along the gravely path behind us gave us pause.

"They are coming!" Andreas gripped my hand. "Not all, but some. They are following!"

Heat filled my chest, swelling me with the burden I had taken up, the burden of leadership. I could not fail them.

I led us in faith toward unseen light. Slowly, we advanced, one hesitant foot placed before the other, blind toes and fingers probing ahead, meeting dripping slime and the occasional scuttling insect or rodent, the echoes of our scraping feet like nails dragged down stony walls.

My toe struck rock. I stumbled, and only Andreas's hand stayed me from pitching forward over a line of stones that barred passage.

Andreas hauled me upward, his questions piercing the stale air. "What—? How did—?"

"It is my marker!" I bent to run my hands over the line of rocks, heart pounding. "Here! Here is my rope!" I clutched it with both hands, careful not to tug it fiercely to my heart.

"Brilliant, Chloe!" He circled my shoulders and kissed my cheek.

I kicked the stones aside and walked forward, gathering the rope slowly to myself as we went, feeling the warmth of Andreas's hand against my lower back. Was it possible we would find our way out?

The torch I had brought seven years ago must have been long lost by now, and my eyes did not adjust to this absolute darkness, but the pressure of the rock was palpable. When the tunnel opened into another large cavern, I sucked in a deep breath with some relief.

Andreas paused at my side. "Do you remember this cavern?"

"I do. There were others here. Wandering."

"Yes, I met them, too."

The little knot of creatures at our backs pulled up short, their breath hot on my neck.

"Are you also searching for the Horn of Truth?"

The voice was clear and strong and bounced off the cavern walls. Impossible to tell where it originated.

"It is Chloe, daughter of Galenus and Harmonia. I've returned, and I have found it."

"We are searching for the Horn of Truth. For the hand of the princess."

I sighed. Seven years, and still the same self-delusion? I spoke into the darkness. "You shall not find it here, shall never find it in the paths you are searching."

"There are many ways to find it."

I raised my eyebrows at the deviation from their well-worn phrase, but there was no one to see my expression. "No. No, there is only one way."

"Perhaps there is no Truth. Perhaps it is only the search that is significant."

Though they had not seemed aware time was passing, still these endless searchers seemed to have evolved in their argument.

I lifted my chin, made my declaration in a tone I hoped conveyed my certainty. "If there is no Truth, then the search for it is meaningless."

Again, as if the earth revolted at my words, a vibration began beneath my feet and shook its way through my core.

Andreas pulled me toward him. "Stronger this time." He tucked my face against his chest, his hand covering my head.

Rocks broke away from where they had spent millennia and crashed around us. The men we'd led from the deeper cavern cried out and their shrieks shook me as much as the tremors.

"This way!" I had coiled my rope loosely around my arm thus far, but now I flung the end across the cavern toward the searchers and wrapped both hands around its taut, suspended length. Following the invisible thread, I moved toward the side of the cavern where it led. Andreas held my elbow lightly, but I could feel the drag of the men who followed, clinging to him in a tattered line of near-senseless panic.

We entered the press of a narrow tunnel once more. Safe from rocks falling from a grand height, we were nevertheless in greater danger of the tunnel entombing us within itself. I paused to shout backward into the cavern. "There is only one way to life! You must follow the blood-red cord!"

Whether any would heed my warning, would trust enough to give up their own efforts and follow, I could not know. But the caverns, the mountain itself, would not wait. We must flee.

The floor beneath our feet gave a mighty heave, and I ducked my head at a deafening crack like thunder.

Behind me, Andreas shouted, "Go! Go!"

I wrapped loose fingers along the life-giving thread, held my other hand aloft at shoulder-height, and half walked, half ran into the dark-ness, trailing Andreas and whoever else might follow.

The mountain bucked and rocked, caught in death throes.

Was this the eruption? Had I returned too late to save my people?

The tunnel echoed with the shrieks of men and the breathless huffs of running, running now along the cord, praying for deliverance.

How long? How long did we race through the collapsing mountain? Fissures opened in the rock walls, their presence announced by a blast of putrid air against my face. The floor cracked and fractured into tilting planes, knocking me left and right and threatening to bring me to my knees.

And then the rope skewed downward, down toward the tunnel floor, and my hand met the boulder where I had tied its end, so long ago.

Andreas shoved into me from behind, and we stumbled, together with the others, into a heap.

"What is it? Have you lost the rope?"

I shook my head even though he could see nothing.

"It is the end. I tied it here."

"The end?"

I heard the note of panic in his voice.

"From here we take all right-turning branches."

"You are certain?"

"Yes, I am certain. Follow me, Andreas. Follow and trust."

I took the tunnel at a trot, fingers trailing the wall at my right. Each time I felt it drop away, I made the turn and called out a warning to those behind.

The tremors, the roar, had ceased but the aftereffects remained, and rocks *cracked* and *popped* and rolled under our feet. More than once my ankle twisted painfully beneath me, but still we ran.

Right-turn. Run. Right-turn.

Did I imagine the darkness lifted? A slight easing of the abyss, as though the air were infused with the lightest breath of angels?

No, no, it was not imagination. There—ahead—

the tunnel lay in twilight, its dripping walls gleaming with a slight sheen.

Another shriek behind and a mighty roaring crash.

The tunnel was collapsing.

As one, we ran faster, harder, with an urgency born of self-preservation. With the gloom cut by half, our steps were more sure.

Like a chaste twin to the evil glow of the beast's lair, the mouth of the Great Cavern beckoned ahead with pure sunlight, inviting us into life and hope. We rushed forward, forward toward the light until we were through it, and in it, and falling to the grassy slope beyond the pit of death.

Blinking and giddy in the sun, I laughed and crawled through the lush green to Andreas's side and collapsed into his arms, feeling his kisses on my face and neck like an anointing.

When I regained my breath, I stood. Stood and faced the sun-washed island of Kalliste, the great mountain, distant and hazy in the center, still intact and unaware of the raging death beneath.

Andreas came to stand beside me.

I breathed deeply of the island's scent, of flowers and grass and sea air. "We have come in time."

In time to save the people from destruction, at least.

"We must go."

He nodded.

I felt his gaze on me and turned to see his eyes bright, dancing.

"What is it?"

He smiled. "The sun on you. On your head. Like your coronation."

I gripped his hand. His words filled me up with all I had sought. Truth. Love. Destiny.

I could not tell if seven years had passed on Kalliste, if my father still lived, if my mistakes had led to disaster or had been redeemed in my absence. All this was yet to be answered. But one thing I knew.

I was going home.

⇥ 41 ⇤

Like a memory arising from a seven-year mist, yet tangible as yesterday's dig site visit, the village of Lycoris appeared at the base of the Green Mountain as we led the captives down.

Long before we reached the outskirts of the village, we were spotted—our ragtag group of survivors, with Andreas and me at the head and the dirty, worn, sun-blind men behind, still dazed and following us like dream walkers.

Villagers poured from homes and streets. Some gathered at the central fountain, others ran to meet us on the hill, with shouts of joy as lost sons and husbands were reclaimed.

I released each of these delivered ones to their families, but a message of warning was still on my lips.

"The island grows unsafe. There is indeed a beast within, and it will rise up to destroy everything here."

Wide eyes, open mouths. Did they believe my words?

"Make ready to leave the island. Pack what you can, but in haste."

Isandros was there, pushing to the front of the crowd, little Selene clutching his hand. "Leave? How will we leave? Where would we go?"

I glanced toward the center of our precious island, the great hill in the center where the palace and temples proudly stood. "I will send word. Ready all the boats you have. It will not be long."

The people fled the square. Isandros remained.

"I did not believe I would see you again." He smiled, but the smile was for Andreas as well and held only friendship. "You are well? And you have found the one you sought?"

I took up his hand in gratitude, for the friendship he offered when I first passed this way, and for the trust I knew he had in me still. "My father, Isandros. Does he live still?"

Isandros's eyes flickered with a moment's confusion. "I have heard no news from the palace. But it is not yet time for the saffron deliveries, and I have not been there since last we spoke."

Andreas stepped forward into the conversation. "How long? How much time has passed since Chloe left your village?"

He furrowed his brow in thought, and in that moment I saw Selene was unchanged. I had not thought of the significance until this moment.

"Seven days, I believe." He nodded. "Yes, it is seven."

A thrill ran through me at this, the best news he could have shared. Surely we were in time to save my father from the Mycenaean assassins.

"We must get to the palace quickly, Isandros. Warn them of the danger." I glanced backward at the remains of our huddled group and counted twelve. Whether they were villagers from elsewhere on Kalliste or suitors from across the sea, I could not say. "Can you take care of these as well and offer us horses to speed our travel?"

Selene grinned at me. "Herakles will be glad to see you. I took good care of him."

I laughed and tipped her chin back. How could I have forgotten? "Of course you did!"

Isandros nodded. "You shall have another as well. For—"

"Andreas." I reached for his hand. "This is Andreas, and he is to be my husband."

Isandros bowed. "Then future king of Kalliste as well. I pledge you my loyalty, my lord."

Andreas nodded, but I knew his thoughts ran alongside my own. There would soon be little left of Kalliste to rule.

We were off within the hour, with fresh food and water for the journey, headed for the Cypress Forest.

Melayna had found some other route, but whatever it was, I did not know it. And the Oracle's words were fresh in my memory. I must pass backward through the trials if I was to be worthy to lead my people. I did not relish more days in the gloomy forest. And yet, like a child who could easily read a tablet that was once unintelligible, Herakles and I found our way through the Cypress Forest as though it were nothing more than a child's tale. Andreas's horse trotted behind, and it seemed only minutes before we were on the other side, headed for the Blade Path, the ridge that would lead us to the palace.

My thoughts grew darker as we progressed. I returned with the Horn of Truth, but it was a warning, a bit of knowledge. How would it help my father? How would it erase the insult I had given to the Mycenaean king bent on annihilating us? Would he not chase us wherever we went? Or worse—prevent us from fleeing to safety?

And I had no prized treasure to loft above the crowds, no Horn to trumpet over them and make them believe my words about the destruction of our beautiful island. Why would they believe me?

Andreas caught up to ride beside me. "You are too quiet, Chloe, for a woman about to ride home in triumph."

"A hollow triumph. I bring only terrible news, with no way to stop it."

"But it will be good news to those who believe it."

I thought a moment, then nodded at his words of wisdom.

When the roofline of the palace emerged against the brilliant sky, my heart soared toward home and family, and I nudged Herakles to greater speed on the upward path.

We thundered into the center of the town, then up the wide Processional Way to the base of the palace steps.

News of our arrival traveled into the palace as quickly as we could alight and hand off our horses to the groomsmen who emerged from the stables.

My mother and father were on the dais before we were halfway up the steps.

Mother. And Father. Home.

I fell into their arms, weeping with the relief of seven years of loneliness ended.

Andreas stood at my back, silent and waiting.

Father pulled away and looked him up and down. "From Athens, wasn't it? I usually take little notice of the suitors, since they never return."

Andreas bowed at the waist. "Yes, Athens, my lord. But I have traveled a great distance more than that, to ask for the hand of your daughter."

Father glanced beyond us, down the steps and the Processional Way. "Melayna? She is not with you?"

I gripped Mother's hand. "She is not. I—I believe she is safe. But I do not think she will return."

Mother gave a tiny gasp, but Father's eyes lighted on Andreas, understanding dawning there. "So. You will marry Chloe. And rule together."

Andreas looked to me, still clutching my mother's hand, and I took Father's hand in my other. "Let us go inside, Father. There is much to tell you, and very little time."

⇢ 42 ⇠

Indeed, there was less time than even I imagined. Within the palace we felt again the rumblings of the earth, and I sounded the Horn of Truth first for my parents—these disturbances were more than slight shiftings under our feet. They were warnings that we must flee immediately.

Andreas stood at my side, but Father turned away, and I could not discern whether he believed my warning or dismissed it. He crossed to the terrace overhanging the grassy hillside that ran toward the sea and searched the horizon as though the answer would come from across the waves.

And a message came, but not a message we wanted.

There on the horizon, lit by the setting sun behind them, a thousand Mycenaean ships in full sail toward Kalliste.

It was Mother, always practical, who spoke first. "There will be no leaving now, even if we had the ships to take all of Kalliste from the island."

Father gripped the terrace wall. "If the ships come, the assassin must already be among us."

My gaze traveled north, to where the little town of Oia would one day be built, where Andreas and I would stand on a balcony such as this one and talk of the truth that this island was home.

I did not travel all this distance, fight my way back through the Great Cavern, to give up my people or my father on the eve of their salvation. Not when their destruction was caused by my own hand.

"Ready messages, Father. Send them through the island. There is no need to convince our people of the danger that lies under our feet, for all can see the danger that comes across the sea. Tell them to prepare to flee, to await instructions."

He turned to me, grief etching his features, aging him. "And what instructions shall we give, Daughter? Where will we go?"

"I do not know. But I will find a way."

I gripped the hands of Andreas. "Stay with Father. See that no one gets through."

His eyes darkened. "Where—?"

"There is one who may have answers. I must find the Oracle."

He inhaled, glanced at the ships cresting the horizon, and nodded once. "I will protect him with my life."

I kissed his cheek, took a last look at my parents, and fled the upper level of the palace, down to the wide veranda and marble steps, along the Processional Way to the temple of the great goddess.

The priestesses had lit the evening torches, and the columns glowed like a white forest, beckoning penitents inward to sacrifices and prayers. I intended neither.

But she was not there.

I had seen her last in the cave on the hillside of the Green Mountain. How had she gotten through to that other world? Had she come back?

"The Oracle?" I asked a priestess.

Her white gown was nearly translucent when she bowed, torchlight behind her. "I have not seen her in many days, my lady. Perhaps she seeks the goddess in one of the caves of the High Place."

To the High Place I climbed, breathless with the journey when I reached the windswept crag over the sea. Nightfall obscured the mouths of caves. This was the night of the dark moon, as though all of nature conspired to keep me in darkness.

"Oracle!" My voice carried over the plateau and was lost at sea. I called again and again, resorting at last to a name that felt clumsy on my lips in this place.

"Judith!"

But there was only the crash of waves far below and the whisper of wind.

I knew she would not be here. Even as climbed, I knew this final battle, this last challenge, was one I must face alone.

I returned toward the palace, raking through my mind for any desperate way to save my people.

The first watch of the night was already spent by the time I reached the palace steps. But Andreas would still be at my father's side, awaiting my return.

On the upper level I nodded to the guard at my father's bedchamber door, and he stepped aside to let me pass.

Inside, my mother rose to her feet at my arrival. She was alone.

And she was crying.

"What is it?" I crossed the room and grabbed her hands. "Where are they?"

"They have gone. To Peleus's men."

I flew to the balcony. "Out to sea? To the Mycenaeans? Why?"

She was at my back, spoke over my shoulder. "Not to sea. Peleus sent a messenger. To kill your father, I suppose, or to make some sort of agreement for surrender. He and Andreas talked with the messenger—I was seeing to the packing of some things—and then he was saying good-bye, saddling horses—"

"But where? Where have they gone?"

She shook her head. "He would not say."

I ran for the door, then slowed. With no direction, it was useless to chase them. The ships had not yet reached the island. Andreas and my father could have gone anywhere. I would have to trust Andreas to keep him safe.

Through the second and third watches of the night, my mother and I gave direction to servants for the packing of crates and sent messengers to all parts of the island to spread the news to our people. How many of them would heed, I could not know.

Every hour found me at a balcony, searching the sea or the streets for ships or men.

And then he was there. Andreas. Alone.

He was dismounting before his horse even reached the steps, and I was flying down, down to meet him.

I ran to him on the wide palace terrace, grabbed his arms, and searched his face for news.

"He has made an agreement."

"Who has? Where is my father?"

Andreas touched my face. "Your father has arranged with the Mycenaeans for them to transport as many of your people from the island as their ships can take."

I shrank back. "The Mycenaeans? Why would—?"

"He has agreed to abandon the island without bloodshed if they will take the people."

I sucked in a breath of salty air. "He believes me, then? About the eruption?" My mind raced through the strange development. "But why would they trust us? Would they not suspect that once upon their ships, our people would turn on them and overpower?"

"Yes."

My heart thudded. "Where is he? Where is my father?" I knew the answer before he spoke it.

"He has given himself as surety."

I made for the steps, as though I could stop this thing, but Andreas held me back.

"This is his choice, Chloe. He does this for his people, and for you."

"They will kill him!"

"He knows that."

I rammed a fist against Andreas's chest. "Why did you not stop him?"

"Because this was his choice. And it is the only way."

"No! There must be—"

"How, Chloe? How can we get an entire island of people to safety?" He waved toward the sea. "Do you not see the hand of the divine upon the arrival of these many ships?"

I collapsed against him, tears choking my words. "All of this is my fault. He pays the price for my mistakes."

Andreas smoothed my hair with his hand. "And yet, the deliverance of your people will come of it." He raised my chin and looked into my eyes. "*Your* people, Chloe. It is time to claim your birthright."

He turned me toward the city, to look out over my beloved Kalliste, with the knowledge she soon would be gutted.

The grassy slopes, dotted with vineyards bursting with ripeness and olive groves ready to be pressed, spoke of tranquil memories and promised a future prosperity that was not to be. The hill where I stood would be flung heavenward and the sea far below, tickling the edges of the beaches, would soon sweep into the wound. How could I let go? The land was a part of me, and there was nothing I could do to save it.

But the people. I could lead the people.

How many years had I resisted the prophecy, insisted I was not worthy of rulership? My own foolishness had a price, and I had brought nothing from my journey to save my father. But I had brought knowledge, and I had returned to the Most Beautiful Island changed.

Ready to lead, wherever it should take us.

✦ Epilogue ✦

The ships landed by daybreak.

Through the cloudless day, my people streamed toward the sapphire sea, following the directives issued from the palace, from the woman who would be queen of an exiled people.

Some will go to Crete, our nearest neighbor.

Some, including Andreas and myself, will go to Egypt—to the Theban king in the desert valley—and bring tribute in exchange for favor.

I stand again now on the hillside overlooking the sea, watching the deliverance take place before my eyes. Andreas is down on the strand, directing and instructing. Ensuring our people are well treated. Looking for news of my father.

Beneath me, the mountain rumbles again. I turn my gaze to the High Place. My journey in that other place and time is already growing hazy, yet I know from my studies the highest point on the island is the likely center of the annihilation to come.

True to my suspicion, a vaporous stream breaks

through and slithers up from the High Place, like a whisper of death.

We do not have much time.

But I will be on the last ship to board. I will not leave my island, my people, until I know I have done all I can to lead them well into our unknown future.

I become aware of another, a figure at my back, and I am not surprised. The Oracle does not speak, only joins me in my vigil.

Is her time at an end as well? Do we leave behind the Great Goddess?

In the millennia to come, I see many will begin to suspect the mystical, to fear it. They will not realize that to pursue their spiritual longings is to take a step closer to truth, not away.

And yet, as I have also come to know, redemption is core to the human psyche, and must also be pursued.

Any religion, any faith that would stand as truth, must offer both. It must be both rational in its atonement but also heavy with the mystical breath of enchantment.

And I see life itself is a maze. It is a theme repeated everywhere—cut into Long Island hedges and laid into Italian mosaic floors, tunneled by canals through the alleys of Venice and channeled into limestone in the depths of Kalliste.

Yes, life is a maze, and always we are trying to

find our way through. Leaving signposts along the way for other travelers, painting our best conception of what lies at the finish.

The ultimate question every traveler must answer is which direction the maze runs.

Do all roads lead inward, into myself, to a higher consciousness where I am dissolved? Or do all roads lead outward, toward a power greater and outside myself?

Andreas climbs the hill toward me, and I sense the Oracle is gone, drifted away during my musings.

I smile on the man whom I journeyed through time and space to find, and he returns the smile, sad but also joyful, if that is possible.

Yes, that is possible. For we will have many years together, to ask our questions, to seek more answers.

To search for the one true story.

⇢ **Acknowledgments** ⇠

Thank you, first of all, to my travel partners who joined me on research trips to Egypt, Venice and Santorini—my husband Ron, and daughter Rachel. I love traveling with each of you and cherish the memories!

John Olson, as the dedication attests, this book would not exist without you. I treasure you.

Thank you to my first "beta readers" on this manuscript, for your invaluable feedback: Lora Doncea, Erin Mifflin, Erin Al-Mehairi, and Beth Goddard. Your insights greatly improved the manuscript, and your encouragement was life-giving!

Thank you to Julee Schwarzburg, my fabulous editor, who takes a manuscript that's rough and messy and spiffs it up until it shines. You are awesome.

And finally, thank you to Holley McEllroy of TreeBranch Media for the gorgeous cover design. I hesitate to tell people your name, because I fear you will get too busy to create for me!

❖ About the Author ❖

TRACY HIGLEY started her first novel at the age of eight and has been hooked on writing ever since. She has authored twelve novels, including *The Queen's Handmaid* and *Chasing Babylon*. Tracy is currently pursuing a Master's Degree in Ancient History and has traveled through Greece, Israel, Turkey, Egypt, Jordan and Italy, researching her novels and falling into adventures. See her travel journals and more at TracyHigley.com.

Center Point Large Print
600 Brooks Road / PO Box 1
Thorndike, ME 04986-0001 USA

(207) 568-3717

US & Canada:
1 800 929-9108
www.centerpointlargeprint.com